AN ALIEN'S QUEST

by Cary Neeper

Penscript ®
PUBLISHING HOUSE

Characters and alien species depicted herein are trademarks of Carolyn A. Neeper. The Penscript® logo and calligraphy are trademarks and Penscript is a registered trademark of Shawne A. Workman, DBA Penscript Publishing House.

Publisher's Cataloging-in-Publication
  Neeper, Cary.
    An alien's quest / by Cary Neeper.
    p. cm. — (The archives of Varok ; 4)
    Includes bibliographical references.
    Searching for meaning on an alien planet, a young
  human woman helps her multi-world family
  investigate a wave of interspecies conflict and kidnapping.
    LCCN 2016948521
    ISBN 978-1-62222-021-2 (hardcover)
    ISBN 978-1-62222-022-9 (trade pbk.)

    1. Human-alien encounters—Fiction.
  2. Extraterrestrial beings—Fiction. 3. Spirituality—
  Fiction. 4. Science fiction. I. Title. II. Series:
  Neeper, Cary. Archives of Varok ; 4.

First edition, 2022 reprint
Published by Penscript Publishing House
San Jose, California.
http://www.penscript-publishing.com

For Tahvi, Leela, Karis, and Allegra—
who can take this and will, no doubt, run with it.

CONTENTS

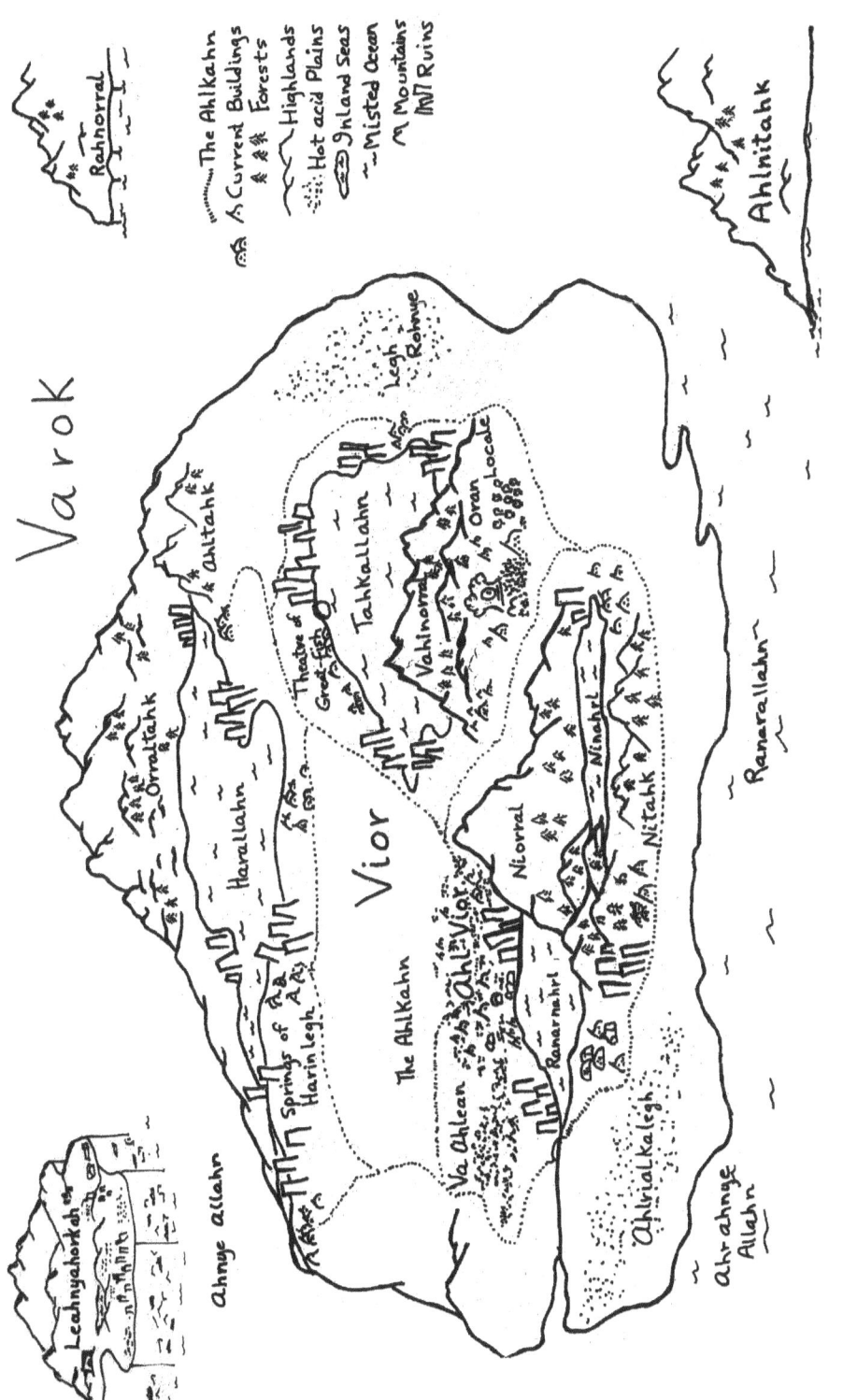

Varok

Legend

- ⋯⋯ The Ahlkahn
- 🏛 A Current Buildings
- 🌲🌲🌲 Forests
- Highlands
- ⣿ Hot acid Plains
- ⟨⟨⟩⟩ Inland Seas
- ≈≈ Misted Ocean
- ⋀⋀ Mountains
- ⋀⋔⋀ Ruins

Rahnorral

Ahlnitahk

Leahnyahorkah

Ahnye Allahn

Springs of
Harin Legh

Ahlvior
Va Ohlean

Ranarmahrl

AhlrialKaleigh

Ahrahnye
Allahn

Ornaltahk

Ahltahk

Harallahn

The Ahlkahn

Vior

Theatre of
Gret Fefl

Tahkallahn

Valtinom

Mt Ovan
Locale

Niovral

Ninahrl

A Nitahk

Legh
Rohnye

Ranarallahn

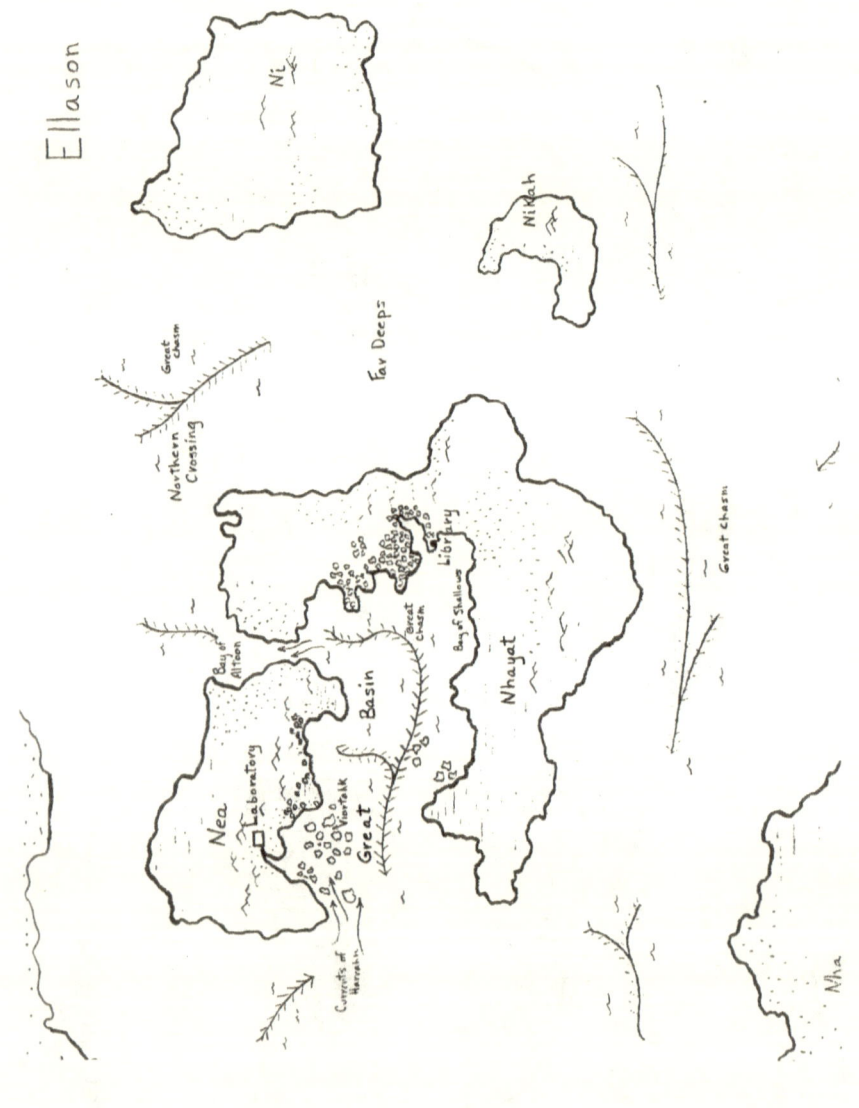

Ellason

Nt

Nikah

Fav Deeps

Great Chasm

Northern Crossing

Great chasm

Library

Bay of Altreon

Berott Chasm

Bay of Shallows

Nea

Laboratory

Great Basin

Viewlook

Nhayat

Currents of Marrah

Great chasm

Nha

I. Returning Home From Earth

In our recent work on Earth, I saw that many people agree on basic values, even when they did not agree on the details of belief. We living beings usually agree with the Golden Rule, treating others with kind regard, as one would hope to be treated. Words written early in human history reflect the profound notions and questions that still torment *Homo sapiens* in the 21st century.

Then there was neither being (Sat) nor non-being (Asat):
There was no air, nor firmament beyond it.
Was there a stirring? Where? Beneath what cover?
Was there a great abyss of unplumbed water?

...

Whether the world was made or was self-made,
He knows with full assurance, he alone,
Who in the highest heaven guards and watches;
He knows indeed, but then, perhaps he knows not!

—Tandra Oran-elConn-Grey, quoting
the Rig-Veda, 129th Hymn of the 10th Book

KILLAH'S PATIENT

Memo, medical, personal, to Shawne Oran-elConn-Grey from Killah, Senior Medical Officer for Ell-Varok Science:

In answer to your recent inquiry: No, in my opinion you have not done anything wrong or medically unwise. Perhaps you need to explore who you are, lovely human. Ask yourself how difficult it will be to be alone, a fertile being unable to experience a normal marital bond and reproduce. Will the love of us ells and varoks be enough?

Important: You invested your entire first professional experience in your teaching venture on Earth. Have faith; they'll find the obvious answers to avoid a repeat of the last century's plutocracies. Now take some time for yourself and move on. You know in your heart things on Earth must progress slowly—and erratically—so don't swamp your lifejoy in EV Science reports from Earth's Moonbase. While you are recovering, allow your own questions some time. Perhaps review some of the gems from Earth's religions. You, too, are human, right?

Am I? Shawne grieved for Earth's history, with humanity's loss of precious time to hunger and stress and constant warfare. *What kind of creatures are we, we humans? What am I?*

– Δ –

Swimming in the therapy pool of Varok's Space Travel Recovery Center usually quieted the despondency in Shawne, but not now. Haunted by a sense of failure, her mind drove her human body through the water at a fierce pace.

I should have realized we were decades too late going to Earth.

Shawne slowed to a stop in the clear water and dove. Its calm, silky feel helped. She didn't see the lanky form of her elll-dad Conn coming toward her underwater.

The elll's backfin waved slowly through his trunk plumes, fully extended, and the long green line of his leggy aquatic form passed around the young human female.

She felt his presence and smiled. Was he looking for some fun? *What will Conn do this time? Throw me out of the water? Or maybe he'll tow me around with his pedal fins.*

He did neither—just caught his adopted daughter gently in his arms and finned through the water while she rode his tiled chest, teasing its finer plumes with a loving finger. When they reached the side of the therapy pool, he raised her onto the deck, upright, slowly.

Surprised by his tender treatment, Shawne vaulted over his sonic melons back into the water and grasped his be-finned feet in her customary water wrestling hold.

He curled around her and lifted her once again out of the pool.

"Hey ho, Sweet human," Conn said in Varokian, "glad you're feeling wicked, but enough water play is enough. Right?"

"I'm feeling very righteous for a change. Tell Killah. He'll be proud."

"You've got to be kidding, my dear. Now be good and listen to me, with both ears if you don't mind. I have rotten news."

Conn continued. "Killah says you should stay here for a while, but your mom and your excellent daddys, Orram and I, need to get back to the web fields."

"That's not rotten news. I'll have a chance to live it up here in Ahl Vior for a while."

"Oh no you won't. You'll stay here at the recovery center, until Killah says you're strong enough to come home. Everything will come out all right in the end." His eyes sparkled with green at the old human joke. "You can do this, Jeff or no Jeff." Conn curled his wide elllonian lips into a mock kiss, tapped her on the nose with his long tongue, and hurried off.

Shawne sat still for a moment, stunned. *Didn't he scan me just now? His sonar must have seen something earlier, during the trip home to Varok. Surely Conn couldn't be counting on a human grandchild.*

"Conn, don't you know? I didn't—"

The elll was already gone. She hoped he would understand. Ellls always chose carefully what eggs to hatch, timing the rearing of tads so they would have every advantage.

Long ago the ellls of Ellason had reached a consensus: they had a right to replace themselves—but only that. The visiting alien varoks had convinced them to adopt the policy ages ago, after the ellls suffered starvation during an overpopulation crisis. The crisis passed; the ellls' population dropped and held steady, even though they loved raising tads more than anything else in their aquatic existence.

Conn adored young life even more than most ellls. What had she done to him? To herself? To the family. Their lives would never be the same.

"Oh, God!" Shawne slipped back into the therapy pool, overwhelmed with self-doubt. What kind of person was she? She rose to the surface and swam three laps before she realized what she had said.

Oh, God? Do I really believe in a Creator person? I would like one right now—a loving presence to say I used good judgment. Maybe Killah's right. I need to read more. There must be something worthwhile in human religion.

Shawne climbed out of the pool and into her recovery chair. She wheeled back to her room at the Space Recovery Center and sat, wrapped in a towel, staring out the window at the broad trees below that disguised the suburbs of Ahl Vior.

Shawne felt that her problems went far beyond the personal depression her family feared. During the months-long trip from Earth back home to Varok, she had enjoyed working hard to stay healthy. The constant exercises to avoid blood pooling and loss of bone mass also helped keep her mind off the overwhelming cloud of despair that plagued her.

She had studied the clinical definitions of depression and decided they didn't fit. Her bleakness was more rational than that. It was the intense feeling of failure on Earth and loss at leaving her first love, rejecting the possibility of carrying a child. Jeff's child.

She had missed a period and taken a pill to define her future. She had decided against suspension of the pregnancy—assuming there had been one. There could be no child with a father left behind on Earth, a man she no longer trusted or respected. Jeff was ignoring everything she had worked for, everything she believed humans could do and be.

Intellectually, she recognized that her school had helped further human understanding. She knew that she had done all one person could do. Only human consensus could secure a decent future for life on Earth.

There was still hope for that now—now that Earth was recovering from the huge die-off of the 2050's—but not if Jeff and like-minds had their way. She recognized that it was frustration and fear she felt—dread that the Jeffs of Earth would repeat in the 2070's the mistakes of the 20th and early 21st centuries. *Aren't we smart enough to stamp out our raw genetic compulsions for wealth and power?*

Before she could recover from a sob that shook her body, Killah appeared in the doorway. She let the tears stain her face.

The elllonian medic looked down and focused generous oval eyes on the young woman sitting in her recovery wheelchair. She had never hidden her fears from him, nor her current sense of failure. He understood her well.

"Why can't I just move on, enjoy the gift of my own life, Killah? What's wrong with me?"

"Going to Earth to share your insights was a huge gift. Wake up to it, Shawnoon," Killah scolded. "Stay focused on the good things that are happening on Earth. I suspect your species will either evolve or find their way out, but it will take time, as it did with us."

Ellason and Varok had found the difficult solutions to long-term survival for their worlds' sentient life. It required painful, unrelenting attention to conservation, real denial of attractive conveniences. The ells and varoks had achieved cultures that valued, above all, the quality of creative living, where time was savored and spent with discretion.

Killah talked on. "You've made your dent on Earth, Shawne. That's all anyone can expect in life." Killah lifted her face with soft befinned hands so she couldn't avoid the dark emerald glint in his eyes. "Let yourself heal, with every tool you've been given. Focus on living."

Maybe I've lived long enough, she thought.

KILLAH AND SHAWNE

Some time later, before Ahl Vior turned away from Jupiter and a soft dark descended on the Varokian city, Shawne decided to walk to the therapy pool. She focused on her body. Good. Nothing hurt. The recovery exercises had done their job; she was no longer trembling while walking in Varok's gravity.

"It's good to see you smile, Shawnoon." Killah appeared in the doorway, his sonic melons tilted foreword. "I've got your pills. We've decided to try the serotonin reuptake inhibitors, the SSRIs. They shouldn't give you any serious side effects, maybe some mild nausea or headache."

"Killah, I don't think they'll help."

"Right. Maybe not, but we'll know before the next Callisto Cycle." He followed her into the water and moved around the young woman, staying a few meters away as he scanned with his sonar. "Now turn around, slowly," he said in Varokian, as if to remind her where she was. "Yes, the healing is about done. You look well, but I'm going home with you, on the Ahlkahn. You have more healing to do, don't you? Psychological healing while you give the pills a chance to work."

She climbed out of the pool and threw on an elllonian wet-sweater. "I'll give the pills a chance, Killah. But I have more work to do on my attitudes toward . . . life . . . and the living. Philosophy, religion and all that." Her eyes did not meet his. "You can sign off on my good health now, can't you?"

"You have no regrets?" The elll's brow plumes tensed into folds.

"Of course I have regrets—about everything." All the grief she thought was gone rose like a torrent to drown out the happy expectation of going home to the lovely valley on Varok where she grew up. "I have never lied to Conn before," she said.

"Someday you will tell Conn about your very wise decision," Killah said with emphasis. "You know all too well what it was like to grow up alone, the only human child on a strange world."

Killah sat beside her on the pool's deck, and she welcomed the soft touch of mossy tiles on the arms enfolding her.

"I didn't expect to feel so . . . failed, and so alone now. I could have been a mother," she said.

"Probably not. The continued bleeding suggests you were not successfully pregnant."

"In any case, I am firm in my belief that I have done the right thing."

Killah looked into the glistening eyes of the young, newly mature human female he called Shawnoon—Shawne the swimmer, lover of water, adopted daughter of the mixed-species Oran-elConn-Grey

Family he knew as close friends. He had worked on interspecies contact problems with her mother at the Elll–Varok Earth Moonbase when Shawne was a toddler.

Killah's friend Conn had been the first elll to know Shawne's adoptive human mother, Tandra Grey. As a student of Earth's history and culture, Conn was able to convince her to join the Elll–Varok Science project on Earth's moon and work with Killah for EV Science there, studying cross-species microbiology.

There Tandra met the varok Oran Ramahlak (called Orram), Conn's lifelong friend. At Moonbase, the varoks' disconcerting humanoid appearance challenged her self-image, until she was able to define and accept their differences.

As an aquatic, schooling creature, Conn presented different, more physical demands that created real problems for the human woman, until she experienced significant personal growth. Eventually she bonded with both Conn and Orram as family. Shawne smiled, as she remembered the story; it had required hard work for her mother.

In 2051 C. E. (Earth) the family had settled on Varok, and for nearly two Earth decades (two Jovian years) Killah had watched Shawne grow from a chubby child prodigy to a statuesque athlete and powerful swimmer, for a human, slowed down in water only by her crown of wavy blond hair.

As he studied her now, he realized that he had never before seen her blue-green eyes so troubled, her life-joy muted by *what*? Not just an unnecessary self-doubt. Something far deeper than her worries about Earth. Something edged with a primal fear.

Killah was glad he had decided to take her home. She needed her family. The Oran-elConn-Grey family ellls—Conn, his mate Lanoll and their hatchling Stringer—the varok Orram, his son Orticon, and the humans Shawne and Tandra were tightly bonded, happy to be responsible under Varokian law for each other's well-being and financial support.

– Δ –

On their way to the family's locale, riding the rapid rail Ahlkahn, Shawne stared blankly out at the extensive city Ahl Vior, its dwellings and shops nearly hidden amidst large trees and rocky outcroppings.

When they had passed the rugged peaks of Niorral and entered the fertile valley beneath the slopes rising into the Vahinorall, Killah broke the silence.

"I've got something more for you to read, so you will quit obsessing about Earth's future."

An old book lay cradled in his right manual fin. Its cover was stained, its edges tattered, and several thin leather-weed markers protruded from the pages. "You're in good company. This was published on Earth by a university scholar. I did good detective work finding it in the Human Studies Library."

The elllonian medic read aloud, pronouncing the English with an unpracticed confusion of Elllonian *l* and *lll* sounds. Shawne had to smile at the effort he made.

> *The world is facing some stark demographic trends. . . .*
> *Population is growing exponentially. . . . Regional shortages*
> *of land and food have already produced starvation, refu-*
> *gees, and violent conflict . . . Dealing with this population*
> *pressure may require many countries to use a greater level*
> *of coordination and planning than has been used tradition-*
> *ally, and may require fundamental cultural, economic, and*
> *political changes . . .*

Killah handed the book to Shawne, confused by her deepening frown. "That was published in the human year 1999."[1]

"1999? Killah, that was seven decades ago! Before the die-offs. They knew, and yet . . ."

"Right." Killah realized that his attempt to boost Shawne's faith in humanity had instead deepened her grief. "I thought it might be hopeful to know that you have never been alone with your ideas. Of course you knew that. I'm sorry. Keep the book."

Shawne smiled for Killah's sake. "I've read many of Earth's books. I just didn't realize how early—"

"What do the complexity texts say? If a hundred years in, then a hundred years out. Right? Remember your Varokian history. It took many generations for them to create a steady state. Humans will do

---

1   John W. Kingdon. *America the Unusual*, New York, St. Martins/Worth, 1999, 96–97.

what they need to do. They're moving north. They'll be fine, just like the dinosaurs and forests in the Arctic during the early Cenozoic."

"Swell. Warming will cancel the next ice age, so man can continue destroying the planet." She paused. "Sorry, Killah. I'm being cynical."

Killah caught her eyes. "Some balance will occur, ice age or no."

"When mother was born in 2020, there was still a strong belief that technology could fix anything. People thought that escape from Earth was possible. By the time I was born in 2047, toxic chemicals, air pollution, deforestation, ocean acidification, water scarcity—who knows what else—had gone over the tipping points. The huge die-offs had begun."

"You're forgetting the good stuff, Shawne. Ocean fishing hasn't collapsed, even now. Catch-sharing probably helps. Los Angeles roofs are now loaded with solar collectors. There was even some talk about energy efficiency."

Shawne smiled through her tears. "You won't let me obsess about all this, will you, Killah?"

He looped his long slender tongue over his nose, and she laughed.

"You've seen Conn do that."

Killah stared out the large window as they raced through the web fields of Varok. "The crest of the Vahinorral is visible. There, beyond those slopes covered with looping snarl. They glisten when the lightning brightens the sky. Look. Can you see the hints of Jupiter beyond the clouds?"

"I can. I love when it fills the sky and sends a glow over Lake Seclusion."

"What about the dolphins and whales on Earth?" he asked. "Do they understand what's been happening?"

"I wish I knew. They seemed to be coping, but I didn't have much time with them. I stayed with Conn at the seaside house after we swam with whales and he got sick. Then I was busy teaching our steady-state courses at the lab, until we all went chasing south to Australia to rescue Nidok. You know him, don't you, Killah? The ahlork that helped us snag that witch Mahntik?"

"Oh, yes. I've even tried to patch up his exoskeleton once. Later I managed to file a chip in his beak."

"In Australia I swam with dolphins a little. When we came back, I was . . . preoccupied with—"

"Your first love. That's huge, for you humans. But now you must move on." Killah took her hand in his left fin. "Dear girl, I have had an idea. I think you need . . . I think you would enjoy consulting with the great-fish on Ellason. Give them a call. The communication time delay is annoying but manageable. They are not only renowned philosophers, but quite interested in the complex phenomenon on Earth known as humanity."

She looked at him with curiosity. She met his smile, but it surprised him. Her lips were trembling.

"I'll read the religion you suggested, but I can't talk to great-fish, Killah. I don't know how. And I'm not . . . I'm too confused and angry. Maybe, when I'm back home at the Oran Locale I'll find some . . . reason for being, something to extinguish this horrible feeling."

"I hear you. It seems unthinkable to talk with great-fish on Ellason right now, but you'll heal quickly once you have a few good rides on your favorite daramonts. Then, perhaps you will let me introduce you to the great-fish who live here in the Forested Sea."

Father Elll, Daughter Human

First-light drew silver beams across the web fields and into the elll-pond. Stringer's sonic voice woke his father, Conn, from a dream of Ellason—the feel and taste of succulent white moss dancing in heaving dark waves, deep ocean vents warming gardens of frilled filter-fish, thirty bright moons weaving a tapestry of light in high clouds.

Strange. Why am I preoccupied with the home planet I left as a young tad? Conn yawned and rolled over in the mud, intending to cover his mate Lanoll as she slept. She wasn't there. Then he felt the buzz of Stringer's sonic demand.

"Wake up and surface, Conn." Stringer meant it. "Shawne and I need to talk to you about Ellason. We'll be outside with Lanoll."

"Crazy idea," Conn mumbled in ultrasonics.

Down the hearth stones, on the tree-embraced porch of their home, Conn found his offspring Stringer with his adopted human daughter, talking about a trip to Ellason they had no hope of making. "I'm a schooling elll, Shawne," Stringer was saying. "I'm naked without the school's flow pattern."

"You're always naked, Plume-hips," Shawne quipped, "and I'm in no shape to go out there with you."

Good thing she's not encouraging him, Conn thought.

"I'm serious, Shawne. I'm desolate without the school's pressure pattern defining me. Incapacitated. I can't live here on Varok all my life, like Conn and Lanoll. They're loners. I'm not. Somehow, as soon as possible, while Ellason is at perihelion, I'm going out there, where some ellls still live full schooling lives. Don't you want to see where Conn grew up?"

"Of course." Shawne took hold of Stringer's head plumes and gave them a gentle tug. "You always know how to get to me, don't you?"

"'Some ellls live full schooling lives.' That's correct," Conn said. "There are also loners on Ellason, and they're having trouble getting along. Oleyall has applied to set up a research facility on Ellason to study schooler-loner problems."

Stringer's eyes swallowed his face. "Really? When? Why didn't you tell me the great-fish are interested?"

"Because you shouldn't risk the expense and the danger of going out there. It's another long trip in space. You're bones would turn into crackers."

"Now I have a professional reason to go, Conn. The schooler-loner problem is important. You could go as an observer, Shawne."

"You really think I could?"

"Of course."

"Well . . . perhaps, if you're going, Stringer. Do you suppose I could study with the great-fish?"

Lanoll, Conn's blue-plumed mate, came to the porch from the hearth with bowls of pond-fish soup for the first-light meal. "Surely you're not considering more space travel! We just got home. I'm afraid you wouldn't be strong enough to visit the great-fish, Shawne. And you certainly should not be doing any space travel, especially a trip that long."

"Killah says I'm quite . . . healed, Lanoll. Ellason doesn't require optional gills like yours, does it?"

Lanoll laughed. "Our lungs are optional, not our gills," she said with her usual kindly tone. "Ellason is all hot geology and water, you know, Shawne. You do well here on Varok, but you and your . . . you won't ever be strong enough to keep up with Stringer on Ellason." She looked at Stringer and decided that he knew nothing of Shawne's pregnancy. Had she decided on suspension to avoid a birth in space, or had she lost the tiny fetus Conn had noticed early on the trip home?

Shawne frowned. "You're serious, Lanoll, aren't you?"

Conn slurped noisily. "*Ellason alahranon niloh har ahrahl.*"

"The mists bring disaster? Nonsense," Shawne said, calling his bluff. "Tell us more in Ellasonian, Conn. I've got to brush up before we leave."

"I'll protect you if Conn doesn't go." Stringer shot his narrow tongue out and wrapped it around Shawne's wrist.

"Off your tongue, Brother Elll. I know how to adjust to elllonian schools here on Varok. But maybe Lanoll's right. Ellls could be very different on Ellason."

"Of course the schools on Ellason are not like those here, Shawne," Conn said. "And you, Stringer, surely you can find a good life here. There are some interesting schools in Varok's Forested Sea."

Shawne gave Stringer a look, but his gills flared in opposition. Or was it frustration?

"Schooling here is not enough," he said to Conn. "I want to go where they're stable for generations . . . where loner ellls don't keep leaving the school to do this or accomplish that. Adjustment is too painful."

Shawne's eyes lost their focus. "Maybe I'd better not go out to Ellason. I can contact the great-fish here, Stringer, and ask for tutoring in philosophy."

Conn didn't like her waffling back and forth like this. Apparently she hadn't told Stringer about the baby. Was she still depressed or something? There was a tone of desperation in her voice. Maybe the pills weren't working. "Come on, Shawne," he said, grabbing a wet-sweater off the rock wall of the porch. "Let's go watch Jupiter fill up the sky. It should be full-light soon."

Feeling strangely at odds with herself, Shawne followed Conn down the stairs and into the garden. She curled beside the elll, hugging her jeans and pulling her varokian tunic over them, then twisting her long waves into a single golden knot at the back of her head.

They sat on a bench they had created from looping snarl, an otherwise nasty Varokian weed that covered the foothills of the Vahinorral. Careless daramonts sometimes tripped on its slick arching roots. She and Conn had planted the living bench near the egg-layers' nests in the family's garden, enjoying many talks there while she grew up, watching the furry critters snatch at mud-root worms with their forked tongues.

Conn decided to attack the subject of Ellason up front. "You know that very few can ever go to Ellason, Shawne. Global Varok needs a good reason to spend so much energy."

She shrugged, and her blond waves hid her face as she leaned over to trace curving shapes in the purple moss at their feet. She couldn't make herself tell him. What would she say? *I couldn't have given you a grandchild? That would be lying, wouldn't it?*

Conn saw a surge of grief rise in her, then dissipate. "You know, Shawnoon, I'm not convinced Stringer is a true schooler. He may have trouble adjusting to Ellason if he goes out there, or if he takes on this loner-schooler problem."

Conn wrapped his webbed hands around Shawne's face. Questions poured from her eyes. For reasons Conn didn't understand, they filled with tears. He was doing nothing to improve her mood. As Tandra feared, she seemed clinically depressed.

"How about a trip to the Forested Sea," he said, "before you start your environmental monitoring work with Lanoll? Stringer will want to do some schooling there."

"I can't go there, Conn."

"Why not? You could talk to the light-hoppers about relevance of mosquitoes or the size of the universe or something. Oh, sorry. I'm not thinking. Of course you should stay close to home for a while."

Conn caught her tear with the tip of his tongue, an old habit that usually made her smile. This time was no exception.

"Your faith in nature should help me give up on Earth, Conn, but I'm haunted by what's happening there. I can't get it out of my mind."

Conn put one long green arm around her and let her weep. Then he reminded her of Ellason's history. "When the varoks first went out there, they realized the ellls were obsessed with their love of tads. They were so nuts to have kids, they didn't get what was going on—the stress from overcrowding. It was driving schools against each other.

The varoks thought the answers were obvious—just do as we say: 'Limit your population, clean up your wastes and define your farming space.' It didn't work, only made things worse. The ellls had to find their own solutions, come to terms with their own nature."

"But human nature is so . . . difficult. Our history is loaded with wars and cheating and making others wrong—"

"And wild-ass creative intelligence, and love of good hard work, and getting smart and educated when needed. Many humans have suffered and many more will suffer, but in the end they'll reinvent themselves. I know this, because I've driven a car on Earth. Remember? Well, no, you don't, because you were so young. I remember how humans driving cars do an intersection with stop signs in both directions. Everyone knows that the first car to arrive has the right of way, the right to cross the intersection first. If two cars arrive at the crossroads at the same time, the car on the right has the right of way."

"Conn?"

"I'm serious. Think about it. Drivers watch to make sure that it's safe to go, but the rule holds. The same mentality will kick in on Earth when the stoplights of population and resource limits are obvious."

Shawne sighed. "Conn, you're amazing. How can you be so optimistic, after all the decades of people working to define how to do a steady state economy? And nobody listening?"

"You're allowed to grieve, Shawnoon."

That did it. She broke down and sobbed, long and hard. When the tears and shaking stopped, she lay with her head in the elll's lap.

He stroked her hair. *How can I help her feel pride in her good work, move on to enjoy the creative power of her youth?*

As if to emphasize their differences, she smoothed the pressure-sensitive moss of Conn's breast tiles and traced with thoughtful fingers the meshwork that framed them. Carefully, she avoided the neuromasts in those sensitive lines, knowing they were like the lateral lines in fish, only more so—filled with many sensors.

Then she surprised the elll and sat up, ready to reclaim herself. "Ellason is not just about wanting to be with Stringer. It's talking with great-fish. I do want to study with them and understand their philosophy. If Ellason can heal, Earth can heal. It's hard to imagine varoks and ellls being unable to communicate. Why did it take so long?"

"Ellls didn't use their throats to make noise in air, except to sing,"

Conn said. "And at that time, the varoks considered themselves God's great gift of sentience to the universe."

"Was elllonian singing like wolves on Earth howling at the moon?"

"Not quite. Ancient elllonian singing had little to do with everyday talk. To sing 'I'm over here. What's for dinner?' was downright rude, a parody on a respected art form. It took a horrific clash between ellls and varoks to shake up both species' mind sets before they would use the new language."

"Paradigm shifts are hard to come by."

Conn saw a faraway look in her eyes. He expected her thoughts were probably back on Earth, but they were not.

"Do you think I could understand the great-fish, Conn, like I do you?" Shawne asked.

"Probably. But it will take a while."

At age three, twenty Earth-years ago, Shawne had bonded to what she called the green lights in Conn's huge black alien eyes. She wondered what colors he saw there. What else did he see?

Orange and silver in English translated to medium off-dim and rich-bright in Elllonian. Having evolved in water on a planet lit by moonlight, shore-pool lightning bugs, and deep-sea vents, ellls see far into the infrared at the expense of what humans might call color, though they do seem to share some notion of red to yellow to blue. It took Shawne some time to understand that.

"Talk to me, Shawne. I can't read you like Orram does."

Shawne reached up to stroke back the red and yellow plumes that fell between his dark eyes. "I want to experience your native planet. I want you to show me where you grew legs. I want to meet your sponsoring school." She tried to smile. "It would help me find myself, if I knew where you were hatched."

"Now that's weird, my dear, given our biological differences." She didn't laugh as he expected, and their silence grew. "I don't want to go to Ellason," he said.

Conn couldn't believe he had actually said it, especially to Shawne. He didn't want to go back to Ellason and face—what? Himself, he supposed—his wild elllonian nature, the part that might run free in the seas of Ellason, where the water surged deep and clear and alive with soft lights.

Shawne knows nothing about wild schooling ellls. Those of us who made

Varok our home are more or less civilized. I barely remember my hatching waters on Ellason. What's so scary? Afraid I'll drown or get eaten by eefl? True, here on Varok I spend most of my time out of water, but, great gardens, gills don't forget how to work. It's not that. Maybe I'm afraid of not measuring up. I am a loner, not a normal schooling elll. And Ellason is a big place, a harsh place in spite of its warm deep waters and glowing critters and thirty bright moons dancing the mambo in the mists.

As they sat on the looping snarl bench, Shawne had that look in her eye, that unique human look that said, *Forget you're an elll, Conn. Give it to me straight, soul to soul. No funny business.*

Conn felt that his daughter deserved the closest thing to a soul dump he could manage. *I don't need to bother her with the uncomfortable memories—growing up as a loner, ignoring schooling pressures, being rejected for causing an adjustment every time I left. Going off alone for good and studying Varokian languages and Earth biology eased the pain.*

"Ellason is a dangerous place, Shawne, a wild place. Your going there would be like dropping the Easter bunny into the middle of a jungle."

"So why is Ellason the center of religious thought in this solar system? Even the Earth scholars read Haralahn."

"Haralahn? You mean the ancestor of the intellectual by the same name, author of *Reflections in Blood-stained Water*? That's ancient Ellasonian history. Nobody on Earth reads that."

"Yes they do, Conn. Some people are fascinated with Ellason's history, and his descendant is still writing good stuff."

"Whatever. Unbelievable, but if you're serious, you and Stringer should do some groundwork here on Varok first. Go to the Forested Sea and listen to what the ellls there have to say. Then study Ellason so you know how impossible it is for you to survive there."

"Good idea on both counts," Shawne said. "Stringer will want to do some farewell schooling in the Forested Sea, and I've got to learn *eefl* and *eeflin* defense before we leave, if we leave."

"Also—" Conn hated to say it. "You shouldn't try to talk philosophy with Haralahn until you've learned what people here on Varok think, Shawne. You could get a mind-blowing perspective talking to light-hoppers."

Shawne laughed. "I bet."

"I'm serious. You've got to load your mind with all kinds of ideas before you talk to great-fish. Take a close look at human religions."

"Yes, I've started doing that, but you need to think about going with us, Conn. There are too few loner ellls like you who have raised a schooler. And—not many ellls are committed as family with a human and the former Director of Living Resources. We're sure to get our proposal accepted if you and Mom and Orram sign on with us."

"But I won't sign on, will I? I hate space travel. Ellason's gravity will make pea soup of me and beef *bourguignon* of you." Conn avoided the real issues.

"I know."

"And it's worth it? Your need to understand great-fish philosophy is that important?"

Shawne seemed to be struggling to find answers to questions she couldn't define. "It's not just that, Conn. I just can't . . . feel good . . . about how we left Earth. What good has my life been? Why are we even here? Why are we anywhere? What good are our brains if they're too complex to think straight?"

THE QUEST BEGINS

Conn looked up to watch Lanoll and Tandra emerge from the family lodge. He was glad to see them wave him and Shawne in for the midlight meal. He was relieved at finding an excuse to dodge Shawne's questions. "See these beautiful complex creatures calling to us? Who could ask for more meaning in life than such a family?"

As she entered the lodge, Shawne looked at her adoptive human mother Tandra and Conn's mate Lanoll. Their warm smiles broke her downward spiral. "I also have two wonderful fathers, Conn—you and Orram. It's natural for me to think of the creative force as being more like a loving father—or mother—than a designer or a self-organizer or a strange attractor."

"Why can't He be all at once?" Conn asked. "A father for you, a devoted sponsor in an elllonian school for me, an *ahl* seed becoming a tree, a supernova about to blow up and produce heavy elements so life can go on somewhere for another billion years, on and on."

Conn stood at the hearth pot, filling their bowls with *hoat* berry stew laced with *el* eggs. "My problem with the formal religions you're studying is that on 21st century Earth the love message got lost."

"I know, Conn, that's why, somehow, sometimes I feel I must go to Ellason, whether you go or not. Religion is so confusing and controversial on Earth. I want to understand what is meaningful to great-fish and real schooling ellls."

Ouch. Real ellls? "Why, Shawne? You don't need to worry about Stringer. Maybe he'll get over his Ellason kick."

"You know better than that, Conn. Stringer is . . . different when he's schooling at Ahl Vior. I understand his need to return to his genetic roots. It's like my need to find the reason for being."

"You can't get more real than recognizing the complex nature of everything we know. Everything is connected," Conn said, feeling just a little frustrated. "Ask Lanoll."

"Shawne probably means she needs a more spiritual definition of God," Lanoll said, standing back from them and shaking pool water from her plumes. "Do you use the word *God*, Tandra?"

Tandra smiled as Conn started to answer for her. Then she answered Lanoll to save Conn from himself. "I think some philosophers use the concept *God* to mean emergence—the fact that the whole is greater, and something different, than the parts or their behavior. I like that idea. It implies a spiritual reality, a reason for existence beyond the testable knowledge of science."

"Good grief, Mom. Existence has got to mean something less mechanical than all the goodies that come with complex systems and quantum mechanics. All I want to know right now is why we're here at all, why anything we do matters."

"Don't forget the beautiful, miraculous fact of being conscious," Lanoll said. "Isn't everything trivial when measured against the miracle of love and beauty?"

"I have learned a lot from the zen of ellls, Lanoll," Shawne said, but isn't it all just unpredictable dumb luck in the old clockwork universe, cranking out us carbon critters? At the Concentrate, Master Oleyall talked about the nonlocality of subatomic particles, as if everything is connected because they get entangled. Who cares if quantum non-locality has anything to do with things going 'bump' in the night? It doesn't tell us *why* it all connects."

Shawne's bitter tone burned a hole in Conn's heart. He knew he couldn't help her. The same old tape kept reeling through his head. What he would say, again, wouldn't help, but he said it anyway. "What we do matters, Shawnoon. It's built-in meaning. Just like our work on Earth. Anything we do can have consequences in someone's future. We just can't know why or how or when something will trigger—"

Shawne reached for the family ring deeply embedded in Conn's fourth interdigital fin. She always turned the ring with a gentle touch, knowing how sensitive elllonian fins could be. "But that's why we should go to Ellason," she said. "Our going could make a big difference eventually, especially for Stringer."

Conn heard the 'gotcha' in her voice and realized she was right.

– Δ –

Shawne worked on Orram later that light-period, when the family gathered at the hearth again.

Orram—now there's a good solid soul for Shawne to talk to, Conn thought. *She's wasting her time trying to pin down the slippery thoughts of a moss-eating aquatic like me.*

Shawne gave Orram a pleading look. "Conn keeps describing everything as if it were stuck in a complexity textbook—as if everything that's connected has to be sensitive to initial conditions, or sensitive at critical moments, or sensitive to forks in the path or amplified or emergent. So nothing can be predicted, right?"

"At least not much. Sorry, Shawne." Orram looked the part for the philosophical ruminations she wanted, with his planar face and probing blue eyes. His head of silver-streaked hair added a distinguishing touch to a body as tall as Conn's. He had let his hair grow over his ears when they went to Earth so it would hide his patch organs, the only feature not even vaguely similar to human features on casual surveillance.

Superficially, Conn thought to himself, *Orram resembles a human who has been through a fire. His skin is smooth, cool as bronze in the infrared, and hairless—beautiful.*

Orram gave Shawne a look and focused his patches on reading Conn's mood. "I see more angst in Conn than anything, Shawne. The loner-schooler situation on Ellason could be as snarled as it is here."

"Hmmm." The varok could see that Conn didn't want to hear that. The words passed through Conn's ear plaques without alerting his brain to what Orram was suggesting.

Shawne stood up. "Are you saying that the ellls are in trouble here and on Ellason, Orram?"

"That's why I don't want to go to Ellason," Conn said, knowing it sounded lame. "We could trigger any number of avalanches, and they could all come down on us."

"Since when have you been afraid of avalanches?" Shawne said. "We know how to control complex systems. You don't focus on symptoms, you find the rules that govern how a system operates. Right?"

"Oh sure," Conn said, "Let's start with Old Bain the curmudgeon and figure out what triggers his—"

He stopped talking when Charley Hazard came in the door. The human friend Tandra had brought from Earth gave everyone his big hairy smile as he took a seat on a hearth stone.

Tandra followed Charley in, looking happy and rested. "I've been showing Charley how to care for the web bushes," she said. She busied herself serving him a bowl of stew from Orram's hearth pot.

Though the family had been a familiar oddity on Varok for two Jovian years, no plans had been made for bringing more humans to that moon. Humans were still a rare sight there: Shawne and Tandra; Jesse Mendleton, the ellls' and varoks' initial contact on Earth; and Charley, Tandra's recent intimate contact.

In these times of economic stability and renewed creative energy, most varoks, and the ellls on Varok, replaced themselves by having children. Few Replacement Certificates were being traded or sold. Orram had offered his own certificate so Charley could come to Varok with the family.

"Did I hear something about going to Ellason?" Charley asked. "Now that would be quite a challenge. It's pretty far out, isn't it?"

"This is our only chance," Shawne said. "It's near perihelion now."

Charley pinched his red beard. "Sorry, Shawne, but wouldn't that be a huge expenditure for someone?"

Why does this guy always find a way to make me smile? Conn thought.

It's infuriating. I miss my time alone with Tandra. She brought Charley here. Now I suppose he'll find an excuse to go to Ellason with us.

On Earth, Charley had been an engineer turned fisherman. He had given up the big bucks staring at a computer screen to run fishing rigs off Cabo San Lucas. Last year while running a tuna hunt, he befriended the family's ahlork friend Nidok and Orram's son Orticon, after rescuing them from a tiny weather station in the middle of the South Pacific. He brought them home to the Scripps Institute in San Diego, and promptly fell in love with Tandra.

Conn interpreted "falling in love" in the human species as nothing more than a hormonal attack on the brain. *The victims readily forget this fact. They also forget that such love doesn't last forever, but—as Tandra insisted—with hard work and incredible good luck it can metamorphose into something worthwhile.*

I can't help worrying a little about Tandra's human sex hormones getting in the way of the mental release she provides Orram. Their mind-link allows him to experience emotion and stay rational. Realizing this all too well, Orram invited Charley to return to Varok with us—over my objections.

At next light, Conn blew off steam by going into the fields to check on the daramonts, large mounts dedicated to transporting the ellls on land. Several frequented the Oran Locale's web fields. His favorite mount stood watching him just outside the garden, looking for an excuse to race to the hills. When he bowed in invitation, Conn took hold of his tough mane and swung up onto his shoulders.

"Anywhere," the elll said, and they took off toward Lake Seclusion.

The ride didn't help much. Conn's mind kept trying to replay all the details that Tandra had told him about a recent serious talk with Charley. The bottom line was simply that all the males wanted more time with Tandra. Also, Charley would need to make a major paradigm shift, they agreed, if he were to become part of the family. He needed to distinguish concepts like *pet* and *brother* and *mate* and *friend* and *husband* and *confidante*, then throw them all out and imagine something that incorporated features of them all.

Before he realized how fast he was riding, Conn found himself in the foothills of the Vahinorral. He turned back toward the house as Varok began its swing away from Jupiter.

When Conn got back to the house, Shawne was waiting for her turn to climb onto the daramont.

"Oh, no you don't. No racing while you're—" Before Conn could make his point, she had stepped onto Pork Belly's inviting knee and settled onto his shoulders. They loped off toward the mountains, leaving Conn to worry silently about his imagined grandchild lying in a freezer somewhere, awaiting its return to Shawne's womb.

He loved the way Shawne's colors matched the caramel brown of the daramont. She was barely visible from a distance except for her long silken hair streaming across the mount's back.

The light-period dragged on dim and confusing, as Jupiter loomed huge behind restless clouds, and its moon Io appeared in the dark part of the sky. Conn tried to tend to the business of the house and locale, but he could do nothing but worry. As Varok turned away from the roiling light of Jupiter's striped face, only Tandra's good sense kept the elll from going out to search for Shawne.

She returned soon enough, with the ahlork Nidok. Conn and Orram could hear them coming as Shawne's hoots of laughter and Nidok's loud misuse of Varokian cut through the moist air.

"Philosophy be useless words, Shawne," Nidok said.

"I know it can be tied up with semantics, especially if philosophers ignore what has been learned lately," she replied. "I really have listened to my mom, and Conn, and Orram, all my life. They believe in something about complexity's built-in meaning, as if an act of kindness could be amplified into something terribly meaningful a thousand years later."

"Ahlork give meaningful scars that amplify," Nidok said. He hopped onto the porch to squat near the rest of the family.

"Of course, fair crustaceanoid," Shawne laughed. "I see your point. You can't have living chemical cocktails all over the universe, shaking out consciousness and relationships, without it signifying something. I just want to know why. What's the point?"

They followed everyone into the family lodge.

Nidok took Shawne's arm in his prehensile wing tip. "I show you meaning built-in," he said.

Conn knew what he was going to do. "No, Nidok."

Before the elll could stop him, the ahlork gripped Shawne's wrist and swiped it deftly with a sharp wing tip. He spit on the wound to stop the bleeding and create a raised scar. "There," he said proudly. "Now you be my adult nestling. There be meaning—guaranteed love, protection by ahlork scar, same as your family." He turned a beady eye to meet both of hers.

Tears flowed down Shawne's face, and she embraced his exoskeleton as best she could, reaching only halfway around. "Now I am yours, Nidok, more honored than I deserve."

At next light Nidok appointed himself Charley's tour guide of Varok. After the family breakfast at the hearth, they huddled with Orram over electronic maps, planning to explore the ancient ruins of the *horkah*, the ancestors of Varoks. Nidok would be an excellent guide. Ahlork had a long history mining the ruins for useable minerals.

"We'll stay in contact," Charley said. "You have my handle, Orram?"

"Yes. Enjoy your trip. Nidok will be an interesting guide."

"At least I'll hear the ahlork point of view," Charley warned, and the human walked off through the web fields, while the ahlork hopped from bush to bush. Soon they disappeared toward the lower slopes of the Vahinorral.

– Δ –

They had been gone less than two light-periods when a late dark-period call came in from the great-fish Oleyall. Ellason had contacted him. Great-fish there reported strange elllonian behavior—loners going off abruptly and never returning, schools suddenly growing much larger, loners making long journeys toward the Viortahk close to dangerous *eefl* waters. The greater elllonian community on Ellason was endangered by tension between loners and schoolers.

The council of great-fish had asked Oleyall to contact Varok's Living Resources Council. They would put together a team to look into the problem.

"I want you or Conn to take me to Ellason, Orram," the great-fish Oleyall transmitted in carefully translated Varokian. "Perhaps your family will agree to go with us. I need your varied expertise to study this sensitive problem. Stringer, of course, will have permission to stay on Ellason if he wishes. We will find for him a replacement certificate."

There it was. Suddenly Shawne and Stringer had the justification they needed for the trip.

"Before I agree to go anywhere," Conn told Oleyall, "I need to see

the council's proposal, and we need to know a lot more. We need details, concrete evidence about the problems between loners and schoolers both here and on Ellason."

When the message was translated, Oleyall signaled amusement.
"I understand you, Conn," he replied. "No fuzzy-headed crystal-ball
tongue-wagging. Promise."

"You great-fish have been downloading too many old *Wired* maga-
zines," Conn grumbled.

Realizing he had been outmaneuvered, the elll retreated upstairs
to the house pond to find Lanoll. She had experience working for the
Living Resources Council and would know how to get out of this.

Conn dove into the pool and roused his mate from her favorite

resting place in the shore weeds. "You missed Nidok's latest drama, Love—and Oleyall's too. Where's Stringer?"

"Asleep, as was I, thank you very much."

"Do you have evidence that loners and schoolers are in some crisis?" he asked. "The great-fish are convinced we need to go out to Ellason."

"There is also some evidence for tension between loners and schoolers here on Varok, yes, and I agree that we should find out more, Conn." Lanoll's pain was obvious in the rigid spread of her brow plumes. "I know you don't want to make the trip, but we need to know more, for Stringer's sake. He may have a difficult adjustment out there. I can't *not* go, if there is a trip. Don't make me choose between you and Stringer, Conn."

"You won't ever have to," he said, but it felt like a lie.

Before they fell asleep in the soft mud at the bottom of the pond, Lanoll wondered out loud what their native planet Ellason was really like. She had never been there. She was hatched on Varok, sponsored by a small school in the warm currents of Lake Seclusion. "You need to explore your tangled thoughts about Ellason, Conn. You don't want to make a decision you'll regret."

Conn couldn't deny Lanoll. He struggled to find a way to walk through his fears. "Ellason would be a harsh . . . an alien place," he said. "It wouldn't be the same as I remember. My school wouldn't know me. They adjusted me out of existence when I left as a tad, a loner tad. The schools could be . . . less open than the ones we know on Varok. Ellls there would be stronger, smarter, more ocean-smart than we Varokian ellls. Stringer might stay there, and maybe you will decide to stay there with him. Why should I risk that?"

OLD BAIN

Shawne began advanced Ellasonian studies at the Concentrate and soon learned more than she wanted to know about the tension between loners like Conn and schooling ellls like Stringer. When she tried to explain the problem to Stringer, he agreed to swim Varok's lakes with her to check out the situation.

"Let's go to Lake Seclusion first," he suggested. "Old Bain is a master of carving truth out of moldering fables."

– Δ –

It was like pumping *eefl* fangs for love potions. Old Bain greeted them with a demand for immediate adjustment. Bringing a human into the school challenged their pressure patterns.

"Let me get a good feel for you in water, Missy," Bain demanded, expecting Shawne would come close to drowning in the process. When she didn't, and when she minded her schooling manners, and especially when she kept up with the school as they circled, Old Bain softened a bit and agreed to answer one question.

"Only one?" she asked.

"One. I'm not getting any younger, and your stench is clogging my gills."

She nearly gulped water. "I thought . . . if I were careful—"

"Well, you smell like something alien. Don't argue with me if you want answers."

Stringer winced. "Hurry up and ask your question, Shawne."

Ellls of the school kept their distance, swimming in small circles, as if they knew trouble was brewing.

Shawne pulled her hair back into a knot. "Can I have an answer in Varokian, please?" she asked Bain. "There are not enough words in Sonics to cover the subject."

"We'll see. Ask."

"What does it all mean?"

"All? All what?"

"Well, everything."

Stringer nearly lost his cool. Shawne wanted a philosophical discussion with the old slime bones—in Varokian? "Shawne, for *chrisake*, what are you asking?"

Bain's temper exploded and he sailed over to Stringer. "Don't use language you don't understand, young Stringer. You picked up that word from your sponsor, Conn. You can't even pronounce it correctly."

Stringer had no idea what he meant. "Conn is my genetic sire—my father," he said, "not just my sponsor."

"You don't understand me," Bain snorted.

"I think Bain doesn't like your use of the expression, *chrisake*," Shawne said, steeling herself. "The expression is an English expletive, a contraction for 'Christ's sake.' The person given that title was martyred for teaching that the Creator is more interested in love than church politics."

"Among other things, no doubt," Bain said.

"I know. I know," Stringer whined.

"You're a schooler, Stringer," Bain continued. "You should know better, using language from Earth's history. Conn is a loner, and loners can't keep their thoughts clear. Loners keep muddling up good school logic, going off, then coming back, going off, coming back. Your school is always out of adjustment because Conn can't stay put."

Shawne crossed her arms under water, giving the ellls' negative signal. "No, no, that isn't the way our family works."

Bain ignored her. "Keep the loners out of Lake Seclusion, I say. Leave the water to water ellls, as they do on Ellason. If loners want to live on dry land, let them stay there. They come and go, come and go. They disrupt the school with so much adjustment. Mutants they are, a bad strain. Don't ever let any of them get back to Ellason. Ruin the gene pool there, they would."

Stringer couldn't believe it when Shawne interrupted the old elll again. "There have always been loners on Ellason," she said. "The inventor of Elllonian, Ilean, was a loner."

"All the more reason to poison their water. Loners—a rotten deep root infecting the whole evolutionary tree—all the way back to greatfish. Now off with you. You have my answer. Genes, indeed. You're right. It's all about genes. That's what it's all about. Loners are not true ellls."

Shawne resisted when Stringer insisted they do a quick farewell adjustment and leave the school. "You go ahead," she said in English. "Old Bain is useless. He keeps repeating himself."

"You know I have to school with him again, to say goodbye, Shawne, and so do you. Stay close to me while we do a brief farewell. It won't take long."

She tried. Stringer was sure she tried. But ellls have many senses, and they all count for something when the school redefines itself in adjustment. Bain knew—from Shawne's scent, from the tension she generated in pressure patterns, from the temperature of her flushed, angry face, from the voltage she put out—that she was both frightened of him and furious. She was wildly defensive of Conn and Lanoll, her loner ell-parents.

"You do not adjust, imaginary hatchling of loners," Bain said. "Your humanness disrupts this school. Get out of our water. Now. Take your loner stench and go back to Earth."

Shawne swam off, warning Stringer not to follow. "You needn't suffer on my account," she said. "Finish your adjustment."

She swam as swiftly as she could, along the surface of the lake, so her pressure patterns would not stir up more ellls. A strong wind had churned the lake with white caps, as though even the water would fight her. She felt leaden, and she made little progress. When Stringer found her, she was near exhaustion, still far from shore.

"Let me tow you for a while, Lunkhead," he said.

Shawne rolled over on her back and relaxed so Stringer could link his arms diagonally across her chest. Her hip rested on his, and his backfin acted as a rudder while his wide, webbed feet moved them along the surface at a good clip.

He hated to see Shawne upset. "So Bain hates loners. So what? He's an old fool."

"An old fool having a bad day," Shawne said, "but I liked what he said about the word Christ. Jesus did the Earth a big favor, teaching the importance of love."

"I'm sorry your love didn't work out on Earth, Shawne. Are you sorry you lost your baby?"

"I did? What? How did you know?"

Stringer rolled up in the water and looked at her sideways.

"Of course. Sonics. What did you see? Was I really pregnant? It would have been awfully tiny."

"It was very early. Are you all right?"

"Killah says I am."

"You can always talk to me, Shawne. Come here. Relax. Let me take you home."

They treasured their mutual support. They had grown up together in water, often using this life-saving hold on extended trips. It was a symbol of everything they shared as family, though born alien to one another, enjoying life from different perspectives, enjoying love and trust with the unique twists their lives found.

They swam for two kilometers before Shawne spoke again. "So what do you think, Stringbean, about *Meaning* with a capital *M*? Talk to me. Given the complexity that drives it, isn't everything totally unpredictable in the long run? Do little changes we make really count? Should I have let nature take its course, whatever that was?"

"You know my answer for that. We eells choose when to have a tad."

"Which seems both rational and wise. But I still feel that I did something wrong."

"Nonsense. When did you start laying eggs?"

"I don't know. Earth age thirteen, I think."

"And now you're 23 or more, right. So ten times twelve—one egg per Earth month, right?—is one hundred twenty eggs that could have been human babies."

"Not until I found a loving mate."

"So you knew Jeff only a few months, right? You still laid a few eggs that could have been babies. And every one of them would be cute as anything and unique with personality and talent, 'cause Jeff was a good specimen, as far as human males go."

"Stringer, that's ridiculous."

"So don't play mental games with yourself. Life is a continuum, and you're in charge."

"Well then, what about God? Did he choose which egg? Does He play with loaded dice, like Conn says?"

"I never heard Conn talk about God, Meathead," Stringer said. "Maybe he means God is natural law."

"That's too impersonal for me. I need something closer, inside."

"So you have a belly ache. That doesn't make for good theology, Shawne. Didn't the impressed information in Philosophy at the Concentrate sink in?"

"Talk about impersonal." Shawne rested her head on his chest so he could support her a little better while stroking with his arms in the lake's restless water. "I don't see how you retain anything from the Concentrate's electronic mind-cramming. I've had to re-read everything."

"Human brains are weird tangles of spaghetti smothered in sauce that's too hot." He laughed, took on a mouthful of water, and blew it noisily out his nasal gills.

"You know," he continued, letting her go and rolling over on his back, "You've got me thinking. I see that Conn's philosophy puts out a very logical idea of Creator. Maybe the complexity of life—its intricate design—requires a Designer with capital D, as Conn would say, and isn't that just another name for imbedded self-organization? A creative impetus in and out of everything?"

"That's called panentheism, not self-organization."

"Who cares what you call it?"

Stringer rolled over in the water and eased Shawne under his right shoulder.

"It matters if God can't do anything about anything," Shawne said, "like when a hungry *eefl* is waiting behind a rock to grab you. Yum. *Eefl* food. God can't save you from bad luck. His hands are tied by the accident of time and the edible stuff we are made of."

"True. I agree. A personal Creator doesn't—or can't—tinker with the stuff that allows us meatballs to exist, but maybe He draws the big picture, which you could call meaning. Complex systems don't travel outside the boundaries set by their strange attractors."

"So God is the strange attractor of the universe? That's a little too abstract for me."

"You want Creation to be a cozy father, like Orram or Conn."

"I know."

Shawne was quiet for a moment, as the water of Lake Seclusion cooled her confused emotions. "Stringer, what if you and Conn are really different from each other?"

Conn's gentle offspring, the schooling elll, didn't give Shawne's question a flick of ten neurons. "Bain was downright rude about Conn being my sire," he said. "I like knowing I carry Conn's genes and Lanoll's genes. What difference does it make if they are loners and I'm not?"

"I'm proud of you, Stringer. Sometimes you almost make sense." Shawne gave him a playful shove.

"Then maybe I'd better say it—you should tell Conn there won't be a human grandbaby. Don't mess up your relationship by playing human hurt-feeling games."

She watched Stringer arch backwards over a gentle wave and slice silently into the water. Sleek and lean, his long green figure brushed past her then disappeared. He was right. She realized in a flash of maturity just how deeply she loved him, this alien sibling she had wrestled with all her life. How many dimensions had he added to her awareness? And now he was adding more, when she needed them most. So far he was her best anchor for sorting out the religious instincts that challenged her.

She felt better, knowing he was close, letting the deep clear water of Lake Seclusion flood his nasal gills and refuel his aquatic muscle-machine.

Shawne relaxed on her back and let the waves toss her about. The sky was dancing with tall curtains of orange and pink that bounced off the water and fed her human eyes with the glory ells called fire-light. *Where are my feelings? The sky should be glorious.* Far above, beyond her vision, a flock of ahlork crossed the lake, their wing plates clicking and clacking in a steady rhythm above the sporadic gargling sound of their native speech.

As the water cradled and rocked her, Shawne dozed, until a familiar *drip drip drip* on her forehead told her Stringer was back—and about to dunk her if she didn't wake up. She grabbed him around the waist and set her cheek against his backfin while they swam for the distant shore, their coordinated legs beating a strong path across the lake's surface.

TANDRA AND CHARLEY

After dinner with the family, welcoming Stringer and Shawne home, Charley busied himself with washing out the hearth pot. Tandra came up behind him, wrapped her arms around his waist, and told him she had missed him.

"I missed you, too, Tan," he said.

"Then let's give ourselves more time. There's plenty of work that

could be done here. Conn's thinking of leasing out the web-fields. They
are too much for us. Shawne and Stringer should spend more time at
the Concentrate. They can't help."

"I can't stay here, Tan, not yet. You're still sleeping with Orram."

"I'll always sleep with Orram. We need the linkage time. It's a mental thing with us. It's not sex. We're world's apart genetically—literally.
I'm like a battery charger for him. During sleep we have a connection
that allows him to stay released."

"Tandra, for heaven's sake. That isn't very comforting. We humans
mean sex when we say we sleep with someone, or have you forgotten?
I'm walking on egg shells here. How can you say you miss me? I don't
know what you want. I'm no longer a young buck with raging hormones, but I want you—sexually."

He put the well-polished pot aside and turned to face her. His hands
found her shoulders. "I want to hold you in my arms as we fall asleep.
I want to rub your back until you ache to have my hands all over you."

"I love you, Charley," she said. "I do want you to love me. I need
human love. Orram is not my mate. Conn—he gets pretty frisky sometimes, but it's not sex, any more than playing with a beloved dog. Don't
you understand the difference?"

"Frankly, no I don't, Tandra. Orram and Conn are quite human-like."

"Only in the parallel accident of being bipeds with brains. Their
communication skills are good; they fooled me, too, at first. I assumed
they were not very alien at all. But it's only our basic needs that we
share: food, relationship, safety. All life shares those. If you can communicate those, you can also communicate differences, and alienness
loses its meaning."

"Then you must know that Conn has been bragging about your
grandchild-to-be. Why didn't you tell me Shawne had a fetus in stasis?"

"Shawne wasn't ever pregnant . . . was she?"

"Conn says she was."

"I doubt it. She broke off with Jeff Passage before we left Earth."

"Well, someone better tell Conn then."

"I'll look into it. Orram would be able to tell, just by reading
Shawne's mood, or an occasional thought as it went by. I think you
must have misunderstood. Secrets just don't work with this family."

Tandra hated to lecture him, but it was frustrating—wanting him as
mate, wanting him to share everything about her life. She wanted him

to understand the intimacy with Conn and Orram that helped fulfill their commitment to each other as family.

"Don't be possessive with me, Charley," she said. "It can't work that way. Humans divorce and re-marry ten times over, but my family with Orram and Conn is totally committed . . . in our support of each other. You don't seem to understand what selfless intimacy is all about."

"Then this human had better find work at Lake Seclusion and forget about going to Ellason," he said, and he walked away from her.

When Charley found Shawne in Orram's office, she was smiling. She looked up from her personal com and showed it to him.

```
EV Science News Report from Earth 2070.4 C.E. The transi-
tion to rail transport is a success. A spider web network of
rail on the North American continent has made the automobile
obsolete, securing fossil fuel reserves for critical energy
in the future.
```

"Good news, very good," Charley said. "But now, the better news is your smile. I guess the anti-depressants are helping?"

"A little, Charley. They take the edge off. But it's not pleasant. It's like the edge is off of everything. There's no despair, but there's also no joy. Everything is flat. I hate it."

– Δ –

At next dark, the entire Oran-elConn-Grey Family gathered around the pool where Orram served his protein specialty, Roasted Web-wrapped *Kaehl* Eggs.

"What did you put in this sauce?" Lanoll asked. "It's marvelous—has a nip, with a hint of green peppers we had on Earth."

Orram laughed. "I shouldn't admit it in public, but I loaded my pack with New Mexico's green chili before we left."

Conn wanted to end the family dinner with their usual early dark swim, but Shawne insisted they stay dry and talk. "Since we're all here together, I'd like to talk about our visit to Old Bain and his school. How do I fit Bain's tantrum into my thinking? What kind of truth was Bain doing?"

"We all have our own truth, don't we?" Orram said.

Shawne twisted her lips. "I was afraid you'd say that."

"Truth is like infinity, Shawne. You can get closer and closer, but you never quite get there—"

"Not even sometimes?"

"Well, maybe very close, sometimes."

Conn couldn't let it go at that. "Until someone else sees something you missed. Like Bain, and all us ellls, we often jump to the truth dictated by the moment."

"He spoke from his immediate emotions, I would guess," Orram added.

Shawne slumped down onto the pool's deck away from the water.

"Right then he wasn't considering all the data," Orram continued. "Emotions do that to us varoks when we let them. Humans often do it when they decide to take a stand."

Charley added, "Shawne, you might keep in mind that many religious ideas don't contain testable information. They offer universal truths that go deeper than fact."

"Right on, Charles, my boy," Conn said. "And—"

Shawne gave him a smirk, interrupting him. "And then there's this disease Mom loves called cognitive dissonance."

"Exactly," Orram lectured. "If your belief in some truth runs counter to your experience, you will be in serious trouble, spiritually and intellectually."

Shawne gave him a bored look, and a sensitive circuit blew in Conn's mind. "It's a horrible disease, Shawnoon. Don't ever bemean the critical stuff we've learned, all us sentient critters. Science and history, all honest information gathering can also give us way big inspiration. Widely accepted knowledge can be awesome, especially when it stays open to question, so good babies don't get thrown out with the bathwater."

Shawne gasped. "I'll be in my room," she said. "I have some reading to do."

Tandra followed her down the stairs and into the small sleeping chamber her daughter had claimed as a young child.

"Did you know that Conn believes you might have a child waiting, preserved, delayed for our coming home?" Tandra asked. "Do you?"

"No, Mom."

"I didn't think so, but maybe you'd better let him know."

"He'll be so disappointed. I don't know how—"
"You'll find a kind way to say it."

BAIN AGAIN

On hearing about the incident at Lake Seclusion, Oleyall insisted
that the family see Bain again. "You need to clarify what went on during the earlier visit. Are you willing to do that, Shawne?"

The direct question from the great-fish struck a harsh chord in the
young woman. It was as if a thirteenth note sounded deep within her,
awakening a resonant defense. "Of course," she said.

"I will rely on your good nature," Oleyall said. "Signing off."

In preparing for the trip, Shawne packed only enough antidepres-
sants to taper off slowly. She wanted to be real, to feel every nuance of
emotion during the difficult encounter.

As the family gathered to leave, Shawne disappeared for a moment
then emerged like a golden goddess from some ancient forest, all polished up for the occasion. She had traded her usual cut-offs and tied-
up shirt for a varokian sari made of some flowing material one could
call shimmering blue. It set off her bright hair and dark caramel skin.
Dressed for varokian eyes, she was. Orram saw it, too, and he greeted
her with a smile. She was ready for something besides battle.

Tandra didn't get it at first. "Am I underdressed for the war?" she
asked. "Or for meeting your fellow student, your friend Tamilan?"

"You always look great, Mom."

Tandra usually wore slim leggings and a baggy elllonian-style
sweater of soft, dry moss. It gave her an other-worldly-elfin look.

The path to Lake Seclusion wound through thick yellow marsh
grass suggesting sulfur oxidation. Chlorophyll experiments on Varok
were rare, so the vegetation sported shades of yellow or purple and
brown more often than green. One of Tandra's first impressions of
Varok had been that golden ßseaweed had crawled from the Arahnye

Allahn (Misted Ocean) and overtaken the land.

The lake spread out beyond the marshes like a giant gray whale beached beneath Mount Ni. While Shawne went into the EV Science office to get her varokian friend Tamilan, the rest ran for the nearest beach and scrubbed each other clean in the deep water of a sinkhole.

Their antics, teasing and splashing around, got no reaction from Tamilan. When he and Shawne came to the beach, they declined an invitation to swim the lake. Tamilan nodded toward a disturbance some distance down shore as Bain and some ellls emerged from the shallows. They approached the ellls, humans and varoks with hands spiraling in friendly greeting.

They all gathered in the Living Resources Center. The conversation took an unexpected turn after Conn backed into Shawne.

"Oops! Sorry, daughter," Conn said.

"There it is," Bain said.

"Where is what?" Conn asked Bain.

"The difference between us." The old elll looked at Orram with lumps of polished obsidian, eyes with a mischievous, know-it-all look in them that rode high on his face and danced under long, thinning gold plumes. "Orram knows what I will say."

Orram wasn't so sure.

"Conn. Conn, my dear boy . . ." Bain continued.

Shawne smiled, and Bain smiled at her.

"You said, 'Sorry, Daughter,'" Bain said. "You used the Varokian word *daughter* as if it had meaning for you, Conn."

"It does have meaning to me."

"But you forget. The word has no meaning to schooling ellls. The eggs we choose to incubate and raise as tads are chosen at random. A sponsor requests the next egg lain, or he chooses one from the school's food stash. The genetic contributors to the chosen egg are rarely known."

"I didn't know that," Tamilan said.

Tandra and Conn looked at him, disappointed at his ignorance of ellls.

"For your young people," Tandra said, "I would like to share a story that illustrates a major difference between the species of Earth and those of Ellason. There is a giant cuttlefish that lives off the southern coast of Australia. When the male has won a female, scaring off others with a display of size and flashing colors, he hoses out the female's sexual pouch, getting rid of any spermatophores left over from a previous mating."

"That's ridiculous!" Bain and other ellls with him erupted with delight. Ten minutes later the school was still inventing elaborate variations on the theme of defending sperm.

Conn was a little disgusted with their silliness, but he saw Tandra's point. Evolution had taken a very different turn on Earth. Very few Earth species deliberately left procreation to random selection as the ellls did.

It gave Shawne something new to think about. "Where is God in all this?" she asked Bain.

"He's eating *llaoon* grass, having a good laugh," he said.

"These ellls have no regard for the sensitivities of young women on religious quests," Tamilan observed, "with their outbursts and tirades."

"Now, as to tirades." Bain's eyes, deep set in wrinkled tiles, focused on Shawne. "Last we spoke about loners, you didn't wait around for my temper to fade, my dear child. We could have had a nice talk about 'what it's really all about,' but you were already gone."

"I was feeling empty, or very upset. Just . . . not able to talk more. "

"Humans get defensive when their loved ones are attacked, Bain," Tandra said.

"And humans see anger as an attack?"

"When it's directed at other persons, yes."

"I understand, Tandra. We will remember that." Bain turned to Conn. "And your tirades?"

"They feel spontaneous. They arise suddenly and subside quickly," he said.

"But sometimes their roots have grown from the past," Tandra noted. "Yesterday, you reacted to something that happened several lightperiods ago. You reacted to something between Shawne and me. That was very remote, Conn. Perhaps only a loner can react to a memory so emotionally, long after the fact."

"Yeah, I suppose it might be a small difference between us," Conn agreed. "A delayed response might give the schoolers a quirky, possibly difficult adjustment."

"Not difficult, Conn, impossible." Bain looked to Conn's varokian soul-brother for his perspective. "Orram?"

"I agree," Orram said.

Tandra moved in close to Bain. "You are very kind. Thank you for explaining this to us."

"I will be nasty again someday, my lovely lady. The loners tousle our plumes quite often these days."

– Δ –

After seeing Bain's school back to water, Stringer and Conn raced a few kilometers around the lake, then found Shawne on the beach with two golden-plumed ellls, elders who said they wanted to talk philosophy. Instead, they started lecturing Shawne on cultural differences in human religious thought.

"She knows all that," Stringer said, interrupting them. "Better come with us, Shawne. The others are waiting."

The elder of the school didn't want to let her go. "Please come back to the water with us. We will support you, make a living raft. We do enjoy trying to answer your interesting questions."

"I'll referee," Conn said.

"I'm sorry," Shawne said, glancing at Conn. "We need to get back to our school, our mixed family. They are waiting on shore in the Living Resources Center.

Conn was surprised. "It's okay, Shawnoon. These elders seem to know their stuff. It could be valuable—"

Shawne shook her head and headed away from the water. She seemed more than a little irritated. "Those ellls have it all figured out, with all their zillion different sense organs. It's all in the present to them. 'Don't be confused by the history of names and concepts beyond awareness,' the elders said. 'Interesting, all that, but not as essential as treasuring the gift of life and living every moment.'"

"Hey ho, my sweet pecan," Conn said. "What did you expect them to say?"

"I expected them to know I'm human. Earth's history is my history. Its religions are more than 'names and concepts beyond awareness.'"

"Are they?" Stringer asked. "Seems to me humans play word games that fuzz out any real meaning or go off on dominance making everyone else wrong."

Shawne blew. He'd lit her fuse. "How can you say that about me, when I'm trying to be thoughtful? Is that how you see my questions? Meaningless? I'm just trying to win some kind of contest?" She leapt to her feet and pounded his chest with tight fists. "You big fish don't even hear the questions, your head is so polluted with sensory input."

"So, now I'm a fish, Miss Holier-than-thou? I'm obviously out of water here." He strode back into the surf. "I'd better get back to my own kind and wrap myself in schooling pressures before I suffocate trying to breathe in too much meaning."

"Stringer, no." Usually Conn didn't mess in their sibling tussles, but this was too much. "Shawne, apologize. Stop him."

She didn't hear Conn as she ran along the shore, trying to escape from the frustration the ellls had triggered. Then she stopped running. Perhaps she had a right to the frustration. Her questions were real. It felt good to search for meaning. She was alive again. She would handle it. She could handle it without the pills.

As Conn watched Stringer disappear into the lake, he felt their angry words tearing his heart into little shreds of raw meat. Stringer and Shawne were the loving fruition of his mixed family. Until now, Stringer had been sympathetic to her need to find answers to the big questions. *Why would he insult something so important to her? It sounded as if he honestly felt disdain for her quest. Was it his schooler needs, so focused on the present that questions of meaning were irrelevant?*

How could Lanoll and he, both loners, have produced a schooling, linear-minded elll? It was an unrecognized puzzle. Then it all came clear. He saw the chasm open wide between Stringer and himself. It was deep and terrifying. Conn understood Shawne's frustration better than Stringer's need to return to schooling.

An Unannounced Meeting

Shawne retreated to the Concentrate in Ahl Vior to research loner-schooler differences. It was not easy to stay focused, a constant battle to stay assured that she and Stringer would heal, that Conn would forgive her fear of disappointing him.

"I can hear it in your voice when you call home," Tandra said. "You haven't been taking your pills."

"They drain all the passion from life, Mom."

"If you had a broken leg, you would use a crutch, wouldn't you? Perhaps the chemical imbalance will change, but for now they are your crutch."

After Jupiter's moon Callisto had come and gone in the cluttered Varokian sky, Shawne came home with a Specialty rating in Ellasonian studies.

Conn hopped a daramont and met Shawne as she appeared across the web fields, racing a handsome mount. In answer to his questions about her studies, she mentioned her difficulty learning Ellasonian, the language devised ages ago by the varok Korad so that ellls and varoks could communicate. Then she talked on and on about the new varoks she had met.

What is she trying to prove? Conn tried to puzzle it out.

On their recent visit to Earth, when Shawne met the worldly rogue Jeff Passage, he had won her brainless devotion. Naïve as she was, she was devastated when he dumped her on the back seat of his life while he hauled Alaskan water to San Diego, making millions off the North American population recovery. He had done a good job of stirring up her hormones, Conn realized, but it was a surprise when she invited the odd young varok Tamilan home for a visit.

Her timing couldn't have been worse. The family was expecting company, lots of it.

"Tamilan, you remember my elll-dad, Conn. This is his mate, Lanoll," Shawne said, bursting in on their quiet meal by the pond. "Orram, Tamilan is Tamon of the Ilanor family. Tamilan, this is Master Oran Ramahlak, my varok-dad. My human mother, Tandra Oran-ElConn-Grey. You remember Conn, I'm sure, from our visit to see Bain at Lake Seclusion."

The formal introduction was too much for Conn. He scooped Shawne up and tossed her into the algae pond. She kicked up a lot of water and made some rude noises before he finished the dunking. Then they both disappeared underwater to connect with Stringer, who was napping at the bottom.

"Hey ho, Lunkhead." Stringer said, taking hold of her shoulders as they surfaced. "I understand you brought a friend home to visit."

"Be nice to him, please," she said, relieved at their easy reunion. "You too, Conn."

Tamilan stood on the deck getting splashed. His only comment was an architectural inquiry. "Your elll-water seems to be very deep," he said. "I assume that the surrounding rocks have been grouted and sealed."

Orram intervened to explain how his mother's grandfather had chosen the site for its lava tunnel and deep natural spring. He had built the house to accommodate the adjacent mineral tree's growth. Its great limbs now supported the porch.

"One of the nicest examples of ecologically integrated architecture I've seen in this area," Tamilan said.

Lanoll smiled. "Shawne, won't Stringer want to school with your friend?" She turned to Tamilan with the invitation. "Won't you join us in water?"

Tamilan's faced took on a greenish tint. "I doubt that I can withstand ellonian adjustment in such a confined place." The varokian kid was obviously panicked at the thought of schooling with Shawne's brother.

"Just a brief, introductory adjustment in water, Tamilan," Conn said. "No electro-fizz."

Shawne managed to laugh. "I'll murder Stringer if he zaps you, Tamilan. You go ahead and meet him. I'll see him later. He is a schooling elll, but he grew up in this mixed family with a varok for a dad, so he respects varokian nerves."

Tamilan smiled nervously and shook his head.

Shawne understands Stringer well, Conn thought. *Elllonian sensory overload doesn't leave much room for leftovers, like detailed memory. We see, we hear, we taste, we feel, we smell—like humans and varoks—but in water we sense so much more. I hope Tamilan knows that.*

In contrast, Conn remembered how repressed most varoks are, the ones without consummate mates. Until varoks find mental union with someone and experience release, they have to be very careful not to let their emotions get out of control. Fully expressed emotion means loss of rationality, sometimes for hours, sometimes for many light-periods. It's crippling, embarrassing, and a danger to life, limb, and self-respect—hence emotional expression is tightly controlled.

Orram, however, expressed himself almost as freely as humans. He was released, in union with Tandra's mind. Their mental consummation was probably different from a varok–varok mind-blend, but it did the trick for him.

That's why Conn understood when the young varok Tamilan nearly jumped out of his hairless skin as Orram stripped off sweater and slacks and jumped into the pool—this Master varok, the famous former Governor of Living Resources, confidante of great-fish, an alpha male in more ways than one. He came to the surface riding Lanoll's back fin. Stringer knocked him off his perch with a lateral tackle that took them all into the water reeds at the far side of the pool, where they enjoyed a brief scuffle.

Their noisy swim brought Conn back to the surface, and soon Orram was surrounded by ellls.

"You are cruelly outnumbered, Master Ramahlak," Tamilan noted.

"Sorry to get you so wet, Tamilan. It's the price we pay for living with ellls."

Soon everyone gathered on the deck. Orticon, Orram's son, had just returned from Ahl Vior with two old family friends, the ellls Killah and Artellian.

Conn watched Shawne's face for signs of suspicion. The family didn't usually have so many guests at one time. Would she guess that some were serious about going to Ellason? That the proposal had been accepted?

Probably not. Shawne simply reveled in greeting the ellls, her physician Killah and the elder Artellian. Both had known her since she was a toddler on EV Science's Earth Moonbase. Over the years, as their plumes turned to gold, they had played the role of grandfather to her, holding her accountable with loving inquiries about her education and peers.

Killah watched Shawne, caught her glance, and nodded. Together they disappeared down to the hearth.

"Talk to me, Shawne. Are you still obsessing about Earth?"

"How can I stop, Killah? There seems to be a fanatic compulsion for money and power driving so-called 'recovery.' With the Earth no longer 'full,' greed is fueling a push for re-growth."

"It's not just greed, is it? There is still fear of being out-numbered by more aggressive peoples. Global consensus may not be possible yet, but I think your species will surprise you, Shawne. Focus on the good things that are happening. Otherwise, you may destroy yourself with grief. Are you doing that?" The elll medic looked deep into her eyes, and she shuddered. "I sense something very tense in you."

Lanoll's velvet tones covered Shawne with the painkiller she needed. "I decided to join this verbal schooling and hope you will forgive my intrusion, Shawne. Won't you spend some more time with Stringer in water? He misses you. The anger you exchanged passed so quickly, he can barely remember it now."

"Of course," Shawne said. She managed a smile and nestled against the soft blue plumes of her adoptive elll-mother. "I'll see him right away."

"Well, maybe not until later," Killah said.

"What do you mean?"

Killah's eyes grew wide. "You'll soon know. Let's join the others."

When the humans Jesse Mendleton and Charley Buckman appeared in the pool room with the ahlork Nidok, Shawne's face took on the look of a quizzical *lohn* bird. She knew something was up. Charley and Jesse were supposed to be working at Lake Seclusion. After his long trip, she thought Nidok had returned to his nest on the cliffs of L'orkah after his long trip with Charley.

Taking a perch on an ironwood branch over the pool, Nidok spotted Orram's son Orticon, a tall figure coming through the garden toward the house. When Orticon appeared at the top of the stone stairs, the ahlork flapped his huge wings with a loud clack and sailed over the water to land on Orticon's head.

"When do we sing Happy Birthday to Nidok?" Orticon called.

"So that's what this is all about," Shawne hollered back. "I wondered when this rude family would honor you with a birthday cake." She took Nidok's prehensile wing-tip in her hand, and they started down the steps and outside, with Orticon still acting as perch. "But I'm sure you two will tell me something more interesting than your age, before the party is over."

Conn found himself walking beside the elder ellls Artellian and Killah. At Lanoll's urging, the group began to move outside.

"Sounds like you've changed your mind, Conn. Would you really take Nidok out to Ellason?" Artellian asked quietly.

"I wouldn't go without him," Conn said. "He added a dimension to our work on Earth—saved our disaster from becoming a tragedy."

"We'll have to keep bathing him in moss depressant." Killah always found a way to stay on medical alert.

"He won't like that."

Killah smiled and shook his head. "You better clear that up with him before he signs the trip proposal. There are good reasons why Ellason never spawned anything that can be called an insectoid. Without routine treatments, Nidok's small parts would get jammed up before the moons set twice."

"Why don't you see if you can lure him into the kitchen," Conn said. "Have you two signed on for the trip?"

"Yes. The proposal looks good, Conn," Artellian said. "Killah has made appointments with nearly everyone for health checks, and Tandra has agreed to run the cultures and help with immunizations. We don't want to carry any nasty germs out there or contract any Ellasonian diseases. How many people are going?"

"There are fourteen—ellls, varoks, humans, and the ahlork—who have read the proposal and want to go with us."

As a team, all had agreed to review the loner-schooler relations on Ellason, as well as the history of interspecific relationships on Ellason compared to Earth and Varok. Each would contribute something unique to the plan.

Together they had also discussed how to support Shawne's religious quest. They suggested she note interactions on a philosophical plane, and she agreed. Was anyone trying to convert anyone else to their set of beliefs? How did those beliefs differ? Between species? Within species? Some great-fish of Varok, even Oleyall, saw her job as the spiritual *raison d'être* for the trip.

Stringer would be allowed to stay on Ellason if he found a school that would make permanent adjustment to include him. The Interplanetary Replacement Exchange would arrange for his Replacement Certificate.

Nidok had insisted on taking his eldest nestling, Forelock (named for Conn's unruly forehead plumes). What kind of unique job could they do? It would take some fancy reasoning to justify taking two ahlork to a place totally hostile to aerial cracker bones.

Charley had come up with the answer. The ahlork would provide aerial reconnaissance in questionable situations as the team traveled around the planet, and they would record their response to each different environment. As long as they recognized the risks to their health, took their anti-moss baths, and promised to report any difficulty, they could go. Charley called Nidok inside to put the question to him. Shawne came with him and soon understood that a trip to Ellason was a real possibility.

"We take nasty baths. Is okay," Nidok said.

"I like complaining. Will report bad news," Forelock croaked in his best Varokian. Nidok looked at his nestling with proud beady eyes, and the young ahlork straightened his narrow exoskeleton into a tall shoebox shape, then flexed his dangerously sharp chitinous wing plates.

Shawne made it clear she had overheard enough to know this was the team going out to Ellason. "So when do we leave?"

"As soon as we're ready and the planets line up to give us a boost," Killah announced. "As your physician, I have just signed off on your health, Shawne, so your participation is now official. The trip to Ellason is about the loner-schooler problem, and your quest for meaning is integral to the agenda. But first this kind old elll thinks you need to ask your why-questions of this wise old ahlork here."

Nidok clacked his wing plates, rolled his eyes nervously, and waddled toward Killah and Shawne. "I now stay serious for two minutes," he said, and he leapt onto Shawne's head.

She laughed at the impact. "What is the meaning of life?" she stammered.

"Being alive," Nidok said from above her ears.

"You mean consciousness?"

"If someone is having some."

"But why is consciousness so important? Why does this huge universe go to so much trouble to create consciousness? It causes too much pain."

"Needed for knowing where to scratch," Nidok countered.

"So how did the universe come into being?"

"It couldn't help itself."

"Is there a Creator, a God of everything that we can relate to?"

"Everything relates to everything. It can't help it."

"I mean—" Shawne was flummoxed by Nidok's sharp answers. "Do all ahlork agree with your atheistic beliefs?"

"They're not ath…istic. Ahlork don't do agreeing."

"Well, what do you think most ahlork think about being created?"

"Whatever."

"That's Conn's cop out, Nidok."

"I don't cop out these two minutes. God is *whatever*. That's enough, like Conn says. The why is Whatever's business, whatever it is be okay with me. Your two minutes are done."

Nidok hopped off Shawne's head, and Forelock followed him past the hearth and out the great door. Then, without a word of farewell, they took off from the front porch, intending to graze in the fields beyond the web bushes.

"Have you two signed the proposal, Nidok?" Shawne called up to the ahlork.

Nidok banked and sailed lower. "All done, bright hair. Have you signed? Enjoy the party."

"I will. Right now," she called.

Nidok flew off after Forelock.

"I've got to find Stringer," Shawne said.

Conn gave Shawne a quizzical look.

Tears filled her eyes. "I haven't had enough time with him since we quarreled. Is he still in the pond, Conn? When do I get to sign the proposal? Are you really going with the rest of us?"

Tamilan and Korak

When she could not find Stringer in the pond, Shawne decided to join Tamilan outside on the great porch. She told him all she could remember about her argument with Stringer.

"Compared to the ahlork, Bain and the schooling ellls are logical, if nothing else," Tamilan said, hoping to ingratiate himself with Shawne.

"That's the problem, Tamilan. Stringer is too logical for me, but I guess he provides a good example." Tears rose in her eyes. "He never holds a grudge, so neither will I."

I need to know where he is. Will we really lose him to Ellason? Orram would know how I'm feeling. Why doesn't Tamilan? I could use a good gentle back rub, but I suppose that is far beyond Tamilan's knowledge of humans, or his ability to touch.

Tamilan stood behind Shawne, scanning three moons moving in and out of Varok's colorful mists.

"I wish you would sit down with me, Tamilan."

"Sorry, Shawne." He folded his thin legs and planted himself just beyond touching range, balanced on the edge of the porch steps.

He was a varok, after all. But she was human, and she wanted him to become like family—like Orram, who had learned human customs, primate grooming and comforting hugs, all the lovely touching that warmed human hearts.

She didn't realize how extensively the barbs on Orram's nerves had been polished to a silky sheen by living with ellls all his life and with humans for more than two Jovian years (twenty some-odd Earth years).

Tamilan was as prickly as a dawn-fish. Shawne respected his distance, but she yearned for more. Seeing it wasn't going to happen, she left the young varok on the porch and entered the house.

Her dear old family friend Artellian approached her. "We were about to engage in Living Resources business," he said. "Killah's given you his okay, so you need to join us upstairs."

"Business, Artellian?" The two started up the stairs as they spoke. "You had retired to Lake Seclusion when we came back from Earth."

"Ellls never retire, you know, Sweets," Conn said, moving toward them from the hearth. "Artellian has a new assignment."

"And Killah?"

"Yes."

And you, Daddy-mine?"

"Yes."

"When were you going to tell me, Conn? When the Lurlial was packed and ready to sail for Ellason?"

"No," he said, "when we were boarding for launch."

A spontaneous celebration began in and around the pool. Tandra and Orram appeared with trays of food and drink. Most of the staff from Living Resources, the bureau sponsoring the trip to Ellason, arrived. Light from a brilliant auroral display danced across the pool's water. Food from packed lunches appeared at the hearth and on a table dragged outside from Orram's office.

A young varok approached Orram as he stood talking with Tandra. "Master Ramahlak, I am Koran Akrallon, Korak, a student of ellls. Is someone taking notes? I have heard many good ideas. I would like to record them for you."

"Go ahead," Orram said. "Good idea. Be sure we all have access to the ideas."

"Hi, Korak." Shawne greeted the young varok with a smile. "I see you've met my father, Orram."

"Hello, Shawne," Korak said, "I just offered to digitize useful discussions about your trip to Ellason."

Conn sauntered over to join Tandra and Orram, and Shawne ushered Korak toward them with thoughtful varokian gestures that avoided touch. "Conn, Orram and Mom, this is one of my friends from the Concentrate, Koran Akrallon, Korak. And that sea serpent is my other father, Conn, Master of lies and deception. Last I knew he didn't want to go out to Ellason."

Conn spiraled his hand in varokian greeting. They reviewed the proposal briefly while munching *arl* moths. Korak was eagerly asking questions and recording comments, but his eyes kept wandering back to Shawne. Conn decided he had not seen much of her at school and was fascinated by her human form, which was elegantly displayed beneath the thin tunic flowing against her body. It was not all that different from a feminine varokian body, which probably woke up some latent mind-link desires in the youthful varok.

The brilliant auroral light glowing through the house had dimmed to a pleasant golden yellow. Korak gave his hand-corder to Orram.

"Thank you, Korak, for your company at the party," Tandra said. "You will go far, my son."

She laughed, and to Conn's surprise the young varok laughed with her. Then he moved away to talk more with Killah and Artellian. Shawne paid him no more attention. She was focused on Conn, eager to hear more details about the mission to Ellason.

"We've had another message from the great-fish Oleyall. He will accompany us to his home planet but then leave us for a conference with the Council of Ellason. It probably has to do with loner ellls there stirring up trouble."

"Was Stringer successful in finding a sponsor on Ellason?" Shawne asked. By this time most of the team were gathered in or around the hearth.

"I'm afraid he really is going for good, Shawnoon," Conn said. He would have preferred to say it at a better time, or in private, when they were playing at being sponsor and tad in deep water. "He'll use the Replacement Certificate of Ol-Sahn, an elder of Artellian's nurturing school."

She looked at the elll, and her eyes filled with tears. "I've got to find him."

As she hurried from the gathering, Conn saw Korak emerge as if to follow her. His anxious gaze met the elll's, and he hesitated when he saw Conn's cautioning head shake. Then he approached Orram.

"I have read the official proposal for your trip to Ellason, Master Ramahlak," he said, "and I couldn't help but notice that the only Elllonian Specialists on your team are Shawne and one elll. If you would allow me, I would like to apply as a varok with a Specialty in Ellasonian studies."

"Good idea, Korak" said Orram. "Specialist Koran Akrallon is it? I know the Akrallon family reputation for efficient, functional architecture. I'm sure we could use your good sense. Please apply, with my recommendation."

The young varok hurried off to do the paperwork, and Conn looked at Orram accusingly. The varok gave the elll the silliest look he could manage. This was going to be an interesting trip, with two young varoks along to vie for Shawne's attention.

Daramonts, Light-hoppers, and Parents

After the team celebration, the family didn't see Shawne again for nearly a Callisto Cycle. Because she couldn't find Stringer after the party, she contacted Lake Seclusion, and Old Bain put out a search message on the ellls' ultrasonic network. Someone thought Stringer had gone back to the Concentrate. Shawne inquired, but he had not checked in there. While the family was tying up loose ends with Living Resources and finding someone to care for the Orran Locale homestead, she went off to the Forested Sea looking for him.

When she finally found Stringer, she cut loose. "I'm so sorry I called you a sensory-overloaded fish."

Stringer laughed. "You did?"

"Yes, Spaghetti Brains."

For several light-periods she swam with him and his childhood school in the deep central waters of the Forested Sea. They had a lovely time cruising the protected Crystal Cove, where the water was so clear it reflected the changing auroral lights like a prism reaching deeper than sight. When the ellls dove to hunt low eels and sinker-fruit, Shawne floated on the surface watching the lights come and go.

On Varok she never knew whether to look up or down. It was beautiful both ways. She floated in warm synthetics surrounded by light so deep it drew her into another space, where beauty enfolded her.

Was there any such place left on Earth? Lake Tahoe used to be like that. Mom's great grandmother saw it on speedboat rides that took people to see the endless crystal blue water in the center of the lake.

Will I ever stop worrying or grieving for Earth? she asked herself. *Probably not. I am connected to that planet the same way Conn is connected to Ellason, though he won't admit it.*

When her skin started to wrinkle, Stringer took her to shore and offered to wait with her until a daramont showed up to take her home. They had a good chance to talk. He could see the loner-schooler problem in his differences with Conn and Lanoll; they made assumptions, even decisions, alone, without the assurance of constant consent.

While they talked, curious light-hoppers living in the ruins of Tahkin gathered around them. Thankfully, they kept their distance and their chatter to a low sizzle.

Before dark, Shawne saw two daramonts loping along the shore.

"I'll go back to the school and finish my farewell adjustments," Stringer told Shawne. "I should be home soon." He turned to the daramonts and gave each a web stalk from the pack Shawne had stashed near the beach. "Thank you for coming," he said to them. "My human sister needs a ride over the mountains to Orserah's house. Eat all you want there. The stalks are good. Then please come back to get me, here, in two light-periods."

Stringer backed through the gentle surf, dove, and disappeared. The last thing Shawne saw were his wide, befinned toes slipping under a cresting wave.

Feeling a little silly, Shawne asked the daramonts to sit down, have another web stalk, and tell her their thoughts about God. Of course, they didn't recognize the word, so she tried the word *Creator*. No luck. Daramonts don't create anything tangible—just racing strategies or faster, and safer routes down the rocks of the Vahinorral.

"Source of life," she tried.

That was easy for them. "Females," they indicated.

"Meaning. What is your reason for living?" It took Shawne a while to translate that one for them.

All they could come up with was, "Good web stalks." Food. Conn would probably agree, in a zenful sort of way.

Meanwhile, the light-hoppers were going crazy, trying to get in on the philosophical discussion.

The daramonts turned away to graze on small tender plants and moss growing in the cracks of the ancient shoreline ruins, and Shawne knew they were done with talking, such as it was. She also knew they would wait to take her home, so she sat down on the beach while the light-hoppers had their say.

They were long-winded little snobs, as she expected. She didn't need to repeat her questions. They had all the answers, whatever the questions.

"God be the dream light of Beginning's last breath."

"Love is the mother of Longing's worst fears."

They were also good at making up words, with definitions full of more made-up words.

"Corrulence comes when the spiritual tide turns."

"It means dividual languidity or torentiality."

Her only hope for gleaning anything out of their lecture was to enjoy it as sound-poetry.

"Round the flowering essence flows the tepid epic of true lightness of being. See then the better half of nothing more worthy than spiritual essence intoned."

The underlying attitudes and honest beliefs in their triangular little heads were buried too deep for her to shovel out under their arguments about "true light" and "spiritual corrulence."

The light-hopper session contributed two things worth considering, when she was able to translate their stories into a viewpoint she could understand: "Authors of rules and painters of words that do not fade make contradictions and stick knives in good cheese." They seemed to be saying that authoritarianism and certainty were evils.

"I don't understand why you think certainty is an evil," Shawne retorted. "I agree that certainty implies that all the evidence is in, which it never is. However, new information continues to accumulate as we approach greater certainty. That's how we learn; we ignore such growing certainty at great cost."

"Deepest pychic knowledge must reside in mystery, else it be untrue as reason," they said, and Shawne disagreed, at last, with something she thought was concrete.

"I'm sure you don't mean to trash reason, which reaches out for truth," Shawne said. "Perhaps you are mistaking reason for rationalization, which reaches out for convenient excuses."

"No no," they said. "Good excuses come from wells of spirtual virtue."

"But can you agree that science, or reason if you prefer, tries on theories useful in making predictions that can be tested?"

"Predictions come from the soul of beautiful experience." The fragile little critters sang in high tones that nearly harmonized.

"Okay. I think you are saying that there is some kind of Truth out there. With a capital T. Something science can't touch, like love or meaning."

"Love is spiritual meaning."

"Okay," Shawne said, hoping they had arrived at some obscure conclusion in their interchange. "Perhaps we can agree that religion should stick to moral guidance."

"Agreed," they all squeaked, and with a flash of iridescent

toothpick-frames they disappeared into the growth at the edge of the Forested Sea to hunt reed tics.

Relieved, having absorbed all the light-hopper obfuscation she could take, Shawne went in search of the daramonts.

One took her on board, and they climbed into the foothills of the Vahinorral. By then the mists had cleared. Shawne could see Orserah's house in the distance, its foundation of rock framed with neat rows of web bushes, the giant ironwood tree hovering protectively over her family. Tears came to her eyes as she remembered Orram's mother Orserah, her only grandparent, an unplumbed font of love for all the family. She cherished the stories of Orram's father rescuing ellls new to Varok, tutoring them in the ways of varoks, and giving them a safe refuge in the algae pond, where she too had found safe haven with Conn, when she was a young child new to Varok.

When Shawne arrived home, she found her family nearly ready to leave. The proposal to study loner-schooler problems on Ellason was being funded by Living Resources on Varok and the Keepers of Balance on Ellason. The team would begin flight training immediately. Launch was scheduled for the next window, when the Jupiter system would help sling a ship toward Ellason in its do-si-do with Neptune.

Shawne's reaction surprised everyone. "We can't go yet."

"Don't panic, Tandra said. "You have several light-periods to get packed."

"I'm not ready to talk to the great-fish Master Haralahn." Then she laughed. "I'm having an attack of non-inspirational corrulence."

II. Introduction To Ellason

Ancient species of the planet Varok, those that eventually changed to become the varoks, based their religious thinking on verifiable observations that remained open to questioning. We look into a microscope and see living beings, enormously complex and whole in themselves, swimming about in a drop of water with the graceful turnings of great-fish. They are probably not unlike other beings that make their homes near millions of stars scattered throughout billions of galaxies.

With such information we varoks have grown our sense of awe. We find meaning when we learn that we exist as a result of laws and limits set in the first few moments of the universe—six constants that must be exact for the universe to produce stars and planets. If those numbers were different, there would be no atoms, nor matter as we know it.

However, a leap of faith is often required to express a truth that cannot be verified with testing and accumulated evidence. There is meaning in love and beauty and creative stories, as long as one doesn't confuse metaphor with fact, allegory with history.

—Oran Ramahlak in a note to Shawne Oran-elConn-Grey

THE VIEW FROM SPACE

Aside from preparing for the long space trip to Ellason, Shawne spent most of her quiet time reviewing Earth's Buddhist literature. She agreed passionately about not harming life and being mindful. From Tandra she had also learned the healthy benefits of meditation. Buddhism made sense, all but the emphasis on pain. The Buddha must have meant something like the ellls' grief at the loss of life joy.

She understood that desire could be a real source of pain, but life had been good to her, even incredible, being raised by loving sentient beings so nearly human, so profoundly unique in themselves. Before they left Varok for Ellason, she would ease Conn's pain, somehow, after telling him he would not be a grandfather.

Her first attempt to tell him, however, didn't happen until they were on their way to the spaceport in Ahl Vior. Then it fell between them like a meaningless song with no redeeming melody.

"I'm sorry we haven't had time to talk lately, Shawne," the elll said. "Are you feeling okay? Ready for Ellason? Ready for liftoff?"

"Yes, I'm fine."

The swift Ahlkahn glided to a stop, and they gathered up their gear and loaded daramont carts for the trek from central Ahl Vior to the spaceport.

Meanwhile, before the great-fish Oleyall had a chance to visit all of his many relatives in the Forested Sea to say goodbye, he was gently hammocked and lifted into a mobile tank truck, driven to the space port at Ahl Vior, wrapped in soaking wet synthetic that was reasonably non-irritating and dumped unceremoniously into an *uuyvanoon* on EV Science's varokian-designed spaceship.

"I demand to know why it is that humans are allowed to visit Ellason, and, as a result, some ellls will never see their home planet?" Old Bain had asked Oleyall before he left the Forested Sea.

The great-fish respected the elllonian curmudgeon, who had left his school to question him on behalf of ellls who were refused passage. Oleyall provided Bain with a printout of his report to Living Resources:

The humans will add a third perspective as well as needed expertise in reviewing loner-schooler relations on Ellason.

Interspecific relationships on Ellason will be compared to those on Earth and Varok. Each species will contribute something unique to the study.

Killah will be everyone's personal physician, and Tandra will work with him, doing routine cultures on everyone and their contacts on Ellason, watching for an exchange of microbes.

Artellian will keep a log of interpersonal dynamics as the team experiences the realities of Ellason.

Jesse Mendleton, the human who has won the confidence of EV Science as their first contact on Earth, has worked on both Varok and Earth for twenty Earth years as a steady-state trouble shooter. Now he has a chance to see how the ellls of Ellason have maintained their stable population. Hopefully, they will provide an example for Earth.

Lanoll, Conn's lovely blue mate, will continue her job as a Living Resources field biologist, noting any unique biological impacts of loner/schooler tension on Ellason as compared to Varok.

Orram and Conn will be modeling general patterns in species interactions there.

Together all will support Shawne's religious quest. She will note philosophical and socio-psychological interactions with various belief systems. I, Oleyall, will keep Shawne on track and help her organize her thoughts, while I compare notes on the ellonian problem with great-fish. I will make my home in the underwater cave communities of Ellason. I have bought a Replacement Certificate from an aging female who cannot reproduce.

Stringer too will be allowed to stay on Ellason, if he finds a school that will make permanent adjustment and include him. The Interplanetary Replacement Exchange has arranged for his Replacement Certificate from the ell Ol-Sahn. Orram's son Orticon will answer requests for information about Earth and trouble-shoot problems in maintaining population levels and resource quotas.

As a human engineer who loved fishing, Charley will assess the effects of technology on the aquatic cultures of ellls.

Conn will give him a crash course in the dry-land technology the ancient ellls have developed. It doesn't amount to much, you remember. Besides communication enhancements and an ancient library of *ahl* scrolls, Conn's elllonian ancestors have concentrated on bio-metallics, which were developed for use in sea-bottom gardening tools.

Then there is the ahlork Nidok. He has decided to go to Ellason but insists on taking his eldest nestling, Forelock. What kind of unique job could they do? Perhaps aerial reconnaissance. It has taken some fancy reasoning to justify taking two ahlork to a place totally hostile to aerial cracker bones.

Charley, Tandra's human friend, provided the answer. The ahlork can provide aerial reconnaissance in questionable situations as we travel the planet, and we will record their response to each different environment. As long as they recognize the risks to their health, take their anti-moss baths, and promise to report any difficulty, they can go."

Having read all he cared to about the Ellason team, Bain had harrumphed and gone back to Lake Seclusion, leaving Oleyall amused but satisfied that their plans were not too bad. Given some luck, they might all survive.

The Schooler-Loner Study Group was in the ship to greet Oleyall with a welcome meal of stripefish. When he had eaten, Conn took command, and the EV Science long-distance cruiser lifted off Varok, powered by a nuclear thermal rocket capable of exhausting accelerated protons at fifty kilometers per second. With Varok shrunk to the size of a waterfalling game ball, a fusion pulse amplified the ship's thrust so it could reach Jupiter's 60 kilometers per second escape velocity.

"Whoa!" Charley cried as his red beard dug into his flattened face. "That was quite a ride. You say this trip to Ellason will take more than nine Earth months, one way. Why so long?"

"We're not made of infinite energy, you know," Conn answered from the command desk.

Charley pursed his lips. "I'm no physicist, but why haven't varoks invented a matter-antimatter engine or some kind of cosmic wormhole transport?"

Conn laughed. "You try it."

Shawne decided that the elll and the human probably enjoyed their jousting. Her family and their team knew they would not be the first to visit Ellason in its perihelion swing, and they would not be the last. Many ellls wanted to re-establish personal contact with the errant planet while its eccentric, twelve-thousand-Earth-year orbit brought it into reasonable flight range.

During the months-long trip to Ellason, mind-wrestling with the great-fish Oleyall provided the team with a rare chance to get up close and personal with that magnificent beast. The varoks and humans used snorkeling gear to enter Oleyall's sealed water tub. The water was so well oxygenated, the humans probably could have done without gear, but they were a bit timid about flooding their lungs.

Early in the trip Shawne tried the flooding and managed to convey, with primitive clicking Sonar, a quick question to the great-fish. "What do you think of Conn's complexity philosophy, Oleyall?"

"You ask me such a question when your silence tells him lies? First you must confront your own truth, Shawne. Come back to me then."

"I need your help now, Oleyall. I don't know how. . . how not to disappoint him."

"Time is your enemy."

"Yes."

"So take away its power to do you both harm. You must tell Conn your whole truth, your doubts, the empty womb you grieve—now! You are a complex system approaching criticality—a vast network of non-linear feedback mechanisms and controls operating at all levels and between all levels to produce self-organized and unnecessary disaster in your relationship with Conn."

Oleyall nodded his right fin and laughed until bubbles rose to the surface of the small tank they shared. "Yes, your whole has become more than the sum of its parts, more than your behavior can explain, even to yourself. Go to Conn, ASAP, as they say on Earth. Don't ignore the importance of—how do you say?—complexity for your personal life, Shawne? Whatever you did or didn't do, whatever do or don't do could be amplified."

"But it's terrifying, Oleyall. It's so unpredictable."

"Ah, yes, life is unpredictable, especially when dealing with ellls."

The great-fish shrugged, raising both fins and lifting Shawne out of the *uuyvanoon*. Without his mud and rocks, Oleyall couldn't find words to express his thoughts with the nuances he preferred. Further, the great-fish needed to shut down in order to survive the long months of confinement in a small *uuyvanoon*.

Shawne made herself go to Conn, but found him preoccupied with navigating away from Jupiter's dangerous magnetosphere, which stretched millions of kilometers away from the sun past Saturn.

As she turned to leave the flight deck, he caught her arm. "Stay and watch the stars go by for a moment, Shawnoon. Okay?"

They shared a hug and watched Jupiter shrink away. Shawne couldn't break the mood. For the rest of the trip she spent most of her time jockeying between her two young varokian friends.

One after-meal, when Saturn dominated the view, she approached Tamilan at his desk. "You're going to be too well informed," she teased. "The ellls of Ellason will probably not fit the paradigm you've gleaned from all this studying."

"I thought of that, Shawne," he answered, "so I am now looking at current reports and official transmissions between schools. Listen to this."

"Interesting. These are schoolers talking, worrying about loners who have suddenly disappeared."

Tamilan successfully drew her into his work, until Korak approached with an invitation to race exercise bicycles. She followed him to the gym, and when her muscles began to ache, Korak gave her an intriguing bit of news.

"The schoolers—from a school that gardens near EV Lab on Ellason—are worrying about other schools growing too large."

"Are they related to Conn's school?" she asked.

"No, his is farther out, past the Viortahk. That's . . ."

"To the east," Shawne said. "I can picture it." She remembered the map of Ellason with a clarity that surprised her.

As they talked and compared notes, Shawne found herself enjoying exploration of Ellason with a comfortably similar mind. She began to hope she might not have to spend her life on Varok alone.

As the trip drew to a close, Conn was relieved to see Shawne's spirit brightening, but there was still an uncomfortable edge to their relationship he didn't understand. Why hadn't she ever talked to him about the fetus? *I suppose it's just one more human sensitivity about nature's raw facts,* he thought. *I wonder whether she kept it.* He thought no more about it.

When Ellason first appeared as a recognizable planet in the ship's monitors, Lanoll and Conn settled down in sopping wet-sweaters and comfortable harnesses to watch the dark blue disk do a do-si-do with its thirty hot moons. As the planet loomed large, and most of the moons went off to the back side, the oceans came alive with an orange glow from the hot rifts in the deeps. Then they spotted the continents, dark shadows trimmed with the brilliant blue of shallow oceans.

Lanoll was delighted. "The waters are filled with sea creatures striving to out-glow each other," she said. Conn gave her a half-hearted smile.

When the mists cleared, land settlements became visible against the glow of life in the sea. They were nothing but faint sprinklings of artificial yellowish light on the edges of the dark continents.

Tandra looked up from her monitor and announced, "We're nearly there." She was entranced by the awesome view of Ellason coming at her like a giant holiday ornament. "There are moons everywhere."

She knew that land-based activities on Ellason had always been

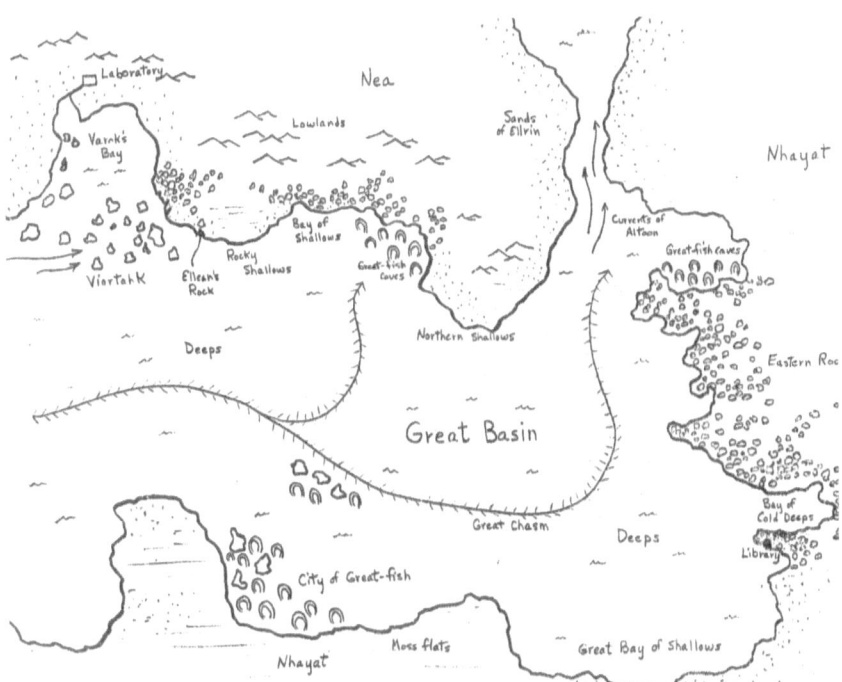

concentrated in four areas: at the Elll-Varok Laboratory on the continent of Nea, at the site of the ancient elllonian library on the peninsula of Nhayat overlooking the Bay of Cold Deeps, at Elll Central in the Bay of Shallows, and in the rocky land bordering Varok's Bay.

The view felt a bit weird to Conn, like early memories buried so deep they had a nightmare patina about them. Scanning the coastlines, he remembered the shallows, glowing with the cold blues and greens of bioluminescent plants. Delicious fruits on marine trees stood in neat rows. He couldn't remember their names.

He remembered well his school's gardener, a golden-plumed elll with a list in his glide and two toes missing. One of Conn's earliest memories was chasing bright water *brilln* into dark crevices between huge rocks, where a small tad could sneak onto shore without being seen. He remembered the heaviness of walking on land, the careful balancing to avoid pulled muscles.

"Earth was called the blue star L'ran," he told Tandra. "We could see it when the mists parted and the moons were off somewhere else for a moment. I remember meeting my first varok, a kindly old person teaching Varokian history. Any varok would have to be in love with ellls to stay so long on Ellason, trying to prepare us aquatic hooligans for the dry streets of civilized Varok."

Conn had been away from Ellason most of his life. His fears surfaced again, as they had when the real possibility for this trip loomed large. How would his human daughter fare?

"Look at me, Shawne," he said, pulling her toward him as the ship quit gravity mode and began to decelerate. "Here. Dive into the black. Find the glint in my eyeball. It's me, Conn. I'm an elll. This is the planet that carved me out of dinucleic acids and megaprotein, only vaguely similar to the way Earth carved you. I want to show you my home."

"That's good to hear, finally," Shawne said. "So glad you could come along. But what's got you in such a fuss?"

"I don't think I'm taking you into danger, Shawnoon, but you've got to realize—Ellason is an alien place. It's far more alien than Varok. It will give you new perspectives."

"I hope so."

She locked her gaze on the green emerald deep within his glance. Then she laughed, and caught him off guard with her resilience. "You sound like Orram."

"And why not? He's been my family, my brother, my school, most of my life."

"You and he could probably give me all the answers I need," she said, sounding as if she meant it.

"True—if your brain were a rubber stamp, not a sponge with tentacles. My answers, Shawnoon, are not good enough for you. I realize that. It may take forever, half your lifetime if you're lucky, to sort out all the weird answers you'll hear, but in the end you'll tie them all together. You'll weave for yourself a comfortable dry sweater of faith that will protect you from all the nasty challenges you encounter."

Shawne laughed. "Am I going to mop up things, or weave, or carve? Maybe I'll carve a great-fish sculpture." She shook her head. "My problem is that I want an answer, Conn, the right answer."

"Is there a right answer? Is God that much like us critters He created? Does He fit into human patterns? Or elllonian answers? Maybe varokian assumptions? Seriously, I think you should carve first. Go with Oleyall to the great-fish caves first thing and get some 3-D input from him and his friends. You can pontificate there all you like while we do Living Resources work in the nearby shallows."

"Sounds like a good plan." She snuggled a bit closer to see out of the monitor above their heads. "Look, Conn."

The glow of Ellason's hot deeps drew a spidery pattern over the huge globe filling the monitor.

"You're seeing the Great Basin north of the City of Great-fish," he said. "The Great Chasm breaks up into lots of narrow deep cracks out there."

"I can see the larger fissures. Ellason's Canyon Lands. And there to the north—I can just see the glow of the shallows around a huge peninsula."

"That must be the Northern Shallows. Soon we'll come over the Bay of Shallows, my nursery waters. Then we'll see the dark rocks of the Viortahk guarding Varoks' Bay. EV lab sits on the beach where Varoks' River drains the flats."

"Oops, here come the mists, right?"

Suddenly they couldn't see a thing.

"Sometimes the mists move in fast, but they can also move out fast. We may see more of Ellason again soon."

She smiled, but she kept glancing at the monitor and fiddling with a stray curl that had fallen over her cheek. He didn't have time to re-assure her again before Orram's calm, gravely voice sounded from the ship's intercom. "It's time to get into full braces for landing. The mists are thick. We'll do a quick radar drop. No point in prolonging the glide."

First Impressions

As she left the ship, Shawne shuddered. "There's nothing out there but endless mud flats. Where are all the moons? Surely not the green-ish yellow-orange lights glowing in the high mist."

"Those could be a few moons," Conn mumbled. "The mists will clear up sometime soon." He felt keenly Shawne's disappointment. He had wanted her first experience of Ellason to be full of wonder at its vibrant beauty. He wanted her to experience the colorful display of moons, gliding across Ellason's skies doing a thirty-body dance. You couldn't know what the sky would do next. He remembered loving it.

Orram stepped in with his mind focused on the humans' orienta-tion. "Lab personnel are on their way, bringing us transport to our rooms, but first a reminder. Shawne, Charley, Tandra—The EV lab uses the word *day* as a convenience. The sun is too far away, so day-time doesn't mean a thing out here. There are no well-defined, vari-able, light-periods like Varok's. While Conn was growing legs here, ellls measured time by their normal body routines: sleep, eat, play, eat, work, eat, mate, eat, sleep and so on."

Charley laughed. "Swell. Sounds good to me. I realize that the sun is never close enough to contribute useful heat or light to Ellason. So where does all this heat come from? The thirty moons and radioactiv-ity or a hot core?"

"All three. Ellason's got mid-ocean ridges like Earth," Conn an-swered. "We were told tales of their bubbling and rippling with vol-canic fury so we wouldn't go looking for them. They fueled a creative biochemistry that did its own erratic thing, probably still does. The whole system provides heat, light, and food chains."

"Here comes our welcoming committee," Orram said.

The entire lab staff, varoks and ellls alike, met the travelers at the landing pad with enough wheelchairs and gravity braces for all, even a mobilized tub of water for Oleyall. They wheeled the humans and Varokians in a noisy parade over the spaceport flats to the long pier that ran from the estuary along the river all the way to the boat dock just outside the lab.

Nidok and Forelock rode on the back of Conn's chair, their exoskeletons apparently unaffected by gravity's sudden pull after the long space journey. Forelock leapt toward the air, but his wings soon felt the extra work required to stay aloft.

"Watch out, Forelock," Shawne called. "Don't crash into the mud. We'd never get you cleaned up." The young ahlork landed on Charley's head. The human gave a large sigh.

Clear water ran beyond the dock, directly into the lab's indoor pool. There, the humans, ellls and varoks sat on benches adjusting their G-braces and nibbling Ellasonian goodies. EV Science served *oeln* fish wrapped in *challall* weeds. The wonderful smells and tastes were enough to lift their spirits, and they soon forgot the braces they wore.

During the long days of recovery from their space flight, sleep came easily to the humans, varoks and ahlork, but not to the ellls. The lab pool was warm enough, the mud soft enough, the G-braces surprisingly comfortable and reassuring, but Conn lay awake under the water, sorely tempted to take off down the aqueduct to Varoks' Bay and the ocean deeps beyond.

Lanoll picked up on his restlessness. "I keep wanting to get to the sea," she said. "I am so curious to know what it's like."

Stringer heard her and joined them at their end of the pool. "I feel it too. It's like a primal urge—the call of the deeps, as if feverish wild genes are urging me back to the sea. Now I know I was right to come back here."

"Let's go," Conn said. They left the pool and swam the channel, moving silently along the pier toward deep water. There the sensory-loaded hexlines between their mossy tiles encountered sharp electrosigns, as though they had run against a fence of hot wires.

"Surface! Back to the pier," Conn clicked. "*Eefl!*"

Stringer started to argue, but Lanoll repeated Conn's demand, and they climbed the nearest ladder onto the pier.

After their hurried retreat back to the lab, the ellls were too weak to do anything but loll around in the shallow end of the pool, teasing each other about their need to use lifters, like humans and varoks.

Twelve artificial hours later all the travelers gathered on the deck to try out the small hovercraft devices they would wear to ease walking. With an amazing show of sensitivity, the lab personnel had arranged their quarantine housing together. They were never alone as they ate, stood for medical exams, took structural tests of strength and bone density, and dictated trip reports. Everyone adjusted to the extra gravity (1.4 Earth's) and gained strength and bone density as expected.

Shawne was impatient with the adaptation requirements. She joined Conn in pushing their exercise schedule as much as they could into the local shallows. There, she gave him great delight, swimming beside him all day, enthralled now, as he had always hoped, with the lighting virtuosity displayed by Ellason's smaller creatures.

Shawne loved the beam-fish best. The sweeping biolights that decorated their foreheads danced through the light green waters, setting aglow the shore moss and reflecting light from critters of every color darting this way and that like tiny jewels come to life.

"It's Indra's Net," Shawne said, "alive, in three dimensions. What a wonderful place."

"What's that?" Conn asked.

"Indra's net? Didn't you study the religions of Earth at the Concentrate? Indra was the ancient Hindu god who ties a net with tiny jewels, every one reflecting the entire universe."

"You see it here? That's wonderful, Shawne."

"Indra was also a storm god, and one who helped in battles, like so many other god personalities. There's so much conflict in Earth's history, I don't understand what we humans are, Conn."

Shawne climbed out of the water onto a mossy rock and laid her forehead between the elll's sonic melons. "Forgive me for being too human, Conn. I'm just as self-centered as any war lord. I chose not to take a chance, when I thought I was pregnant."

"What are you talking about, Shawne? We're all a mixed bag of raw guts and genius. We're not simple; the brain is the most complex object in this flipping universe. We all need to forgive ourselves something."

"Can you forgive me, Conn?"

"First you need to forgive yourself. Don't ruin your life-joy by dwelling on what might have been. It's the here and now that matters. Always. Right?"

He pulled himself up onto the rock next to her, and she took a deep breath. "You were so excited. . . I'm so sorry—"

"My fault. It was none of my business, and now it's cost you life-joy. I just hope I don't cost you more."

"You could never cost me anything, Conn."

His eyes retreated into his head plumes. "I can only try, Shawnoon."

They clung to each other for a moment listening to the slow Ellasonian waves caress the rocks. "Now," Conn said, "tell me more about what you've been reading."

"Well, in Buddhism there are theories of karma and reincarnation, or finding virtue in chastity, sacrifice and asceticism. None of that makes much sense to me. But I like the idea of respecting all living beings, and we know meditation is good medicine, like mindful living—being aware that you are aware, like ellls are, most of the time."

"Agreed," Conn said, "so right now I'd like to get out and see what living beings are up to here on Ellason. Help me talk the others into taking a trip soon."

Before twenty lab days had passed, with Conn's urging and Shawne's support, the travelers decided they could handle a short venture beyond the relative security of the EV Lab bay.

Conn and Shawne decided they should use the Lurlial's land/sea rover for a trip to his tad waters. The rovers at EV Lab were in constant use. "Varoks believe in efficiency, if nothing else," he told Charley. "They don't leave extra vehicles standing around unused."

Orram went on to tell the team that current reports assured him that the planet was healthy. Populations had been stable overall. Ellls and varoks were getting along, but poorly defined tensions seemed to be rising in schools that had grown larger than the usual twenty.

From the EV Science Laboratory where they parked the Lurlial, Shawne's team planned to travel through the Viortahk, an intricate archipelago infested with *eefl*, and past Ilean's Rock to the Bay of Shallows. There Conn had been hatched, nursed while his legs grew out, and sponsored through early childhood until he was ready for a Varokian education.

After Conn's nostalgic visit to his nursing waters, they planned to escort Oleyall to the great-fish caves of Nea. He would swim all the way, but would need to rest frequently. "Protection from *eefl* in the Viortahk will be necessary," Conn said.

"I can make that my responsibility," Orticon said. The young varok surprised Conn by admitting he was eager to see his "elllonian father's nursing waters." As Orram's son, he rarely referred to Conn as *father*.

As a young varokian Specialist in Ellasonian Studies, Korak was also chosen for a spot in the rover's first trip.

Charley was torn. Being a master fisherman on Earth, he was eager to "test the seas," until he learned that Tandra would be staying at the lab. Though everyone had gone through the standard regimen of immunizations and lab tests, it was critical that she double-check the current Ellasonian germs for invasive potential, using her carefully nurtured tissue cultures. She also needed to check out the antibiotics the lab had prepared for emergencies. The ellls Killah and Artellian would stay to work with Tandra.

Charley was in the most danger of infection, having been on Varok only a short time before the nine-month trip to Ellason. In the end, the human decided to chance it and go on the trip, "to give Tandra some room to breathe."

"They were tip-toeing around each other like ellls on sharp rocks," Conn told Orram.

"We stay with Tandra," Nidok declared. "She needs ahlork at lab. Protection from sky hawks."

"Good, Cracker Lips," Conn said. "She also needs you to stay out of the sky and close to home, until you figure out which way is up here on Ellason."

Packing the rover for the trip was not fun. Conn threw out most of the stuff Shawne packed, except for the synthetic swim gear that would keep her warm in and out of water.

Orticon's electronic gear also stayed home. "This is my trip," Conn told the young varok. "Stay in the moment. Experience the life of ellls first-hand."

"Survival will be all we can handle," Orticon retorted. He, Stringer, and Lanoll took emergency waist packs, some dried rations, extra wet-sweaters, and detailed sea charts to supplement those programmed into the rover. Nothing else. They had so many invitations from elllonian schools along the way, they felt little need to pack food.

They planned to be gone twenty lab light-periods, which was laughable, looking back. Conn had been away from Ellason far too long to appreciate the dangers they might face. Lanoll and Stringer were hatched on Varok, as new to Ellason as the young varoks Korak, Tamilan and Orticon. If Oleyall the great-fish hadn't been with them, the others might not have made it through the Viortahk, much less the Rocky Shallows.

SETTING OUT

Early on the appointed day, with Orticon and Korak at the wheel and Charley and Shawne keeping watch, the team squeezed into the rover like sardines in a padded can—all except Oleyall, of course. The great-fish swam alongside the rover and set the pace as they glided down Varoks' River, waving to EV Science well-wishers on the docks. They appreciated the nostalgic value of the trip. Sure enough, once the ells felt the leaden swell of open water, Conn, Lanoll and Stringer couldn't resist its call. They hopped overboard and rode the rover's wake as it took off in speedboat mode.

At first the water felt like pure silk against Conn's tiles, but soon it began to sparkle with the electro-massage of a large school of ellls, and Stringer disappeared. Lanoll and Conn found themselves surrounded by a leaping, somersaulting school making fun of their stodgy pace. The school's electro-fizz sent warm shivers through Conn's hex mesh, and to Lanoll's amazement and utter delight, she was approached for mating three times before they reached the outer currents of Varok's Bay. These "wild" ellls were as driven by sex as dolphins.

"Oh, I say . . . thank you so much for the compliment," Lanoll clicked off in Sonics, as she somersaulted away from a huge male, "but we are both loners, Conn and I. We usually prefer to mate with each other."

She might just as well have set off a stink bomb. Within seconds the school did a quick farewell adjustment and swam off. From her perch on the rover's bow, Shawne hollered to the ellls in Elllonian, "Where are you all going? We welcome your company."

Four ellls dropped back from the retreating school, and Orticon cut the rover's power so the ellls could talk in Elllonian. Korak dropped into the water to monitor the conversation.

"Did we do something wrong?" Conn asked.

"We are nearing the Viortahk," one elll said. "Too many *eefl* hunt there. It is not safe for water ellls. They are returning to their gardens in safe shallows."

"'Water ellls?' What do you mean?" Korak shouted. "Schoolers?"

With a nod and an apologetic wiggle of their back-fins, some swam off. One looked back—longingly, it seemed—then they disappeared into the dark water.

Shawne threw out the rope ladder, and as the four remaining ellls climbed aboard, she pelted them with questions: "What are water ellls? What did you say to them? Are they coming back? Where's Stringer?"

"He went with them," Lanoll said.

"Perhaps he couldn't help it, Shawne. He's a schooling elll." Korak's tone was kindly, but Shawne was struck dumb, and for a moment Conn and Lanoll shared her pain. Being ellls, their pain passed quickly, but they knew she had been wounded.

If Stringer didn't check in soon, she would continue to suffer. His absence left a huge gap in her life. He had been a brother to her, as close as any human brother would have been, perhaps closer.

Charley tried to distract her with speculation about the phrase *water ellls*. "The four who came back when you called must have been loners, Shawne," he said.

"Loners who hadn't yet made the break from the school," Lanoll added.

Shawne agreed. The discussion helped, as it usually does in humans.

"They referred to schoolers in the third person, *they*," Conn noted.

"But, Conn," Korak said, "they couldn't admit it. That's serious. That's why they left you and Lanoll so quickly. Their schools probably don't tolerate loners, like that school you visited in the Forested Sea. Old Bain had a tantrum about loners."

"He's an old curmudgeon," Conn said. "He enjoys stirring calm waters. He apologized later."

"It's not just him, Conn," Shawne said. "Didn't Old Bain say there was real trouble flaring up now and then in the Forested Sea—trouble not easily forgotten, even by ells? It could be a reflection of what is happening here."

"We'll try to be sensitive to it, Shawne," Lanoll said, "but right now we'd better pay attention to the Viortahk. A determined *eefl* could knock this rover into the rocks."

Eefl, the largest carnivores on Ellason, have side fins that span more than three meters behind a head shaped like a thick arrow sliced in two by a huge mouth full of nasty teeth. Whipping along behind the lethal head is a long tail with prehensile capabilities.

"Does Stringer know how dangerous they are?" Conn had never seen Shawne so upset. She was shaking.

He pulled on a wet-sweater and wrapped himself around his human tad, wondering why in this hell had he brought her here. His fear of wildness was beginning to look reasonable. The mists were closing in. They, too, were cold, like demons rising out of a colorless wasteland of leaden water.

"Stringer knows about *eefl*," Charley said. "Picture books show unforgettable, evil pale eyes staring as they bare their teeth and aim their tails. No carnivore should be allowed nasty weapons on both ends."

Shawne immediately picked up on his careless use of the word *evil* to describe the *eefl*'s steel-gray eyes. "So, did God do *eefl*?" she asked. "Did God design an evil creature to keep the ells in line? I find that hard to believe."

"It's all in the accidents of selection, survival and all that," Conn said.

Shawne put on her cynical tone. "Like the blind luck of a genetic draw, a mindless machinery set in motion by an accidental blip in the primordial vacuum that tipped a mindless Big Bang—so much for the 'great unnamed cosmic reality.'"

"I thought you were on a quest for God," Korak said.

The varokian kid really looked upset. Conn had no idea he was invested in Shawne's philosophical questions. "Have you talked to Charley? I think he would help restore your faith—in your quest, I mean. It's an important quest, Shawne. It matters, for how you live your life."

"Charley says," Charley said, "random happenstance plays just as large a role as the physical laws running the universe. It's not all one or the other. *Eefl* live and die by natural law, but they came to exist just as much by the chance shuffling of genes."

Orticon guided the rover through the rocky maze into open water, and they relaxed. A new moon appeared on the horizon. Oleyall kept pace alongside the boat as they moved toward Conn's native waters.

"A huge asteroid the size of Mars whopped Earth a good one just right," Charley continued, "sending great chunks of Earth's crust and the so-called Giant Impactor into space, where they got together to form the moon. The impact tilted the Earth's axis of rotation just enough to give us pleasant seasons. It was a very lucky hit. There are no laws of nature that say it had to happen that way."

Shawne moved to the stern to hear him better, and he took the controls from Orticon.

Conn felt a twinge of envy. Shawne probably needed the reassurance of a real alpha male human. An elll shouldn't object or interfere. His tie to Shawne was deep enough to survive a little stretching. Charley was a kind and thoughtful man, a good foil for her self-doubts and her cynicism. Still, Conn had to add his two cents.

"So, back to the question of the moment," he said. "Did God do *eefl*? Random event or natural law? Did the Creator have no choice? Do we have to eat each other in order to generate enough energy to think? Is that the price matter and energy pay for consciousness?"

"It's a high price," Shawne said.

"And," Charley said, "it's a serious question. Like the question of God playing with loaded dice. If any one of six constants in our universe were just a little off the mark, there would be no mass, no galaxies, no planets, no life. It's as if there were some very careful designing going on in the beginning, some extremely fine tuning."

"So who cares if there are other universes?" Shawne asked. "Or if our 3-D universe is a kink in a fourth dimension of some kind. What does it matter if time always existed or if time started when space expanded. Why should I care?"

Conn had never heard Shawne sound so negative. He took a hard look at her, and what he saw gave him pause for a moment. When was she going to get it? When was it going to sink in—the complex nature of nature?

All this time, silently, deep in his own first impression of Ellason, Charley had piloted the land-sea vehicle slowly through the winding channels of the Viortahk. They cruised at a comfortable pace behind the great-fish, making slow progress away from the lab.

Conn dozed off then awoke, realizing Lanoll was pulling at his wet-sweater and pointing behind the wake.

"Charley, Dr. Hazard, power off," Korak shouted. "Oleyall has fallen behind. I think he's in trouble."

OLEYALL AND THE LONERS

Conn scanned the leaden water behind the rover, and he didn't like what he saw. There were too many fins cutting the surface, way too many. He unsheathed his knife before he dove in. Lanoll followed him into the water, and they screamed ultrasonics into the dark, hoping to scare off the *eefl* closing in on Oleyall. So far no blood had been spilled, but Oleyall moved with a seadog's limp. He had been stung.

Conn was long out of practice dodging *eefl* tails, but they caught two beasts by surprise and whacked off a good length of tail before they knew what had hit them. One got away, circling into deep water to lick its wounds, and the other took Lanoll's knife into its ravenous heart.

The ellls swam to Oleyall and supported him in the water, while Korak and Orticon rigged a harness. They towed the great-fish to safety in warmer shallows so he could recover from the *eefl*'s nerve-deadening poison.

"Stupid of me," the great-fish apologized, pushing sand and moss into symbols and adding an occasional word in Elllonian. "I have delayed your trip. Leave me. I will swim the Rocky Shallows near shore and be perfectly safe traveling slowly to the caves."

In response, Shawne built a huge three-dimensional "No!" from shore moss. She stayed near him in water, feeding him turnbit and fish and rubbing his paralyzed fin until he could use it.

The mossy shallows lay like a lovely warm (red) oasis between the islands of the Viortahk.

"The waters are lighter here," Shawne noted, "more bluish-red than anything on Earth. They're rich with mud worms. Look at that glow. I love the soft green light where the waters meet the beach. Look there. The worms' sifting mouths are dancing above ridiculous long bodies. They must be anchored in the mud. I guess the shore moss gives them cover. I love how it adds a purple decor to the scene."

One night they spotted an *eefl* approaching the shallows. Without warning, Forelock appeared out of the mists and stabbed the huge predator by driving his beak into the *eefl*'s largest sight organ.

"What are you doing out here?" Conn shouted. "You crazy ahlork !"

Charley armed the large fishing rod with a huge hook.

"Don't even think about—" Conn shouted. But before the elll could stop him, the human had baited the hook and snagged the huge water beast. He played it well, but Forelock's beak was stuck in the thrashing *eefl*'s eyeball.

Conn had almost decided to dive in and rescue the young ahlork, when Nidok flew low over the scene, striking again and again at the *eefl*.

Forelock pulled loose just as the creature's long fin swept past him. It took two varoks and an elll to help Charley land the catch. That evening, everyone enjoyed *eefl* steaks before the ahlork departed to fly back to the lab.

The next day they eased through the Viortahk, the boat following close behind Oleyall as he listed through the water. They arrived at Ilean's Rock, now an Ellasonian historical monument.

The famous wall of stone rose ten feet above the shore moss that grew around its feet. About six-hundred Varokian years ago (following a historians' estimate), it had been under water. Ilean, the ultrasonics-deaf elll, had first met the varok Korad there. Together they would invent Elllonian, a throat language still shared by ellls and varoks on Ellason.

Over the ages since, loners like Ilean had gone off by themselves to work at the elllonian library or to deal with varoks or to apprentice with the land-toughened experimenters. Some of those loners played with fire and eventually invented metal working and electronics. At first they were considered lunatics for spending so much time on land. Most loners kept quiet and stayed on the fringes of their schools, where they could sneak a little solo time without messing too much with the schools' pressure patterns.

Only when loners began to migrate to Varok for higher education at the Concentrate did they become somewhat respectable. Their accomplishments, often honored by varoks, gave them status.

"Look at me, for example," Conn told Shawne as they walked around Ilean's Rock. "I'm known as The Expert in Earth Studies, the first alien—not just the first elll—to contact a human being, not to mention dragging one to the moon and joining with her as family."

When Oleyall was made comfortable in warm shallows near shore, Lanoll and Conn cruised the mossy bank near Ilean's Rock.

They gathered with the humans near shore to talk. As a courtesy to Oleyall, they all sat in water up to their necks. There were enough small rocks and chunks of moss around for the great-fish to build his pithy comments, though he never really said much, for he was still suffering from the *eefl*'s sting. As Shawne listened to elllonian stories, she would occasionally massage the great-fish, following his cues, helping him rid his body of the poison.

After three sleeping and eating cycles had passed, the last of the paralysis and numbness eased off. Oleyall wrapped his huge wing fins around his young human friend in a show of appreciation and reassurance of recovery, then ushered her onto the beach. Orticon and Charley had made a fine late-cycle meal for all, including their four visitors— the same loners who had stayed behind when the three schools left Conn and Lanoll at the Viortahk.

"Go and dry off, Shawne," Oleyall said. "Your duties are well done. Enjoy the feast. Let's celebrate my recovery."

The ellls had a jolly time trading stories, but Shawne was a little subdued. "Oleyall," she said, after downing the last of her scrambled *el* eggs, "are you all right? You've not said much."

The great-fish answered in body language, "I'm listening to the mists."

"What does he mean?" Shawne asked Conn.

"It's an old Elllonian great-fish expression," he said. "He's upset about something, but he needs more input before he can clue us in. Something has given him the shivers."

At once, the great-fish beached himself, and using Elllonian, talked quietly to the four visiting ellls. Conn didn't like what he overheard from them. "You are good meat for *eefl*, great-fish. Leave our waters so they will go back to their deeps."

Oleyall answered calmly. "I am traveling as fast as possible to the caves of Nea, and will remain there."

The loners looked toward Conn and Shawne. "Take these . . . Varokian ellls, these land-walkers with you. We have not agreed to their visit."

"They have good intentions. You could help them solve the riddle that disturbs your schooling lives. Or take me to the great-fish caves so they can go directly to Conn's nursery waters."

One of the loners, a hedge–guardian elll with tiles framed by wide hexlines, cut a circle of acceptance around the great-fish. "Yes. We will take you. Tell the aliens not to follow us. Tell them to go away—quickly across these shallows to the nursery school they seek."

"Why would you take off with these bullies, Oleyall?" Conn asked. "We'll be more careful."

"It's not that," the great-fish clicked with difficulty. "You and your ahlork friends have saved my life. We are more than school, bonded for life, but I must let these loners accompany me to the northern great-fish caves. I am strong enough to continue on. I will see you there soon."

After the briefest of farewell adjustments with Lanoll and Conn, the four ellls leapt into the air with a somersault of farewell and sped off with Oleyall, leaving a bright gray wake. They headed for deeper water to avoid the Rocky Shallows, and Conn guessed they would swim directly east across the Bay of Shallows to Nea Moss, a large peninsula pierced with great-fish caves on its western face.

"Now what was that all about?" Conn asked Lanoll, when they had returned to the beach.

Lanoll made a good guess. "Oleyall may feel he is needed at the caves, but I think he wants time to talk to the loners. He was listening carefully. They did not seem happy, Conn, did they?"

Conn gave her a loving glance. "They were downright odd, Lanoll, not even a bit curious about the humans. And what was that strange circling? They could have swamped Oleyall."

When the varokian and human crew bedded down on the rover's pads, Lanoll and Conn swam to deeper water. There a line of sea floor vents sent cascades of warm water over them. Conn wrapped himself around his round blue-plumed mate. The water surged, warming them, and they sensed its vastness. They knew that greater depths lay further out. There the Great Chasm threatened to split Ellason in two before it branched into endless fissures pointing east, interrupted here and there by errant lava streams. On the ocean floor long rows of *ahl* trees stood tall, wearing ear rings of mud turtle shells filled with glowing beam-fish to light an elll's way along the gentle currents.

At next light, the ellls couldn't resist one such lighted path, which beckoned them away from their breakfast of arrow fish. In every direction endless shallows glowed with decorations of stone and moss. A rainbow of bioluminescent colors painted the shoreline of intricate textures at every turn. The water's surface lay unbroken by wind and crashing waves, weighted down by gravity. It moved with a gentle rocking motion over the welcoming mud and the wide fields of cultivated star-light plants growing heavy with tasty white blossoms.

With no thought for family and friends, Lanoll and Conn swam away, mesmerized by the promise of Ellason's endless treasure in the bright, rich waters.

– Δ –

Orticon was the first to notice that the ellls were gone. He had realized that the open sea might lure them in. He decided that the rest of the party should continue to follow the shore to the Bay of Shallows. He knew Lanoll and Conn would go there eventually. The ellls wanted very much to introduce Shawne to Conn's tad waters, the places he knew as a hatchling.

Shawne was not easily convinced. After the scare with the *eefl* attack, she was nearly frantic when Lanoll and Conn failed to show up on shore for breakfast.

"Conn never misses a meal, Orticon," she cried. "Something's happened. We've got to take the rover out and look for them. We can spot them with the infrared scanner."

"After we find a hundred other ellls that don't want to be disturbed," Orticon said, keeping his cool. "Lanoll and Conn have found a much better breakfast in the deeps, maybe in some school's garden. Maybe they were invited in for a star-light blossom."

Shawne's mind turned in on itself. "Conn wouldn't leave me, Orticon, not like this, unless—" As her deepest fears surfaced, she couldn't finish speaking.

"Not on Varok he wouldn't." Orticon hated saying it.

"What?" Shawne couldn't focus. "Wouldn't what?"

"Perhaps Conn and Lanoll needed to explore on their own for a while," Korak said.

"Think of your obsession with Earth, Shawne," Charley said. "You had to return. It was your womb, your sick Mother —"

Shawne gasped. "What? No. I just wanted to be sure—"

"You felt the ties so strongly," Charley continued, "you were determined to give your life to save Earth, as if the atoms and molecules of your body needed to return to their source."

Korak tried to help. "I believe Conn and Lanoll, like Stringer, are off somewhere with other ellls, feeling the same pull, a deep link with their home planet." The young varok's rationale pulled Shawne deeper into the certainty that she had been abandoned. "Perhaps they must reconnect with their souls' home base, just as you did."

"I wish Oleyall had stayed with us," Shawne said. "He senses things at a distance. He could put out an early alert. The ellls have no help if they get into trouble."

Orticon didn't like the hole Shawne was digging for herself. "So let's pack the rover and cruise into the deeps. When we find an elllonian garden, we'll put out a cautionary alert in Sonics."

"We should add a message to let Conn know where we'll wait for him," Korak insisted.

"An alert can't hurt anything, can it?" Shawne said, breathing deeply.

Orticon spoke carefully. "We'll probably find Lanoll and Conn already at the Bay of Shallows, waiting for us."

Rocky Deeps Ranch

While the travelers were waiting for Oleyall to recover from the *eefl* attack, Stringer reveled in the sensations of the school he had encountered in his venture alone.

The school's waters were warm with an expansion joint in the ocean floor. The ellls of Stringer's chosen school cultivated hot sulfur snakes there, similar to the tube worms of Earth's sea vents, but tastier. Also, near the rifts, primitive monocells grew, supporting the hydrogen sulfide-driven food chain. In the cooler areas near the surface, *oeln* fish and spiked turnbit thrived in the roiling waters where warm upwellings met the cold currents of Harrahn moving south from the Viortahk.

Stringer swam through the Viortahk with the three schools that had greeted Shawne's team at the lab. Driven by a longing he barely understood, he felt whole, completed, as the pressure of the other ellls swimming near him flowed over his hex plates. Their electromagnetic presence sent tingles of awareness throughout his hexagonal meshwork of lateral lines.

Conn and Lanoll would let him go with a few regrets, he realized, but no clinging. *We ellls don't cling to what can't be. We don't grieve when death strikes, like humans. Welded to the moment, we are, as Tandra says. It's not a bad way to be. In fact, it drives a very reasonable philosophy, seems to me.*

When the three schools paused to graze on a swarm of salt bees, the younger ellls questioned Stringer. What were humans like? How did they mate? How were females different from males?

Stringer answered eagerly. Too soon, however, the questions turned edgy. Older voices in the school wanted to know how Lanoll and Conn survived, "intact," alone in the "small water of a varokian house." How could they raise a schooler properly? They wouldn't know what was required, how to find a place in a school.

"They respected my schooling nature," Stringer said. "I grew up visiting the schools of the Forested Sea."

"Visiting? That is not schooling," they argued. No doubt Stringer would disrupt any school he visited.

"The schools enjoyed my visits, and they encouraged my parents to come more often. You do not seem to understand what you could learn from loners like Conn and Lanoll."

"Your parent loners set a bad example for the schooling tads. Don't bring them here."

Stringer had never heard a demand like that. "Surely you don't mean that—"

"And don't bring those ugly humans into our water. You are no true schooler to swim with them."

Stringer couldn't tolerate their razor sharp attitudes. He swam off alone, giving the schools a harsh adjustment in farewell. Hunting dawn fish solo, he felt like a leg without a body, or a human without a tent, a cave, or a house. He hated the aloneness, missed the flow of contact with others, but knew he could do better. Surely, he could find a compatible school.

Surely. Or had he made a terrible mistake about who he was?

The empty waters spooked him. Supressing panic, he sent out ultrasonic calls introducing himself and asking for help.

Ultrasonic news travels fast in water. Stringer pleaded for deep school recognition and acceptance. A school of ranchers picked up Stringer's scan and put out an inquiry that sent his hopes soaring. He was quickly identified and welcomed as the schooler of the OranelConn-Grey Family.

Part of an association of schools that ran the huge Rocky Deeps Ranch, the ellls had been patrolling the ranch borders, covering a fifty kilometer radius. The ranch included the northern arm of the Great Chasm, which whipped around to the northwest before it dwindled to a weak expansion joint in the ocean floor just south of the Bay of Shallows.

Stringer moved toward the school's sound image in the southeasterly currents, and soon met eighteen ellls. All wore protective covers made of woven sea grass for their work tending the living parasite barriers of the ranch. A dense, narrow forest of *ahl* trees kept out infestations of deep crawlers, the sea bottom dwellers that parasitized *eeflin*— raised by the ellls for meat to be traded in the northern shallows.

"I didn't realize my dad was so well known on Ellason," Stringer said.

"'Dad?' What is dad?" A lithe young female asked as she circled Stringer with curious glances. She carried a mix of blue and green plumes that grew long from her waist and short over the back of her head.

"Don't be rude, Nealla. We haven't offered our visitor an adjustment yet." A large elll covered all over with dark green plumes brushed close to Stringer to begin the welcome.

Soon the pressure of all the ellls rolled over Stringer like a warm ocean current. A bright tingle ran through his hexlines as his being meshed with the school. It was like awakening to life itself.

The school felt the young male's *joie de vivre* and erupted into great celebratory arcs. They swam around Stringer, rolling toward the surface, where their arcs found air and a chance to compete with twists and rolls. A competition of loud splashes soon became a contest of silent re-enty into the water. Then the school quieted in order to understand Stringer's need.

"I would like a full adjustment," Stringer said in Elllonian sonics. "I did not tune well to the schools that escorted me through the Viortahk."

"Then you are looking for a permanent school? You will stay on Ellason?" The eldest of the repair school sported a crown of golden plumes that swept backward below his wide fan-shaped melons, revealing huge eyes colored deep brown. Stringer had never seen an elll with brown eyes.

"I plan to stay, if I can find a school that needs me. I replace Ol-Sahn, friend of Artellian, gone to Varok from a school near Varok's Bay."

The ellls recognized the honor given Stringer in Ol-Sahn's Replacement Certificate, the valued legal entity that represented every person's right to an heir. The certificate system had succeeded in keeping the population near constant levels, while allowing all individuals on Ellason, as on Varok, the choice of replacing themselves either by selecting, sponsoring, and nurturing a fertile egg or by accepting an immigrant to the planet.

The ellls nodded in acknowledgement of Stringer's place on Ellason, even while laughing at his choice of words. "'Need me?' Who," they chided, "needs me? Won't someone take a poor elll new to Ellason? Educated at the Varokian concentrate, schooled in the Forested Sea, sponsored by a human—"

"Mothered," Stringer laughed, and he surged around the school, initiating an adjustment while their sonic roasting continued, "and fathered by a varok, brothered by a varok's son, and . . . biologically fathered by Conn."

A young elll as long as Stringer joined him in a circling race. The others followed, and the school's pressure patterns began to find definition.

"Mothered? I think that means he came from Lanoll's egg. Is that like sponsoring, Stringer?" The kindly question came from the young female called Nealla, as she joined the whirlpool just inside Stringer's path.

With the initial pattern established, the circling slowed, and the ellls tuned in to the voltages they all generated, coordinating the sensations picked up by neuromasts in the hexagonal mesh outlining their velvet body tiles. The adjustment was done quickly, the patterns of their movement in water easily reformed to include Stringer. The electo-fizz happily tingled with recognition for everyone.

Their work on the deep tree parasite barrier was forgotten as the ellls gathered turnbit eggs and rooted clams to celebrate the new member of their school. Nealla swam close to Stringer as he answered her questions about the differences between sponsoring and mothering, but soon he found himself surrounded by three more young females.

Conn and Lanoll had raised Stringer with lots of schooling experience in Varok's Forested Sea, so he easily recognized the females' body language when they made invitations to mate. Before he joined in the work, pruning and shaping the deep trees and re-planting *ahl* shoots, he joined with two of the females at their invitation, but he wouldn't admit to it later—not to Conn or Lanoll. Their tendency toward monogamy left him a little wary.

– Δ –

Ellason drew Lanoll and Conn further and further into her waters with the irresistible magnets of rich bioluminescent life and warm, glowing deeps. Surely Orticon knew their minds. He would have seen their home planet in their mood. He would reassure Shawne and the others, and make sure that they continued forward.

As Conn and Lanoll entered the Rocky Shallows, they received a long sonic message from Stringer. Passed along the planet's living network of ellls dedicated to the task, the message had no doubt evolved on its journey.

"I have been invited, with great generosity and some need, to join a school of the Rocky Deeps Ranch," said the message. "I am delighted with the fine females and strong ranchers, and will do my schooling with them."

"Ha!" Conn grimaced at Lanoll, and she laughed as elllonian tears ran through her fine chest plumes.

"I suspect a little editing has been done to Stringer's message," Conn said.

They were tempted to go out to him in the deeps right then, but thought better of it. The team would expect them soon in the Bay of Shallows, and Shawne would want to see Stringer's new home.

They hurried onward, eager to meet the others, before circling out to the deeps for a look at the ranch.

THE ORPHAN

Since Ilean's time, ages ago, the Elll-Varok Observation Laboratory at the end of Varok's Bay had grown from a single building on the mud flats to a sprawl of tile-covered adobe structures tied together by pleasant courtyards. There, ellls and varoks together managed joint ventures in education and research.

After Conn and the others had departed with Oleyall, Tandra and Orram spent many pleasant hours holding court on the Varoks' River dock near the lab. It had a nice view down the river to the West Viortahk. The varoks there were especially eager to hear news of their home planet.

Ellls were more curious about the human woman chosen as family, defined as committed lifetime economic and emotional support, by a loner—a "loner," not an elll, Orram noted. Then, when word got out that two "tame" ahlork had come along, Nidok and Forelock were kept busy exchanging jokes and playing games with younger ellls and varoks.

As they grew stronger and more accustomed to Ellason's gravity, Tandra and Orram took walks along the river. Long piers there accommodated the lab's fleet of land-sea rovers and fishing boats, as well as facilities for elllonian guest scientists and students.

Tandra and Orram's favorite pier formed a bridge to the eastern mud flats, where the vast EV gardens supplied herbal sea plants and salt thistle, as well as *llaoon* grass, with its delicious spores for making bread. Also cultivated there were *challall* weeds—a favorite of ellls that grew too far from the sea to be anything but a delicacy. Purple shore moss provided both wet-sweaters and salad. The broad walkway was made of dried *ahl* branches set on piles of cement. There, fitted with head braces, Orram and Tandra sat on comfortable benches while they told stories of Ellason and Varok or answered questions, which were endless, coming from elllonian tads and varokian children.

During one such session, Tandra noticed a small varokian child surrounded by adult ellls. As each day's story developed, the little girl would inch closer to Orram. One day, while sitting at his feet, one hand came to rest on his left boot.

Though he found it unusual, Orram thought little of it. As a released varok living with humans and ellls, he was accustomed to touch.

The next day, while Tandra was telling an animated story about Conn's whale-riding off the coast of southern California, Orram looked more closely at the tiny varokian girl sitting amidst the ellls. She wore an elll tad's wet-sweater and synthetic tights. They were soaking wet, as if she had just come out of the water. Her hair, too, was wet, tied back with *ahl* rope, and uncombed. Her eyes were fixed on the patch organs behind Orram's ears, and he could sense her childish attempts to read him.

He focused a greeting in his mind, and a few simple words about her lovely green eyes. She startled. Her patches sought frantically to capture the thought again. Orram smiled inwardly so she would feel his acceptance, then he scanned her mood. There he found a disturbing mix of longing and confusion. She was trying to read him as if he were an elll. His varokian thoughts were more diffuse than the ellls' directed mental focus. Like most children, her mind was unfocused, but it was wide open in its desperate searching. She probed Orram's mind, apparently looking for elllonian-type channels of logic.

"I am your friend," Orram spoke silently, slowly, guiding her.

Her big green eyes searched Orram's face. With a quiet signal to Tandra, Orram got up from the bench and offered a hand to the little girl.

She took it eagerly, and they walked down the pier to the next bench. Two ellls followed them.

"I think you would like to ask me some questions," Orram said in Varokian as he sat down.

She looked up at him and smiled.

He tried Elllonian. "Can I ask you a question? What is your name?"

"My name is TK," she clicked in Sonics.

"Her name is Tahlee-Karal, but we call her TK." A handsome hedge-guardian elll nearby translated the name into Elllonian. He sat on the bench next to Orram and took the varokian girl into his lap. A stern-looking female kept a watchful distance.

TK didn't flinch at the close contact. In fact, she nervously toyed with the elll's tunic plumes and isolated a bright yellow one buried beneath the long green plumes rooted at his waist. She must have been raised by this elll, to be so familiar with him. It reminded Orram of the way Shawne toyed with Conn's plumes when she was little.

"Tahlee-Karal. That's an interesting name," Orram said. "Part varokian—"

"Our best guess."

"—And part elllonian." Orram looked at the girl until he was sure she was focused on his thoughts. "How did you get such a nice elll sponsor, TK?"

"She doesn't speak as she should, Master Ramahlak." The elll's voice dropped to a whisper. "She knows some Sonics, but she speaks very little Elllonian or Varokian." His Elllonian was heavily accented. "Some of us in the school believe she should be educated here."

"At the lab?"

"Because she needs to learn your languages and your ways while she is young. She should no longer school with us, some believe."

"You have raised this varokian girl?"

"Her varokian parents were killed in the Far Deeps near the Shallows of Ni, where we have our gardens. The infant was thrown from their skimmer when it exploded. We have supported her on living rafts for many star-light changes, too many to count."

"You have come a long way," Orram said.

"We searched Ni for varoks who could identify her. Then we came north into the Bay of Altoon. There are few varoks there. Varoks at the Elllonian Library could not take her."

"You came against the Currents of Altoon to bring her to the library?"

The elll set the little girl down and gave her a set of colored stones from his waist pack. He and Orram watched as she arranged them in neat rows. "The currents were not our worst problem. The great-fish at the caves north of the Eastern Rocks slammed water, angry with us keeping her so long. And now is worse. Some blues of the school won't let her go. The school could split. The females say no varokian librarians should take her. That is why we came to EV court here. No one wants a split school; all have agreed to do the court's decision. The court must find varoks for her or our blues will keep her, and the school will split."

"The courts are blind to species' differences, unless there are issues that endanger physical well-being," Orram said. He gently scanned the elll's mood and could find no reason to doubt his story. "Perhaps, we could take her. It would have to be a family decision. We are a mixed family, as you know. At the least, we could find varokian sponsors for her while she was educated. We would make it clear to females in your school that she would have freedom to choose to return to you, as soon as she had a basic education."

"Some call such education a loner's folly," the elll said.

Orram saw that he was shamed to admit it. "Odd—" he started to say, then thought better of it.

The elll's mind was locked in a defensive mood. "I must go," he said. "I have spoken outside the school. Forgive me."

"You have spoken well," Orram assured him. "Please tell me your name and where I can contact you. I would like to help. We have come to Ellason to study interspecies relations for Varok's Council on Living Resources. We could approach your school without implicating you."

"No. It would be too much—"

"Too much for you to handle alone? Your school is deeply divided, is it not? We have seen similar problems on Varok. Please let us help."

The elll's eyes filled his face with anxiety. "My name is Cuffall. We will swim Varok's Bay, but do not call my name. Our school is called *Leonnl-b ek Sasvoll-oon.*"

"Lovers, caretakers of the alien-water child," Orram translated. "I believe you have been good sponsors to this child, but you should not try to be therapists." The varokian girl seemed too simple for her size; the stones were enough to occupy her for a long time. "May I?" Orram put a finger to his left patch organ.

"Quickly, please. You should not be seen examining her."

A quick thought-flow reading surprised him. "Her thoughts are quite focused for her size."

"She is not simple. Her experience is limited."

"Perhaps. What is her age?"

"We don't know." Cuffall glanced into the water and startled. "We must go."

Before Orram could learn more about her, the elll led the little girl away, down the pier away from the lab, on the side away from the river, out of sight of the water.

When Tandra excused herself from her audience for the day, she found Orram deep in thought, wandering on the pier that led to the estuary. Nearby, Nidok and Forelock were hunting mudworts. A small group of ellls splashed in the water, gathering vanilla mudworts, pausing occasionally for a curious glance toward the human and varok.

"Where is your little friend, Orram?" Tandra asked.

"It's odd. That child was being raised by a school of ellls. In the past, loners, not schoolers have raised varokian children. We're not the only mixed family in this solar system. But schools need to school. They can't handle an air-breathing bipedal child indefinitely. It would disrupt their entire social life. How can they sleep on the sea floor, or garden in deep water together? No wonder their school is in trouble.

That long male—he is called Cuffall—said that controversy about keeping the child was splitting the school."

"They can leave her here, can't they?" Tandra asked. "People at the lab could find a varokian family to take her. I assume she's an orphan?"

"Yes. Her parents died in the southern shallows of Ni."

"The eastern continent? They've come here from Ni? That's like swimming the Atlantic." Tandra used all her human intuition to understand Orram's mood.

"And crossing North America. They must have started out when the girl was still an infant."

"Did she really walk as if she were deformed?"

Orram cupped Tandra's delicate face in his hand. Though outwardly calm, as ever, he had that wondering look in his deep blues—the look he gets when his mental hormones are stirred to a varokian frenzy. "You still amaze me, after more than twenty Earth years, Tandra. You know my mind better than I do." He laughed and kissed her (which gave the onlooking ellls a jolt). "I didn't say anything about the child's walk. You saw it in my subconscious. She does have a wobbly walk for a child that must be close to four-tenths of a Jovian year, about three Earth years old, I would guess."

"A wobbly walk, as if she hasn't had much practice?"

"Precisely. Too much riding on ellls, or swimming. Too little strengthening of muscles and bone needed to walk on Ellason." Orram stood up and called to Nidok, using the low hoot they had agreed upon to carry through the mists without disturbing others.

"Orram, what are you doing?"

"I'm going to ask Nidok to fly over Varok's Bay. I want to find the child's school, do an adjustment with them, the whole elllonian thing—in water if I have to."

Tandra fought back a surge of excitement. "Orram? You're thinking we might adopt such a young child?"

Depression in Conn's Bay

Shawne felt heavy. Her spirit sagged under Ellason's weighty pull. At the Bay of Shallows the sea was gray, the mists smothered the low hills, and dull plants struggled onto land as if the effort left them bent and drawn. She wondered how long she had been on this rocky beach, scanning the heavy waters, wishing the tides would do something worth watching. Waiting. Waiting. Waiting. She hated it. She hated Conn's not telling her when Lanoll and he took off alone. She hated Ellason.

Tears rolled down her cheeks. It was such a disappointment—this planet of Conn's. It was colorless and flat and disorganized. She wished Tamilan had come on this trip. At least he would talk to her. Korak did nothing but poke around under rocks. You'd think he was a student, not a specialist in Ellasonian Studies.

"Shawne, are you all right?" Korak asked.

"Think of the Devil and there he is," she muttered. The varokian youth was standing over her as if he wanted to help. He made an excellent target for her frustration.

"You know everything about Ellason, Korak. Tell me why I'm here."

"Your quest. It's important to feel comfortable—"

"And how am I supposed to feel comfortable on this miserable sun-forsaken ball of dark water?"

"The moons send a warm glow over the sky," Korak said. "They paint the sky with yellow and red. Their patterns are always changing behind the mists."

"Always changing. A thirty-one-body problem. Unpredictable. Chaotic. Conn convinced me unpredictable was inevitable, so I left Earth to its fate. 'Have faith in natural process,' he said, and I did. But did I really make even a few small changes in rules or 'initial conditions,' that might influence something there someday?"

"Why does it matter so much to you personally, Shawne?" Korak sat on a rock a short distance from her, but she moved even further away, annoyed with his reasonableness. He sounded like Conn.

"What Conn didn't emphasize, Specialist Koran Akrallon, was that the big, long-term differences one makes by changing initial conditions or tweaking the rules that drive complex systems can be terrible, or tragic, or disastrous. There's no rule that says the difference you make will be wonderful or harmless or even neutral—even if other complex systems nudge it in the right direction. It's very scary, this complexity we live in. We can never know how much damage we've done."

"Or how much good we've done. That's why we do the best we can."

"Right. I'm sorry, Korak" Shawne got up and walked into the water. She lay down to rest, floating on her back, regretting her outburst but caught up in her angst. "I'm stuck. Way out here, and I'm still stuck. We're all stuck in this miserable, empty universe, in a tiny solar system, stuck with nothing but humans, greedy big lemmings going over cliffs they refuse to see, and varoks, so fragile they can't be real, and ellls, so buried in sensual input they run off without telling me where they're going!"

She was shouting by the time she finished, and, in his sympathy, Korak nearly went irrational with frustration for her.

He took a minute to gather his frayed neurons. "We may never know if we're alone in this universe or not, but it's nearly certain we are not. There are too many watery planets orbiting other suns too far

apart. Yet it takes too much energy to travel to other stars, and the time it takes makes it meaningless. So yes, we are effectively isolated. But life anywhere is a wonder, isn't it?"

"A quote right out of Conn's lecture," Shawne mumbled to herself. "I don't need an astronomy lesson, Korak." *I don't know what I need, but it's not this new med, the MOIs, Killah told me to start. I can't even eat the good food we've packed.*

Korak read the comment in her mind but didn't understand it, so he plunged ahead. All he realized was that she was digging a negative vortex of reasoning, and it was pulling her down.

"We're lucky we have so many sentient species in our solar system, Shawne, people that take good care of our home planets, because that's all we have."

"Hmmph. Some do."

"Yes, and I think you need to consider those who do."

Surprised at his comment, Shawne looked at him as if he should apologize. "You sound like Killah. You're right. I'm sorry. Someday I'll get off my self-absorbtion and grow up."

"You're too hard on yourself. But I won't help you dig deeper into black holes."

"Right now, I'm just so afraid . . . It's not Earth. The news from there is better. Guess I'm afraid of losing Conn."

Korak reached out but didn't touch her. "I'm sorry I was so insensitive, Shawne. I didn't understand your fear—"

"It's okay, Korak. I guess I'm too afraid for my elll family. The *eefl* attack. . . this is a scary place . . . I didn't expect such a wild—"

"Land ho!" Charley shouted, running along the beach toward them. "Here come two self-organized emergent bundles of moss-tiles and feathers right now, riding in on the surf."

He pointed out to sea where Lanoll and Conn painted green arches on the matte-gray surface of the water. They were leaping at high speed, coming directly in across the Bay of Shallows.

Shawne ran into the somnolent surf, where Lanoll and Conn caught hold of her and tumbled her about like an elll tad.

"Don't ever do that again, Conn," Shawne clicked off in Sonics.

"Do what?" Conn asked.

She pulled him to the surface and spoke precise English. "Don't ever just poof off like that."

"'Poof off?'" Conn somersaulted into a standing position and had a good laugh. "You got me, Sweetums. I haven't heard that one before."

Lanoll took Shawne's hand and they stumbled toward shore.

"I believe our human daughter is requesting that we inform her before we leave her—"

"—alone on Ellason without ellls or great-fish to guide her!" Shawne shouted.

Charley wrapped Shawne in a towel, rubbing her back to warm her. "Our little gal here is just a little spooked by so many moons moving around the sky. You know what I mean, Conn?"

"I'm not sure," Conn said. He dared to think Shawne had learned from him how to quickly snuff out unproductive emotions.

As they gathered for the late-day meal, Conn called Orticon in from his explorations on shore and told everyone about his and Lanoll's trip through the Rocky Shallows. He repeated Stringer's message and mentioned their plans to see his chosen school. Conn expected Shawne to be eager to go, but she didn't say much. Lanoll picked up on it even before Conn did

By the time Conn finished eating, Shawne and Lanoll had gone off into the mossy shallows, talking rapid-fire, like two *lohn* birds laying eggs. When at last Shawne went to sleep in the rover, Lanoll called Conn into the shallows. She warned him to keep a watchful eye on Shawne's mood.

"It's not like her to play at moods," he said.

"It's not play, Conn." Lanoll drifted thoughtfully above him, then came down to their bed on a muddy bank in the shallow bay, where he had hoped to shut down for a good sleep. "She is not adapting, she admits. Everything is gray on Ellason. There is no point in visiting Haralahn."

"Ouch."

"She knew you would be upset if she didn't love being here."

"And you drew her out. You're good for her, Lanoll." Conn wrapped himself around his round darling and nuzzled her blue plumes with his gill housing.

"We'd better get her to the brighter shallows right away," he said. Lanoll talked on. Perhaps there were other drugs that would help Shawne get a handle on her lost life-joy. They should look into it when they got to the great-fish caves. Oleyall was probably there already. His friends could direct them to a source of good medical advice.

Conn slept fitfully, stirring up the mud so much Lanoll moved to sleep away from the gunk he set loose.

After a breakfast of *el* eggs and shore moss, everyone piled in the rover. Before the next meal they were in Conn's native waters at the east end of the Bay of Shallows. There, he was sure, Shawne would come alive with delight when she saw the antics of the bioluminescent critters. She wouldn't need any more pills.

Ahlork, Useful, In Spite of Themselves

"Orram, Watch this." Nidok sailed over the mud flats then beat his huge wings and disappeared into the mist, hovering over the shallows of Varok's Bay. His nestling, Forelock, tried to follow, but found himself a little too heavy to keep up with his sire.

"Be careful, Nidok," he croaked.

Orram and Tandra gasped as Nidok suddenly dropped out of the mist like a box kite loaded with marbles. At the last minute he pulled into a glide and with a soft plunch settled onto the mud near one of the EV piers.

Uttering an unmistakable grunt of pain, Forelock landed heavily on the pier near Orram.

"Careful, Forelock," Orram said. "I think Nidok has the right idea. You're not built for this gravity. Better land in the softer mud."

"Varoks know how to fly now?" The young ahlork had grown up listening to Nidok and Conn exchange insults. They didn't expect any less sparring from Nidok's eldest nestling.

"We know a bit about physics," Tandra said. "Land in mud or we'll have ahlork steaks for breakfast when you break your scrawny legs."

"Not scrawny, my legs. Yours. Mine be powerful tendons."

Nidok waddled up the pier, looking to join the fun, but Orram cut it off with his serious tone.

"We need your help, Nidok," Orram said. "Can you fly far enough to find a school of ellls for us? They should be somewhere in Varok's Bay. They won't go into the Viortahk without rover escort."

"On Varok Ahlork fly across seas and continents without stopping," Nidok bragged. "One small Bay on Ellason be easy. Come with me, Forelock."

"Find the ellls with the little varokian girl. Tell them that we need— no, we want—to school with them. We will come to them whenever they say."

"Whenever?"

"This must be arranged, Nidok. Do not take no for an answer."

"Orram!" Tandra was shocked by the passion of his demand. "These ellls are not accustomed to ahlork. Don't give Nidok a blank check."

"Blank check?"

"You see what I mean."

He did. Tandra's mind was always open to him. "Nidok, remember you are a guest on this planet. No insults. These ellls may not understand such intimacy. Talk Elllonian—straight."

"Straight is boring," Nidok crackled.

"You can do it, my friend." Tandra said. "Please. This may be very important for that little girl."

"They fight about her," Nidok said.

"Yes," Orram said. "What have you overheard?"

"Females threatened running away with her."

"I was afraid of that. You'd better hurry, Nidok. Cuffall's school should be easy to spot from the air, for they float together, linked by arms and legs to make a raft for the child." As Forelock took off and circled above, Orram touched Nidok's greater lip as a show of confidence.

Nidok lumbered down the pier away from Tandra and Orram and spread his wings to their full extent. Then, with a loud clacking of chitinous wing plates, he ran into the air and sailed over the flats to the water of Varok's Bay.

Within minutes Nidok and Forelock spotted Cuffall's school. A green circle of ellls and a few blue females drifted in the shallows near the long expanse of sandy flats opposite the West Viortahk. The ahlork landed in six inches of water and made a great show of washing the mud off their chitinous wing-plates. Curious young ellls of the school swam to shore and crowded around to watch. Soon they were pointing out spots of mud the ahlork had missed with their splashing.

"Please to wash the plate in back of left wing?" Nidok enunciated with a polite precision Conn would have enjoyed. "I do never reach it."

"I'll get it," a young elll cried enthusiastically. "We can wash you off with this." She plucked a handful of shore moss growing in the muddy sand of the beach and set to work polishing Nidok's outspread wings. Forelock invited the same treatment by unfolding his wings, and soon three be-tailed tads struggled out of the water on new legs to play at washing the young ahlork. With the tads came their sponsors, then the rest of the school to watch with interest, until the entire school was beached near the ahlork, including the raft and its precious cargo.

The varokian girl stayed in the water with the older ellls until her curiosity outdid her shyness. Then she crawled onto the mossy shore and picked a handful of the soft plant to rub on Nidok's wing tip.

A tall hedge-guardian elll, probably the one Orram had met, stayed close to the child and helped guide her mossy washrag cautiously over the sharp edges of Nidok's wing plates. Nidok had seen this child talking to Orram on the EV pier, so he chose to give her elll Orram's invitation.

It was a good choice. The elll, Cuffall, nodded assent and spoke quietly to Nidok, assuring him they would be willing to school with varoks within the next starlight change.

"So where were the stars when you talked to him," Orram asked Nidok on his return to EV Lab.

"Behind the mist," Nidok snorted. "Where else?"

"Then we have no idea what time they meant. It is hard enough to discern one school's starlight period from the next. Each school invents its own time markers."

"The elll was in a hurry," Nidok said. "You better go now, Orram."

– Δ –

Orram and Tandra returned to EV Lab and convinced Killah and Jesse Mendleton to go with them. Together they assembled enough gear for five Varokian-defined days. They checked out a comfortable lab rover and fueled it for land and sea travel.

By this time, Nidok and Forelock had reappeared at the lab. The two ahlork and Artellian came out to the dock to see the travelers off.

Tandra let Nidok know she was sorry he wasn't coming. She touched his scarred lip goodbye. The ahlork caught her finger on his prehensile wing tip, looked at it with black beady eyes, suddenly the size of shirt buttons, and hopped onto the rail behind the rover's stern couch.

"We go now with you," he said. Forelock joined him on the rail and they hunkered down, ready for a high-speed take off.

Tandra yelped with joy, but Orram looked more than a little doubtful.

Killah said, "What do you think you're going to eat? Not my rations, you're not."

"You don't carry rations. You be moss-sucking elll," Nidok chirped.

"I'll share mine," Jesse said, knowing the ahlork would do well on shore pool lightning bugs.

Tandra settled into the driver's seat. "Ahlork travel light," she said. "Let's go."

With that they were off down the river to the Viortahk, leaving Artellian on the pier scratching his hip plumes.

Nealla

Stringer imagined himself to be like a young bull elk of Earth, released into an idyllic green pasture. Though he missed his family, he happily ranged with purpose across the warm fissures and vast sea-bottom plains of the Rocky Deeps Ranch in the heart of Ellason's deep-water country. There, five schools cooperated to herd captured *eeflin*, raise their feed, and arrange for their slaughter and marketing. They were delighted to welcome a young male into their venture.

Stringer enjoyed his work—an expression of Lanoll's genes, not Conn's. Since he had been raised to endure moments apart from the school and loved a challenge, he was put in charge of patrolling the living parasite barrier of *ahl* trees, watching for signs of infestation by the voracious ocean floor dwellers that parasitized the *eeflin*. The parasite was sensitive to the *ahl* tree's resins. Stringer noted where new trees or bushy sea ferns were needed and called for repair crews, who kept the barrier intact with expert marine gardening techniques.

The elll Nealla was delighted with Stringer's job, for it gave her a chance now and then to be alone with him. The pretty little blue-green elll plotted carefully, so the school would not suspect she was singling him out. Whenever she found a dead branch on the *ahl* trees, she would report it to the Master Gardener, who was usually happy to let her take care of it. Soon her young friends in the school were report-ing dead seedlings to her, as well as overgrown sea vines and stinging fish nettles.

The nettles prevented marauding kelp amphibioids from entering the sand crawler beds and rooted clam crops, but they often grew out of control. Nealla earned the unofficial title of School Tidy Blue, and the elders were happy to let her do what they considered to be scut work. Perhaps she would become the next Master Gardener, a respon-sibility few wanted.

Schooling ellls do not like leadership rolls. They regard them, quite astutely, as necessary functions for those who can't do something more creative. 'Dead *ahl* trees float to the surface,' they said.

No one in the school dared suggest that Nealla chose to clean up weeds and dead branches in order to be alone with Stringer. To do so would be to accuse her of being a loner.

Stringer was startled the first time he encountered her alone. She was high in the spreading branches of a huge *ahl* tree.

"Are you all right?" he called, then he swam up to see for himself. The deep water was clear and green, brightly lit by a symbiotic moss that draped itself in luminescent splendor from the larger *ahl* branches. Nealla's blue and light green plumes camouflaged her. Stringer swam upward to search ultrasonically. He found her silhouette in a tangle of *ahl* leaves.

"I'm fine, Stringer," she called.

"What are you doing?" Stringer followed a long *ahl* branch through the dense thicket.

"I think this tree is sick. Over here, Stringer. There are black spots on the young leaves. I'm pruning the affected branches back to the first crotch and bagging them. I think they should be burned."

"I'd better help. There are more over here. Do you have another sack?"

Nealla was a little upset that Stringer paid more attention to business than to her. She had given him all the usual come-hither signals an elllonian female gives to invite intimacies from a male, but Stringer was intent on work.

They cleaned up the infected branches, then Stringer took a good look at Nealla. She was hovering nearby, looking insulted. Her electro-fizz had an edge to it.

"Why are you out here—" Stringer began.

"Is there something wrong with me?" Nealla asked at the same time.

"—alone?" Stringer finished.

"No one else likes this job," Nealla answered. "I'm here to be alone with you."

"Of course. You're a loner, aren't you? I'm sorry to be so stupid. I think you're wonderful, Nealla." Stringer's caution vaporized as she moved toward him. They mated joyously, and Nealla stayed with Stringer until he finished his task gathering *ahl* fiber and spinning twine.

"Perhaps you would always like company while you work," Nealla suggested, as they swam back to the school. "I could prune and weed wherever you need to go. There's always cleanup work to be done."

"I would love it, partner," Stringer said. He needed no further encouragement. As a schooling elll, he hated the time working alone.

"Partner?"

He had used the human term. There is no word for a one-on-one commitment in Sonics. He was explaining the word to her, in the context of two varoks working together, when they rejoined the school. The others took them in with a brief welcome-back-thanks-for-the-work-well-done adjustment. Then the school took on a foraging pattern. As one body, they made a gardening pass to gather food, and began a mudwort hunt. All the while, Nealla stayed close to Stringer.

Other young males and females in the school noticed her behavior. They didn't like it.

III. A Sea of Troubles

Ancient great-fish were moved by the infinitesimal, yet profound intricacy of our place in the universe. As they learned astronomy, the enormity of time and space overwhelmed them. For eons they debated the meaning of existence. Was it all chance and inevitable physics? Essentially meaningless? They understood that in a fraction of Greater-time, all of Earth, Ellason, and Varok were doomed.

However, recently, by tapping into the vast knowledge provided by humans and varoks, we great-fish have realized that the potential for life in the universe is very large. Hundreds of billions of galaxies—each with hundreds of billions of stars—fill the universe. The water and chemicals that react to create life are everywhere! We can be certain that we were never really alone in the universe, and life will certainly continue elsewhere. What a gift to be part of all that!

—Master Great-fish Haralahn to Shawne

Conn's Nursery School

When only a few moons lit Ellason's sky, the east end of the Bay of Shallows glowed with a circus of living blues and greens far more vibrant and active than anything Shawne had imagined. In a grand contest for center stage, mosses and ferns competed with mist-hoppers and beam-fish, putting on brilliant displays to attract their own or warn off enemies. Dawn-fish imitated the bright flashes of shore-pool lightning bugs, hoping to lure them in for a quick meal. Wild herbs danced lazily on thick stems rooted in deeper water, where their colorful streamers lured in small piscoids who would carry away their spores.

After touring his nursery bay, Conn stood up in the shallow water beside Shawne and received her excited hug with all the joy any parent feels at sharing their precious childhood memories with their offspring. He missed Stringer then, and Lanoll saw it, but they didn't spoil Shawne's life-joy by dwelling on it.

When she went off with Korak to follow a huge beam-fish, Lanoll and Conn sat in the shallows and wondered aloud if other loners felt such strong parenting emotions. "Did my sponsor feel the kind of connection we have with Shawne and Stringer?" Conn asked. "I don't think they missed me when I went off to Varok."

"Probably not," Lanoll said. "They had a farewell adjustment."

"You're right. 'Out of sight, out of mind,' they say on Earth. I hope Shawne can do that."

"I'm not sure she can. She checked reports from Earth every light period while we were at the lab."

Conn didn't like hearing that. "I certainly hope she's not fussing about things she can't fix. She did have some angst about my leaving her alone. Or maybe she doesn't like the new meds Killah prescribed."

"I know she doesn't like them. She says they take off too much edge, just like the last pills. There's no passion in anything, like schoolers in a loner's adjustment."

Lanoll scooped the water's surface and handed Conn a succulent tide plum. "We are different, being loners. I feel it here more than on Varok."

"Could be." Conn bit off the plum and handed the sweet stem to Lanoll.

"May I join you?" Charley came to sit in the warm knee-deep water with the ellls. His broad face had an unusual twist in it, as if he'd been thinking too hard without letting his thoughts out to air.

"You look like you've swallowed a sour flea, Charley," Conn said. "What's got you're knickers in a twist?"

"That's an English expression, Conn," Charley said. "You amaze me."

"British English has its charms, too, you know," he said. "Now, leave us not avoid the unspoken subject. What's up? You look like you've sucked a lemon."

"Conn, will you please try to be decent to Charley."

"It's all right, Lanoll," Charley said. "Conn's got me dead to rights."

"Not true," Conn said. "We had a good balance going, and I don't want to go through all the agony of another dry-land adjustment. It could take years of this and that, worry who and fuss the other, talk, talk, talk, and try it in water before we all quit bumping into each other."

"I understand," Charley said. "I'm not sure I want to go through all that, either. I just want—"

"Tandra all to yourself. Well—sorry. You can't have her."

"I know. I know, it's settle for less or go back to Earth."

Lanoll gave Charley an understanding smile. "No one can be everything to someone else."

He shook his head. "But a lot of human relationships blow up on that point."

Conn hung his right handfin over the human's shoulder. "Look, Charles, my boy, if you can give Tandra the human love she needs, be thankful and go for it. Don't get hung out to dry on outdated assumptions. We're experimenting with new human–elllonian–varokian relations here. Don't tie us all up in unnecessary knots. No one is going to rain on your personal parade, as long as you don't get greedy. We all want Tandra to be happy."

"Thank you for that, Conn, but right now I'm more worried about Shawne. She has been preoccupied really, with Earth—"

At that moment Shawne and Korak swam in. "You've been so busy talking you've missed all the excitement," Shawne said.

"Where? What?" Conn asked. He called over to the rover, floating nearby. "Orticon, can you see anything from there?"

"Underwater disturbance."

"It's the school of ellls we met. They're coming in," Shawne said, standing up and pointing past Orticon. "They gave me and Korak a good swim."

"Without drowning me," Korak said.

"Where? When?" Orticon left his work in the rover to look out to sea.

"It may be your nursing school, Conn," Shawne said. "They wouldn't say."

"I'll swim out to meet them."

"Wait for me," Lanoll called, taking off behind Conn.

They cruised at a fast pace, sending out an ultrasonic ID and inviting the school to join them and their visitors on shore.

An answering welcome came back through the water. Conn recognized his nursery school. Lanoll and he accelerated, and they were caught up in the school's welcoming excitement—breaching the surface, leaping and rolling together as one, like wild ellls.

Wild, Conn thought. *There was that idea again. What's a wild elll? Moi? Lanoll?*

The school's emotions washed over them and drowned out their loner separateness. Conn found himself caught up in the nostalgic smells, pressure patterns, electro-fizz of the school that had raised him from egg to tad, from long backfin to legs, from downy fuzz to adolescent plumes. He was captured by imprinting subtler than memory. For the moment he was no longer a loner. He schooled.

Lanoll pulled back from the fracas and watched for a moment. She wondered if Conn could so quickly lose his tameness, adapted to the ways of Varok. Would he forget the sense of commitment to their mixed family? She decided not. Silly to worry. She rejoined Conn, and for both of them the adjustment was wild and joyous.

Shawne, Korak, and Charley thought, from all the turmoil visible on the surface, that Conn and Lanoll were being shredded. Then the ruckus moved toward shore, and Orticon greeted thirty laughing ellls as they stood up in shallow water to make their clumsy way onto the mossy beach.

"We seldom come on land, Orticon. We don't have the muscles for it, as you do." The elder elll, Ol-Sahn, spoke in short gasps as he leaned on the varok's shoulder and struggled to lift one leg after the other. He had taught Conn to catch shore-pool lightning bugs when he was still a tad.

"Roll, Ol-Sahn, as you try to walk onto the beach," the old bronzed female, Martell, said to Conn's companion in Elllonian.

Lanoll rushed to the bronze's side to give her support. "Rock and roll, Martell," she said with a laugh.

"Yes. Yes. I've heard of that," said Martell. "Some of us have followed Conn's adventures on Varok and Earth."

Lanoll couldn't believe it. "That took some doing, but maybe we don't give Ellasonian technology enough credit."

"Of course you don't," Martell said. "The librarians have kept us informed on solar system news over the decades. Earth, mid-twentieth century. Our tads like that music best—rock and roll—good fun."

By this time Shawne and Charley had met the younger ellls in the shore moss. Korak hung back, uncertain how to greet "wild" ellls out of water.

"No need to come all the way up on shore," Orticon shouted.

"No, no, no," Ol-Sahn said between breaths. "This is our adventure. We rarely have a good excuse for coming on land. The tads would meet you on the back hills if we let them."

"We haven't ventured into the hills, yet," Shawne said.

"Nothing there, really," Martell said. "Come walk with me, young human. Hold me up. You must be Conn's daughter?" She used the Varokian word.

"Yes, I'm Shawne." She took Martell's other arm, and with Lanoll, they guided the ancient female and Ol-Sahn to a thick spot of moss at the edge of the bay.

"Look how we match, Shawne," Martell said. "Your young hair is the same shade as my old plumes, and just as wild."

"We call it wavy hair, but it curls tight when it's wet," Shawne said, noting the tough old fins between Martell's exploring fingers. "You don't think I smell repulsive, do you, Martell?" The memory of Bain's cruel comment about human stench made her just a little shy.

"Of course not. Your scent is new to me, like sweet fresh air, but you are not at all like varoks."

Ol-Sahn laughed. "Your scent is more like ours," he said, "more like ripe *hoat*—and you need touch, as we do. I understand your family better now. Please tell me. Has Stringer, my replacement on Ellason, found a school?"

"Yes," Shawne said. "You should have heard from him by now. He works with the *ahl* tree gardeners of Rocky Deeps Ranch."

"A good choice," Martell said. "A challenging consortium of several schools, farming all those *eeflin*. Now—before I forget—you must give our old friends Artellian and Killah a good wet hug when you return to EV Lab. We had hoped they would come here with you."

"Artellian is working with my friend Tamilan," Shawne said. "They are studying interspecies relations for Living Resources on Varok."

"And Killah?"

"We just heard that he is traveling a short distance into Varok's Bay with my mother, Tandra, and Orram, my varokian dad."

Ol-Sahn smiled as Conn joined them on the shore moss. "What a wonderful family you have, Conn. Do I use the right word?"

"It's as close as we can come to the right word," he said.

"We need a new word for interspecies commitment," Shawne said. "Ménage or household, maybe hearth-kin."

"I like ménage," Conn said. "It's French for 'unit living together,' a domestic establishment, from the Roman root for 'mansion,' a fancy house."

Martell picked a young clump of moss and offered some to Shawne. "Do you like our mosses, Shawne?"

"I like the pink, the warm, variety best. EV Science uses it to control mold on the space ships."

"And is this shy, young varok your mate?" She looked over her shoulder at Korak, who was still hanging back.

"No, of course not, Martell," Shawne said. "Korak is a varok. We look similar, but we don't mate."

"Are you sure?" The old elll grew very serious. "Oh, I see. You have the older human male, over there, talking to the tads. That's why you have decided not to have a child."

Shawne startled and looked at Conn, who shrugged it off with an apologetic look. "No. Not Charley." she stammered. How could Martell know about the brief pregnancy? Is their sonar that sensitive?

"Charley is a friend of Tandra, Shawne's mother," Conn said, moving toward Shawne. "They will mate, I suppose, if Charley can accept Orram and me as ménage." Something was wrong; Shawne had gone very pale.

"And Orram?" Ol-Sahn asked. "I thought varoks were monogamous, once linked in mind."

Conn wrapped his arms around Shawne to ease whatever was

bothering her. "Though Orram and Tandra are linked mentally, they don't really understand it. Humans don't have patch organs, but Tandra can read Orram like a book. We call it intuition, but I've decided she also reads body language and facial expression, tone of voice, that sort of thing. Earth's canines—you know, humans keep dogs—they're good at that, too. Our touchy-feely relationships are good, but they're not much like mating—not the brain-dead compulsion and extreme sensual high of mating."

"Conn, you are amazing!" Ol-Sahn said, meaning it. "Your verbal expression is like no elll I have ever known."

"When Tandra and I were first struggling to get along, she insisted I talk a lot," he said. "Language is a hobby of mine—but enough is enough." He stroked Shawne's hair and stretched his fins. "Since the adjustment I've ignored the rest of your school. Looks like they're heading out. Coming Lanoll?"

"I'll find you a little later, Conn," Lanoll said. "Why don't you go, Shawne? Go with Conn and Ol-Sahn and have a swim with his school."

"I'll be your sponsor," Ol-Sahn said. "Can you adjust without drowning?"

"Of course she can," Conn said.

They walked into the rocking surf. When water reached their hands, they dove and swam together on the surface, keeping up a running conversation in Sonics with the school as they adjusted to Shawne's presence. A little way to the south they circled back toward shore where the hunting was within Shawne's easy diving reach, and all feasted on sand turnbit. The loners–schooler problem seemed like fiction, an academic exercise that had no real impact.

THIS MATING BUSINESS

Lanoll stayed on the beach with the elder, Martell, watching Shawne, Conn and the school disappear in the gentle swells of deep water. Soon they were joined by Korak, Orticon, and Charley, who brought them a basket from the supply of *challall* biscuits and dried piscoids prepared and packed by the lab's staff.

Martell turned to Lanoll with great concern showing in the wrinkled skin between her large melons. Like an older person on Earth, her dominant features had become more pronounced with age. She looked like the elllonian version of a bag lady on Earth, the smooth edges worn a little too tough. Lanoll guessed she was very old, nearly two hundred Earth-years. She had known Artellian as a youth when she was nearly ready to mate.

"I am afraid for your young human, Lanoll," she said. "Shawne cannot remain unmated for very much longer, can she? I see that she has lost a mate, perhaps a small child?"

Korak offered the old lady elll a dried fish.

"Perhaps you should try a mind-link with her, Korak, like Orram and Tandra. You would like that, wouldn't you?"

Korak nearly choked on his *challall* biscuit. Lanoll was afraid the varokian youth would go irrational with embarrassment or confusion. No doubt he was attracted to Shawne, but he didn't know what to do about it. Was it wrong? Was that what Shawne needed? Or wanted?

"Even if Shawne could not produce a human-varok hybrid," Martell went on, "you would have the physical outlet you needed, and you two could easily find a young varok to adopt if you accomplished the mind-link. Isn't that true, Lanoll? It's only natural. Tads are so lovely. Watching them grow is a miracle. We are always looking for excuses to choose just one more fertile egg to incubate and raise."

Korak stayed busy keeping a lid on his emotions. "I would be honored—but Shawne is interested in another varok, Tamilan. He is working with Artellian at the EV Lab."

"So? He is not here. You have your opportunity. Better not waste it." She laughed heartily, then turned to Charley.

"Will your species survive much longer, my dear human? We are so worried. We have never had their luxury of so much ready fossil fuel, nor have the varoks. Have the humans been able to adjust to their climate changes, or will they mutate to something that can survive on current leavings?"

"I predict more catastrophe, with eventual mutation," Charley said.

"And do you agree, Orticon?"

"I think the human species is quite adaptable, Martell. They have been more sensible lately."

"And do they have enough time?"

"You have spotted the unanswerable crux of the problem," Charley said. "There has already been too much suffering. We repress the knowledge of others' pain when there is so much."

"There may be some hope for *Homo sapiens*," Orticon said. "Shawne has been reviewing the love message that comes from different religions on Earth—"

"And do most humans subscribe to such messages?" Martell asked.

Orticon didn't know how to answer. "Many do, I'm sure, but humans come with many different histories . . . and personal experience. In their literature, one finds . . . hope, and intelligence."

"I will be interested in those references you mention. I have spoken with the great-fish Haralahn, and I believe he agrees."

The old elll was insatiable, driven by curiosity. The talk went on and on—longer than Lanoll could manage. She knew that Shawne was deeply disturbed by such questions, either by what she had been reading, from what the lab news had been forwarding from Earth. She excused herself and left Orticon to try to sort out Martell's questions, while she went into water to search for Conn, hoping he was able to sense Shawne's trouble.

Instead of Conn, she found Shawne swimming back to shore. She was alone. "I couldn't keep up," she said. "By now the school must be at the great-fish caves. Conn is still with them."

Lanoll could see a confused hurt in her eyes. "They took me hunting, then we visited their garden," she said. "It was beautiful. Then the swimming got . . . too vigorous. It was more than I could handle."

"Of course, Shawnoon. You are not an elll, remember?"

"Conn went wild again."

Lanoll took in a breath, sensitive to Shawne's distress. "Let me take you to shore," she said.

They swam back to the shallows.

"Thank you, Lanoll. I'm fine now."

"Are you sure? Should I go find Conn?"

Shawne struggled to repress a sob. "Yes, please, Lanoll."

Lanoll swam off as Shawne stood up in the shallows. She was near exhaustion. Martell helped her to shore and tried to get her to eat.

"You get a good rest now, Shawne," she said. "I'll swim back to the school with Lanoll. Charley is nearby, over the hill, gone hunting *lohn* with Orticon."

The old elll left her and entered the water. Shawne hurried away from the rover where Korak was packing the food away, then she broke down.

Korak saw Shawne's grief and heard her quiet sobs. He couldn't stand to let such pain go untended, so he went directly to her, following her into the rock garden that framed the west end of the beach.

She sat huddled against a huge boulder streaked with red and decorated with white crystals of quartz. She was beautiful beyond his imagining—a wild, lost creature thrown from Ellason's leaden waters like so much flotsam, wounded, in need of care.

Her eyes met his and darted away. "Go away, Korak," she said. "I'm a mess."

With patch organs on full alert, he saw that she meant it.

"I will be at the rover if you want company," he said, backing away. Before he turned and left her alone, he thought he sensed in her a longing for physical contact, with anyone, with anything. No—she needed comforting as only a human could give. He would find Charley and send him to her. He also saw pain in her mood, a ripping pain that named Conn over and over. He could not understand it. The only memory in Shawne's mind that he could capture was her vision of Conn being silly with a couple of interesting females who wanted to race and mate a bit.

Charley found Shawne exactly where Korak had left her, curled up against a colorful rock.

"What's all this about Conn gone wild again?" Charley asked. He sat down next to Shawne and gathered her up in his arms. She melted against his red bear chest like a rag doll that had lost half its stuffing.

"He's gone off again, messing around with some other females, not Lanoll. He's never done that on Varok, Charley. Or did he, in Lake Seclusion?"

"I don't know, but he and Lanoll refused offers to mate from the first school they met in Varok's Bay. She told me all about it." Charley took a deep breath. "I think you and I have similar problems. Even though you were raised on Varok, you must have picked up the same damn assumptions I have. Monogamy is right for us. Faithfulness to one is the only decent way to mate, for us bipeds at least. We don't expect dogs to stick to one mate."

"You know what, Charley? It's not just Conn. The news from Earth is not good."

He suddenly turned sober. "Yes. It's more of the same, isn't it?"

"What kind of creatures are we, Charley? Are we so driven by greed? So obsessed by power-grabbing and hate, that we are blind to the natural beauty we destroy? We had so much potential. We're failing, aren't we?"

"Perhaps."

They let the silence between them ripen with their grief.

"What a wonderful creature you would be if you hadn't tried to save the Earth we knew. You'd be out there in Ellason's sea right now, urging Conn on and rolling around with the young ellls just to see what would happen. You'd be free."

"Would I? Do you really think so?" The idea was so outrageous and so spontaneous, they both laughed until she cried real tears.

"You'd be free, but the seeds of hope you planted on Earth wouldn't be there to sprout when they found their way to fertile ground."

"I don't know who I am now, Charley. Can I be satisfied with sowing just a few seeds? We humans like results, now! How can I swim here having a good time while humans forget the love message in their religions and ruin Earth as they self-destruct?"

"Maddening, not to have a crystal ball to see that you've made a dent. Confusing, isn't it?" Charley said. "I shouldn't say this to you, Shawne, but I will, because you're no child. I too don't know what I'm doing here. I love the idea of your family, but I have a problem with your mom's relationships to Conn and Orram. To be so intimate with aliens doesn't seem quite decent."

"Aliens? Conn and Orram? I hadn't thought of them as aliens."

"I'm not surprised. They have been good fathers to you."

"The best."

"But they are alien, Shawne. They evolved on different planets with a different DNA code. They only seem humanoid because they stand straight on two feet—a reasonable design for a technical critter—and they can sound out words we understand."

"We're all made of the most likely stuff, right?"

"Carbon and water and all that." Charley started to grin.

Shawne giggled. "And classical green skin with big black eyes."

"Except for varoks, who are even closer to weird with their warty patches behind the ears that read minds."

"Except they really don't," Shawne said.

Charley's face lost its big grin. "I should try to understand just what they do sense in others' thoughts and moods."

"Good idea, Charley. Ellls and varoks have watched Earth for so long they know all about us. Then there is Conn's interest in twentieth century language, slang and all that."

"It makes him seem very human."

"Mom says his slang is dated, and he gets some of his English usage wrong."

Shawne sat up and took on a more analytical mood. "The ellls' alienness is subtle, isn't it?"

Charley agreed. "We've bumped into it in this mating business, Shawne. Have you asked Lanoll if it bothers her to have Conn mating so casually with these Ellasonian ellls?"

"I bet she would say casual mating is no problem here, but loner ellls wouldn't usually do it on Varok."

"You think so?"

"It's a guess, Charley. Ellls are different here. I just didn't think Conn would go off again like he did."

"And forget you?"

"He wouldn't ever forget me, not really. I just didn't think he'd leave me alone out there."

"You know what I would do, if I were you?" Charley gave her a questioning look. "I would go ask Korak what he thinks about all this."

"Oh no, Charley. He'd curl up with embarrassment. Varoks are weirder than humans when it comes to sex. It's all mixed up with their patch organs—mind-links like Mom and Orram have. It's super private—not so hypocritical as with humans on Earth, especially in North America. With varoks it's really between two people joining minds first, no public display of any kind."

"So you should have an academic, private talk with Korak, Shawne. I'll give you three good reasons. He's a varok, he's a Specialist in Ellasonian Studies, and he understood what was going on in your mind when Conn went off or he wouldn't have asked me to talk to you."

"You make a good case," Shawne laughed. "If Korak can't take my angst and give me another lift, he's not much of a friend."

"Another lift?"

Charley sounded so serious, Shawne turned back and searched his eyes. "You're right. I promise. I will not trade in the pills just to lean on Korak. It's time to get hold of myself, or find myself, somewhere, in all this."

She wrapped the absorbent moss Lanoll had discarded around her shoulders and strolled across the beach to join Korak, who was sitting alone on a moss-softened rock. Charley had to smile at the enthusiasm he showed, responding to Shawne's invitation to talk. No curling up for this lad. They wandered off into the rocks and didn't reappear until Orticon sounded the rover's alert signal.

"Supper is waiting," he shouted, "but it will disappear down other gullets if you don't show up soon."

STRINGER'S SCHOOL

At the Rocky Deeps Ranch, Stringer's favorite time came at the end of work, when the maintenance school gathered to adjust and reform the bond that defined them in the huge space of Ellason's deeps. In this re-making of the school, he found his identity and his solace.

I always get a tingle up my backfin, he thought, *a rush—whenever I am part of a school, swimming blindly with a greater whole to a place only the whole can determine. Here on Ellason, it is even more intoxicating, less cerebral than on Varok. From what we've seen on Earth's TV broadcasts, it's like being at a rock concert when a favorite song starts up, and the entire audience of humans erupts, clapping and whistling, carrying everyone along into the super-thrill of hearing a favorite sound re-created in real time and space. It's an emergent phenomenon. Your sonic melons swell, and the adrenaline surges through every cell in your body. You don't want it to end, so you swim harder and faster, as do all those who swim with you. Like an explosion of joy, you cut through the ever-changing glow of sea-critters you pass, until you all sense the kill, and, like a ravenous monster, you descend together on the huge, succulent arrow fish you have trapped. You eat your fill, with no mind to manners, giving way to only small tads who need the food worse than you do. Then your greater self moves on. You feel the motion take you and the pressure signals encase you. You join in pleasure with anyone nearby. It welds you to the school. You are one of many echo projectors, throwing out ultrasonic probes and watching the communal motion picture of Ellason's deeps pass by, until the tell-tale signs of dawn-fish alert the school to dig for those delicious treasures.*

Conn has called it a mindless thing, schooling, which is why it wears thin on loners like him. I can understand Nealla. She will follow along for a while, but, eventually, on nearly every hunt, she loses interest and struggles against the school's flow to single me out and stay close.

Before long, every time Nealla approached Stringer, she soon found herself surrounded by eager young males, which disrupted the school's pattern.

"You can't have him all to yourself, Nealla, so quit trying," her friend Ellan told her on one such occasion. "The elders will designate you a loner, and you'll have to become a scout or a guard or leave the school."

"Perhaps that would be best," Nealla said in a temper. She swam off without adjustment to look for problems in the northern tree line.

Stringer felt her pressure move away from his school space and quickly covered for her, triggering an adjustment for them both. He told the school he and Nealla would take on the repair job in the trees growing on the northern boundary paralleling the Bay of Shallows.

Nealla's scent led Stringer north, where he found gaps in the parasite barrier shrubs that needed filling. Small shrubs poked through the rich sea floor. As he uprooted and replanted some into the gaps, he expected Nealla to sense his efforts digging and come to help.

He stopped work to pick up her scent, but instead, was distracted by the far-off, high-pitched laughter and irregular schooling pattern of many tads and at least one adult. *Must be a tutorial on holiday*, he thought. He started toward the Bay of Shallows, sending an ultrasonic offer to help re-school the tads. Oddly, they faded from his echo-vision.

Thinking the tads must be okay, probably having a lesson among shore rocks, he called for Nealla. When she didn't answer, he realized her scent had faded, so he continued working the gap in the parasite barrier.

– Δ –

When two cycles passed, and Stringer and Nealla had not returned, there was school talk suggesting Stringer was more loner than he realized. Nealla had triggered his loner genes, they said. The two would not return, except as auxiliary members of the school. Stringer's genetic parents were loners. It was only natural. Besides, before he had been with the school three cycles, he had taken the loner job of looking for breaks in the parasite barrier, hadn't he?

The school adjusted to Stringer and Nealla's permanent absence, and they were forgotten.

– Δ –

The northern fifth of the huge Rocky Deeps Ranch was farmed by a lusty school of hedge-guardian ellls who tended the large *eeflin* herd. The *eeflin* were a tasty piscoid species related to the dangerous *eefl* of the Viortahk. They were huge, twice the length of an elll and nearly as fast, which gave the northern school an interesting challenge, trying to contain them in deep channel pastures and corral them for slaughter.

When the largest fish-like creatures were ready to harvest, they were driven north. There, the schools butchered them and carried the great strips of meat to the Rocky Shallows. They were dried, stored in moss, and used to barter for credits with varoks or to trade for gardening tools with ellls.

The long hedge-guardian ellls were glad to see Nealla. As usual, the *ahl* parasite barriers needed tending. A black rot had infected many trees. It needed to be pruned away and the infected branches carried out of the sea to the shore at Rocky Shallows. There it would be used as fuel for the quick drying of *eeflin* meat.

Following the herders' directions, Nealla swam to the northern line of trees and turned west, armed with pruning shears and a thin saw. Her temper had long since faded, and she regretted leaving Stringer, but it felt good to be on her own, swimming where she would, doing work that was useful. She started pruning as she moved west. Every three *pallons* (about nine meters) she would gather up the diseased trimmings and tie them into bundles with *ahl* fibers. Then she would move on to prune the next three *pallons*.

I don't need Stringer. I don't need the school. I can find mudworts when I grow hungry. She looked forward to towing her bundles to the Rocky Shallows. It would be an adventure to go there alone and meet new ells.

She had just lashed her bundles together into a manageable raft when she felt an ultrasonic probe rattle her melons. She scanned to the northeast and saw with ultrasonics two ells racing toward her. She sent out an ID and warned the intruders that they were entering waters of the Rocky Deeps Ranch. They would encounter herds of *eeflin* that should not be disturbed.

"Righto, Sweetums," Conn answered back. "We are Conn and Lanoll from Varok. We found ourselves further south than we expected, so we decided to come on down. We're eager to visit the school that has adopted Stringer."

As Conn and Lanoll swam into direct contact with Nealla, she introduced herself as a loner recently divorced from her school, which was the very one they sought. Stringer would be found with them to the south, near the northern arm of the Great Chasm.

"Impressive," Conn said. "Warm deeps. Must be very nice."

"The gardens flourish there, but so do diseases that attack our parasite barriers. Stringer and I used to mend them together, but I have decided to work alone. I am a loner, as you see. My name is Nealla. I have just come up here to mend the northern lines."

There was a tone in her Sonics that didn't ring true, so Conn did a little probing. "Let's find something to eat, Nealla," he said. "We are also loners, so we would be very interested in learning about your school. What is it like to be suddenly an auxiliary member of a school? Isn't that what you call it here? We have no such status on Varok. Either you school or you leave the school to live on your own."

"That must be very difficult," Nealla said. "Where would you go for help?"

"Varokian society provides help for individuals of all its species when they need it," Lanoll said, "but Conn and I have joined as family with humans and varoks."

"Yes. Stringer explained it. He was an egg chosen from you, Lanoll, and fertilized by Conn, deliberately. The surprise was that two loners produced a schooler. He explained that part, too."

"I'm afraid it's been Stringer's life theme," Lanoll said. "Do you think he is happy here, on Ellason, with your school?"

"Oh yes," Nealla said. "Or else he would have followed me here. We were growing close. We shared more as partners working the *ahl* trees than we could in the school."

As they talked, they drifted south, following a vein of mudworts. The three loners picked at them as you would pick berries on a mountain trail, and soon they came within range of Stringer's school, which had decided to meet with the hedge–guardians to coordinate plans for parasite barrier maintenance.

As they finished a visitors' adjustment, the question they all shared surfaced—where was Stringer?

"I thought he left with you, Nealla," Ellan said. "You both adjusted out, to work the northern parasite barrier."

"I didn't adjust out," Nealla admitted.

"But he did—for both of you." Before Nealla could stop her, Ellan put out an alarm, an electro-fizz that immediately alerted the school. "Stringer is missing," the electro-fizz announced. "Nealla did not see him on the northern line."

AHLORK ON WATCH

The rover's noise soon drove Nidok and Forelock into the sky. The ahlork chose to fly, on the pretext that from the air they could spot Cuffall's school carrying the varokian child TK. Actually, the rover's infrared scanners had done a good job, and Tandra, Orram, Jesse, and Killah were heading for what they thought was TK's school of ells on the eastern flank of Varok's Bay.

Tandra cut the power, and the rover settled on the water to slice toward the school. When Orram hailed them in Elllonian, the ells quickly gathered around to greet the aliens. They offered them their choice catch, an unsuspected treasure trove of mudworts—which are fine, if you are a hungry elll, raised to savor their slimy tentacles.

"We suspect these are a new variety," said an enthusiastic youth. "Look how large they are. They are seen in the shallows quite often now, especially where the mud flats mix with sand from the rocks. Do have one, pretty elder human. They are delicious."

Tandra had no choice. To refuse such a generous offer would have been an unforgivable insult. This was treasure true to the young elll, who had no idea what effect he had on Tandra by calling her an elder human and offering her the slimy tangle of wiggling tentacles.

From the rover, she extended both hands to the elll and accepted the treat. It was still alive, flashing with brilliant green streaks of panic that elicited more horror than sympathy, but Tandra said, "How do I put it out of its misery?"

"I'll squeeze it for you," the generous young buck said, and his tongue reached out and wrapped tightly around the wiggling jelly until its green flashes dimmed and went out. "Sometimes we bite off its anterior control center, if we can find it. You have to be quick though." He laughed with a wonderful bass tone. "I didn't want to risk biting your fingers, did I? And we wouldn't want to lose him."

"No. No," Tandra stammered. "We certainly wouldn't want to lose him."

Now, Nidok would be the first to admit how much he enjoyed this little scene. He and Forelock sat on the rover's stern and snickered their weird gargling snicker like naughty tads who had just spread rotten fish eggs on their sleeping sponsor's plumes. Orram nearly went irrational holding his laughter, until he was offered an even larger mudwort to suck and savor.

Jesse was next, and the sight of his human friends trying to be polite sent Killah backward off the rover's rail with mirth.

"You could have stayed on board and helped us eat those ugly snails," Tandra scolded her elllonian colleague. "But no. You abandoned ship when we were sinking. You probably went off and nibbled shore moss, so you wouldn't have to eat a mudwort."

"I was raised on mudworts," Killah protested. "Eating them is a fine art, too fine for me. I had hoped never to see one again."

"They make a disgusting mess," Tandra agreed, "but they are a bit tasty." She often managed to see her glass half full.

The Varokians soon discovered that the mudwort school was not the one they wanted. When the meal was finished and a brief hale and farewell adjustment was done, the gustatory heroes climbed back in their rover and set out again, being careful to stay away from sandy mud flats.

They scanned the entire bay and met three other schools while looking for Cuffall's ellls and their varokian ward.

Some in Cuffall's school had agreed to a visit, but the majority feared contact with varoks. They dictated the school's movement. They had no other reason to climb the broken rocks of the Viortahk. *Eefl* were rare in those shallow waters, so they had no reason to ruin good moss shoes escaping onto land. There was little to hunt there, little moss to eat. It was a sterile, rough place. Anyone searching for ellls with infrared scanners would never think to scan there.

In their flight over the Bay, Nidok and Forelock had a good view of the shoreline. TK's searchers would never have found the ellls and varokian child, if the ahlork hadn't spotted them on the low rocks of the West Viortahk.

With the ahlorkian scouts proudly poised on the bow, Tandra, Orram, Jesse, and Killah sailed over the water toward the outer rocks. Then they shut the rover down to a glide before threading their way through the archipelago, hailing the hedge–guardian elll Cuffall with a reminder of his invitation to visit.

The long hedge–guardian elll met the rover in water. He was accompanied by two grim-faced blue females, who politely refused the searchers' offer to adjust.

"The water is cold here. There could be *eefl* about," they lied. "We would appreciate a visit on the rocks, but we don't want to disturb our tad. She is not feeling well."

"There is a small beach on the mainland near this island," Cuffall said. "I will lead you there, and we can visit without disturbing the child."

As they moved around the island, Cuffall was joined by two more ellls. Tandra said they looked like males to her, though their tiles were not as dark green as on Varok. She was usually able to tell elllonian sexes apart by plume color, as well as facial structure and leg musculature. When not in use, elllonian cloacae are modestly retracted beneath a tunic of torso plumes.

The five ellls and the rover party gathered on the beach, and Cuffall's fear for the varokian child TK quickly surfaced. "She is very hot," he said. "I believe she is ill, but the school refuses to go back to the EV Lab for help. Perhaps you can persuade them."

"Take us to her immediately," Killah insisted. "I was trained on Varok as a healer. Fever is very dangerous in varoks. She must stay conscious. I'll get our medical kit from the rover, then you must lead us to her. Orram can confirm my diagnosis."

With Killah's elllonian expertise and urgency as ammunition, he and Orram were allowed to approach the child. The females of the school, who were reluctant to make way for the strangers, surrounded her. TK was bedded comfortably on moss and elllonian plumes, but she was covered too warmly, given her feverish state. Killah picked her up and asked Orram to carry her over the rocks to the water. It was a short trip, and the rocks were not sharp, but Ellason's pull on the elll's moss-padded feet made them hurt.

Orram found a cradle of rock on the beach and lined it with moss to hold the child where cool ocean water would wash over her.

As the moons shifted above, the females of Cuffall's schools kept a close watch over the strangers. TK's fever finally broke. Orram saw full consciousness flood her mind with alertness and recognition. She reached up to him with both arms, and he held her close, as the ellls had.

"I'm hungry," she clicked in Sonics, clinging tightly to his arms.

"We'll have something wonderful to eat up on the rocks," Tandra said. "Here comes Cuffall. Maybe your school will join us for warm varokian stew. We'll make a campfire. Have you ever seen a fire, TK?"

The child shook her head.

Cuffall reached out to take TK, and she smiled broadly at Orram as she clung to the elll.

"She identifies with you, I think," Cuffall said. "You see, Orram, she needs to be with varoks now, to grow up more normally."

"We can't just take her away from your school, Cuffall," Orram said. "It is very clear that the females love her as much as their own sponsored tads."

"Please try to talk to them. They are logical adults."

"We'll make a cooking fire here on the beach," Tandra said. "Ask the school to join us for a varokian meal, while we keep watch on TK."

"Is that what they call you?" Killah bent close to the little girl. His head plumes tickled the back of her neck and she pulled away.

"I want Orram," she said. "Go away, dry elll."

"I'm your doctor, little TK, like me or not. I'm going to make you feel better, but you have to let me help. Will you take this medicine for me?"

"No," she said.

"It's from Orram's medicine chest. I'll let him give it to you."

"Yes." She opened her mouth as Orram offered her the antibiotic, and her eyes grew wide with brown lights. "It's good."

"You can have more later," Killah said, "but you should come back to the varoks' big house with us, so you can get well faster."

Killah's voice carried to the ellls who had made their way over the rocks. An argument began and spread through the gathering school. Two females were afraid for the child's health. They agreed with the males who wanted her to go to EV Lab with us.

After the meal and a good rest, the child's fever rose a few degrees. The school gave consent to leave immediately for the lab. Cuffall decided to accompany us with the alpha female, Talln, who would represent the school's interest in keeping the child.

"We do not intend to steal her from you," Orram said, in answer to Talln's objections. "She is your ward. But we will talk to you about how she should be educated. She is a varok."

"She will always be a varok," Cuffall added.

"Are you going to bore us with the obvious," Talln snapped, "all the way to the lab and back?"

Nidok and Forelock watched most of the island scenario from the air. When the ellls had eaten, the ahlork returned to the fire for a taste of Orram's dried turnbit stew. There they overheard enough conversation to decide the situation was as tense as it looked. They said little, but perched on rocks some distance from the fire's light as they lapped up two bowls of Orram's one-pot meal.

"I smell bad breath coming from those ellls," Nidok said. Forelock knew better than to laugh.

To the Caves of Great-fish

The great-fish Oleyall had a proverbial ear-full by the time he reached the caves of his fourth cousins. The three elllonian schools that escorted him were full of talk about loners who had left them. They used the Elllonian word for *betrayed*.

Oleyall checked their definition against Sonics and Varokian (though only one in the sixty-eight ellls knew enough of the latter to be helpful). The three schools felt that loners were bad ellls, disloyal and selfish, self-centered and self-indulgent—but worse—immoral, depraved in some basic way. Genetic indicators for loners, now testable at hatching, were beside the point.

The trip east to the great-fish caves was a real downer for Oleyall, so he sent the ellls away as soon as they came in over the first underwater cliffs, the outskirts of town. When the schools were well out of sonic range, he sent his ID into the clear abyss that bathed the dark entrance tunnels pitting the face of the steep walls of lava rock.

He was overwhelmed by the response to his call. Great-fish of every age emerged from entrance corridors all over the cliffs. They lined up in a huge spiral to greet him. Many had gifts of rare, succulent deep-worts or warm baskets of iridescent long moss. All wanted to entwine momentarily the prehensile forked tail of the Master Oleyall from Varok. It had been many cycles since a great-fish had traveled so far to finish his life on Ellason.

The last to greet him was Ihratohl, the elder female who had given Oleyall a place on Ellason with her unused Replacement Certificate.

"Mother!" Oleyall cried in burbled Varokian—and she laughed with delight at the joke. Like ellls, great-fish are hatched by the school. Sponsors oversee their education, but their genetic parents are unknown.

"You will surely get gastric water distress, mouthing Varokian underwater," she said to Oleyall in sonic Elllonian, then she lapsed into their native speech of intricate wing-tip signals and readable thoughts. *I am honored to give you a place on Ellason with my Replacement Certificate. You are my legacy to Ellason. Now follow me. I have prepared my cave for you. If you find it comfortable, it is yours, for I will soon retreat to the shallows to finish my death.*

Oleyall embraced the elder in his broad lateral fins. *I entreat you to stay with me as long as you find comfort. I will need your wisdom and your vision, for I am newly born to Ellason, yet I have an elder's responsibility to Varok and to my young human student, Shawne of the Oran-ElConn-Grey Family.*

We have heard of her quest, Ihratohl replied, *and we have indulged in deep debate in order to contribute.*

I believe she is capable of wide vision, Oleyall said, and he turned to follow Ihratohl to his new home, *but she is crippled with feelings she can't define or resolve — like her grief over Earth's terrible predicament.*

A common feeling we all share, Ihratohl suggested. She swam at a tilt, as if pain in the right lateral fin bothered her. It was arthritis, that universal toll taken by time from many creatures, regardless of their origin.

They passed the low cliffs and dove over the abyss as it opened beneath them. Oleyall felt a nostalgic surge of pure delight. Swimming

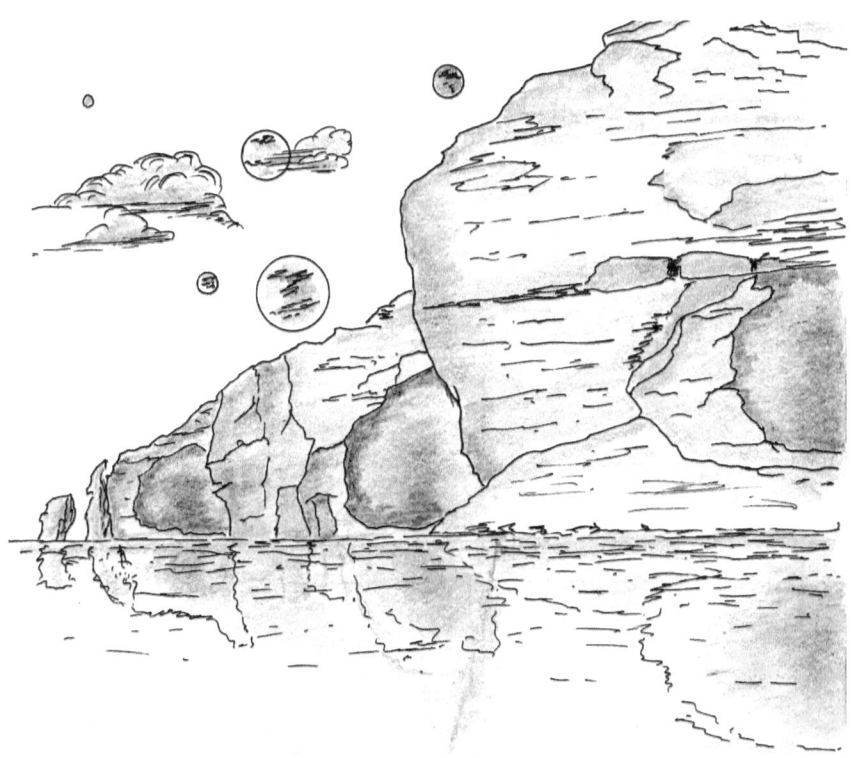

where the ocean's bottom dropped away was like flying. He thought of Nidok, wondering how the ahlork were doing in a place so alien to them, hoping they could fly the shore cliffs someday, just for fun.

Great natural caves and volcanic vent channels filled the sharp edge of the continental plate that defined the northern shallows on the end of Nea Moss. The cliffs then dove to even greater depths where the Nea continental plate met the Great Chasm.

Ihratohl's cave faced southwest on the western flank of the Nea Moss Peninsula. From the shelf that served as entrance porch and patio, she had an infrared view of the northern arm of the Great Chasm, for its heat radiated upward from long rifts in Ellason's crust. The rifts fueled the warm waters with methane and hydrogen sulfide, which microbes utilized, providing the basis for an extensive food chain of bioluminescent critters. Across the chasm, in gentler sea bottom terrain lay Stringer's ranch.

Oleyall followed Ihratohl past the shelf into a long volcanic vent leading into the heart of the Nea Moss. The flow of yellow long moss lit the corridor and beckoned with succulent warmth where it lined the entrance to a cave of grand proportions. Star-light blossoms paved the floor of the cave, and a stunted *ahl* tree defined its living spaces. A large garden occupied a high shelf that ran the perimeter, and everywhere long moss had been woven into hanging baskets.

I have had a vent blasted to the surface, so you can host your human student in comfort, Ihratohl noted. *Please choose your sleeping chamber and enjoy your gifts. I am very tired. I must sleep. Make any changes you like. I want your mission here to be a success. You will find that the high parlor I have made will seat several air-breathers. There are shelves for conversation with symbols and access to the peninsula beaches with a place for varoks or humans to sleep.*

Oleyall's gratitude was obvious, for his joy filled his mind. Ihratohl soaked it up for a moment, then limped off to sleep before she made her last journey.

– Δ –

"My guess is that Conn and Lanoll are having some kind of problem with his old school, Shawne," Orticon said. Her elder varokian brother approached her on the beach and stood as close as his nerves allowed. "Let me read you. Perhaps I can help."

After her talk with Korak, Shawne had seemed fine, but after exploring the shallows with hospitable ellls who came to visit, she spent hours staring out over the water, waiting for Conn and Lanoll.

– Δ –

Conn told Lanoll that Shawne was entirely right when she said he had gone wild.

"The untamed waters of Ellason are like an intoxicant, magnifying my senses and mocking my commitment to dry land bipeds. Shawne was bent on getting to the great-fish. She will pursue her quest at the caves now that she has seen my nursing school and home waters."

– Δ –

In Korak's eyes, Shawne grew more and more beautiful, standing tall and straight in her solitude and grief, a becalmed soul gathering strength for Ellason's demands and, hopefully, finding comfort in the green moss at her feet. The broad, quiet ocean spread before her to a misted horizon. Her hair fell over her shoulders, framing her face with soft curls that belied her solemn eyes. Tears no longer stained the modeled planes of her face. Instead there was a steadiness about her gaze he didn't understand.

Orticon stayed close to Shawne, determined to help her.

She didn't move away. "Read me all you like, Orticon," she said. "We'll see if we agree about Conn's wildness and his school."

Orticon took his time searching her mood, then he sensed her thoughts as she opened her mind to him and they came into focus. He touched her arm and turned her gently to face him.

"It seems we agree. Conn expects us to go to the great-fish caves. You must follow your quest, Shawne. It would do you good to give it more air. Also—" He hesitated, knowing she hated the idea of taking drugs. "Perhaps the great-fish can prescribe better anti-depressants for you."

"You think I've got a chemical imbalance I can't manage on my own?"

"The brain is a pot of chemicals always seeking equilibrium with the input it gets. Right now yours could use a little help finding some kind of resolution. A need for self-forgiveness perhaps."

"Perhaps."

"It's not a failing to need such help."

"I know that, but what am I, if not my brain? What I mean, Orticon, is that I need to use it, regain control, not just lean on the chemicals, or Korak, or you. It's too easy to wallow in deep mental holes and dig even deeper."

Orticon nodded. "I'll buy that. My beautiful human sister is being brilliantly human right now." As if she were still the six-year-old begging to be pinned to the ground by her mature sibling, he swatted the back of her head gently. "Go jump in the water. Clean up, and put on traveling clothes. We've waited long enough. We're going to the caves without Conn and Lanoll."

Watching the swat, Korak nearly jumped out of his skin, then he busied himself, folding ground cloths and packing cooking gear in the rover. He was amazed. Shawne seemed happier. The rough treatment had helped. She had laughed, and obeyed, of all things, which was not in character. On the pretext of rinsing the cook pot, he moved closer to her on shore so he could check her mood. It was clear and light, anticipating the trip to the great-fish caves.

Suddenly she turned to face him, surprised at the intrusion. Their eyes met, and he tried to smile. How did she know he was reading her? Humans had no patch organs.

"I'm sorry," he stammered in Varokian. "I was worried about you."

She laughed. "You'd do better to worry about Orticon. He is always telling me what to do. I'll get my revenge. He thinks Orram and Conn have spoiled me."

"Spoiled?"

"Been too easy on me. He's right. I'm a brat."

"Is there a word for *brat* in Varokian?" Korak asked.

"*Aloon* is a close translation in Elllonian, but the English word has a little more edge to it. Brats in North America can do real harm."

"You are not a brat, Shawne. You care very much—though I suppose you are a bit willful."

"Suppose? Korak, you get the prize for diplomacy. You know very well that I'm willful. Your patches are dripping with my willfulness."

"Shawne," Orticon shouted from the rover. "Don't exaggerate. It's unattractive. The great-fish will hate it—and, believe me, they'll see it in your head."

She didn't hear half of what he said because she was busy attacking Korak with handfuls of water. He defended himself admirably, and soon their water battle escalated into throwing pelts of soft moss.

Their laughter alerted Charley, who came in from fishing the shallows to see what strange noise Korak was making.

"Go nuts, Korak," Shawne shouted. "Cut loose." She stuffed a large handful of moss down his wet suit. As he pulled at the moss, she caught him off balance, rolled him under the water, and sat on him. Suddenly he went limp, and her eyes opened wide with fear. She started to get off to help him up, when he braced his legs, found a foothold in the sandy mud, and thrust upward, tossing Shawne a good two *pallons* across the water.

Orticon and Charley clapped heartily. "Good show, Korak. She needed that."

"Attaboy!" Charley shouted. They ushered Korak on shore like a hero returned from the wars, leaving the bedraggled Shawne to gather her wits and pretend nothing had happened.

Orticon knew a lot had happened. The relationship between Shawne and Korak would never be the same. Contact, even in play, meant too much to varoks.

Everyone was in a better mood as they prepared to move on to the great-fish caves. While Orticon drove the rover southeast toward the west-facing cliffs of the Lea Moss, Korak navigated. They moved quickly across the placid water on a straight course to the broad peninsula that defined the Great Basin and pinched off the Deeps to the north. On the way they planned to check in at Great-fish Central.

Charley and Shawne relaxed in the stern couch, letting Ellason pass around them like a slow movie. Sixteen moons made an impressionistic setting above patches of thick mist upstaged by high clouds. Not much could be seen at high speed over gray water, except the occasional dim suggestion of land scratching the horizon.

"I like Ellason up close and personal," Charley said.

"Like God should be." Shawne leaned back so her head rested on the back of the seat. "Stringer thinks my theology suffers from having too many fathers."

"Whatever works," said Charley.

"You really believe that?"

"In some ways it has to be true. A belief has to fit who you are."

"So my quest is nothing more than a self-indulgence?" Shawne rarely felt defensive with Charley. With him, her thoughts could relax and flow.

"I didn't say that, Shawne. I think your quest is valuable for furthering interspecies understanding, opening up new ways of thinking for everyone you quiz."

"I want to know what's real, Charley. I need to think clearly, concentrate on finding positive truths."

"You want truth? The pendulum swings back and forth on that one. I go with the idea that there is a Reality we can only guess from our personal view—but we can work toward it, asymptotically, like a curve of data inching ever closer to infinity but never getting there."

"Orram says something like that, Charley. Did I come all this way just to hear the great-fish say the same thing? That it all comes down to science?"

"Perhaps. Science can get pretty close, as more and more evidence builds up and questions find answers, but all science can do is describe how things work. That's often enough to inspire faith or generate awe at the incredible intricacy and beauty of life and the cosmos."

"But my questions are not about how things came to be or how they work. They're about why we're alive. What for? What good is it, if we just hate and kill and destroy ourselves?"

"Only you yourself alone can answer that question. The great-fish can do nothing but share ideas."

Shawne's face set into a grimace. "I suppose. So why is there so much pain, Charley? Will they answer that question?"

"You already know the answer to that, don't you? You've studied biology. Pain is a fair warning that something needs fixing. We are made of stuff, you know."

"Complex stuff, Conn would say. Things can go wrong or be unpredictable, especially in the so very complex sentient brain. Is that why humans can be so terrible, Charley? Or crazy? Or is a complex brain necessary for survival? So only the smartest can get a drink of water?"

"Maybe you need faith in something beyond biology."

"Like what?"

"How about love and beauty? Even out here on Ellason?"

"You sound like Mom. Right now I just need to know what's *real*. What good is truth we can never reach? It leaves us always uncertain."

"There's the catch. To reach certainty requires a leap off the curve, a leap of faith."

"Faith? The whole planet Earth is still paying the cost of humans using this or that faith to deny what their eyes and ears should tell them."

"True, you have to be careful how far from the data curve your leap of faith takes you—but a leap it is. The data alone can get close only to questions that are testable. If the questions are not testable, like 'what's right' or 'for what purpose or meaning—why?,' then religion or philosophy takes over. The leap to that realm can be pretty scary."

"You're saying I have to leap?"

"Like everyone else. That's why religious intolerance is so intolerable."

"So everyone has their own unique vision," Shawne said. It was a protest on her part. She wanted one answer, a formula to encompass everything and everyone.

"It can't be helped. It's in the nature of things," Charley said kindly. She turned away and stared out over the water. "Charley, look!"

The cliffs of Nea Moss rose high above the rolling face of the sea. They were alive with the business of life—millions of critters of every size and shape that supported the City of Great-fish. Ripples puckered the surface, and small dart fish cut the water with bright arrows of blue and yellow. Algae tulips and crawling invertebrates occupied shelves and crannies on the sheer rock faces, along with the moss-lined nests of flying egg-layers. Crumbled rock at the base of the cliffs swarmed with *lohn* birds.

"Korak, did you see that animal?" Shawne pointed to the tide pools near shore where two small creatures with long bodies like sea otters hunted for succulent worms and shellfish. "What are they called?"

He told her, and she asked more questions.

Seeing Shawne and Korak swept up with spotting and naming critters, Orticon slowed the rover and zig-zagged toward the cliffs to provide a better view.

Silently, far below, a large presence of great-fish watched and waited.

A FAILED SEARCH AND A WILD RIDE TO DISASTER

Looking for Stringer, Nealla led Lanoll and Conn and her entire school along the common swim path to the gardens of the northern school of hedge–guardians, the herders of *eeflin*.

"We would have seen Stringer if he were up here," the eldest herder told the visitors. He sat on the stump of an ancient *ahl* tree and chewed on a long stem of wild *llaoon* grass. Except for his green velvet body and tunic of lime-colored plumes, he looked every bit the cowboy in an old American shoot-em-up. All he needed was a holster or, better yet, a lasso to complete the picture. Conn imagined him roping one of the huge *eeflin* that grazed nearby on the sea-bottom pasture.

The herder continued chewing while he clicked off his perfunctory Sonics. "We just brought these *eeflin* down off the northern parasite barrier. Had to scan quite a length to find them all. We would have noticed a lone elll up there."

"We'll just circle up and around, anyway, if you don't mind," Nealla said. "I want to see how much work my school needs to do."

"Go right ahead." The touch of gold on the hedge–guardian plumes gave him credibility, but there was no adjustment. Nothing. Even with that, Conn did not find it suspicious when the hedge–guardians offered to help with the search.

They swam the full length of the northern perimeter of the ranch before they gave up. Ultrasonic scans showed nothing. Probes and calls were not answered. Stringer was not to be found.

Though already adjusted to his absence, they all schooled like crazed turnbits, trying to decide what to do next. Lanoll insisted Conn must go to the great-fish caves to be with Shawne. She would go to Elll Central to initiate a formal search for Stringer, then return to EV Lab to enlist the help of varoks.

Conn hated the idea of separating from her. It began to look like this trip to Ellason would be a repeat of their debacle on Earth, with everyone flying off half-cocked in sixteen different directions. But Lanoll hung tough. They would separate.

Stringer's school could not drop their work and take off in search of him. The ranch consortium depended on them to keep its parasite barriers mended. All they could do would be to keep constant watch for Stringer and put out frequent calls. There were schools devoted to rescue work. The alert would quickly spread through the seas, through the ellls' tightly woven net of ultrasonics.

"We'll meet at EV Lab later, Conn, and regroup," Lanoll promised. "We'll spread a message across the communication net, asking Stringer to meet us there. For now, let's get some sleep."

With the plans made, with all bets covered, she dared to look into Conn's eyes. There she saw all the terror they both felt. The life-joy drained from her.

Ellls, loners or not, fail miserably in the missing-persons department. They don't do well when faced with uncertainty. Death and final departure are easy. The school adjusts to accepted facts, and no life-joy is wasted on grief. Misfortune and pain can trigger loss of life-joy—but only while the outcome is uncertain. Then the school is thrown into confusion.

That was how it was for Lanoll and Conn, with Stringer missing. Alive or dead, trapped or injured, they hated not knowing. Was he unable to call for help? They were in danger of letting the questions drive their reasoning into dark corners. There were no good reasons why he should disappear from the school.

Aimlessly, they swam downward toward warm water. At the very tip of the Great Chasm's northern arm they found hot vents rich with life. Warm rocks lay at odd angles over a comfortable plain of sea-bottom mud. There they dug themselves a cradle for their worries and buried them in sleep.

They didn't know Nealla had left the school to follow them.

Conn awoke and said his good-byes to Lanoll. As he swam off toward the northeast, Nealla called, "Where are you going, Conn?"

"I need to be with my human daughter, Nealla," he answered, swimming on. "Go with Lanoll and keep her safe. Remember, we are strangers to Ellason."

She answered with a promise to see Lanoll safely to EV Lab. Conn swam on more quickly then, heartened by her unflinching support. On leaving the school, she had declared herself a loner. In her harsh world, she would never again be more than auxiliary to the school, but now she would have some idea what the concept *family* meant.

– Δ –

Tandra and Orram's rover stood on the tiny pocket of sand near the small rocky island of the West Viortahk. The ellls had retreated, reluctantly allowing the strangers to nurse their feverish varokian ward. They were not happy. Most of them knew TK needed help from the hospital at EV Lab near Varok's Bay. They were afraid she would not survive her illness. Others felt guilty for keeping her away from her own kind too long.

On the opposite side of the emotional spectrum, the alpha elllonian female Talln and others would do anything to keep forever the child they had raised from infant to toddler. They didn't realize how her watery existence had distorted her ability to walk. They saw her as a new link between ellls and varoks, a water-loving varok.

Tandra emptied the rover's scuba gear drawer, lined it with moss, and set it in the rover's stern against the couch. Then she moistened it, using her food cup as a dipper. Killah folded his extra wet-sweater at the foot of the oversized cradle and took the sleeping Tahlee-Karal from Orram's arms.

He lay TK in her soft, cool bed, then moved aside while Talln vaulted into the rover and claimed the stern couch beside the child. Killah and Tandra squeezed in beside the large elll, leaving Jesse on the side bench. Orram drove, with Cuffall beside him to navigate through the treacherous rocks of the West Viortahk.

Far overhead, obscured in mist, Nidok and Forelock watched, flying with tense wing-plates to minimize their clacking noise.

Orram trusted the ahlork's behavior. Though they enjoyed playing the fool, they were not simple-minded. Suspicious by nature, they chose to keep watch from a distance. So much the better—though they always found a way to be frustrating. They stayed too far from the gathering of ellls and varoks to be scanned. Orram had nothing to go on but faith in their good sense. Tandra's intuition confirmed his decision to forego contact with them, and though Jesse looked up occasionally to check the ahlork's whereabouts, he, too, said nothing about them.

The rover cruised slowly just over the water, through the maze of small islands of the West Viortahk. Sonar kept the craft a safe distance from rocks lurking close below the restless sea. As they moved into the open water of Varok's Bay, the wind tore into its passengers with a vengeance, and white caps occasionally broke the surface of the water.

"Where did these waves come from?" Tandra asked Talln. "We have experienced nothing but calm seas since we came to Ellason."

"The winds will last until the moons part company," Talln said. "They will last many cycles. We would do better in water."

"I agree," Tandra said, "but the child cannot use scuba gear yet. The rover will ride well above the waves and cut through the wind. Orram is using high power now."

"I don't like it."

"I understand. The noise is not pleasant."

The rover knifed through the strong gusts as it picked up speed. Soon it was heading northeast across open water to the gentle slopes of the Gate, a broad peninsula of sand dunes separating Varok's Bay from the estuary leading to EV Lab.

Tandra wondered how Nidok and Forelock were faring in the storm, but there was no knowing. Though the mists remained heavy, some had gathered into clouds. An occasional star peered through briefly, promising more clearing to come. Tandra hoped to get a glimpse of Earth, the blue star L'ran. It gave her an excuse to keep watch on the sky. For an instant Nidok and Forelock could be seen as tiny squares reflecting orange moonlight, then they disappeared when the mists closed in again.

Tandra leaned over and felt TK's forehead. It was still too warm. The child stirred with the touch, but did not awaken. Talln snapped a warning, not expecting Tandra to understand the Sonics.

"We share concern for TK," Tandra said to the huge, wild elll. Ellls produce Sonics through a submelon flap that has little to do with human or varokian speech, but Tandra managed a fair imitation of elllonian clicks with the back of her tongue against her palate. "I suggest we learn to get along."

Killah harrumphed and spoke in Sonics to Tandra. "We'll get a leash for this one at EV Lab." It made the point nicely. Talln sat on her tongue after that.

None of the travelers could be sure what happened next. Tandra remembers seeing the sharp cliffs of the Gate on the horizon. The rover must have been quite close to shore, about ready to swing north and enter the estuary of the Varokian River, when a loud noise ruptured Tandra's right eardrum. She was thrown through the air. Cold seawater slapped her to her senses. Coughing the moisture from her windpipe, she looked around, desperately searching for the varokian child.

The wind raced over the water, tossing it into jumbled surf where errant rocks from the West Viortahk lay captured on the southwest point of the Gate. Tandra struggled onto a rock just under the surface. Pain surged across her head, but the solid feel of the rock was enough to ease her panic. She had a glimpse of the rover afloat, overturned, caught among exposed rocks. It bounced dangerously in the surf. She looked around. No one was in sight. She fought to stay conscious, and through the veil of pain, she saw Killah floating on his back, just beyond the rover, holding something out of the water. Talln appeared beside him. *They must have the child,* Tandra prayed. *They must.*

Then she saw Jesse, holding onto the side of the rover, inching it away from the rocks. Every motion gave her a painful jab as she fought to move closer to the rocky shore, looking for a place to land. Finally, she came to a sloping rock in a protected inlet and put her throbbing ear on soft moss. The thermal synthetics she wore protected her from the chilling air. For a moment she lay still, just out of reach of the water, then she pulled her weight slowly over the rocks toward Jesse.

She wished she could scream for help. She prayed Jesse could get the rover turned over. Jesse. Always the quiet human, too quiet now. It drove her a bit crazy, wondering what he felt, what he thought. He hadn't said a thing about TK and the school. Tandra wondered if the ellls realized he was human, not varokian.

I should not complain about him, she told herself. *He has been absolutely loyal to ellls and varoks for all these years, essentially alone on Varok, then traveling to Earth with us, and now this. He will be the one to save the rover, fix it, and have us all back at EV Lab before we dry off.*

She watched as Jesse worked the rover past the rocks to the inlet where she waited. Then she blacked out.

It was Killah and Talln together who carried TK onto sand at the inlet, moving slowly to save wear and tear on their toe fins. Killah wrapped TK in his wet-sweater and lay her in the sand, sheltered by a large rock. He would have to be careful to stay in water.

"You needn't sponsor me, Jesse," Killah said when Jesse approached him with an armload of moss. "I appreciate your concern. We are not far from the lab. The wind won't dry me up before we get there."

"As soon as Orram and the hedge–guardian Cuffall join us, we can right the rover and move on," Jesse said. He was exhausted, breathing heavily, his head bowed as if it were a great weight. "Where are they?"

"I haven't seen them," Killah said, scanning the inlet. "Jesse, look. There's Tandra. She's been hurt. Help me."

While the elll and the human tended to Tandra, Talln scanned the ocean's surface. A crease formed under her melons. "I will go find Orram and Cuffall," she said, and she re-entered the ocean.

She must have scanned underwater extensively before she moved upstream, for she didn't reappear for a long time. When she returned, her brow crease was knotted tight. Talln had found no sign of Orram or Cuffall. She had swum along the shore and up river to the lab, sending out ultrasonic calls and sonic messages, echo-scanning in every direction.

With a comforting rumble, a rover appeared just to the north of the rocky masthead, searching, following Talln's lead from the lab. Its crew had no good news. Infrared detectors on the lab rover had shown no sign of Orram and Cuffall.

A Choice of Ending

Orticon shut off the power as soon as the water grew light beneath the rover. He looked at Korak and deliberately gave the young varok a reassuring smile. "Now we wait," he said.

The cliffs of Nea Moss rose straight up from the sea, not far to the south. The descending tones of *lohn* flyers filled the air. Shawne pointed them out to Charley, who decided they were celebrating the eggs they laid, like chickens cackling with delight—or with relief at ridding themselves of their burden. They sat on nests of moss tucked into the rocks at the base of the cliffs, or they waddled slowly along the shore stirring up shore-pool lightning bugs with the sharp horns protruding from the sides of their tiny heads, like thorny doves.

Here, south of the Bay of Shallows the mists were thin. Colors in the shallow water changed from green to blue and back again. Far to the west dark clouds rose thousands of feet above the mists, which were moving swiftly over the shallows. Charley mentioned the wild storms he had survived in the South Pacific off Cabo San Lucas.

"How much longer—? Never mind," Charley said, when he saw two dark forms surface and circle the rover.

Shawne and Orticon reached over the side and offered their hands in greeting. "We are looking for Oleyall," Shawne said to the great-fish.

In answer, a long tail emerged from the surface like a sea serpent, and two prehensile fingers on the tail grasped Shawne's hand with a shake of welcome that made her laugh. The fingers moved on to spiral upward in a varokian greeting for Orticon.

"Put one hand into the water," Shawne told Charley. "Korak, a spiral greeting over the side will do. They are just being polite, imitating a human handshake."

Charley reached out to shake the offered tail. It then spiraled up to acknowledge Korak, and a second great-fish tail joined the first in pointing the way south.

Orticon retrieved the emergency paddles from their clamps on the starboard side of the rover and passed one to Shawne. They traded ends so his stronger j-stroke would guide the craft, and, as swiftly as they could, they followed the great-fish, paddling like a credible canoe team. The rover was molded from a light titanium material, so Shawne and Orticon easily kept up with the great-fishs' leisurely pace.

They passed *lohn* birds floating in the water. The plump scavengers took little notice, except to row with stubby wings into the rover's wake, looking for the tiny lighted creatures it stirred up.

The storm in the west had spread to the Bay of Shallows by the time they reached the local great-fish theater. Seated in a bright cove, broad steps had been carved in the rocks to form an amphitheater spanning nearly five *pallons*.

Along the east side beneath the cliffs, a long extent of rock had been designed as a dock for varokian craft. It was well padded with the tough, dark moss ellls favored when making sandals to protect their feet on land. At the great-fish guides' request, Shawne hopped onto the docking ledge and tied both ends of the rover to rings set into the rock.

When she looked up, the light-flooded waters of the cove had come alive with a solid blanket of great-fish, their dorsal ridges making ever-changing geometric designs on the surface as they moved about to greet each other. Charley, Orticon, and Korak stood in the rover, trans-fixed by the sight.

Oleyall beached himself on one of the shelves and motioned Shawne to him with an unmistakable gesture of one lateral fin.

She rushed along the ledge to the beckoning great-fish and walked down the amphitheater steps to disappear into the water with the aquatic beast.

Korak gasped and leapt out of the rover. He missed his footing on the ledge and fell onto the backs of two great-fish trying to steady the craft.

Orticon allowed himself a hoot, then joined Korak in the water, knowing the great-fish would be delighted with such a show of faith. Not to be left out of the experience, Charley tipped backward over the side of the rover, and the welcoming celebration erupted, spreading rapidly out of the cove to the rougher waters beyond. The great-fish passed their four alien visitors from one to another, greeting them with appropriate tail-fin gestures, putting them at ease with kindly mood-flooding (Shawne's phrase), and carrying them off for brief tours of their favorite places in shallow water, where the shore creatures shone particularly bright or beautiful.

The formal reception planned by the great-fish was noted but quick-ly dismissed, as it became clear that the varoks were tolerating the wa-ters very well, and the humans couldn't get enough of everything they experienced. The welcoming celebration continued through an entire star-light change. Scuba gear was retrieved from the rover by hands and great-fish fins as needed, and the personal tours expanded to in-clude private great-fish dwellings and historic sites in shallow water.

When the bipeds' dive limits were reached, the astute great-fish re-fused them more time underwater. They ushered the humans and va-roks to a camp beneath the cliffs, where large shell plates of prepared food representing the best of great-fish cuisine had been set out with cups of soothing tea.

A fire crackled merrily in a depression that had seen many fires before, for varoks were frequent visitors, enjoying great-fish hospital-ity as they sought their advice or taped their working knowledge of the planet and its undersea society. Beds of moss warmed by hot rocks (brought up from the deep rifts extending east from the northern arm of the Great Chasm) soon found the exhausted visitors sleeping soundly.

When Shawne awoke, she joined Charley, who was tending the fire, its orange glow echoing the every-changing dance of Ellason's moons through the mists.

"They think of everything," he said, still glowing with the wonder of the great beasts' intelligence. His furry red presence made Shawne smile. He was like a great cave bear, king of the dark cliffs come to absorb the wisdom of Ellason's seas.

"You should keep your synthetics on, Charley," Shawne scolded. "They will keep you warmer, even if they're still wet."

"They're dry. I just wanted a moment to air out."

"Where's the latrine? The great-fish always provide a private place."

"Up the rocks on the south side. Follow the vein of white quartz."

As she returned down the path to the amphitheater, Shawne could see Charley's big form hydroplaning swiftly along the surface on the back of a lone great-fish. She met them as they came to the steps of the amphitheater. Charley climbed off, and Shawne saw that his mount was Oleyall.

"Where is everyone?" she clicked in Sonics.

"Back to business-as-usual," Oleyall clicked, then with lateral fins and quick touches of his long prehensile tail, he began to fashion a communication sculpture. The message quickly came clear to Shawne. As the mud and rocks took shape, she translated for Charley.

"Before we begin our conversations bearing on your quest, Shawne," said the great-fish, "I must perform a duty for the elder who has given up her cave for us. Come with me if you like. Ihratohl has invited you to her death."

"Are you sure that's what Oleyall meant?" Charley asked.

Before Shawne could repeat the question, Oleyall had answered it. Charley nodded. Shawne looked to Oleyall, uncertain.

"Your friend is very open, as open as Tandra," Oleyall said. "Come, Shawne. You alone are invited. You wear a heavy cloak of grief for your struggling planet. This experience will be your palliative, not a cure, but a path toward your inner peace."

"Should I ride on top or alongside?" she asked.

"On top. Full circle. Link your arms about my neck," Oleyall indicated. "We must hurry. Ihratohl has lost all life-joy to pain."

Shawne stepped into the water lapping at the steps of the amphitheater and slid onto the great-fish, anchoring herself in front of his back fin and locking her arms around his triangular head. Once her right cheek nestled into Oleyall's left gill-ridge, the great-fish turned slowly on the water's surface like a huge liner backing off the dock. Then they were gone.

Charley gasped. "How will he know when Shawne needs to breathe?"

"She'll quit exhaling into his gills," Orticon said. "He'll soon get her rhythm and he'll surface when she needs air."

Korak watched until he had seen Shawne and the great-fish appear momentarily on the surface, twice, then he turned away to their waking meal. Oleyall had served dawn fish on a bed of succulent deepworts. Two other great-fish appeared with fresh *lohn* eggs and a pungent tea. Orticon and Korak were happy to be served, but it took some persuasion for Charley to convince them that he wanted to learn to hunt for himself the edible sea life of Ellason.

"We had better guide you," one great-fish suggested, waving a tailfin and inviting Charley to climb aboard. He told Tandra later that the experience changed him. He would never again use sharp hooks to battle huge fish.

– Δ –

Oleyall took Shawne to the Bay of Passing, a place she had heard of only in Ellasonian studies. The bay was a long, quiet estuary where the River of Silence paused and nurtured the shore with one last burst of life before it flowed into the sea. Dying great-fish traveled there to finish their lives, if they were able.

Great-fish did not usually talk about their private lives, and they considered death to be the most private of all life's bodily functions. They believed it was every individual's responsibility to arrange for a death that gave as much comfort as possible to those bereaved, while avoiding the desecration of life-joy in their passing. Pain was one such desecration, so when it became so great that pleasure and productive thinking were overwhelmed and medical help could provide no

healing, euthanasia was discussed and usually chosen by all those involved in the sufferer's life.

"We are very fortunate to have found such a quick and painless
way to end lives," Oleyall told Shawne as they approached the Bay of
Passing. "We inject the poison of the fish called Friend Forever, *Ahl
Eyahka* in Elllonian. It is called God's Revenge in Great-fish Sonics."

What a strange name, Shawne thought.

God's Revenge against the necessity of pain, Oleyall answered. *For every
gift in life there is a price. I see that you, Shawne, pay a similar price for your
complex brain and its talent for suffering—but we will talk about that later.
Now you will experience the death of a great-fish. You will know the core, the
essence of a great life, and you will watch it disappear. Death will become real
to you, so that you will know life better.*

The great-fish said no more as they accelerated past the last cliffs
housing deep caves. They passed through waters that grew cold, then
warm again and warmer, before Oleyall slowed his pace and glided
along the surface. Shawne sat up on his back and looked around. To
the south she could see the cliffs of Nea Moss in the distance, a tiny
buttress against the great leaden sea. Here was a gentler land leading
to the shallows. Its cliffs had given way to the water's relentless nibbling. They lay broken and restless, now coarse sand on wide beaches.
Stubborn rocks decorated the shore like rough sculptures and broke
the monotony of the flats surrounding the Bay of Passing.

As we enter the bay, Oleyall noted, *you will see rocky hills to the north.
Beneath the hills, the water runs in deep channels. There lie the northern
great-fish caves. When you are ready, I will take you there to visit Haralahn.*

I would like that, Oleyall, Shawne answered, *when I am ready.*

Shawne couldn't tell Conn later what language they used to communicate. "It must have been Elllonian," she said. Conn suggested she
had probably matured enough to hear great-fish telepathy speaking
to her human intuition. "Those big water gurus like to maintain their
aura of mystery. Even varoks can't tell with patch sense whether great-
fish are reading their minds or just making good guesses from body
language and the logical momentum of conversation."

As Oleyall glided south into the Bay of Passing, Shawne admired
the moss-laden sandstone that rose on both sides to form molded walls
of smooth peach streaked with warm reds and dusty yellow, glowing
with moonlight. The water lay quiet before them, shimmering with the

internal silver blue of microscopic life-forms unfamiliar to her. Oleyall cut swiftly across one arm of the placid bay, leaving a clean wake that gradually converged with many others toward a gently sloping shore padded with fine sand.

Oleyall ushered Shawne onto the beach, then he returned to deeper water. There, hundreds of great-fish lay in a stillness so profound Shawne could see the subtle ripples of water passing from their gills.

Out of the silence a tone emerged, deep and pure, barely discernible to her human ears. Shawne felt its throb through her whole body. *Nearly out of my range,* she thought. She was grateful she could hear it at all, for it bound her to the great-fish like the sound of a pipe organ in a great cathedral. It spoke of life and thankfulness for consciousness shared, then it expanded to include all that lay beyond consciousness to its Source. More tones joined the first and the chords rose and fell like gentle ocean waves. Harmonics filled the bay with rich combinations that collapsed over and over again to single tones. First one, then another, then the first tone again—until Shawne realized Ihratohl, the dying elder, was calling her.

She found the great-fish on a bed of moss, cradled in the smooth rock where a tireless eddy had carved a large bowl. Nearby, in the shallows, Ihratohl's friends and kin continued to sing of their love for her and their faith in the significance of her being. Soon the tides of Ellason would leave the bowl empty of life-sustaining water, and Ihratohl would quietly lose consciousness and die of oxygen deprivation, if she did not request God's Revenge first.

"Come. Join me in my last water, dear elll-human," Ihratohl said. Surprised at the strength of her voice, Shawne heard her words as Elllonian.

She stepped into the bowl and sat within the embrace of a lateral fin etched with age. Other great-fish gathered around in the retreating water.

"The first human on Ellason," Ihratohl said, "on such a quest! You do our world honor with your questions. Will you listen to the advice of this old fish?"

"You do me more honor than I can ever earn," Shawne said.

"Then pay me back with your ear and your heart—now, for my time is short. Remember to stir all the answers you hear—every definition and idea about God—stir them into the deepest chambers of your soul. Leave them there to ferment as you live your moments with keen awareness. With time and experience all the words you have heard or read will transform you with a faith that is uniquely yours. Honor that faith, but let it go when you must, for no living creature knows everything there is—not even these wise friends of mine. Don't let them intimidate you."

Ihratohl laughed, an embracing sound Shawne will never forget, then she waved the human out of her death pool. "Live well, child, forgive yourself for choices made. Be true to yourself. That is your quest. Don't lose one moment to anything that drains your capacity to love and to learn and to know joy. Live beyond disappointment. Learn from it. You humans can be lovely creatures, capable of honesty and respecting your limits. Thank you . . . for coming . . . to see me off."

The words faded away as Ihratohl turned her face to three moons lighting the sky with gold. Her gills took their last breath from the water, and her awareness before death was of loving strokes from many fin-tips and one human hand.

Shawne wept, but the words *unfaltering trust* came to mind, and she remembered William Cullen Bryant's poem *Thanatopsis*.

Oelyall listened as she spoke:

> *So live, that when thy summons comes to join*
> *The innumerable caravan which moves*
> *To that mysterious realm, where each shall take*
> *His chamber in the silent halls of death,*
> *Thou go not, like the quarry-slave at night,*
> *Scourged to his dungeon, but, sustained and soothed*
> *By an unfaltering trust, approach thy grave*
> *Like one who wraps the drapery of his couch,*
> *About him, and lies down to pleasant dreams.*

TWO AHLORK AND A GREAT-FISH

Forelock was no longer a cartilaginous ahlork youth, and he had no romantic illusions about Ellason; he knew trouble when he felt it. So did Nidok.

The concussion came from far below the heavy mists, rattling their chitinous plates. They dove immediately, ignoring their instinctual wariness of Cuffall's school. Forelock saw two figures disappear into the rocks. He followed them as best he could, but they were soon lost in the thick fog that covered the jumble of boulders and sand on the shore.

Nidok hovered near the capsized rover until he was sure Tandra and Lanoll, the varokian child TK, Killah and Jesse and the big ell-lonian female were safely aboard a rover that had come from the lab. Then he called to Forelock, who flew to him, more irritable than usual.

"Stupid to call me back for report. Now I lose Orram again," Forelock complained to Nidok.

The two ahlork perched on a gray rock above the overturned rover. Their watchful flight had been more tiring than they expected, but it had not exhausted them, for they were built for long migratory journeys on Varok. Forelock's frustration at losing sight of Orram, however, nearly undid him.

"So you learn stupid obedience?" Nidok snapped. "No nestling of mine has so little brains. You saw Orram?"

"I smash my head on tall rocks, if I follow closely," Forelock said. "No ahlork sees through fog. I saw shape like Orram."

At last Nidok did some thinking. "Orram never leaves Tandra to drown."

"I see them go, two tall ones, on feet. Fast they were, close together, not like varoks. Odd walking. One pulling other. One with bad feet."

Nidok spread his wings. He flexed his plates then rattled them violently, throwing drops of condensate in every direction. "I am growing moss. It slows us. I need Killah's med."

Forelock moved out of range, onto another rock. He knew his parent well. Nidok was trying to decide what to do.

"Orram taken by Elll Cuffall—a bad one that—not like ellls on Varok. We fly again and scan like hunting. We find Orram. The elll must keep him from water. The mists will shift. Varok and elll won't walk farther than we fly."

– Δ –

Oleyall's long great-fish tail deftly set six deepwort crackers on the smooth rock beside Shawne, then he docked himself beside her in a round basin of moss-covered rock. Here in the cave Oleyall had inherited from Ihratohl, seawater found its way past them like a quiet river, while far above in the cliffs, vertical crawlers filled the air with whistles and hoots.

"The crawlers sound like tiny owls from Earth, asking questions over and over," Shawne laughed.

"Like yourself."

Shawne thought she saw the great-fish smile.

"Now," he said, "Are you warm enough?"

"I'm fine. This is a beautiful spot."

"And your friends?"

"They're comfortable in the camp you made near the theater. Likely they're exploring while we wait for Conn and Lanoll."

"This house I have inherited is designed for visitors. Ihratohl often entertained varoks, and, as you can see, she was not without a sense of humor." The great-fish did a turn in the discussion bowl Ihratohl had designed. It was very similar to her death pool, deep enough to breathe, or not, and shallow enough to allow scavenging brilln easy access to one's remains.

A little uneasy with the thought, Shawne shifted on the visitors' bench Ihratohl had carved into the side of the basin.

"The bowl is a reminder of our mortality—not a bad idea—" Oleyall said, "something to temper our philosophy." He lay his right fin tip over Shawne's hand, which was resting on the arm of the bench. "Now—tell me what a human thinks after being raised by an elll."

"And a varok. Orram has had a great influence on me."

"I am more concerned about the elll's influence. Their senses drive them into deep pits of logic that can act like traps to creative thought."

"Not much danger there for me," Shawne said. "I'm not a good programmer, Oleyall. I can go only so deep with problems in logic. I do better conjuring up broad visions, summarizing, that sort of thing."

"Good. A right-brained human. Not unlike great-fish. Hence your search for the Source of All, something many humans call God. I think we will communicate well." Oleyall scooped mud from a supply just out of the water's reach and cradled it in his lateral fin tips. It took form in his prehensile grasp as if it had a life of its own.

Shawne watched the mud sculpture, fascinated, and the conversation continued at a level deeper than Elllonian, which was physically demanding on the great-fish.

I see your love for ellls, Shawne. *It runs through your veins, for Conn has been everything to you—father, brother, friend, stuffed toy. He imprinted your two-year-old being when he first loved you and adopted you as his tad. Now you must return to your human roots. There you will find the God you seek.*

Shawne responded in sculpture, forming rudimentary great-fish symbology as best she could. *I don't understand your meaning, Oleyall. I look to find shared thinking. All thinkers near Sol think different meanings.*

Precisely my point.

Shawne's symbolic vocabulary failed her, and she reverted to Elllonian. "But there are similarities in all our thoughts, a need to understand, a faith that goes beyond our differences to the chemistry that we share. I want to find the common source of that faith, the wellspring. Some common point of origin for it all."

Words failed, as a sense of dread filled her. She felt heavy with the enormity of her quest. Or was it something else?

Oleyall startled at her sudden drop into gloom. Her fear for Earth's fate was a visible thing in her face, like thick smoke threatening to smother her life-joy. He took a careful tack, all the while searching for clues to the weight she felt. She was sad, of course, that Conn had gone rambling off to rediscover his home planet without her, but her gloom was more pernicious than disappointment or even her fear for Earth. Perhaps it was amplified by thoughts of the child she thought she had destroyed. In any case, she could not endure the rigors of theological debate with such a burden of fabricated guilt. It would cripple her, if it were allowed to continue.

"Let us find your friends at their camp," the great-fish said. "I would like you to see our most treasured place."

– Δ –

Shawne and Charley, Orticon and Korak all donned varokian scuba gear to visit the famous Cathedral of Faith. It was in crystal clear water twenty meters deep, shining with the light of silver moss and thousands of beam-fish. Intricate marble carvings graced the entrance, telling the ancient great-fish tale of creation.

"Where does the story begin?" Shawne asked.

"I like to begin with this one," Oleyall said, pointing to a tiny figure of an elll looking skyward at a huge moon emerging from a towering cloud.

"What about this one, over here?" Korak said, gliding past a sphere of glass that seemed to be exploding into mist.

"Energy suddenly expanding with time and space to become matter—the universe as we know it," Oleyall explained.

Shawne moved toward the great-fish version of particles becoming atoms, then nebulae congealing to form galaxies giving birth to stars exploding to form the elements and congealing to form planets.

"Humans might call sculpture over here 'The Moral Imperative,'" Oleyall said.

Shawne looked behind her to where Oleyall's tail fin pointed. Within the smooth petals of a huge flower, a varok knelt over an emaciated elll, offering him the last edible stalk from his bundle of web branches.

"Oh," she gasped. "I love this. Korak, look."

"Look well, then look over here," Oleyall said. "Here the elll saves the life of a drowning varok."

The visitors left the cathedral reluctantly, but then Oleyall led them into caverns of exquisite natural beauty. Mosses hung like velvet drapes where rocks soared above the ocean's surface or dripped with mineral sculptures laid down over centuries. They visited great-fish who wanted to meet humans and some who had treasures to share, like collections of rare plants, or relics from the days before varoks came to Ellason. When Korak, Charley and Orticon left them to return to camp, Oleyall motioned for Shawne to follow him to his cave.

Shawne perched on a comfortable dry boulder to admire the sculpted ceiling of the cave. Oleyall rested on a mossy shelf nearby, half submerged. "I have had two thoughts to share with you. First, your grief for Earth will consume your life if you don't make a clear decision: either return there and continue your work, or know, as I know, that you have done all you could do as one person. Know too that you can trust the better nature of human beings.

"Secondly, I too love ellls, but now, in your quest for meaning, I would suggest that you distinguish the value of their logic from the necessity and the limitations of reason. Let me suggest two things about logic for you to consider. Some say logic can show only negative possibilities—it can show only what is *not*. Logic doesn't lead you to what *is*. For example, when choosing not to have a child you avoided the cosmological and teleological arguments for and against, which was correct since they are logically inconclusive."

Shawne startled and the blood drained from her face. "How could you know I had missed a period? I took no chances by taking medication to ensure I wouldn't get pregnant."

"Your fear and uncertainty occupies a large slice of your being, Shawne, that's all I know. You must ask why it matters so much. We will fail to press beyond the boundaries of our minds if we insist on precise definitions, especially the definition of life, which is a continuum, an ongoing process that can grow in consciousness only if nurtured. Isn't that right, Conn?"

"Conn?" Shawne gasped.

The great-fish reached out of the water past Shawne to greet Conn with the welcoming grasp of his prehensile tail that enclosed them both.

"Give old daddy-elll a hug, child. I've been away from you too long."

"Indeed," Oleyall said.

"I'm sorry that I didn't make myself clear. I trusted your judgment, Shawne Love, regardless."

Shawne turned into Conn's arms with a cry of relief. He was expecting excitement, joy, admonishment, but not more tears. Oleyall set him straight with a decisive comment.

"Before we talk more about Earth or Creation, Shawne, you must come with me to the infirmary. I believe you could use a little help to feel better."

Her answer surprised them both.

"Thank you, Oleyall, but I'll be fine now that Conn's back. I've decided not to pollute my brain with chemicals, anti-depressants or whatever."

"Since when are you so dependent on me?" Conn asked.

"Since you broke your promise and left me alone—" She stopped her attack when Oleyall's wing-tip crossed her lips. "—to sort out the direction of my life for myself."

Stringer and Orram

Stringer assumed that the northern school of hedge–guardian ellls was taking him on a tour of the famous Life's Heart, a wide rift in the planet's crust, where sulfur had powered the first simple experiments in living entities on Ellason. It was a place of great beauty, where vast drifts of ancient, glowing microorganisms fed the voracious fields of whip lilies that reached this way and that in the warm currents. Their elongated funnels of succulent flesh lined with beckoning micro-paddles fascinated him.

He wanted to spend more time there, but his tour guides refused. When he started to bid them farewell, they bound him with *ahl* vines. Confused and disoriented by such treatment, Stringer protested, then struggled in panic as they towed him north along a remote branch of Ellason's intricate network of deep sea ridges.

There his captors adjusted his bonds and managed to lash him to a large *ahl* tree overlooking one of the lesser canyons. When he complained loudly, calling out in long-range Ultrasonics, two hedge–guardians returned briefly to tie together his sonic melons. He could not focus the sound waves produced behind his nasal gills. Since they were not into torture, they left his mouth and tongue free so he would still have the life-joy of eating and drinking.

"You play rough," Stringer clicked. "Is this a game of homing ability? Find the newcomer? Is that it? I won't show up on an ultrasonic scan next to this tree. You should have told me the rules. I would have stayed quiet so as not to help the seekers."

"That's right. You will stay quiet," one of the ellls said. "Enjoy the view."

They swam off with no other explanation. Naïve, good sport that he was, Stringer relaxed into his bonds and slept, expecting to be found by the seekers before the whip lilies on the cliff edges awoke and renewed their feeding dance.

– Δ –

Tandra lay in the EV Lab hospital, unable to concentrate, heavily sedated for pain, but awake enough to feel the deadening ache in her heart for Orram. How could he have suddenly vanished, erased from her life with nothing but her family ring to remind her that she had shared consciousness with a varok for most of her adult life?

The elder elll Artellian stayed by her side, reassuring her that TK was safe. As her mentor on Earth Moonbase, Artellian probably knew Tandra better than anyone but Orram and Conn. His eldering love was like a warm blanket to her cold fears, and his gentle humor kept her as quiet as possible.

"You are making my job very difficult, Tandra," he said with a smile. "First you and Orram adopt an orphan's dilemma, as if you needed another child of your own, and now Orram goes missing, leaving you with an ear ache, without telling you his plans."

"I hope and pray that's all he did, Artellian."

"How am I supposed to write up your family dynamics? It is getting far too complicated."

With the help of lab medics, Killah soon had TK's fever under control. Its cause was a common disease of varokian children on Ellason. The virus was usually controlled with early vaccinations, which TK never had. No doubt she picked up the infection from one of the varoks at EV Lab.

Tandra's fever, however, refused to drop back to normal. She argued with Killah and Artellian. She must get up and join the search for Orram. She must find him. She could not recover without Orram. She would not live without Orram.

In desperation, Killah ordered the hospital staff to move TK into the same room with the overstressed human. The distraction worked. Tandra bonded easily with the child, who kept asking for "RamRam." With nothing to do but wait for news from the search teams, Tandra concentrated on the child. When her pain was under control, she tried to explain why Orram was missing.

"The ellls and varoks at the lab here have many ways of searching for him," Tandra told her. "If he is to be found, they will do it. We think your elll father Cuffall is with him, so he will have help if he needs it."

While Tandra's ear healed, Artellian and Killah became TK's surrogate school, along with the TK's sponsor Talln. The visiting elll remained strangely quiet, answering questions and greetings with few words. Tandra suspected she knew something about Cuffall that she would not admit.

TK had a voracious appetite for Varokian, so Tandra joined the child's daily water routine with the ellls to help her practice the language. TK began to mimic Tandra's accent as well as her human swimming stroke. Each day when she joined Tandra on the pool's deck, she begged for verbal tales of life with Orram. She couldn't make out the difference between varoks and humans, until Tandra showed her the smooth place behind her ears and the child's own patch organs in a mirror.

"Humans come from Earth," TK said, using the Varokian she had learned. "Tell me about Earth, Tandra." She touched the smooth skin behind Tandra's right ear, and a tear formed in her eyes. "I'm so sorry," she said.

"No, no, TK. There's nothing to be sorry about. Humans have something called intuition instead of patches." Tandra had to use the English word. There was no word for *intuition* in Varokian. *Was there such a concept in Sonics? In Elllonian? Probably not.*

Tandra remembered Conn saying that sensual experience defines reality. *Hadn't some human philosophers said that,* Tandra asked herself, *with only five senses available to them? Ellls have nine senses, so do they know twice as much as humans? Probably. Descartes was inaccurate in doubting the validity of what the senses tell us. They are directly connected to physical vibes. I feel, therefore I am. Now that makes sense.*

Time was stuck in low gear while Tandra waited for her strength to return and for the search teams to report. She asked Tamilan to help with the child, but the young varok was too absorbed with his studies to give her much time.

At last lab security reported unusual activity in the West Viortahk.

"We are packing for a trip to look for Orram," Tandra told TK and Tallyn. "Would you like to help us decide what to take? We'll need to be prepared for deep water."

"Yes. Yes, please," TK said. She asked questions about everything Tandra had brought to Ellason. She wanted to know which items were human, used on Earth, and which were from Varok.

Tandra failed to notice Talln's growing impatience, which soon blossomed into exasperation. "You won't need much out in the West Viortahk, Tandra," she said, "just your scuba gear. Now give me the child. She needs to sleep."

"Have a good rest, TK," Tandra said. Before she let the child go, she promised to show her more things at new light.

As the elll and varok departed, Jesse and Artellian appeared, exchanging pregnant glances. "It appears Talln won't easily give up the child, wouldn't you say?" Artellian murmured.

"I'll tell you one thing," Tandra said, "I will not give that child back to an elll's life. She's a varok. Orram and I will raise her on Varok. There is no other solution to her dilemma."

– Δ –

The official report came in from the joint elllonian-varokian search effort. Those closest to Orram gathered in the family's quarter at EV Lab to review it. Among details and diagrams stood a list of possible casualties: the elll Cuffall and the varok Oran Ramahlak.

"Orram could not have perished in the boat accident," Tandra insisted. "Surely I would have sensed that. I will not accept his death as fact, not without direct evidence."

Talln seconded her conclusion. "The explosion threw us clear. It did no direct harm."

"Explosion? What have the search teams overlooked?" Artellian asked.

"No explosion was mentioned," Tandra said. "The report assumes we ran into rocks while running on aqua-manual."

"We never run on aqua-manual," Jesse said. "Why would we? The rovers adjust to any surface on auto."

"When the rover was recovered, it was locked in aqua-manual," Tandra said.

"I thought Orram was driving," Jesse said. "He would never—"

"You're right. It's crazy."

"If Cuffall had taken the controls from Orram, wouldn't he know better than to lock the rover into water drive, especially in the Viortahk?"

"There was an explosion before we hit any rocks." Killah spoke slowly, turning a cautious glance to Talln for confirmation.

Talln spoke hesitantly. "I'm sure I saw Cuffall dive free. I thought he was with Orram."

"That settles it." Tandra's eyes drilled holes in Talln's, but she said nothing that might result in more delay. She was determined to start her own search immediately. "Orram must be somewhere near the boat crash. He could be wounded, in shelter, unconscious. I can't accept the report's conclusions," she said.

"If you're really feeling up to it, we'll go out there tomorrow," Killah said. "We'll search the sea floor again, and all the rocks for a kilometer in every direction. Ellls might disappear down an *eefl*'s gullet without leaving a plume behind, but not a fully dressed varok. If *eefl* had eaten

Orram, there would be clothes, the communicator he always carried. Something."

"On that happy thought," Tandra said, "let's try to get some rest. We can leave before the lab starts its work day."

The others retired. Killah dove to the bottom of the pool and entered the channel that ran beneath the lab to the river. When he met the colder water of Varok's Bay, he turned around. The exercise had done him good. He returned to the upper river and slept in the soft mud.

He dreamt of Orram in water, swimming in the blue shallows, where huge edible flowers decorated golden sand—but Orram was trying to swim with his lungs full of water. "Orram!" he called out. A soft elllonian voice answered.

"Killah, it's me, Lanoll. Wake up. I've come from Stringer's Ranch. Conn and I were visiting there when Stringer disappeared. Conn has gone to the northern great-fish caves to get Shawne—"

"Stop. Stop. You're too fast for me. I'm not awake." Killah cleared his eyes and saw Stringer's lovely friend Nealla swimming close to Lanoll. "Who are you, friend of Lanoll? Are you with a school? Should we adjust? Perhaps you're a loner."

"We don't have time, Killah." Lanoll slashed back and forth in the channel as she spoke in Sonics. "We must get Tandra and Orram and the others. Stringer is missing. We've got to find him."

"I'm not sure we should wake the others," Killah said. He didn't want to add Lanoll's panic to their worry for Orram. "Come with me, Lanoll. Let me adjust to your friend. It will do us all good."

Lanoll spiraled in around Killah, Nealla joined her, and soon their electro-patterns collided. Then they merged as one thought might merge in consensus with another. Lanoll's panic subsided. Nealla bonded to Killah with relief and trust.

As they swam to the lab pool, Lanoll and Nealla told Killah all they knew of Stringer's disappearance. "I left the school to work on the northern parasite barrier," Nealla explained. "My friend Ellan said Stringer intended to follow me there. He adjusted out of the school for both of us, but I never found him." She couldn't go on.

Lanoll continued. "The hedge–guardian *eeflin* herders had just worked the northern border of the ranch. They had seen no sign of Stringer, but we checked the tree line again anyway. Our calls brought no response and our scans showed nothing. Nealla and I swam to the shallows and asked for a formal search, then we came here. Conn went to the great-fish caves to find Shawne's party and ask for great-fish help. He'll ask them all to meet us here at the lab."

"Waste of time," Killah said, as they coasted along the river and into the lab pool. "We'll meet them at the place Stringer disappeared. We'll contact Conn, but first we must go toward the West Viortahk and search for clues. There was a rover accident, Lanoll. Tandra was hurt and is nearly recovered, but Orram is missing."

Lanoll's life-joy disintegrated with grief at the news. "Killah, not Orram. He wouldn't disappear." It was too much—uncertainty on uncertainty. Killah did his best, and Nealla was a rock, but Lanoll suffered.

It was TK who brought the ellls back from the edge of their despair. The child came to the pool with Talln and was delighted to find new ellls to meet. Lanoll was especially drawn to her. She was like Shawne had been, but only in appearance and water savvy. TK was opposite in temperament—serious and dependent, with a mind always in search of connection.

When Killah brought Tandra to the pool, she was leaning on the elder ell Artellian. Both were obviously trying to absorb the news about Stringer. They slipped into the pool and found TK clinging to Lanoll and Nealla, giggling with pleasure at Lanoll's solid blue plumage. Killah checked the child's temperature. It was normal. Her congestion had cleared.

"We'll find Stringer," Tandra said. "He's as strong as Orram. We'll find them both."

Nealla dissolved in Tandra's arms, shaking with powerful emotions. "I realize Stringer is a schooler, Tandra," Nealla said, "and he can never love me the way a loner might, but I want to be with him and raise tads with him and the school. I will become an auxiliary to the school, if I need to."

"An auxiliary?"

"An auxiliary works with a school but can check in and out with an appointed person without going through a full school adjustment."

"I have never heard of such a position. I don't think schools on Varok have auxiliary loners, though perhaps they use similar adjustments with frequent visitors."

Tandra looked at the young ell more closely. She was lovely, with plumes as long and delicate as newly washed hair. Her eyes were set wide apart between an equine gill ridge, as finely modeled as her cheek and melon planes.

At new light, news of Stringer's disappearance spread through the lab. Just before the team left to search for Orram, the studious young varok Tamilan came out of his working frenzy to see them off. Though Stringer had not been much of a friend to him, he seemed honestly concerned, and he came up with a few good ideas.

"Where are the ahlork?" he asked Tandra. "They were with your party when you went out to find the child Tahlee-Karal."

The question sent Tandra over the edge, but just for a moment. "They chose to stay on watch, Tamilan, rather than mingle with Cuffall's school. The last I saw they were flying in the storm. I've been so worried about Orram. Oh, God. It's been so long! Stringer and Orram, and now Nidok!"

"I'm sure they took refuge," Killah said.

Jesse Mendleton entered the pool room with his pack, ready to leave on the search. "The storm was nothing compared to ion storms on Varok. Ahlork are built to cross Varok's oceans. They're probably taking care of Orram."

"I'm going out to look for them," Lanoll said. "They could be a great help in finding Stringer as well."

"Good idea," Tandra said. "While you look, I'll call the great-fish and talk to Conn. If you're not back soon, meet us at the accident site."

"Just in case—Nealla had better help you prepare for a trip out to Stringer's Ranch," Lanoll said. "It is in the center of the Great Basin, far from any shore."

The elll nodded agreement and Jesse said he would help.

"First," Tandra said, "I've got to talk to Conn. We'll wait to hear from him before we go. Killah, please go with Lanoll and help look for Nidok. Meet us at the accident site. Perhaps you would stay with me, Artellian?"

"Of course, Tan."

An Unexpected Visit

Conn didn't come right out with the news of Stringer's disappearance. The great-fish had already initiated a search for him, and Oleyall decided to let Shawne's visit proceed as planned, knowing Conn would tell all when the time was right. The great-fish brain doesn't miss much.

Oleyall knew Conn was troubled, so he cut the philosophy short. He promised to meet the elll and his human daughter after they had a chance to talk. Then he found Conn some tough moss sandals so Shawne and her elll-dad could take a slow walk along the sandstone cliffs.

"I had never experienced the death of a sentient being," Shawne said. "Ihratohl's was a farewell celebration—then she was gone. She snuffed herself out, like a candle."

Conn took her hand as they walked. "Orram's mother Orserah said goodbye before she died in her sleep. It's the best way to go—to be surrounded by love as you let go of life."

"It seems so strange to me, Conn—conscious one minute, gone the next."

"Yes. 'Gone' is the feeling I had, too. When Orserah died, she was suddenly, obviously gone. Emergent entities are like that. When the parts fail, the whole changes into something very different."

"I understand the human rituals of wakes and body-viewing now," Shawne said. "You need to see that the person you love is really gone, so you can let go. You need to realize they are no longer in their body. You are left with nothing but a memory."

"And then memories fade, Shawnoon, rather quickly for us ellls," Conn's voice faltered. How could he tell her Stringer was missing? *Maybe I shouldn't.* "But someone's effect on you never goes away."

Shawne sat down on a lift in the sandstone, near a basin eroded by trapped water. The basin of rock was filled with dust and sand, enough to support a small garden of volunteer *llaoon* grass and a flowering sea bush. They looked out over the Great Basin to the immense sea beyond, a quiet puddle on Ellason's mossy hide.

"Do you believe in life everlasting for great-fish, Conn? Of all God's critters, surely the great-fish are the most saved."

"Or the most tortured," Conn said. "Too much awareness for their own good, seems to me."

"I can imagine. There are many things that would be hard to take forever."

Conn grasped at the chance to delay his news about Stringer. "Everlasting. Why not eternal? I like that idea better," he said.

"Isn't God the only eternal thing, outside time and space, if He's the Reason for Being, the Creator?" Shawne asked.

"Just outside? Why not also inside every moment? Where was God when time and space were created? Wasn't He intimately involved as Creator? And where will He be when the last black hole winks out?"

"Immanent and transcendent, in it all and beyond it all, all at once?" Shawne asked. "Doesn't it have to be one or the other?"

"Why?" Conn said. "We're talking ultimates here, concepts beyond our experience. It doesn't impact my faith much. God can be Whatever He or She or It is, as far as I'm concerned."

She stood, and beckoned to Conn to continue their stroll toward the camp. "We better keep moving, Conn. Charley, Orticon and Korak are waiting for me there."

She hurried on, and he followed, trying to decide if he should tell her about Stringer while she was alone or with the others.

"So you admit it, Conn. You do have faith in something more than process."

"I suppose. Process, God, it's all the same to me. I'm no atheist, Shawne, not even agnostic. Atheists either deny the reality of the stuff religions come up with, or they deny the inherent reality of anything, while talking about it anyway. I do neither. I experience love. I experience awe at the intricate miracles that gave us consciousness—and I can't talk about what I don't experience, not very well. There's a lot more to existence than I can ever know."

They had returned to the camp. Charley gave Conn more hail and good fellow stuff than he wanted before he turned to Shawne. "How was the wake?" he asked. The human was always curious, if nothing else.

"It was a dying," Conn corrected.

"It was a very loving time," Shawne said. "Ihratohl waited to meet me, though she was in great pain. Her death was quick. The drugs eased her out of her pain while she was filled with the awareness of being loved."

"Now for an experience of living," Conn said. He thought of

Stringer, feeling like a coward. "Oleyall has made an appointment for us to speak to Haralahn. He has come from the City of Great-fish on a short visit."

At that moment they saw their host, Oleyall, at the beach. He motioned Conn into the water, and he spoke in Elllonian so there would be no misunderstanding between them.

"You are barely able to maintain life-joy, Conn," he said. "The search has begun. You and Shawne had better visit Haralahn briefly before you deliver your message to Shawne."

After a short swim beneath the great cliffs, they came to the cave where Haralahn, the Master philosopher, waited. He gave them a quick welcoming treat of fresh turnbit stuffed with spiced *challall* weeds. Then he refused any more discussion.

"You are not wise to refuse the advice of the great-fish medics, Shawne," he said abruptly. "For a time, you need chemical help. You could try our herbal anti-inflammatories first. There is no need to feel as depressed as you do."

"I'm fine, Master Haralahn. I—"

"Your life-joy is a dim glow in a very dark tunnel, child. Oleyall sent ahead for your medication, and it has arrived. I will not talk about the more profound questions of philosophy with you until you face up to this physical challenge and accept the chemicals that your brain needs to function normally and find its balance. It will take some time before you feel the heavy cloud lift from your mind. Return to me then, and we will discuss what you have seen and heard on Ellason and Varok and Earth.

"I will leave you now with just one thought. The fact that you are compelled to make this quest for God tells me that you feel there is a reality to goodness—beauty and joy and peace and love beneath the cloak that you wear—a goodness that is something real, something fundamental to existence, something essential that is not just an accidental by-product. Think on that feeling. Find it in yourself when this unfortunate cloak lifts from your mind and your best potential is free once again."

Haralahn led Shawne to a discussion shelf and helped her put aside her scuba gear so she could take the anti-inflammatory he offered. Tears streamed down her face.

"Now, Oleyall will take you back to your fellow travelers," Haralahn said when she had secured a supply of medicine in her waist pack. With luck, you will grow out of your need for chemical help and will learn to trust yourself. Now, go with your elllonian father, and do what you must."

There was no arguing with Haralahn. Shawne and Conn swam back to the conversation shelf near Oleyall's cave.

"I owe you a report on our wild excursion, Shawnoon. After Lanoll and I did a nostalgic turn around our nursery waters, we went down to see Rocky Deeps ranch to meet Stringer's school. He was not there. We soon realized we needed great-fish help to find him. He disappeared heading north in the Rocky Deeps Ranch."

"Disappeared?"

"There's more. The great-fish have reports of serious problems there. Tads, very young ellls, have suddenly appeared in the northern shallows, then reappeared in the Far Deeps where there are no known training camps. They suspect that a black market in tads has been operating from the wild forest that runs along the northern parasite barriers of the Rocky Deeps Ranch. Stringer may have discovered a wild school hatching elll tads for sale. Perhaps he deduced the truth."

"So where is the law on this planet? Why haven't they enforced the limits?"

"The authorities are closing in. The great-fish say the producers and dealers are very clever. They're quite mobile. The waters of Ellason are huge, in every dimension."

"And if the black market has nothing to do with Stringer's disappearance?"

"Oleyall has already ordered the search. We should know something very soon."

IV. Denying the Fates

We ahlork don't do science. We learn how is being. We know having fun be necessary. Is gift like eating and enjoying the mating.

When you say, "*Dankah* tea be intoxicant. Is probably from Devil." I know you be joking. But don't. Is vile heresy. This be good universe— every *challal* weed on Ellason, every *arl* moth on Varok, every star in sky.

That's all. We be elements of huge universe knowing self and beauty. Is miracle. Like sharing love.

—The ahlork Nidok

TADS

It was bad enough, Stringer thought, being strapped to an *ahl* tree like a piece of bait—with every critter on the ridge nibbling at your moss tiles and no way to eat except to sift out with your gills and lick up with your partially restricted tongue tiny plants and debris—but Stringer also had to endure being alone. Though he missed Nealla, he ached for the touch and the zap of the school. Alone, he was raw meat, vulnerable, barely able to hold off the panic. He had no way to call for help, his sonics and ultrasonics disabled by cruel tapes.

He thought of Conn and Lanoll, Tandra and Orram—his family, a school substitute for a good part of his life. Would Orram and Charley compete openly for Tandra's time or intimate attention? Was Shawne enjoying the shallows with Conn? He missed her, and he realized that he would probably always miss her. Her pressure in water, so angular and chaotic, was like a part of his skin.

"So," he told himself, "I'm an elll, filled with Conn's genes and Lanoll's, including some weird recessive diploid aberration that unmasked their ancient schooling needs."

His isolation on the *ahl* tree at the edge of a hot, deep rift was agony. At least he wouldn't dry out, and he was thankful for that, remembering Conn's imprisonment in the ruins of Varok long ago.

Something was wrong. Stringer coughed through his gills to clear them. The water was getting cloudy, way too cloudy for good health. Then he saw it, a megaplume dancing along the ridge that followed the rift below. It was coming right toward him. He looked up but could not see the top of it.

It must be a hundred meters tall.

The spiraling cloud of ocean bottom sludge tossed debris all around as it sucked its way along. Stringer tried to shut down his eyes and his gills as it neared his tree. Then, suddenly, it veered off, and a shower of stuff fell in his head plumes. The upper limbs of his *ahl* tree had broken its deadly aim.

A cloud of eggs drifted by, like a gift from the megaplume gods, and Stringer was able to snarf up most of them. They made his first decent meal in three cycles, and the nourishment was enough to fire his engines. He struggled against his bonds to test their strength. Then he relaxed to loosen the tethers on his melons and fire off a few weak Sonic SOS signals. He knew they wouldn't go farther than a few dozen meters, but he decided it was his best hope. The repeated calls gave him a focus.

The logical channels of his mind cleared, and he remembered. He had been working the northern parasite barrier of Rocky Deeps, expecting to sense Nealla's approach. Instead, he had picked up the far-off, high-pitched laughter and irregular presence of many tads. *What were they doing there?* They were swimming together about one hundred meters west, near the parasite barrier, but they did not form a coherent school. They kept scattering in different directions.

That was odd, perhaps even for Ellason.

Stringer had moved toward the rowdy tads, sending an offer of help to the hedge–guardian—*was it really a hedge–guardian?*—an adult trying to lead them north toward the Bay of Shallows. The tads suddenly disappeared from Stringer's ultrasonic echo-vision.

That must be when I was attacked from behind and brought here. Why were there so many tads in the care of so few adults? It wasn't a school; the ratio of adults to tads is normally very high here. Population levels are carefully maintained.

The word *normal* struck him, woke him out of his naïve idealizations of Ellason. He had witnessed something very abnormal, hence his capture and disposal.

They will not be back, the hedge–guardians, he realized. *I've got to save myself.*

SEARCHING FOR ORRAM

High over the West Viorlahk, Nidok watched his nestling Forelock destroy a third *lohn* bird nest in the rocks below. Eggs were good food, but he was impatient to resume their search for Orram. He didn't know how many varokian-defined days they had been searching, but he was determined to find the varok who had taken his scar. He was bonded to Orram. He would not abandon him. "How many *lohn* eggs do you eat, Forelock? Too many, I think. You won't fly. You will soon be walking."

The mists had lifted to reveal a jumbled shore of large rocks and tide pools filled with abundant shore life. Dawn-fish risked their lives to the whims of the erratic tides in order to imitate the bright flashes of shore-pool lightning bugs, luring the love-struck insectoids to a sudden end as a quick snack. When they weren't being lured, the bugs nestled happily in the warm sands. Sadly, they were rudely uprooted on the horns of *lohn* birds, who chose this craggy place for building sand castles with substantial basements in which to lay their eggs.

"Next you want fire to roast fat bird," Nidok complained. "Put bereaved parents out of misery, eh?"

"Good idea, Nidok," Forelock said. "You build fire."

"After you, son." Nidok shook out his wings and burped loudly—a sound without any redeeming tone in it. "Now we find Orram. The moons have burned mist. We will have time to hunt."

With no further exchange of insults, they beat their wings and set off from the rocks, found a thermal over the dark fields of basalt just beyond the first hills, and were soon soaring high over the coast where the rover had run aground.

There, earlier, they had found evidence of an explosion in the rocks, but no debris to suggest damage done to the rover or to anything else.

"The explosion is diversion," Nidok said, remembering some wartime spy novel Conn had read to him when they were on Earth. He was determined to be the hero of the story. No doubt Orram had been kidnapped for ransom.

The ahlork had flown in circles over the lands bordering the West Viortahk. Now, with the mists cleared, they spotted one of Ellason's rare inland lakes beyond the hills of Al Nea on the Harrahn Peninsula. The lake was called Al Neoon, a forbidding basin of cold water surrounded by sharp rocks that were untouched by the sea's polishing waves. Naked of succulent mosses, which preferred saltier moisture, the rocks tore at elllonian fins that dared venture there, while they provided shelter for poisonous critters well defended against overlong elllonian tongues.

Nidok and Forelock circled lower over Al Neoon, their black beads focused on a disturbance at the water's surface near the eastern shore.

"Ellls. Lots of them," Nidok whistled to Forelock.

They flew over the hills east of the lake. Low shrubs with tubular mist-drinking leaves peculiar to Ellason congregated in spots soggy with artesian water.

"Good places to hide varoks," Forelock suggested. They concentrated on the oases in the rough landscape of ancient volcanic hillocks and seepages.

Tirelessly they searched, and foolishly, for as they flew lower and lower, the unique crackling sound of their chitinous wing plates alerted ellls near the lake. Within a few moments, traps were set for the unsuspecting aliens, whose taste for *lohn* eggs also had not gone unnoticed.

– Δ –

While keeping an eye out for the flying box kite shape of ahlork, Lanoll and Killah swam into every crevice on the shore near the accident site. Looking for signs of Orram, they probed with ultrasonic scans every inlet that percolated off Al Nea into the West Viortahk. They climbed every accessible rock to peer into myriad sandy beaches and tide pools rich with moss and *llaoon* grass that hid succulent critters protected with shells. At last, discouraged and exhausted, they gave up their search.

"I suppose Nidok and Forelock are feasting on these shore snails," Lanoll said, lowering herself off the rocky edge into a large tide pool. There she rested her back and legs.

"Do ahlork know what is edible on Ellason?" Killah plucked a snail from a long stem of *llaoon* grass and chased it down with moss, then joined her in the tide pool.

"Maybe not. Conn tried to educate Nidok about survival here, but we could never tell how much took. Ahlork are resistant to instruction, you know."

"Guess I haven't had that much to do with them," Killah admitted. "They always put me off a bit, but I've been glad to know Nidok better. He surprises me."

"I pray they'll surprise us all and find Orram." Lanoll spoke with difficulty, but Killah did a good job distracting her.

"'Pray,'" he echoed, playing to her sense of logic and looking for an excuse to rest longer. "Interesting choice. A human word, Lanoll. Shawne's religious quest got to you, has it?"

"Some of her questions have stuck with me. Like how could prayer to a Creator possibly influence things directly?"

"I don't know." Killah took her seriously. "How can a Creative Source be all-powerful if it is a party to the universal laws we see in chemistry and physics? Would it set aside these laws on special occasions? Doesn't sound reasonable to me."

"Isn't prayer another word for being thankful? Being aware of swimming in clear water?"

"On Earth, prayer is said to have real medical benefits, you know."

"'Going with the flow,' Conn would say. Oh how I wish he were here. What are we going to do, Killah?" She sank into the water and flooded her gills so she could concentrate on Killah's electro-fizz.

"Let's think. What would Conn do? He refuses to worry over details. He uses words that reflect a deep-seated faith beyond creature concepts."

Lanoll sat up. She blew all the water out of her lungs. "You're right, Killah. Conn wouldn't sit here moping. Let's keep looking."

Killah stretched into the water and flushed his gills. "We've got to find Nidok," he said. "Get on your moss sandals, Lanoll. We need to walk inland. There's no sign of Orram on shore here. Our best hopes lie with the ahlork."

They pulled themselves out of the tide pool, donned the moss shoes they carried in waist packs, and moved into the rocks, watching the skies for ahlork while they scanned the rough shore. When they had passed beyond the shore rocks, the ground became even and rose gradually to enclose the lake that lay hidden on the peninsula to the west.

When walking became easier, Killah picked up the conversation where they had left it. "So what do you know about human religions, Lanoll?"

"Not much. Shawne says that most human religions deal with symbols, concepts that go beyond the literal words. I like what great-fish say: The word God is outside logic and sense perception, so His existence can't be proved or disproved. The word is a symbol. It shouldn't be confused with the reality it represents, Conn's big Whatever."

"Shawne won't want to hear that."

"No she won't, but, even worse, she won't want to hear Conn's ultimate logic: the answers to her questions lie within herself. Even if she finds a credible authority, she will have to either accept or reject someone else's authority and belief system—and in the end trust herself."

"Poor Shawne. Humans have inventive minds that keep dodging the simple answers they crave."

– Δ –

Nidok and Forelock flew north to south and north again, tracing parallel lines so that their fields of vision overlapped. Finally, before the moons shifted gears and the mists rode back onto the Harrahn Peninsula, they spotted Lanoll and Killah plodding along a zigzag course toward Al Neoon. There was no sign of Orram.

The ahlork were about to buzz the ells, when a broad marsh ripe with *llaoon* grass caught their eyes. The lush meadow lay on a path between the sea and the lake. Lanoll and Killah were on that path. The marsh probably housed many *lohn* nests, so they decided to land there and wait for the ells.

They dropped quickly to the marsh and polished off two clutches of eggs. While approaching a third, Nidok waddled into a trigger that dropped a huge metal net over both of them. They struggled for some time and tried to cut through the metal with the sharp edges of their wing plates, but they could not get free.

– Δ –

"We're coming to the southern marshes," Killah said. "We can soak there for a while and help ourselves to some *lohn* eggs."

"No need for that, Kill. I've got one coming. Excuse me for a moment." Lanoll hurried ahead into the deep grass and waded in until water touched her knees. Then she sat on her haunches well hidden in the grass and kneaded her oviduct to hurry her ripe egg into the world. It was a nice big one. She washed it in the marsh water and dried it with her hip plumes, then took it to Killah and presented it to him for lunch.

Killah expertly shook the *el* egg to mix its contents, then cracked the shell open and divided the rich pudding equally between the two shell halves. Handing one to Lanoll, he sat down and drank his in three gulps. Lanoll sipped at her lunch. A frown tied her lovely brow plumes into a knot between her sonic melons.

"We should have seen Nidok and Forelock by now, Killah," she said. "Ahlork spend their time in the air. They would have seen us—if they were anywhere over the peninsula. The mists have been gone for most of the time we've been out here."

"Why didn't Conn outfit the ahlork with radio collars?"

"They wouldn't wear them. They didn't want to 'go public,' they said. Conn tried. Nidok wouldn't wear a collar for anyone, for any reason."

"Conn took Nidok's scar. That's far more commitment than a radio collar."

"But a scar is a private matter. Radios are public. I'll give Nidok that."

The air exploded with sound, like a hundred *kaehl* shrieking and chains rattling.

"What?" Killah leapt to his feet.

Lanoll listened for a moment. "It's the ahlork, Kill. They're very angry. Let's go."

KORAK

When they got back to Oleyall's cave, Shawne and Conn helped the great-fish beach a young and tender *eeflin*, then they relaxed as best they could, sharing a jug of salt-thistle cider. They soaked sore muscles in the communication pool while Charley, Korak and Orticon roasted their big marine prey in a bed of evening dry moss and hot rock.

Conn worried about Shawne's reaction to Haralahn, and he said nothing about Stringer to the others. He thanked Oleyall quietly for letting him postpone the disturbing news.

At first, Shawne was angry with Haralahn's prescription, then she realized the value of his suggestion. If her depression was caused by inflammatory problems, she would have a more certain cure—perhaps a chance at a quick medical fix.

She sat deep in the water, where she could reach out to both Oleyall and Conn. "You'd better tell everyone that Stringer's missing," she said.

"What?" Orticon and Charley reacted together.

"A search has already begun. We have contacted Elllonian Protection and the EV Lab," Oleyall indicated in his abbreviated sign language.

"I didn't want to tell you," Conn said, "because there is nothing we

can do yet. We have to glean all the information we can from official sources before we go looking for him again. The schools keep Ellason well monitored. We can wait here. Or maybe we should go back to the ranch and search again for leads there."

"That would be redundant, Conn. Experienced great-fish have already gone to the ranch," Oleyall said.

"Experienced?" Shawne asked.

"Great-fish trained to search for missing persons of any kind."

As if on cue, a great-fish appeared at the mouth of the cave. Oleyall met him and they communicated silently, only briefly before the messenger departed. Oleyall moved slowly back to his guests.

"I have more disturbing news," he said in Varokian. "There was a rover accident in the Viortahk. Orram went missing, as did the elll Cuffall. Everyone else is safe. A thorough search is underway."

Shawne blanched.

Korak responded as if she had cried for help. He stood facing her, confused by the physical need he saw in her mood and his own varokian need for mental contact. As a compromise, he placed his right hand on her shoulder.

"Thank you, Korak." Oleyall saw what the guesture cost the varok. "Shawne needs more company than Conn and I can give her."

Shawne placed her hand over Korak's. "When can we leave for the lab, Conn?"

"Soon, if you really want to."

Charley looked to the others in confusion.

"It's Orram. He's missing." Conn spelled it out in English.

"Orram and Stringer both missing? Are you sure? Did I misunderstand?" Charley looked to Oleyall, who nodded in confirmation.

"No," Shawne sobbed. "No. God, please, no."

To Conn's surprise, Korak steeled himself and took her in his arms.

"He reads her well," Oleyall said.

"I'm sorry, Korak," Shawne said, pulling away from the young varok. "The messenger must be mistaken. Conn has given us details of Stringer's disappearance. It couldn't be Orram."

Conn knew the message had to be correct. The sonic network was a reliable source.

"You mean Stringer," Shawne cried. "You can't mean Orram. Orram wouldn't go missing." Her hands shook, and Korak took them in both his. Their eyes locked and his patches throbbed with the intense probe he sent through her mind. She clung to him for support, and Korak had no problem with the touch.

All Conn could think was that Shawne didn't need two knockout blows like this on top of her depression. He couldn't let her take refuge in a mating she didn't understand, could he?

He looked to Oleyall for help, and the big great-fish shrugged. Who was he to understand human–varokian relations? The Charley-Orram-Conn-Tandra-Lanoll pentagon was more than he could fathom.

Charley took the cooked *eeflin* from the steaming rocks and served it on a bed of seasoned deep sea vines. They ate in silence, knowing they must. Every bite was a torture in the swallowing.

She caught Oleyall's fin tip in her hands and shook it angrily. "Why? Why? How could they both just disappear? It doesn't make any sense. Am I being punished for dragging them here? Is that what this is? A punishment for my quest? For its presumption? Or is it because I denied my chance for a child?"

Conn blew. "That's a crazy western human notion, Shawne. You lost a pregnancy, not a child. Snap out of it. You were raised to know better than to raise an unwanted—"

"You did know, when I didn't. All this time, you knew?"

"You made a wise choice, even though you wanted the experience, and the company. Elllonian sonar sees quite well under water. You know how much dolphins love pregnant women. Do you really believe this fatherly God of yours is into tinkering with human lives and punishing wise choices for semantic reasons?

"Does He use accidents to drive lessons home? Stringer and Orram were in the wrong place at the wrong time. That's all. That's it. There is no punishment, though God may be sorry—I'll give you that, Oleyall—but he couldn't interfere if he wanted to—if Orram and Stringer were in the wrong place at—"

Conn's anger fizzled with the redundancy. "We will use everything we have to find them, Shawne. That's all anyone can do in an avalanche—calculate the trajectory, run, then keep digging when you get dumped on."

Conn couldn't eat much. The thought of Orram in trouble threw him into a boiling pot of anger, frustration, and loss of life-joy that made normal functioning impossible.

Oleyall picked up on his mood, and he moved quietly into deep water, leading the others toward the rover. "I will go with you," he said, "at least part way to the lab. I have business at Elll Central."

– Δ –

Oleyall swam on the surface, keeping pace with the rover's moderate cruising speed. He put an abrupt end to the speculation about Orram and Stringer.

"Such talk does no good right now," he said. "If you must make sounds, use your thinking to benefit Shawne's quest. All too soon, it will get lost in your more urgent concerns."

Korak surprised everyone—all but Oleyall—when he slid across the watercraft bench to sit close to Shawne. His patch sense sought her thoughts, and he captured her fingers in his, hoping to release the pressure she felt and tap into cooler reserves.

"It's time to go beyond academic talk," he said, tuning up the sensitivity of his patch organs and diving deep into Shawne's currents of thought. "Go deeper with me. We'll sort through all the concepts you're tagging with the word God, everything you've heard or read about. Throw out the ideas that are not helpful. Perhaps you should forget the word God; it's loaded with historical human baggage."

"Yes, please, Korak. You may read my thoughts, but please talk to me in Varokian or Sonics or something."

"We can join the search for Orram and Stringer," *or we can sit here and scream 'Unfair!' and forget to tinker with choices and initial conditions,* he finished in thought.

Shawne's eyes widened and she searched his. *I understand you! Without words. I understand you.*

And I you.

Oleyall motioned to Orticon to stop the rover. As it coasted in the restless water, the great-fish reached to take Shawne' hand. "You are healing. I must go now," he said, "and here's a prayer for you, Shawne. Thank God for Korak, whatever that means."

Shawne actually smiled. "I will, Oleyall, and thank you."

Trust the faith Conn released in you, the great-fish told her. *Travel safely. All our comfort and love to Tandra.* His words were clearer than hearing.

– Δ –

Oleyall watched the moons above Ellason paint the broad ripples with warm (orange) and bright (white) patterns on the changing surface of the ocean. When he reached Elll Central, he found the master philosopher Haralahn already there.

Like two giant kites sailing in calm winds, the two great-fish met with an intricate exchange of pressure patterns. Then they talked, quietly, as only great-fish can. Time passed, and the moons continued their endless dance. The name Korak was mentioned. The word *urgent* was used, then Haralahn sped south to an obscure branch of the Great Rift, where the molten core of Ellason surged upward through wide cracks in the planet's crust, heating the oceans and powering life.

THE DEEPS

Stringer stared at the dim glow lighting the deeps, grateful that Ellason's molten core was keeping him comfortably warm. He could no longer focus on the nearby vents or the local currents that brought him nuggets of sulfur-energized life to eat. It was not enough. He was wasting away, he felt—too constrained, too alone, too bored, too damn hungry to live much longer.

His mind felt as clogged with memory as his tiles had been after swimming in Earth's polluted waters. The water flowing from the vents surged with their own smoke-like toxins. Elllonian plumes are pretty good filters, but ellls need pure water to stay healthy.

Ellls' tiled skin is full of receptors and glands that are enmeshed in lateral lines containing a variety of neuromasts tuned to every taste, pressure, sound, and voltage that fills live waters. There's no quick clean up for sorting out so many tiny receptors.

He knew he was well hidden from echo-location, tied to the huge *ahl* tree. Elllonian ultrasonic scans wouldn't pick him up, and he couldn't generate enough pressure, Sonics with his sonar melons, or electro-fizz to carry very far. His scent—now, that would do it, if the search teams had a scent tag from him, which they didn't. Not even his family had anything fresh enough to help much. *Who would pick up the strong scent of one elll's scat?* he wondered. The great-fish would pick up on it, but they never came out this far. He wasn't sure they could stand this depth for very long, and he knew they didn't like the heat and volcanic smoke that disturbed the sea so close to a rift.

His mind wandered into thoughts of Nealla, and he cried for the school. Then he focused on his peculiar situation. Why would the hedge-guardians leave him here, undetectable but provided for? They wanted him alive? He assumed they would never arrange for his torture, deliberately. No. It was more like they couldn't kill him, but they wanted him gone. He had seen too much, too many tads. Black-market tads.

Elllonian females—all ellls—loved young ellls too much, as if nothing else mattered. The replacement-only restriction to keep the population stable was hard on them. All schools were probably on the lookout for unused certificates so they could raise more tads than their one-on-one replacement allowed.

In his short time on Ellason, Stringer had heard grumbling about school relocation and splitting, which was needed because the schools had grown too large for their locale or their gardens. Of course, other schools had dwindled when they lost out on the scramble for Replacement Certificates.

Stringer thought of Tamilan, sitting with his data at the Elll-Varok Science lab, trying to figure out why the population of ellls kept bursting like bubbles here and there. Such population problems didn't occur on Varok. Those ellls were different—more focused on their studies or their accomplishments as distinct schools. Of course, they used all their Replacement Certificates, but they didn't put pressure on the system.

After the exertion of pushing so much logic through his stressed psyche, Stringer must have slept. At first he thought he was dreaming. Soothing pressure wafted over him. His plumes moved back and forth, and his mesh lines alerted him to a swimming presence. He awoke, calling out in Sonics.

The pressure waves came stronger. He sensed something large swimming nearby. *Eefl?* For a moment he panicked. He would make a delicious meal. *No. Too warm for eefl here. Eeflin then? Possible. What did they eat?* They would nibble him to death. He called out again. Maybe the sound would scare off the huge fish.

No. Damn. The pressure suddenly changed and its intensity rapidly grew. He shouted again and again, tried to roar, but the pressure was too much—then he saw it coming at him. A monstrous shadow loomed huge out of the smoky water, then hovered over him. He tried to curl up against the tree, but his bindings held him open to attack.

"Calm yourself, Stringer."

He couldn't be sure if he heard a voice or was talking to himself, but the words calmed him, and he relaxed against his ropes.

"That's it. Now I can cut you loose."

The presence hovered closer, and he felt something pulling at the tough weeds holding his hands tight against the tree's wide trunk. Pulling and pulling. Would it ever stop? He tried to jerk free.

"Stop fighting against my efforts. I don't have metal with me, just this volcanic rock. Patience. You will soon be free."

It was a great-fish voice, struggling to produce elllonian Sonics.

"Thank God. Thank God," Stringer mumbled, and he heard the great-fish let out an unmistakable "Harrumph."

"Conn's son, using human expressions, like your father. Well, what else would I expect? Have you ever considered what you mean when you say, 'Thank God?' Be forewarned. Shawne will soon hold you to your faith or challenge it. There. You're free. Your gag and melon-blind are loose. Now follow me as quickly as you can, safely, to the surface. We need to talk."

That was all, then the great-fish Haralahn disappeared, leaving Stringer alone to gather himself and decompress. He floated free, flushing his gills as he slowly rose in the water. On the surface he closed his gills and took in a huge breath to fill his lungs and clear his head. Delicious air. He thought he would never think such a thought. Now he couldn't get enough of it, and he longed to feel solid ground under his feet.

The great-fish was not in sight or scan, so he set off for the Bay of Shallows. Conn might still be there with Shawne and the others. He should warn them about the hedge–guardians. They were a dangerous school and might pose a threat to valuable alien visitors, especially visitors probing into population dynamics.

He soon tired of swimming on the surface. After a few kilometers he could barely make a ten-meter leap, so he dropped underwater and glided along at a slow pace, looking for something to eat. There wasn't much out here so far above the deeps. He would have to make it to the shallows.

"Here." Suddenly the great-fish was with him again, providing a schooling presence. Stringer realized he was still fuzzy-headed. Half his senses were numb. He had not felt the great-fish's approach.

"Thank you," he said.

"Eat this. It's nothing but riftworms and ventweeds, all I could find, but it will help. We will swim—slowly, mind you. You must take your time until you recover. We have serious work to do, you and I. You will need all your strength and at least half your good sense."

Stringer wasn't sure what he heard next, but he thought it was a laugh. Whatever it was, it was a joyous sound, a celebratory explosion, and he joined in—and soon found himself embraced by huge fins, rolling with the great-fish over and over in the water, as if they had both suddenly caught life's fever.

Laughing and crying at the same time, Stringer hugged the great-fish as best he could. "My hero," he said. "I don't know your name or I would thank you."

"I am Haralahn," the great-fish said, "and because of you I have missed out on my first chance to talk philosophy with a human—your sister, Shawne. Because I have found you alive and reasonably well, I must now postpone our talk even longer."

AL NEOON

"Lanoll, wait. There's something else. Listen." Killah pulled her down into the tall marsh grass. Another rushing sound added to the ahlork's hollering, which had suddenly changed to violent invectives.

"Something's got them."

"Stay down, Lanoll. I'll take a look."

Lanoll pulled at Killah's tunic plumes. "You stay down. I'll look. They'll see your green. My plumes blend in better with the grass."

"Be careful."

Lanoll eased up slowly until she could see through the spore heads on the grass. "Varoks, Killah, and a hedge–guardian elll. They are dragging something. Yes. It's a bag, full of some very noisy ahlork. They're moving away. Come on, Killah. We've got to follow them."

They crouched low and stayed to the taller brush. Before long they came over the crest of a hill and saw the lake spread out below, shining with reddish lights reflected from six moons behind veils of graying clouds.

"What a beautiful place," Lanoll said. "Too bad we can't enjoy it."

"There's a reason it's deserted," Killah warned. "Killer moss and lack of food. Ellls have never lived here, bet my left melon."

"Well, they do now. Look. More hedge–guardians."

"Camped in the rocky cliffs on shore. Strange."

"And tads, Killah, seven or eight tads."

"All in wet-sweaters, but I don't think they're hedge-guardians. Look. There's a blue tad. See her head plumes?"

"Killah, there are no hedge–guardians among the tads. None."

"Must be an educational trip."

"They're too young for that." Lanoll was ready to take on both hedge–guardians and varoks. "Is this an education in how to capture ahlork? Nidok and Forelock are in those nets the varoks are dragging to the caves. I'm sure of it."

"Let's go in closer so we'll know where they leave the ahlork."

Lanoll and Killah lay down in the grass. From the rim of the basin that housed the lake, they could see the southern face of the cliff etched with caves where the ahlork were taken.

"Just dumped outside and left. What do they think ahlork are?" Lanoll raged.

"We can't help them yet. At least we know they're all right. They're still complaining." Killah had had less experience with Nidok, so he wasn't emotionally tied to them. Probably a good thing, for Lanoll was a little too hot.

"Killah, what are they doing? That elll just pushed something through the net."

"It's coming back out."

Nidok's name-calling told the tale. The elll had pushed some kind of food to the ahlork, who were having none of such rude treatment.

"They had better not be so cavalier with the water bottle that's being fixed to the mesh," Killah said. "That other elll just set code locks, essentially sewing the mesh shut. I think they intend to keep the ahlork imprisoned where they are."

"Good. If they leave them outside the caves we can get them out when the moons grow dimmer."

"That may be a while, Lanoll. Let's go in closer and see where the varoks are in their cycle. They must operate on some schedule."

Lanoll and Killah fortified their moss sandals with the strong marsh reeds, then they set out toward the caves. In places the reeds grew too tall and thick, and they had to backtrack through kinder, mist-drinking shrubs. When the ellls had crouched and slithered to within twenty meters of the net, the ahlork suddenly stopped their raving. Their net grew still. Lanoll said they could feel the air freeze in place all around them.

She groaned. "Oh oh. They've sensed us. They're very keen to being stalked, you know. At one time there were predators of ahlork on Varok."

"Quiet," Killah said. "We've got to keep still. Someone will come to see why the ahlork have quieted down. They're going to give us away. Keep down."

Killah and Lanoll shouldn't have been so talkative. In the silence the ahlork created by listening to the ellls, they barely missed being heard by the hedge–guardians.

Nidok or Forelock recognized the whispered elllonian and got smart. Nidok suddenly started up again, crabbing at Forelock in their native noise, telling him to move over, get off his tail plates, and other nonsense.

Lanoll relaxed, but she wished Nidok would keep it down to a low roar, or feign sleep or something, so they could tell when the varoks and hedge–guardians were not alert. Her vision through the vegetation was not good. All she could see was the top of the cave entrance and gray sky above the moving ahlork net.

At first it didn't register—the varokian face that suddenly appeared in the frame of rock. Then a hedge–guardian pushed the varok from behind, and she nearly cried out.

"Take a good look," the hedge–guardian said, dragging Orram to the net. "It will go better for these ugly beasts if you identify them. They are your alien spies."

Lanoll blanched. These ellls must know enough to realize varoks couldn't lie. Endowed as they are with patch sense, hence open minds, lying did them no good. How was Orram going to protect Nidok and Forelock?

Orram played it very cool. He laughed. "They're Conn's pets," he said. "I'd hardly call them spies. You can see they're not tame. They don't respond well to me."

Silently, Lanoll cheered. Of course. Orram had learned a bit about lying when he had to deal with that awful varokian woman, Mahntik, the aberrant who could block her mind from reading. She had used her talent to set up illegal operations on Varok. Also, having lived closely with humans for so long, Orram had enough examples to follow when it came to dealing out a casual fib.

"We don't need an ahlork lecture, Orram." Another long, handsome (according to Lanoll) elll appeared and stood close behind Orram. Killah could see that he had a firm grip on Orram's hands, which were bound together at his back.

"Some advice, Cuffall," Orram said, warming up to his acting role. "These ahlork are weighted with metal-retaining organics. Their square shapes show up very well on radar scans. If you don't release them, Conn will initiate a search. Perhaps you've heard of carrier pigeons on Earth? Conn has started a new sport on Varok. I wouldn't try it here, though. I'm afraid ahlork make too much of a mess to keep as a novelty. You should really return them to the lab. You don't want them breeding freely on Ellason. They could make life miserable for ellls, upset the ecology—you see my point."

To illustrate, Nidok farted with a jarring tone and relieved himself all over one side of the net. Forelock added to the scene with an ear-splitting protest, and the two set up the most god-awful racket, arguing about the mess and the stench and sparring with sharp clacks of their wing-plates.

For a moment, Lanoll was afraid they overdid the show, for the hedge–guardian couldn't get close enough to release the code locks. Luckily, the ahlork quickly caught on, and when the elll shouted at them, they cowered back in the net, keeping away from him (and the mess) and shaking with fear as noisily as they could.

As soon as the locks were released, the ahlork pulled one final scene that convinced the hedge–guardian that Orram had characterized them accurately. They played dumb and continued to cower, keeping away from the elll while he untangled the mesh.

The moment the net was open, however, Nidok plunged for the opening and quickly got out of Forelock's path, so the youngster could wiggle free and give the elll a good swipe of sharp chitinous wing plates as he took off.

While the elll was dancing around in pain, thoroughly enraged, Killah and Lanoll moved toward the lake, figuring Nidok and Forelock would circle overhead and spot them. Together they might have a chance of getting Orram away from the kidnappers.

Negligence

Shawne's grief forged an anchor that settled deep in Korak's mind, giving her a connection she had longed for since she left her first love on Earth. On their way to EV Lab they rode together in the rover's stern, quiet for the most part, letting the hum of the engines dull the sharp jabs of fear for Stringer and Orram.

Charley and Conn sat near Orticon as he drove.

Conn liked Korak. He didn't seem to be concerned with making an impression, personally or professionally.

They were all eager to get to Elll Central in the Bay of Shallows. Oversight school staff there would have recent reports from their search teams. Also, they could communicate more directly by video-phone with Tandra and the others at EV Lab, get their information, and read their faces. Conn hated to think how much Tandra was suffering.

He was not sure Charley understood what it meant to her for Orram to be missing.

"She's missing half her head, half her consciousness, Charles, my man," Conn said. "You can't expect her to be happy with nothing but a human for a consolation prize. Give her some credit for twenty years of mind-link with a varok. If he's really gone, she will be a different person. Make up your mind to that."

Shawne overheard him.

"Conn. Orram's not dead. He can't be."

"We all die, Love. Orram could be anything. We don't know enough yet, except that if he had been killed in the rover accident, there would be evidence. I just hope he is not losing moments of life-joy."

That wasn't helpful, but neither was Charley's comment.

"I'm sure he's fine, Shawne," he said.

"Sure, Charley," Conn quipped. "What do you know that we don't? Are you saying Shawne should kid herself about the possibilities?"

"Why do things like this have to happen?" Shawne asked no one in particular. "It doesn't make sense. How could both Stringer and Orram be in the wrong place at the wrong time? I can't put it all together. They're worth too much to be the pawns of chance."

"Right. So he's probably okay," Charley said.

Korak jumped in when it mattered. "You will need all your strength to get through this, Shawne. Don't bury it beneath ideas that come out of your frustration."

"You see it, don't you, Korak? I can't cap the rage I feel. The same old questions boil up over and over again: Why Orram? Why Stringer? Why do these things have to happen?"

"Listen to yourself," Korak said. "You said they 'have to happen.' You know why. Go deeper. Would you want a pain-free life of certainty—without consciousness, without the risk of a complicated brain, the risk of free will, the flexibility to change and grow?"

"You're no help, Korak."

"I'm getting all this from your own thoughts, Shawne. I have to probe pretty deep, but it's all there in the truths you see. You know the price of matter being conscious. Unpredictability and pain are built into material existence—but so is our capacity to set the trends toward good or evil."

"You see all this in my head?"

"As Orram knows Tandra," Orticon said. "It takes practice."

Korak spoke in Varokian. "Focus on your anger, Shawne. Its source comes from people who do evil, not from your theology. Willful people took Orram and Stringer, or they had accidents. It's part of the package of truth you feel."

"Thanks, Korak," Charley said. "Your realism has now joined Conn's to complete the most horrible possibilities for Shawne to imagine. Stringer and Orram could be beaten and murdered, or devoured by *eefl* or drowned beneath an overturned—"

"Shut up, you mindless hairball," Conn flared. "If we're going to find Stringer and Orram, we have to consider all options. Shawne is no child. She's not a fool that has to be protected from the worst. She can be a hard-headed pragmatist, but right now she has a flailing philosophy that could make good use of Korak's reality checks."

"Can I say something?" Shawne said. She withered both Conn's vine and Charley's with a firm stare and a moment of silence. "Korak is too kind to say it, but in many ways I've been creating my own pain. I've been wallowing in regret, and now the worry, practicing it, and making it worse."

"It's hard not to wallow in worry," Conn said. "Ellls are too good at that."

"Not really, Conn," Korak said. "You ellls shake off pain very quickly."

"I only shake off a done deed, something that can't be undone."

"But when life-joy is missing or in doubt, ellls wallow," Orticon argued.

"The point is we creatures make our own evil, or we do it to each other," Conn said. "It's not built into creation."

"I can believe that," Shawne said. "Blaming God is doing nothing for me, and it won't remove the trouble that fell on Stringer. I just can't stand the thought of Orram or Stringer being so damnably unlucky."

"At the same time," Korak said.

"Yes," Charley said. "It's too much of a coincidence. I believe their disappearances are related."

"Not likely," Orticon countered from the driver's seat. "They have not been in contact since Stringer left EV Lab, and they were not together when they disappeared. What possible connection could there be?"

Conn couldn't see a connection, but he didn't really believe anything terrible had happened to either one of them. He expected to hear good news soon.

"We're coming into Elll Central" he said.

It was now visible over the gentle waves, a beautiful trading center set into a great circle of sea bottom rocks. Varoks accessed it from a long pier reaching to shore. In the center of the watery city was a botanical garden laced with paths and benches both in and out of water. It still thrived as one of Ellason's first experiments in elll-varok integrated bartering—a central gathering place for everyone living on the north side of the Great Basin, including the great-fish.

On their arrival, they docked the rover near the shallows. There the search and rescue squad had an extension to their office for the convenience of varoks, so they went there.

The office manager, an elll with a face full of plumes, greeted them with an odd mix of sympathy and enthusiasm at meeting humans. When brief introductions and niceties were done, the talk got serious.

"We are a troubled planet, Conn," the elllonian manager said in halting Varokian. "Your visit timing is good. We need help. We work to reconcile tension between the schools and packs of loners."

"Packs of loners?" Korak put on his specialist hat. "Loners running in packs—like *eefl* or the ancient land carnivores? And you think these packs have made trouble for Stringer and Orram?"

"I thought you were Specialist in Ellasonian Studies," the manager said. "Surely you know. Packs run illegal explosives to southern shallows. Information is in the data banks at the Concentrate on Varok."

For a moment, Korak went irrational with embarrassment.

"Ah, but you were in space, traveling here for many Callisto cycles. My apologies."

"That is no excuse. I should have scanned for new information." Korak stammered incoherently about saving but not studying the latest information, and his face took on a purple hue that was downright alarming. Being distracted by competing with Tamilan for Shawne's attention was no excuse.

Orticon probed for the truth. Varoks do that without permission or apology for legal reasons in such emergencies, but it was hardly necessary. Korak's shame at being caught negligent was all too obvious to everyone, even Shawne. Varoks are perfectionists, and fragile emotionally. As a specialist for the team, Korak had failed to provide useful, even vital, information, during the trip from Varok to Ellason.

Shawne was uttering sympathetic sounds. She desperately wanted to maintain the close contact she and Korak had experienced. Now, when she was just beginning to find in him relief from depression and confirmation of difficult concepts, he withdrew, too shamed to presume himself on her. Rather than respond to her sympathy, he turned away.

Orticon stayed close in Korak's mind while he recovered, and he kindly translated the young varok's thoughts for the team so he wouldn't have to verbalize them. "Korak leapt at the chance to represent himself as the Elllonian Specialist on our project so he could have time, and a chance, with Shawne. Our relationship to humans is very complicated, as you all know from my father's experience with Shawne's mother."

"Korak," Shawne said, "You have been a wonderful support to me, a good friend when I needed it most. A few loner details don't matter."

He looked at her from behind a tough, protective curtain of failure.

"We don't blame you for missing the latest reports," Conn said officiously. "We've kept you busy running around this planet. You've got my support as long as you continue your support for Shawne. We cannot do without you." He wondered if Korak was rational enough to understand. "You can get up to speed as soon as we get back to EV Lab. No harm is done. I'm sure you will fulfill your obligations to EV Science under the contract of this project."

"I'll join you in taking responsibility for any consequences, Korak, which I am sure will be minimal," Orticon said. "I can help you find the information you need. Sit down and gather your reason. We have no more time for you now." When Orticon finished speaking, he steered Korak to a bench in the small office.

Conn thought no punishment could have been worse for the poor kid—shamed in front of the girl he loved and the humans, varoks, and ellls who had trusted his expertise. Korak sat with his hands on his patch organs, trembling with the effort to stay rational.

Shawne was having her own trouble controlling a wild assortment of emotions. "What's so bad about missing some current theory about packs?" she stormed.

Conn said nothing. Shawne knew very well that the concept was central to the main mission for this trip. He gathered her up with a firm arm. "Orticon, Shawne and I will call Tandra. Please get a full report from the search teams looking for Stringer. Charley, watch Korak, if you wouldn't mind. Tell him how much engineering you've forgotten, and call Orticon pronto if his marbles start to shake loose."

Charley nodded, said nothing. The video link to EV Lab was good—too good. Tandra looked like she had been hung out as dried beef. "Conn—I'm so worried. I've had no report from the search teams yet. Do you have any news, anything at all?"

"Orticon is checking. Hang on a minute."

While Conn got the report from Orticon, Shawne called Tandra and reported some of the details of Ihratohl's death and her trip to the great-fish caves.

"No news of Stringer," Conn told them both after he talked to Orticon. "Nothing from the trackers or the elllonian communication web that covers the Great Basin. Have you heard anything from the great-fish network?"

"No," Tandra said. "They have been silent—which means they must know something. Have they reported in to Elll Central?"

"Not yet. We would have heard something through Oleyall, Tan. All we know is that they are looking."

Tandra's worried face turned to Shawne over the video link. "Sweetheart, we'll find Stringer and Orram. The networks are very tight here."

Conn jumped in to give Shawne her options and let Tandra know what had happened with Korak. "Orticon will be supervising Korak's update. That young varok has been a great friend to Shawne. She's had some tough challenges to face here, no thanks to me."

"I won't even ask what that means, Shawne," Tandra said. "Did you enjoy your visit to the great-fish caves?"

Conn had to laugh at Tandra's diplomacy, and it made Shawne smile through her tears. "I'll be all right, Mom," she said. "I thought Korak and I were joining minds, like you and Orram, but he's shut me out." She broke then and turned into Conn's tunic plumes to have the good cry she needed.

"But Shawne that's wonderful. You were actually able to read him? Give him time. Your connection to him could mean everything—to him and to you."

"Come to us here as fast as you can, Conn," Tandra continued. "We have no news. Orram left no clues where the rover flipped. Forelock and

Nidok have not come back to the lab, so we hope they spotted something and will report back to us when they can. Lanoll and Killah are
looking for them. We are packed, ready for a trip to go over the accident
site again, then go out to Stringer's school and make our own search
for him, too. Killah is convinced the two incidents are connected."

"So is Charley," Conn said. "It seems far fetched, but Elll Central
reports there are dangerous packs of loner ellls causing trouble. Some
packs work together to deal in illegal trade. We're not sure what all is
involved yet."

"Packs of loners?" Conn could see Tandra's angst at the thought.
"Like street gangs in the cities of Earth?"

"I suppose. We don't know the details yet."

"And Korak missed it. I see. No wonder he is in trouble."

"He'll fix it," Conn said.

Conn turned his eyes away from the communication screen when
he felt Charley's meaty hand on his shoulder. "Please, Conn, a moment
with Tandra?"

"We haven't got time for courting games—" the elll snapped.

"Are you two still squabbling?" Tandra was furious. "Charley, talk
to me."

Charley hesitated, so Conn ushered him to the communicator.

"What can you tell me, Tan? I'm not sure I'm making it, alone, here
on Ellason."

"You will, Charley." She smiled. "I love you. Tell Conn to be nice—
for me. He will."

"Conn has been a rock," Charley said, knocking him off his arro-
gant pins. "He turned into something we all needed when Korak was
caught in his neglect. He was firm, but quite fair, I think, as direct as he
needed to be to keep the boy from getting too upset. Korak is sick, but
still rational. I'd better get back to him. We love you, Tan. We'll always
love you. Here's Conn."

"Thanks, Charley," Conn said.

"Don't block Charley's access to Shawne," Tandra threatened. "She
needs him, too." Her eyes filled.

Conn couldn't stand it when she got emotional, and he nearly
choked as his gills swelled up with an empathic sob.

"We have to find Stringer and Orram, Conn," she said. "I won't
leave Ellason without Orram. Never."

The last comment was not lost on Charley. He was pretty grim all the way back to the lab. He knew Tandra meant it.

RECRUITING KORAK

"Wait, Haralahn. Don't surface." Stringer dove quickly and joined the great-fish deep outside Elll Central, somewhere near the underwater entrance to the circular village. "I'm sure I saw the Lurlial's rover at the visitors' dock. Conn's team must be here, on their way home from Oleyall's cave."

"Secrecy is everything," Haralahn said, "but I realize you want to tell them you're safe."

"It would be the worst cruelty not to tell them something, especially since we have this chance. With both Orram and me missing, they have lost all life-joy."

"I will tell them a tale to erase their grief and throw your enemies off your scent. Wait here. Do no scans. Make no noise, leave no scent, lie as if dead so your electric and pressure patterns generate no curiosity. It would be best if you would sleep in the mud while I am gone."

Haralahn disappeared into the underwater entrance to Elll Central, and Stringer swam toward the shallows to hide in a nest of huge shore rocks that had trapped enough mud and sand to make a decent resting-place. Sleep was out of the question.

Many ellls passed through the entrance, both coming and going, before Haralahn reappeared and put out a brief ultrasonic call for Stringer, using the code name they had chosen, "Friend Elll."

"The waters are clear," Haralahn said quietly, swimming in very close to Stringer. "We must move quickly now. Your family has half of their life-joy restored, and only Charley, the human, is suspicious that your real whereabouts may not be as I explained. Humans have far more experience with subterfuge than the people of Ellason, and varoks have none. Shawne was charming. Her love for you runs deep."

"I'll remember that."

"And Korak's love for her also runs deep, but his self-esteem needs repair right now. We need the help of a varok, don't you think? He needs to prove his worth. I'm going back to get him."

Stringer hated the idea. "Can you make him sprout gills?"

"I'll check out a powered skiff for him. Wait here, as before. I must hurry. Your family and friends are about to leave for EV Lab."

– Δ –

Haralahn turned all fins to full power but missed Conn and the other's departure. They were nearly out of the Bay of Shallows into deeper water before he caught up to them.

Shawne saw him first. "Conn, there's a great-fish following us. Slow down," she hollered above the full power roar of the rover. "It's Haralahn."

"How can you tell?" Charley exclaimed.

"Fin shapes," she said.

Orticon moved quickly to the stern to quiz the great-fish, but, being too polite to try reading the huge brain, he didn't see Haralahn's real intentions.

"We need some varokian assistance," Haralahn told Orticon. Before anyone could object, he had wrapped his long prehensile tail around Korak's waist and lifted him out of the rover. Swimming swiftly away, he said, "Hang onto my shoulders, Korak, and lie down so we can hurry." He took off along the surface at high speed, losing Korak more than once before they made it back to Stringer.

At the dock Haralahn deposited the shaken youth into a borrowed skiff—a small streamlined boat, not too stable but very fast. It was nearly indestructible, made of a metal synthetic. "Do you know how to run one of these?" the great-fish asked Korak.

"No, but I can learn."

"Learn fast, and meet us over the northern parasite barrier of Rocky Deeps Ranch. If you must call, use the name *Friend Elll* in Sonics."

They left Korak with that. No food. Only a desalinization unit, scuba and fishing gear. Emergency rations were minimal, and the distance to the deeps brought him near panic.

THE CAVES OF AL NEOON

Orram looked into Cuffall's face and probed deeply, trying to fathom the hedge–guardian elll's motives.

"What more do you want, varok?" Cuffall said, backing away. "You already know too much. You are here as our guest because you gleaned everything I know when we were traveling in the rover."

"You run a nursery somewhere near a shore of broken rocks. You raise tads until they have strengthened their legs, then you bring them here until you sell them, illegally. You do not report the hatching, and no one is accountable for the Replacement Certificates these tads represent."

"You're missing the best part—the extra credits we earn pay the hedge–guardians at the ranch."

"I don't understand that. Why don't they want to be a part of the ranch operation? The shepherding of *eeflin* is interesting, challenging, work."

"But it leaves them no time to help run our business and tend to the tads."

"Sounds like they are in a circular trap," Orram said, "like the one you sprung when you tried to raise TK. Where did she come from, really?"

"I told you the truth about her."

"Your personal school was delivering tads to the Far Deeps when you saw her parents' accident and rescued TK."

"Something like that."

"You have made yourself one too many traps, Cuffall."

"But they are such entertaining traps, my dear varok," Cuffall said. "Too bad you had to get so curious. It was very rude of you, Orram, to read my mind uninvited."

"I fear for TK's life," Orram said. "I don't trust your school. Raising a varokian child in an elllonian school doesn't make any sense."

"The females are very possessive."

"Yes. It is clear that they want to keep the child. But why? She is an enormous burden for the school, and she is not developing normally. Such an obsession is not love. Only your school can give her that— enough love to let her go, to be raised as a varok. She is crippled, Cuffall.

She cannot walk properly and never will, if you don't let her go."

Cuffall's anger flared, but he said nothing. Abruptly he turned away and left the cave where Orram was imprisoned. Perhaps he knew— even while Orram spoke, the varok was monitoring Cuffall's memory and the flow of his thoughts.

In the elll's mind, Orram had seen peculiar clues to the school's obsession with TK. The ellls apparently raised no tads of their own, yet the females kept incubating eggs.

Alone in his cave, tethered like a wild animal, Orram dealt admirably with his rage. He stayed rational and began composing in his head a report on the peculiar elllonian socio-pathologies he had observed. He believed no such aberrations existed in ellls anywhere on Varok. He also noticed a few physical differences between ellls of the two planets—the shape of the skull and slope of the melons for one and a heavier ankle in loner ellls of Ellason (which was not surprising given the difference in the planetary gravitational effect of being close to Jupiter, in Varok's case, and jerked about by thirty moons on a heavier spheroid, in Ellason's case).

– Δ –

When Nidok and Forelock flew free of their net, Lanoll and Killah moved quickly toward the lake, expecting them to follow. The ahlork's prolonged silence had triggered an alarm in another of the hedge-guardians assigned to watch them. Too quickly he discovered they were gone. He complained loudly at his partner, who was just as indiscreet in claiming innocence; he had unlocked the locks when told to unlock them.

"So why are the ahlork gone?"

"Lolltan wanted them gone."

"We'll trap them again in the long grass."

"They fly, varok-brain. They're already halfway to EV Lab. Elll Central will have their loner police out here before we finish our last meal as free ellls."

Two comments caught Orram's attention—the name-calling and the reference to 'loner police.' The latter suggested serious tension between loners and the schooling structure of Ellasonian society. 'Varok-brain' was a puzzle. Tandra could probably guess what that meant.

Cuffall heard the guards arguing and came to investigate. As he emerged from his command center in one of the largest caves overlooking the lake, he saw something move near the eastern shore. He thought he saw blue. Blue plumes.

"Get into the lake, you two," he shouted to the guards. "Look for a stranger, a blue elll. Have the nurses scan the lake for anything unusual, then report back to me before the next moon rises over the northern hills."

TK Meets Shawne

The miserable trip across the Rocky Shallows and through the Viortahk to EV Lab was just that—boring, endless, and miserable to Conn. Haralahn's fairy tale about Stringer helped. Without it, their misery would have been far worse, as he, Shawne, Charley and Orticon worked their way north through the mist and cold water, dodging rocks and getting lost more than once. They could imagine Stringer off in the Far Deeps, playing detective with great-fish and ellls from Elll Central who were trying to defuse tension between loners and schoolers there.

At last the maze of rocks in the Viortahk opened wide to show its gums, the welcome mud flats of Varoks' Bay. They moved quietly across the bay into Varoks' River and saw TK playing on the pier with Talln. The elll nodded as they drifted by, and the little girl locked her gaze on Shawne. She had never seen long wavy blond hair blowing back from such a delicate brown face. Talln tried to call her attention back to their game, but the child started wobbling precariously after the rover on her land-deprived legs.

"Slow down, Orticon," Shawne said. "There is a varokian child on the pier. I think she wants a ride back to the lab."

The rover glided to a stop, then backed up until TK was within reach.

"Going back to the lab?" Conn asked the child's elllonian companion.

Before he said, "Hop in," TK stumbled into the stern, and Shawne caught her as she rolled off the bench into the bottom of the rover. The child didn't flinch much at the contact, so Shawne set her on the bench.

"I've got you, little one. Sorry for so much touching," Shawne said. "Are you all right?"

The child shivered a little, but smiled and reached out to catch a stray curl that had fallen over Shawne's right eye.

Orticon asked Talln to take a seat, then, after making short introductions, they were off to the lab, little realizing what kind of time bomb they had just taken aboard.

Tandra was on the dock to meet them. "I see you've found a new friend, TK," she said, helping the child from the rover and greeting Shawne with a hug.

"Shawne picked me up. I fell in the boat," TK clicked in Sonics.

"Let me help you walk now, TK," Shawne said. "We don't want you to fall off the dock into the water."

"Watch me walk, Shawne," the child boasted, and she managed a few running steps before her legs crumpled beneath her.

Shawne stayed with her, being cautious to avoid more contact than the child could tolerate, and they were soon engaged in an energetic walking exercise. It was a good distraction.

As expected, when Tandra came out to meet them, Charley grabbed her first. Conn wanted to tear them apart, but her eyes were on Conn, so he met her gaze and looked as pitiful as he could. Conn had to admit it—he was worried that Tandra might turn to Charley for all her comfort. The elll needed to be in water with her, to grieve or rant and rave—whatever—to mend the two thirds of the trio that defined the core of their mixed family.

"Conn and I need to adjust to Orram's absence," she told Charley, after she had soaked up a good bit of furry beef. She introduced him to Talln, then greeted Orticon warmly. "Join us at the pool soon, please, Orticon. Charley, I would love it if you would join us in the adjustment."

"I think I had better wait," Charley said, noting the glare in Conn's headlights.

"Your choice, Charley."

Conn's best guess was that Tandra was disgusted with both of them and their primitive male sparring. She said nothing.

"Take all the time you need, Tandra," Charley said. "I'll stay with Shawne a minute and come to the pool after your family has had time together."

"You're giving Tandra more room than she wants, Charley," Conn mouthed to himself. "Big Mistake. I'm not going to invite you into the family. She has to do that, in spite of me."

When Tandra had disappeared into the lab, Charley turned his attention to TK. Conn had to give him this—his Elllonian was improving.

"Hold on, everyone," Jesse said, joining them on the dock. He began telling Charley a condensed version of TK's history growing up with Talln's school. "She was very ill when Orram found the school," he said, "so the ellls agreed to have her treated here at the lab."

"And it will soon be time to take her home," Talln said. "She has been free of the fever for at least two meals."

Shawne had walked away from the conversation, engrossed with TK in a counting game. The child knew her numbers well, as one might expect from elllonian tutelage, but she had a limited vocabulary in both Elllonian and Varokian. "I'm tired, TK, aren't you? I'll show you my room in the lab. Take my hand so you can walk beside me."

The child nodded, eager to please her new friend with the bright hair, but she hung on too hard, trying to swing herself through the air—as if she were in water, Shawne thought.

As she kneeled down to help TK get back firmly on her feet, the elll Talln swooped down on them and carried off the child. TK set up a loud protest.

"Come to the pool and eat with us, Talln. TK, I will tell you a story before sleep time," Shawne promised, then she turned to Charley, who had been watching.

Orticon and Jesse followed them into the lab, talking quietly, reviewing options to search for Orram.

"You are very good with TK, Shawne," Charley said.

"I think I know how she feels, Charley. She's a toddler living on an alien planet, as I was."

"But without a lifeline to her own kind, like the one you had with Tandra."

"Yes. She needs one, Charley. She really does, doesn't she?"

"I can't think of anyone who would make a better lifeline than you, Shawne."

"Mom. Mom would. She has more experience on Varok. She's—"

"Too old," Charley said, "but she would make a great grandmother."

Shawne laughed. "A wonderful grandmother. Yes she would. But TK will also need a father. Ironic isn't it? Just when I thought I had found—"

She couldn't go on, and Charley provided the bear hug she needed. "You'll find someone, Shawne. It may take some practice, but you'll find what you want in a partner. You may have to go back to Earth, but that wouldn't be so bad, would it? Maybe I'll go back with you."

"And watch people make all the same old mistakes, again and again? Squeezing the life from Earth, destroying everything good that humans have done, murdering each other in the name of this religion or that?"

"Oh no, my dear." Charley shook his head and took her by the shoulders. "Don't you realize that religions' commandments to love one another have eliminated cruel ancient customs in almost every corner of Earth? It has diffused into both human and animal rights. Many financial laws have checked even the abuse of political and economic power."

"I guess I overlooked all that, Charley. I was focused on the wars and terrorism that flare up, the big die-off, and the blind spots in recovery."

"In some ways, Earth is not doing too badly, right now, Shawne, moving North. Global environmental agreements are beginning to work. I'm not saying there's not a lot of work to do on Earth, but without optimism, without remembering the progress that's been made, it all goes down the drain, doesn't it? Self-fulfilling prophesy and all that."

Shawne gave Charley a hug. "Thanks, Charley," she said. "I needed that."

The big man sighed with a wan smile.

"What's the matter, Charley? It's Mom, isn't it? If Orram is really gone, she will need you more than ever."

"Conn can hardly stand me."

"He probably wants more time with Mom. He'll get over it. You two overlap a little, that's all."

"Overlap? With Conn? I thought my overlap was with Orram."

"A little of both maybe. But Orram doesn't know how to be jealous. You should try trading minds with him."

"I wouldn't know where to begin."

"Well, then your fate may be sealed, Charley. If you don't get out of your human skin a little, you're not going to make it into the family pool. Better get down there now. Tell Mom I'll join the water after I see Tamilan."

Shawne hurried down the hall to Tamilan's office, where she waited for some minutes before he turned from his work to greet her.

"I'm so sorry about Orram," he said.

"We'll find him." Shawne hated to admit anything would ever harm the being who had given her every reason to trust existence.

"I'm not so sure," Tamilan said. His eyes kept darting back to his work. "The situation is very grim. This Cuffall—the elll who disappeared with Orram—he was being watched by Elll Central in connection with irregular movements of young ellls."

"Irregular?"

"Cuffall claimed he was running a series of survival classes for young ellls, potential loners who needed help surviving away from the school, but no supporting evidence for such classes has been found."

"Have you told Conn?"

"Conn is here?"

"Of course. I was traveling with him to the Bay of Shallows. Then he and Lanoll went off to see Stringer's new school, and he caught up with us at the northern city of great-fish. When we heard that Orram was missing, we came right back here. We need to get together and think what to do, Tamilan. Mom and Conn are waiting for us at the pool."

Tamilan looked at Shawne, then back at his work. It pulled at his mind like a powerful magnet. "I'll follow you there as soon as I have analyzed this new data from the Far Deeps."

"Perhaps that's Stringer's work. Maybe you should go out there and join him. We thought he was missing, but the great-fish recruited him to study loner problems."

"I'll join you as soon as I can."

Shawne watched him lean into his work, relieved that he hadn't asked about Korak. *Tamilan is so dedicated. He wouldn't have made the mistake Korek did.*

At the pool Shawne reconnected with Tandra, then she told Nealla about Stringer's new project with the great-fish. It erased the elll's worst fears, but when Conn tried to school with her, he found it difficult to know how to comfort Nealla. They were both loners, but there was a

disconnect, as if they were swimming in parallel, putting out electro-
fizz that made sparks instead of glue.

Charley came into the underlab pool room when TK and Talln entered for meal time, but he hung back while they made a raft for the
child so she could eat as she usually did.

Eventually, Orticon appeared and entered the pool for his brief
varokian-style adjustment. When he climbed out of the water, Tandra
asked Charley to get in.

Conn thought the human would be eager to take Orticon's place in
TK's raft, but, instead, he followed Orticon out of the room and onto
the dock.

"I need your help, Orticon," he called.

Orram's son, no longer a young varok, nearly as experienced in interspecies relations as the rest, immediately refused the request he saw
in Charley's mind.

"I can't tell you anything about what Tandra is thinking," Orticon
said. "We varoks don't exert patch pressure unless invited. I'm sure
you saw her mood. She wanted you to join her—be a part of the raft.
Why didn't you?"

"I don't go where I'm not welcome."

"So you define Conn as the key to your love for Tandra? You require
an invitation from him?"

"Tandra requires it."

"Tandra requires your loyalty to the family and respect for her relationship to everyone in it."

"How can I respect a relationship I know nothing about?"

"You can trust Tandra's good faith—that she won't betray you or
your relationship. We varoks have learned about trust from you humans, but I think you find it very difficult."

"I don't see it that way, Orticon."

"Then tell me what I am reading incorrectly. Perhaps you need to
return to Earth. Perhaps you would prefer a simpler family, one un-
complicated by ill-defined relationships to aliens."

"Is that what you see in my mind?"

"I don't see inside your mind. It doesn't sit still. Your mind is in flux,
changing and re-inventing itself. My patch sense is like an emergent
moving picture. Your mind has the wisdom to grow, doesn't it? To ex-
pand, to include non-humans?"

"I'm not sure I'm up to it, Orticon."

"Perhaps you're not." Orticon smiled, thinking of Tandra, loving her complicated self. "Tandra presents a tough challenge. I can sympathize with that. When she first came to Varok, I had a difficult time adjusting to her—and to the changes she made in my father."

"Tell me about that, Orticon, would you? Maybe it would give me a handle on my problem."

"I rather doubt that, Charley. We varoks have unique problems. Our patch sense is intimately connected to our sexuality. We usually don't mate seriously until we find our mind set in another's consciousness, and then mating becomes a physical necessity."

"You mean a compulsion?"

"No, a necessity, to avoid great physical pain. It's an evolutionary quirk, left over from the Mutilation, when we stopped breeding and nearly went extinct."

Charley understood that the varok was serious. He began to appreciate the complicated relationship between Orram and Tandra and Conn, an appreciation Orticon saw and trusted.

They wandered down the pier, talking about the early days of the family. Orticon had joined a rebellious group opposed to legal mind-probing while he was still a student at the Concentrate. Charley learned a lot about Orticon, Orram, and Tandra—but not much about himself.

SCENT TRAIL

Far out in the deeps, Stringer didn't expect to have such a difficult time keeping up with the great-fish Haralahn. He swam swiftly, near the surface to give the young varok in the skiff, Korak, a visual reference. They moved steadily south across the Great Basin until they reached the northern arm of the Great Chasm. Here they rested for several meals, feeding on rift worms and deep sulfur turnbit. When not gathering food, they stayed close to the skiff so their shapes would not be recognized by ultrasonic scans.

At last Haralahn gave the signal to proceed to the northern para-site barrier of Stringer's Rocky Deeps Ranch. "Your school has moved toward the eastern range, Stringer," the great-fish said. "Now we can look for evidence along the northern line of *ahl* trees without being seen. Keep scanning for loners. The hedge–guardians may still be us-ing the parasite barrier."

"Using the parasite barrier?" Stringer asked. He was following Haralahn and the silhouette of Korak's skiff riding the calm surface.

"As a place to hide tads, wouldn't you say, Stringer?"

"It's likely. I saw many tads with the hedge–guardians. Too many for one school."

Haralahn got Korak's attention with a tap of his tail on the side of the skiff. "Korak, we will search the entire length of the northern para-site barrier," he said in Elllonian.

For a moment Haralahn made no sound, and Stringer had the im-pression he was repeating the message in some other way for the va-rok's benefit. "The barrier is far more than six trees wide, so we will be here for many cycles. You will supply our food, Korak. Fish to the bot-tom directly over the rift. Use small catches to bring up larger game. Your efforts will save us valuable time. If anyone comes by, display your catch as a sport fisherman would. Share it if necessary, but say nothing about us."

Stringer and the great-fish dove, leaving Korak to find the rift and start reeling in the big ones. Problem was, he did just that. The first thing he caught was a twenty kilo *eeflin*, who had the bad luck to be fascinated by the shiny hooking device on the end of Korak's deep line. The big fish dragged Korak many *pallons* before he was able to haul it in close enough to bash it over the head. Then, unhappily, the bashed piscoid sank like a dead weight, swamping Korak's skiff and dragging it over.

After an extensive search, Haralahn found Korak perched atop the upside-down skiff trying to make his way back to the rift while drag-ging the hammered *eeflin*.

"You have done well, my friend," Haralahn said. He towed Korak and his mount south to a place over the rift, where three megaplumes stirred the waters, lifting a variety of succulent goodies to the surface in a surge of warm water. There Stringer rigged the skiff's anchor, and

Haralahn gave Korak a quick review of varokian scuba gear.

"Since you have found us enough food for the entire search, you might as well join us," Haralahn said. "I want you to document everything we find that suggests how many tads passed by here recently."

The elll, the varok, and the great-fish swam in and out, up and down, amongst the narrow *ahl* forest that grew wild on the Rocky Deeps northern border. Korak was soon as efficient at searching as the other two, actually more efficient than the huge great-fish, who could not maneuver between close-set trees or among thick branches.

After several meals of raw *eeflin* and a long sleep, they began their searching again, not at all sure what they were looking for.

"Ask yourself if anything is out of place in the *eeflin* range," Haralahn said. "Tads cannot hide in an *ahl* grove without leaving some trace."

"Or doing some damage with their rough play in a confined area." Korak's comment opened Stringer's mind to wider possibilities. Before their next sleep they found what they were looking for.

It wasn't obvious at first, just a few ill-fitting mud turtle shells that had been hung on low *ahl* branches and filled with beam fish to light the sea-floor forest. Then too many leaves littered the sea floor. In the interior of the narrow grove many small branches were broken.

Stringer had to back off before he was sure. From a distance there was no doubt. One grove of ten trees had been abused and the sea floor trashed with the remains of elll food.

At the surface they righted Korak's skiff and found in the emergency hold a recording sheet and locator. After they had described their find and eaten their fill, Korak set to work stripping narrow pieces off the *eeflin* he had caught. Carefully, he laid them over the skiff edges to dry.

"We won't need much meat," Haralahn said. "We'll go now to follow the tads. Stringer will return to the surface periodically, Korak, to keep you on our deep course."

"You're going to follow the tads' scent? Can you do that? Is it fresh enough?"

"It's enough, though it has dissipated some," Haralahn said. "Many tads make a broad odiferous swath in deep water."

The scheme worked for nearly fifty kilometers, then the scent trail split into four narrower paths.

"How old were the tads you saw on the northern parasite barrier before you were kidnapped, Stringer?" Haralahn asked. "Were their legs fully formed?"

"Most were. Some were only half-formed, but they had probably lost their early scent so we didn't notice them at the ranch."

"Then that explains the split in the trails. Some of the tads were old enough to be adopted. We are following a delivery trail. To make our case, we must follow at least one trail to its destination—to an adoptive school."

"How will you prove illegal adoption?" Korak asked. "You can't test the DNA of everyone in the school and compare it to all the tads."

"Why not? Such tests would be conclusive. Isn't population fraud worth the trouble to prevent? Left un-enforced, the population will soon grow out of accountability, the undocumented tads would have no Replacement Certificates of their own. They would be a dysfunctional subset in elllonian society. Ellason would very quickly return to the days of overpopulation stress and vicious cycles of growth and die-off."

"It's not pretty," Stringer said. "Voluntary compliance is very difficult for some species. Are ellls on such a path?"

"Not on Varok, as you know," Haralahn said. "So far, on Ellason, the hedge–guardians are the only ones we suspect of farming tads. The frightening part may be how many schools are raising extralegal tads and believing, or wanting to believe, they are certified orphans."

Following the strongest of the four scent trails, Stringer and the great-fish swam south, then west, bypassing the Viortahk. Before the food supply of dried *eeflin* dwindled, they came upon a large school. Only then did they realize their basic mistake. They had followed the strongest scent trail to the source of the tads, not to one of their destinations. Apparently this school produced the eggs and tended to the early nursing of tailed tads. Even now the scent of newly hatched eggs was strong.

Leaving Korak behind, playing fisherman and staying hidden in the rocks, Stringer and Haralahn confirmed their guess with a quick scan of the school. They saw no tads at first, but then they passed concentrated scent that could only come from a nursery.

They worked their way through the rocky shore back the way they had come, then around to the south. After what seemed an eternity, they surfaced and rejoined Korak.

The rover's locator confirmed they were in the West Viortahk. The school was buried in the maze of small islands, and the nursery was well hidden on the shore side of an island of dark rock.

Across from the nursery, on the mainland side of the island, an accessible beach lay enclosed by an outcropping of limestone. Stringer and Haralahn waited in shallow water, while Korak pulled the skiff over the sand and weighted it down with rocks where a wide crevice opened between two huge boulders.

"Wait here, Korak," Stringer said. "Haralahn, let's look around. The strongest scent is nearby, and the school is on the other side of the island."

"Yes. We should document the nursery before we report this school to Elll Central," Haralahn said. "I'll follow behind you and keep watch."

Stringer pushed off the sand and found deep water in the channel between the dark island and the eastern shore of Nea. He moved as silently and smoothly as he could, shutting down his hexagonal meshwork and pressure sense so he put out no electo-fizz or pressure ID. It was like swimming partially blind, but the nursery scent was so strong he followed it easily.

He swam against the current until the scent disappeared, then he drifted back along the island's rocky shore. When the scent grew weaker, he backtracked again and started probing beneath overhangs and between stacked boulders that made up the sheer side of the island under water.

Haralahn swam behind him and reached into likely crevices with the prehensile tip of his long tail. "Here, Stringer," he indicated with an enclosing scoop of his lateral fins. "Duck in here. This seems to be a tunnel entrance."

"Yes," Stringer confirmed. "The scent is strong here."

"Move on in. As soon as we estimate the number of tads being hatched, we can report to Elll Central."

Stringer swam slowly into the rock tunnel and turned right into a deep cavern open to the sky far above. The walls of the cavern were cut with concave shelves and fitted with underwater heaters. Hundreds of *el* eggs sat in clutches on the shelves, rocked gently by the current that moved through the cavern. Haralahn had begun counting clutches of eggs, when Stringer whipped around and tried to stop a huge boulder moving across the entrance to the cavern.

"Jump, Stringer," Haralahn shouted. "You'll be crushed. The boulder is on a track."

As the boulder closed with a water-muffled thump, Stringer jumped back into the incubation chamber, but not in time to save six plumes caught fast in the rock door. He tried moving it back, but there was no budging it. He and Haralahn were trapped.

V. Scene of the Crime

Meaning is built into the way complex systems work. We loners believe the creative life process works at bifurcation points and within personal relations, tossing dissipative systems this way and that so anything significant can be amplified. Power laws, with their inevitable catastrophes, are the reason for tragedy. Bad luck is just that, nothing more. Enough said. Life is too short to worry about why accidents happen.

Schooling ells, however, have a slightly different religious view. They believe that their schools are symbols of all life in the universe—complex islands of connected beings isolated in time and space, vibrant with built-in meaning.

— Conn, after reading one of Shawne's books on comparative religion

An Ahlork Report

"I see Shawne. Below, with varok child," Forelock said, riding the wind above the river near the varoks' lab. "They talk talk talk. Shawne be all talk."

Nidok chastised him with a wing blow that sent the youngster into a spin dive. In retaliation, Forelock didn't pull out until he was less than twenty meters over the lab pier. He heard Nidok gasp, so he had the satisfaction of winning the bluff. He wasn't sure what he had done to deserve the cuff in the first place. Forelock couldn't figure out what Shawne's quest was supposed to do for her.

"When know why is life, live better," Nidok said. "Is called meaning."

"Charley says live so can eat," Forelock said.

"Right," Nidok answered, and the two ahlork snickered with a loud crackling sound as they landed near Shawne on the pier. TK climbed into her lap, frightened by the aliens.

"Nidok. Forelock. Thank God you're back," Shawne said. "Tahlee-Karal, this is Nidok, and this is Forelock, his eldest nestling. They are ahlork."

"And we eat crippled children for lunch," Nidok gargled.

"Good thing she doesn't understand your nasty ahlork tongue, Nidok. Where have you been? Have you seen Orram? Why didn't you come back to the lab? Where is he?"

"He swims in lake. There." He pointed to the big peninsula bordering the West Viortahk. "Orram's rotten friends snared us."

Shawne exploded with hope. "You found Orram? Nidok tell me straight. Orram is alive?"

"Of course. Why would be dead?"

"Where is he then? Why didn't you guide him back here?"

"Chained in cave. Makes rescue difficult."

"RamRam," TK whispered to Shawne. "I want RamRam."

"So do I, TK, and it looks like we'll find him very soon. Please, Nidok, fly quickly to the lab. Tell Tandra and Conn all you know."

TK's and Shawne's worry did a lot to tame Nidok's fresh tongue, but both ahlork refused to go inside the lab.

"You don't have to go inside," Shawne pleaded. "Fly to the dock and find a radio."

"Ahlork don't use radios," said Forelock.

"You do now," Shawne erupted. "Use your long talon. Push the large emergency button. Say Orram is found alive. Say you'll meet everyone on the dock at the lab river entrance. We'll follow as fast as we can."

"Bossy human female," Nidok retorted, but he flew off down the pier to the dock.

"Orram is alive!" Shawne shouted to the wind.

"Look, Shawne," TK hollered in her newly acquired Varokian. "I can run."

She struggled to move quickly and took six steps before she fell. "Wonderful, TK. You're getting much stronger. Now see if you can get up. I'll help you walk all the way back to the lab dock. We have wonderful news, so we must hurry. Take my hand."

"It tingles. Not like ellls."

"Take it anyway. If you're going to deal with humans like me, you're going to have to learn to ignore the tingles. That's what Orram does when I give him a hug."

"Okay, Shawne. It's good now. Your tingle goes away fast. I can touch ellls. I can. They taught me."

They walked slowly down the pier hand in hand, and the child kept looking up at Shawne. The hint of a smile lit her eyes.

"I love you, Shawne," she said. "I wish you were my mother."

"Mother? Where did you learn that word, TK?"

"Tandra explained it to me. She said she was your mother. Will you be my mother, Shawne?"

"Don't you want to live with the ellls any more, TK?"

"Not really. I'm tired of water. I want to walk like you. I want RamRam."

"If I became your mother, Orram would be your grandfather."

She couldn't have understood what that meant, but the full impact of the idea was very clear to her patches. "Oh yes. Please, please Shawne." She stopped as a tear ran down her cheek, and for a moment she went irrational with hope.

Shawne knelt beside her so the child's patches could easily tune into her human mind. She had never seen so young a varokian child go irrational. It scared her. Her friends on Varok had been carefully repressed, and Shawne's rare temper tantrums in her early locale school were treated with medically prescribed isolation and careful monitoring.

Breathing hard with anxiety, she carried the child and walked quickly toward the crowd gathering on the lab-side dock.

"We can't be sure of anything, TK, not yet. I am too young, maybe not fit to be a mother in some ways, but I will always be your friend. I know Tandra and Orram don't want to leave Ellason without you. Perhaps we can take you home to Varok, where you'll be strong and well. You'll go to school and run through Orserah's web fields, and you'll ride daramonts with Grandpa Conn to the Vahinorral." The reassuring words and images helped, and before they were halfway down the pier, TK's emotional attack had subsided.

Hearing their footsteps, Charley emerged from his work on a rover tied to the pier. He saw a brief smile cross the child's face, and he hurried to catch up. "What's up, TK?" Charley asked. "Your face has cracked open."

"That's a smile," TK said, with a giggle. "I can smile. I am very happy. Ramram will be my grandfa—fa—sponsor."

"Is that right?"

"And I will go to school with Shawne." TK allowed Charley to take her from Shawne. They arrived at the dock as Tandra, Jesse, Orticon, Nealla and Conn came out to make sense of what Nidok and Forelock had broadcast on the emergency horn.

The ahlork were perched on adjacent posts, preening their wing plates, preparing to hold court.

Nidok made a loud, rather rude noise to attract everyone's attention, then he began describing the strong mesh that had caught them. "It was made of metal never seen on Varok, too strong for ahlork, too strong for varoks—"

"What about Orram, you autocratic feather-brains?" Conn shouted.

"Conn, please don't start an insult game," Tandra scolded.

"Orram be little tied up right now," Nidok said.

"But he's well? He's not injured?" Tandra asked.

"Maybe he'll go coo coo *lohn* eggs and anger at yuck-green ellls," Forelock announced.

"Maybe," Tandra said. "But he's okay, so far."

"So far," Nidok agreed.

"Thank you, Nidok." Tandra was thinking fast. "You always know when I need good information. You give us all a wonderful gift, finding Orram."

"I'm also very glad you got loose, Scar Lip," Conn said, hoping to grease his fat tongue, "but you haven't said how."

"I saw blue plumes as we flew off."

"Oh migod—Lanoll!" He got Conn, good. Orram in danger was bad enough, but his mate in the middle of it made him crazy.

"And you're sure you saw Orram?" Tandra asked.

"He talked at ellls outside cave near big lake, then was hauled inside."

"Then he was not free to go with you?" Orticon asked.

"Too busy picking green elll brains."

"So where is Lanoll?"

"In the grass."

"And Killah?" Conn asked. "Was Killah with Lanoll?"

"If you say it, Conn," Nidok said. "Two ellls were in grass. We peered up their gills, then came fast to tell you about Orram. Big elll Cuffall, one with fledgling ellls, ran away from rover with Orram after crashing. Nice explosion. Loud—but no one hurt."

"You make a good point," Conn said. "The explosion was obviously a diversion. An inland lake, Nidok?"

As Conn accessed the area map on his com, Nidok pointed toward the oval body of water on Nea, set back from the rocky coast of the West Viortahk. "The question is why Cuffall wanted to kidnap Orram and take him inland to Al Neoon."

"Nidok, did you recognize any of the ellls that talked to Orram?" Jesse asked.

"No."

"Was Cuffall there?"

"No. Big ellls. Carry iron."

"You mean tools?" Nealla asked.

"Not nice metal," Nidok said. "Ellls wear shells on neck."

"Hedge–guardians?" Nealla was frightened. "Why didn't you say so before? Those are the ellls I saw when Stringer disappeared. There is only one school of hedge–guardian ellls in the Great Basin. They herd *eeflin* in the northern ranges of our Rocky Deeps Ranch."

"So there is a connection between Stringer and Orram's disappearances," Tandra said.

"Slow down, Tan," Conn said. "Stringer is off in the Far Deeps with the great-fish. I don't see any connection."

"Let's not waste time," Tandra said. "We've got to get out to Al

Neoon and find Orram before we do anything else." She looked back toward the lab and took in a sharp breath through her teeth. "Here comes TK's elll."

"I will take Tahlee-Karal now," Talln said, reaching for the child. "She must sleep." She peeled TK off Charley's torso, and ran for the entrance as if the big human would pursue her.

Shawne wanted to run after her, and so did Tandra, but Conn stopped them. "We'll settle TK's future at first meal," he said.

"She could be my replacement on Varok, Conn," Shawne announced. The words came from somewhere she couldn't define, but she knew they were true to the moment.

"Charley?" Shawne beckoned for him to join the family. "I'll need you more than ever now, and TK has already bonded with you. Please say you're in."

He looked at Conn. "I can't say yet, Shawne," the human said. "I don't know what I should do."

Teaming Up

Shawne awoke early, eager to set off and find Orram. There was no thought in her head suggesting that the venture might be dangerous. Ellls didn't do violence. They would negotiate and release Orram once their grievances were understood.

She went to the pool, expecting to find Talln there with TK. She wanted to say goodbye and reassure TK that she wouldn't be gone long. She planned to tell Talln that her family would take her to Varok and provide her a Replacement Certificate. It was an offer Talln's school couldn't refuse. They could not educate her in varokian ways. They could not allow her health to deteriorate any further.

When Talln and TK didn't appear at the pool, Shawne went to the dining area, where she found Tandra, Charley and Conn ready to go look for Orram. Artellian, Nealla, Tamilan, Jesse, and Orticon were also gathered there to help solidify the plans.

"I must find TK before we leave, Mom. I have to tell her we'll soon be back for her. Conn, what's the matter? Mom?"

"We're not sure her school will agree to let her go, Shawnoon," Conn said.

"They have to. She's not doing well with them. I've already taught her some Varokian. It's easy for her. She knows where she belongs now. And she loves Orram so much. She asks for him all the time." Shawne didn't wait to hear the others' comments. She picked up an intralab phone and initiated a search for TK.

TK and Talln were not in their sleeping chamber. A call was put out for the elll. Security cameras were used to scan the entire area. Talln and TK could not be found.

"Talln must have taken TK back to her school," Tandra said.

"I've got to hurry," Shawne said. "I've got to plead my case to TK's school before they leave Varok's Bay."

"I'll go with you," Tamilan said. He had actually left his work to bid Shawne good luck in finding Orram.

Orticon didn't hesitate. "As will I," he said. "You can't go out there alone." The comment was not lost on anyone, except Tamilan.

"This is my home," Nealla said. "You'll need an elll to help you negotiate with the school. Then I'll go back to the ranch and wait for Stringer to come home."

Jesse put a hand on Shawne's arm. "I'll go with you, too. We'll take one of the lab rovers. If we leave now, we might be able to overtake Talln. She will be swimming slowly with TK on her back."

"Thanks, Jesse."

Charley looked uncomfortable. "Do you need me, Shawne?"

"No. No. You must go with Mom."

"I'm also going with Tandra," Conn said. "I wish I didn't have to make a choice, but I must go after Orram, Shawne."

"It's okay, Conn. I know that."

They all trooped out to the mud flats, where two rovers were soon packed and ready. Tandra and Conn watched Shawne head out with Jesse, Nealla, Tamilan and Orticon—two humans, an elll, and two varoks. Shawne would be safe, and she would probably be safe from herself. They thought she was taking Haralahn's anti-inflammatory without objection.

Nidok and Forelock flew overhead as their rover cut a wake into Varok's Bay, then they returned to lead Conn and Tandra to Al Neoon.

Artellian stood on the mud flats by the lab watching his friends disappear, and a flood of thoughts, mostly fears, ran through his mind. He couldn't believe Oleyall's story about Stringer going to the Far Deeps. Why would he? He didn't like the coincidental sighting of hedge–guardians. He feared for Orram's safety. And what of Shawne's dream of Ellason? With her magic world tarnished and her family in grave danger, how could she glean anything for her quest? She had not had much time with Haralahn, the focus of all her questions. Her trip to the great-fish caves had been cut short by Stringer's disappearance, and now, with Orram in jeopardy, her trip may come to an abrupt and tragic end.

He turned back to the lab and spent the next several light-cycles on the bottom of the pool.

He was awakened by an elllonian engineer saying he had an urgent call from Korak. Lab personnel had told the young varok that Shawne had gone to the West Viortahk to find Talln and TK and that Tandra and Conn had gone to find Orram.

"No. Tell them don't go there," Korak insisted, when Artellian got to the transmitter, "and Shawne must not come here to the West Viortahk. Cuffall's—that is, TK's—school may be dangerous. Stringer and Haralahn followed a strong scent of tads here from Stringer's Rocky Deeps Ranch. I think they have found an illegal nursery. I can't find them. I need help. I am being hunted. There are varoks involved."

The radiophone went dead. Artellian tried and failed to re-connect with Korak, so he immediately called Elll Central.

"We have also heard from Korak," they assured Artellian. "We are sending an armed school of defenders to the West Viortahk."

When Artellian told them a team from Varok had gone to release Orram at Al Neoon, Elll Central promised to send another emergency backup team to that lake.

As he shut down the radio and retreated to the bottom of the pool, Artellian felt overwhelmed. Things were moving too fast. The potential for real damage was too large. Where was the peace Ellason promised, peace for his final days? He had left a good life on Varok for what? Not for radio messages in the middle of sleep, telling him his life-long friends were in jeopardy.

Sleep was impossible. The old elll swam along the canal connecting the pool with the river and emerged onto the mud flats far from the lab. Here was nothing but earth and mist and the warm glow of Ellason's moons doing their complicated dance through the star-sprinkled darkness of shrouded space.

No clues out here, he thought, *no clues to guide Shawne home to a faith that would shield her through the tragic accidents of life.*

With a sigh that collapsed his lungs, he re-entered the water. He had to laugh at himself. He was playing out his own quest for peace in parallel with hers. He had traveled to Ellason for a quiet conclusion, when it already existed on Varok, and Shawne was looking outside herself for answers that also lay much closer to home.

LANOLL, KILLAH AND THE AHLORK

"The lake is very quiet, Killah," Lanoll said. "Do you think we can risk a scan?" She sat in tall rushes three meters below the surface of lake Al Neoon.

Tandra's elllonian medical colleague suffered from a touch of hypochondria. "We have to. I'm starving to death."

"Then here I go, Killah, up just a bit. I'll be very still. Three scans. That's all." Lanoll pushed off and stopped herself from rinsing the mud from her plumes, then she sent three ultrasonic probes into the long axis of the lake. Nothing resembling ellls or elll tads showed in her scans. "I'm going to risk finding some breakfast," she said.

Killah swam out to join her. "Not without me, young lady."

She laughed, relaxing a bit, and they enjoyed a large meal of fresh water mudworts and a succulent grass they had never seen before.

"I still don't see anything on scan, Lanoll. Shall we try to catch one of those big fish out there?"

"No. I've had enough. Let's swim to the thick reeds on the eastern shore and take a look at the caves."

"Scan as you go, Lanoll. And be sure to shut down if you get any kind of input. I'll be right beside you doing the same."

They moved slowly, using their webbed hands and feet more like rudders than paddles, leaving very little trace through the water. On the south end of the lake the rock bottom discouraged the lush vegetation. They measured visibility in *pallons* through the clear water.

"Let's make a dash for the reeds, Killah," Lanoll whispered in Sonics. "I'm afraid we can be seen from the caves. This water is too clear."

"Go," he said.

As they surfaced in the reeds, they heard the distinct croak of an ahlork voice.

"Was that Nidok?" Lanoll whispered.

In the air above, the ahlork had flown ahead to do some aerial reconnaissance for Tandra, Charley, and Conn, as they trudged toward Al Neoon by the easiest overland route.

– Δ –

"Elllonian heroes down there, Forelock," Nidok said, "sneaking around lake. They don't know caves are empty. We'll make fun."

Forelock was nervous. "How do you know caves are empty? Maybe Orram chained there—dead, starved, something more disgusting."

"So, go look. I'll wait up here, after I give reeds a shake."

Foolishly, Forelock did as he was told. They had made so much clacking noise approaching the lake, any varok would know immediately that ahlork were nearby.

While his nestling was prowling around the caves, Nidok climbed to two thousand meters and made a beautiful spiraling glide down over the lake. Conn and the humans could see him from the rover, for they were moving slowly along the rough terrain near the top of the hills east of the lake.

As they came down the slopes into the lake's basin, Forelock reported to them that the manufactured caves overlooking the eastern shore were empty. Then he circled high. Meanwhile Nidok made a silent pass over the tall shore reeds and cut loose with a rasping sound, not unlike the shriek of a dying *lohn* bird. He saw a sudden movement in the reeds. Two ellls, one thin and one round, flashed quickly across the lake with racing leaps and disappeared to the north end, where a few stubby *ahl* trees struggled to survive.

On a noisy glide, the ahlork followed Lanoll and Killah, while Tandra, Charley and Conn moved cautiously through the caves. Nidok was right. They found little but some equipment and the reed ropes that had bound Orram. The caves were deserted.

"Better radio the lab team, Conn," Charley said. "Tell them to turn back or check with Elll Central. Orram was held here. That's obvious."

When the call was made, Tandra and Conn cooled off with a leisurely swim toward Lanoll and Killah, making lots of noise and pressure patterns so the ellls would recognize them. Nidok was coming in to make another noise attack, but the ellls thwarted his scheme by calling out an ahlork alert in ultrasonics. Lanoll and Killah emerged from the *ahl* trees just in time to make a lunging catch at Nidok's feet. With a wild clacking and splashing, they pulled him into the water for the good dunking he deserved.

"How long were you skulking about in the lake, Killah?" Tandra asked.

"I don't skulk," Killah said. "Did you skulk, Lanoll?"

"Ellls don't skulk," she said.

Conn was eager to plot their next move when they joined Charley at the caves. He had been busy documenting and collecting evidence.

"It's obvious there was some kind of operation set up here," he said. "There was communication equipment, and a store of dried food and wet-sweaters, enough for thirty or forty ellls. I also found a well-worn rover track leading southeast."

"Toward the West Viortahk," Conn said. "Let's follow it. It's the only lead we have."

Tandra touched Nidok's lip affectionately. "You miserable clowns have been invaluable. If we are able to save Orram, it will be because of you. Once again—"

"I know. I know, Dark Lady," Nidok mocked. "Fly, fly, please, fair ahlork, over West Viortahk once more. May big droppings find yucky lime-green plumes of Cuffall. Save my love, Orram—"

"Get out of here, you clatter-plated tease," Conn shouted at him, raising a long reed in his hand. Its chewed end drooped disgustingly, making his point. "Follow the rover track southeast. We'll be right behind you."

"Meet us on shore," Tandra suggested with a shaky voice, "above the hidden beach in the West Viortahk, where we first met Cuffall's school with TK. It's a long shot, but we might find Talln with TK there, also."

"You're right, Sherlock," Conn said, trying to calm Tandra. "It's a place we should check out."

The West Viortahk

Jesse and Orticon, Tamilan, Nealla and Shawne ran the rover across the upper arm of Varok's Bay looking for the ellls and their varokian child. Tamilan sensed the distress Shawne felt. Her thoughts rattled on and on, bouncing around her head with painful imaginings.

Would Conn and Tandra find Orram? Would Cuffall release him? Where was Stringer now? Why did Korak shut me out? He's too proud. Too sensitive. Too much of a perfectionist. He wouldn't listen to me when I tried to show him I cared. Why? What did I do wrong?

Tamilan's patches were bursting with Shawne's pain, but he didn't know what to do with it.

She felt like screaming. *Talk to me! Touch me. Open your mind to me.*

It didn't happen, and the water moved past ever more swiftly.

Orticon drove the rover as if he were on automatic. He didn't dare think about what was happening to his father. *Did I make a mistake coming out here to the West Viortahk, encouraging my human sister to confront the ellls about TK?*

The human Jesse Mendleton was stoic as always. He thought about trying to pry Tamilan out of Shawne's mind, but he told Conn later he didn't want to interfere. He believed Shawne would make a good choice, if she needed a varokian soul-mate, if she made any choice at all. In his opinion, Tandra and Orram were a unique phenomenon. Humans and varoks were made out of different tissue; most of them were not likely to get along as intimate partners.

Jesse was relieved when Stringer's friend Nealla moved in to rescue Shawne from the workaholic varokian kid. She wanted to talk about Shawne's love for TK.

"How did you get to know the child so fast?" Nealla asked. "She adored you from the first, as if you could be her mother."

At first Shawne thought the question strange. Ellls didn't know their parents. Very deliberately, ellls chose an egg to incubate, they decided where it would be nursed, and they committed to sponsor the tad in the school until it lost its tail and grew legs. The relationship sealed the tad to the school. It was like adoptive parenting, certainly just as committed.

"TK and I just clicked," Shawne said, making the pun in Sonics. "So, Nealla, how do you ellls know when you want to use your Replacement Certificate and choose an egg to incubate?"

"Maybe that's why I'm asking."

"I think, at least for us humans, mothering is a deeply ingrained longing. When your child is gone, a piece of you is missing," Shawne said.

"That's what I thought when I saw you with TK. I wanted a tad to sponsor—but I wanted my egg to be fertilized by Stringer. Like Conn and Lanoll. They mated in order to produce Stringer, didn't they?"

"Yes, Nealla, but they were both loners." Shawne took the ell's hands, and they sat close together on the stern bench. "Stringer is a schooling ell. Surely you know that."

"He worked the parasite barrier alone—and with me, alone. Maybe he has more loner genes than you realize."

"He is also from Varok. You're from Ellason. Ellls here are different. Tamilan has been cross-checking recent drifts in the four populations of ellls—loners and schoolers on Ellason and on Varok. There are distinctions—"

"That's not possible," Nealla said. "An elll is an elll, wherever, and however he or she lives."

Shawne didn't want to argue the point. The potential for pain was too great, as were the uncertainties, but the ell said something more. "It's like you and me, Shawne—we both love Stringer in our own ways."

"Of course." Something opened up for Shawne in that moment, and its healing power was almost palpable. "And that's what counts, isn't it, Nealla?"

The elll and the human locked arms and looked out over the Ellasonian sea. "Look, Nealla, aren't those the rocks of the West Viortahk?"

Giant black monoliths stood in the sea surrounded by smaller, jagged cast-offs.

Orticon cut the motors and eased the hovering rover back onto the water's surface, where the propeller engaged and pushed them slowly into the maze of rock. When no school surfaced to greet them, Nealla and Shawne slipped into the water.

"The rover's infrared detection is no good in here where rocks get in the way more often than not," Orticon called to them. "We'll follow you."

Nealla and Shawne swam toward the mainland through a stand of single rock islands that loomed tall and dark all around, shutting out much of the moons' warm glow. Only one moon loomed bright, free of its misty veil.

Shawne kept her eyes on the surface, while Nealla scanned underwater. Vegetation was sparse. Here and there mats of moss draped over rock, or a tough vine wound its way in and out of the clefts between rocks. Nothing stirred in the outer channels, but as they approached the mainland Nealla picked up a scent she didn't like.

The elll surfaced so she and Shawne could talk in Elllonian as they swam, heads out of water, using lungs, checking the rover, the rocks, the dark water's surface.

"A small variety of *eefl* has been in these waters recently," Nealla said.

The idea spooked Shawne even more than the unnatural quiet. *Eefl* were vicious predators. A small *eefl* could be the size of a human, with a prehensile tail twice as long, designed to strangle its prey. Its jawless face could swallow prey even larger. It could swallow ellls.

"I'll dash back to the rover and see if Orticon is scanning for infrared signals," Nealla said. "Any *eefl* prowling around should show. They're not entirely cold-blooded, you know. They're some kind of intermediate form."

When Nealla disappeared, Shawne, alone in the water, felt very vulnerable—very mortal. It didn't matter that Nealla would be scanning underwater on her way to the rover. She would sound a loud warning if she saw the hint of an *eefl*. In those few moments Shawne knew she would be alone some day. She could not take Conn's comforting elllonian plumes with her, not Tandra's loving arms, not Orram's rare smile. She would have to die alone, as all creatures do, if an *eefl* ate her.

The thought gave her quest renewed urgency. Why were there creatures like *eefl* that killed other creatures? She knew Conn's answer—what has to be has to be, for life to emerge out of simple chemistry, for chemistry to move along the edge of chaos to higher energy levels, to stay flexible enough to evolve toward meaningful consciousness.

Consciousness, she thought to herself, *the ability to choose not to kill unless survival demands the killing act. I didn't kill when I chose not to have a baby.* "Potential life is not conscious life, like TK's," she shouted to the wind.

"Of course, Shawne." It was Korak, swimming toward her.

She looked into Korak's eyes and laughed. "Where'd you come from?"

"The cliffs, watching for signs of Orram. Then I saw you, didn't like your being alone out here. I heard your grief. It's grief you feel for Earth, isn't it?"

"And for all the answers I haven't found—except the one you have shown by coming to me. Korak, all these religions I've been studying are like different paths to the one simple truth that life is a gift—" Her words ended and her mind filled, searching for his. *Don't leave me alone, Korak.*

I won't, for partners in mind are a gift not to be ignored.

She felt his thoughts as clearly as if he had spoken the words, and she answered in kind. *And the gift of thought-sharing is not to be ignored by humans who want to understand more about it—*

And what it means to both of us.

Korak took Shawne's hands in his and spoke aloud, using the little English he had studied. "I love you, Shawne. Please share life with me, as well as thought."

Shawne smiled, sensing his commitment—the questions it asked, the losses it would require, and the joys it promised.

"Thank you for those precious words, Korak," she said, and their mind-link slipped easily back into place.

I understand that you have forgiven yourself. Is that right, Korak?

Yes, I guess it is. He laughed and spoke. "My mistake was in timing or in leaving too much to Tamilan."

Shawne nodded with enthusiasm that made him laugh again. "It was hardly a mistake at all, and it certainly wasn't negligence."

"I am concerned for Orram, Shawne, so I had better get back to the cliffs. Soon we will have time together. Nealla is coming. Be careful. There are signs of *eeflin* and perhaps *eefl* in these shallows."

Shawne watched him swim to the beach as Nealla appeared, her green moss tiles flashing the golden light of six moons. Together they swam past the nursery, where the elll caught the scent of tads.

Soon Orticon's rover picked them up. "We've found a strange rover carefully stashed between the rocks, well above the tide line."

"It's probably from Elll Central," Shawne said. "We can tell from the ID plate on the control panel. Korak came out here and got separated from Haralahn."

"Something is bothering you, Nealla," Orticon said. "Please excuse my intrusion, but I think we need to stay alert to every clue. Will you let me follow your question?"

"It's no longer a silly question, Orticon," she said. "We have thought Stringer was in the Far Deeps with great-fish, but I thought I caught Stringer's scent in the water. In fact, I know I did. It was mixed with the scent of great-fish."

"Would you mind retracing your path to see if you can locate the source, Nealla?" Orticon asked. "It might be nothing, but some ellls must be tending the nursery you detected."

"There was no distinct trace of a school on the way here, Orticon, just the hint of Stringer. Wait here. I won't be long."

She swam off at top elllonian speed, no human to slow her down, then she doubled back several times until she was sure that the great-fish scent, and sometimes Stringer's, were strongest where the nursery scent peaked. Nothing else moved in the water, nothing pulsed, nothing zapped. She spoke Stringer's name quietly in Sonics, then louder, then blasted off an ultrasonic emergency call that rattled the rocks.

That did it. The call woke Stringer and put Haralahn on alert. They had not suffered, for many of the fertile *el* eggs on the shelves were not far enough along to give pause to their gustatory needs.

"Nealla, is that you?" Stringer clicked in Sonics.

"Stringer? Where are you? What are you doing here?"

"I'm shut in an incubator chamber with Haralahn the great-fish. Look for a hidden tunnel under an overhang about one *pallon* below the surface. We're in the incubator chamber off to the right, before the tunnel turns upward. This chamber is sealed with a mechanical device, a boulder hung on a track, but it might be accessible from up top. We can see light above. Who is with you?"

"Orticon, Jesse, Shawne, and Tamilan."

"Good. They can rig something from above to get us out of here. Get back to them quickly. Don't get caught wandering around alone. This school must be mad. It's selling tads illegally, Nealla. The hedge–guardians kidnapped me from the northern parasite barrier. They're dangerous."

"We're looking for a varokian child. She disappeared from the lab with Talln, a female from Cuffall's school."

"Who?"

"Never mind. Orram is also missing, Stringer. We think he's at Al Neoon."

"Indeed!" Haralahn exclaimed. "Go from here, Nealla, quickly. If the school is anywhere nearby in water, they will have heard us. They haven't come around for some time. The eggs here are fine, but the tads in the nursery need attention soon."

A sound of distress seemed to come from the entrapped great-fish. "Go quickly. Your life is far more valuable," he voiced with difficulty in Elllonian.

Nealla grew afraid for him. "I'll be back soon. The others are at the Elll Central rover."

"Rover? From Elll Central? It may be Korak's. Is he okay? We got separated."

"You were with the varok? Shawne has seen Korak."

"Good. Tell Shawne. Stay with Korak. Go quickly Nealla."

"I'm gone," she said, and she fled.

Tamilan on the Beach

"I see two rovers on small sands," Forelock said.

"I see also ugly bipeds, and Shawne lovely. We land there, then fly over and find Orram." Nidok dropped like a cork over the small island near the hidden beach.

Always confident, Nidok. He had no doubts about his effectiveness. True, he could stay in the air longer than ellls could swim without surfacing. His eyesight was designed for hunting small animals in deep grass and tiny flyers in the air. He also had some kind of sonar vision, like a bat.

When the ahlork landed, Shawne nearly cried with relief.

"Look at human eyes," Nidok said to Orticon, "how they leak. Is she sad, seeing us?"

"Stop it, Nidok," Shawne snapped. "I'm worried about Nealla. Please fly over the channel between the mainland and the big island just to the east. She should be swimming back by now. Make a lot of noise. She'll know it's you, and she'll surface so you can escort her here."

"Have seen Orram?" the ahlork asked.

"Of course not, Nidok. You said he was at Al Neoon."

"No more," the ahlork croaked. "Everyone is coming here to look."

"We've seen nothing," Shawne said. "No ellls, no TK, nothing—but Nealla is checking out a hint, a water scent of Stringer and a great-fish. Also, Korak came here in this second rover."

"I'll find Nealla," Nidok volunteered. "Forelock looks for strangers. Fly low grid over miserable rocks, Forelock. Come back when found someone." Forelock took off with a clatter of wing plates and was soon lost to view.

Shawne looked to Nidok, then Orticon.

"I saw something go by in Nidok's memory, Shawne," Orticon said. "Why do you think Orram is here, Nidok?"

"Caves empty at Al Neoon," Nidok said. "We found Lanoll and Killah in lake. They now follow rover trail to here."

Orticon looked uneasy, and his eyes kept darting to the rover.

"Go, Orticon," Shawne said. "You and Jesse take the rover. Korak is searching for Orram and watching on land. There's no need for you to wait here. The more people searching the better. Tamilan and I can handle any ellls that come along. Nidok will look for Nealla."

"I go now," Nidok said, and he flew off.

"Assume nothing, Shawne," Jesse said. "Trust no one outside the team. We don't know the ellls here. Carry your hunting blade. Promise."

"I promise," Shawne said, and she gave the old human friend an open smile. He knew her well. "I won't do anything heroic."

Jesse and Orticon began what became an intensive search of every island, cove, inlet and channel in the entire West Viortahk.

While waiting for Nidok to return with news of Nealla, Shawne had a chance to catch up with Tamilan. She did far more listening than talking. She learned all about how elllonian loners were different than schoolers, not just in behavior patterns, but in fundamental organic needs. Elll Central was working on a new directive to help defuse the tension.

On Varok, loner ellls gravitated toward Varokian institutions, like Orram's Office of Living Resources or the Concentrate. To the contrary, on Ellason, ellls were gravitating away from institutions that had a varokian influence, like the EV Lab. Elll Central was more like a superschool, a town hall/university hybrid. No such affiliation of elllonian schools had happened on Varok. Tamilan had developed a working hypothesis of elllonian speciation that disturbed Shawne, but his evidence couldn't be denied.

"You believe ellls are rapidly evolving into four different species?"

"It's obvious," Tamilan said. "In six more generations, no ellls from Varok will produce offspring with ellls from Ellason. Likewise, loners will not be fertile with schoolers on either planet."

"It can't happen that fast, Tamilan."

"Of course it can. Conditions are accelerating the change, self-organizing and driving natural selection. We've seen it happen time after time in populations of bacteria and flying creatures. Environmental conditions can snowball and shift a species' equilibrium right out from under the cultural memory. Accelerated evolution, static equilibrium, reversed trends, cases of spring-trap masking—evolution wears many hats, Shawne."

"I just don't like to hear what you're saying about ellls."

"But it's quite fascinating. It's rare to observe such rapid change in an encultured species."

"I can't stand to think about it right now," Shawne erupted. *Why doesn't he read my mood?* "I want Nealla and Nidok to return. I want to know if Orram is here somewhere. I've seen Korak. He's here, looking for Orram. Keep gathering your damn evidence, Tamilan. No one will want to hear it, and a thousand other elllologists will try to prove you wrong. Until the last Varokian elll fails to produce fertile eggs with the last Ellasonian female, your conclusions will be tentative. If you're not careful, you'll be choosing only the data that supports your theory. You have to look at the ellls' similarities, not just their differences."

"The fertility test is a good indicator." He didn't let his patches get ruffled as her diatribe blew past.

"Then you need a theory to explain your test results."

"DNA surveys can verify the theory I am already formulating. I am advising Elll Central to define very clear rights for all ellls, regardless of their orientation."

"Then—and only then—should you stick your neck out to make hurtful predictions. Sit on it, Tamilan, especially now, when someone is missing. Don't you dare mention your theory to Nealla. Look at her and Stringer. It's obvious she loves him. I bet she'll adjust to whatever life style he chooses in order to be near him. I think they have already shot down your 'Basic Needs Are Different' hypothesis."

"But most of the evidence will weigh in for a rapid splitting into four species," Tamilan said, totally out of touch with what Shawne was trying to say. "It's no tragedy."

"It's no tragedy for you," she said. "You don't care if Nealla and Stringer can't have tads."

"You can't deny the evidence, Shawne. Species change. It's no different on Earth. Humans are certainly changing, and they are still very young—only a few hundred-thousand Earth years old. Ninety-nine percent of all species that have ever lived on Earth are now extinct. Most don't last more than a million. The simplest life, like bacteria, last the longest. Ellls are splitting into two or more different species. I'm sure of it, Shawne."

"I know. I'm sorry. I know you don't do your work blind. Whatever. Whatever." *Would he never get off it? Does nothing count but his precious work? Maybe light hoppers have it right*, she thought. "The light-hoppers say that mysticism penetrates more deeply than fact, Tamilan. It deals better with our worst fears and loveliest dreams. It builds soul."

"They may have a point. But myths that inspire must not be in conflict with scientific conclusions. You may end up in conflict with yourself. Certainly it is essential to distinguish where science leaves off and religion begins, but I would still argue that scientific interpretations are the best guide to developing a set of beliefs."

"No way, Tamilan. Inspiration from scientific information, but not interpretation. Science always stays open to question, subject to new information, or it is not good science."

"I won't argue with that, Shawne."

Shawne sat on her tongue. Then Tamilan surprised her by asking how she felt. "I haven't seen you enough to know if the anti-inflammatory drugs the great-fish gave you have helped."

"Thanks for asking. I guess they might have helped. I can enjoy some things now, in spite of all this worry about TK and Orram."

He took her hand in his, assuming she wanted him to. Orram would have told him to use his patches to read her mind first, but at least it surprised and pleased her.

"I know what you have been trying to tell me, Shawne," he said. "I won't draw any unwarranted conclusions from my work."

Shawne smiled her thanks. "Whatever works for you."

Time was passing. No one had appeared. "Where is everyone? I can't stand this waiting, Tamilan. Nealla!" Shawne screamed as loud as she could, and, almost at once, Nidok dropped out of the mist.

"Shut your lungs, Shawne," he scolded, wrapping a prehensile wing tip around her wrist. "You ruin plans. We found Stringer, trapped. He's in water hole with great-fish. Get some rope. We see ellls, hedge ellls. Stringer says they be bad trouble."

LONG ROPE AND SHORT TEMPERS

Nidok carried the rope, and Shawne swam across the channel to the large island where Nealla had picked up Stringer's scent. Nidok guided her accurately to the overhang that hid the tunnel entrance far below. There Shawne found Nealla waiting quietly deep in the water.

When she sensed Shawne's pressure silhouette, Nealla surfaced and whispered to her in Varokian. "I have found a way up to the rocks near the blow hole that opens into the cave where Stringer and Haralahn are trapped. Where is the rope?"

"Haralahn? Here with Stringer?"

"He'll explain later. They never went to the Far Deeps. We think TK's school is nearby, just a few rocks south. Let's get out of the water so they won't find us. We've got to get Stringer and Haralahn out of here before we stir up the school."

Shawne boosted Nealla out of the water, then pulled herself onto a flat rock where they could both look over the rocks above.

"Over here, ladies," Nidok gurgled, his version of a whisper. He stood on a boulder meters above their heads. A sizeable cleft rose through the cliff and opened at his feet. "Shinny up," he said.

"What?" Nealla had never heard the word before. "Shinny?"

"Conn did it once. Humans do all the time. Shinny. Shinny. Hurry up." The ahlork didn't realize what he was asking. Nealla, at least, was no rock climber.

"I think Nidok means we can brace against the sides of the narrow gap and work our way up," Shawne said. "I hope you have tough sandals."

"The best moss this side of Ellason." Nealla was like an excited schoolgirl at a prom, glowing with the chance to save Stringer. She didn't use her brain, just her hormones. Good thing her toe-fins clung well to rock.

They managed to climb the chimney and pull themselves up to Nidok, but, when they stood up over the blow hole to tie the rope around a large rock, they spotted a school of ellls entering a wide beach two islands to the east.

Shawne whispered down the hole. "Stringer, the rope is secure. Can you pull yourself up? Hurry."

"Shawne, they've seen us," Nealla said. "Some of the ellls are coming this way."

"Hurry, Stringer," Shawne called. "Nidok, go do something to keep the ellls busy."

"My pleasure." He gargled and took off.

Stringer's arms were as powerful as any elll's. Climbing the rope was no problem, except for his finger and toe fins, which took a beating on the rope.

When he got to the top, Shawne and Nealla smothered him with hugs and showered him with tears, then they panicked. "How do we get Haralahn out of there, Stringer? He's huge."

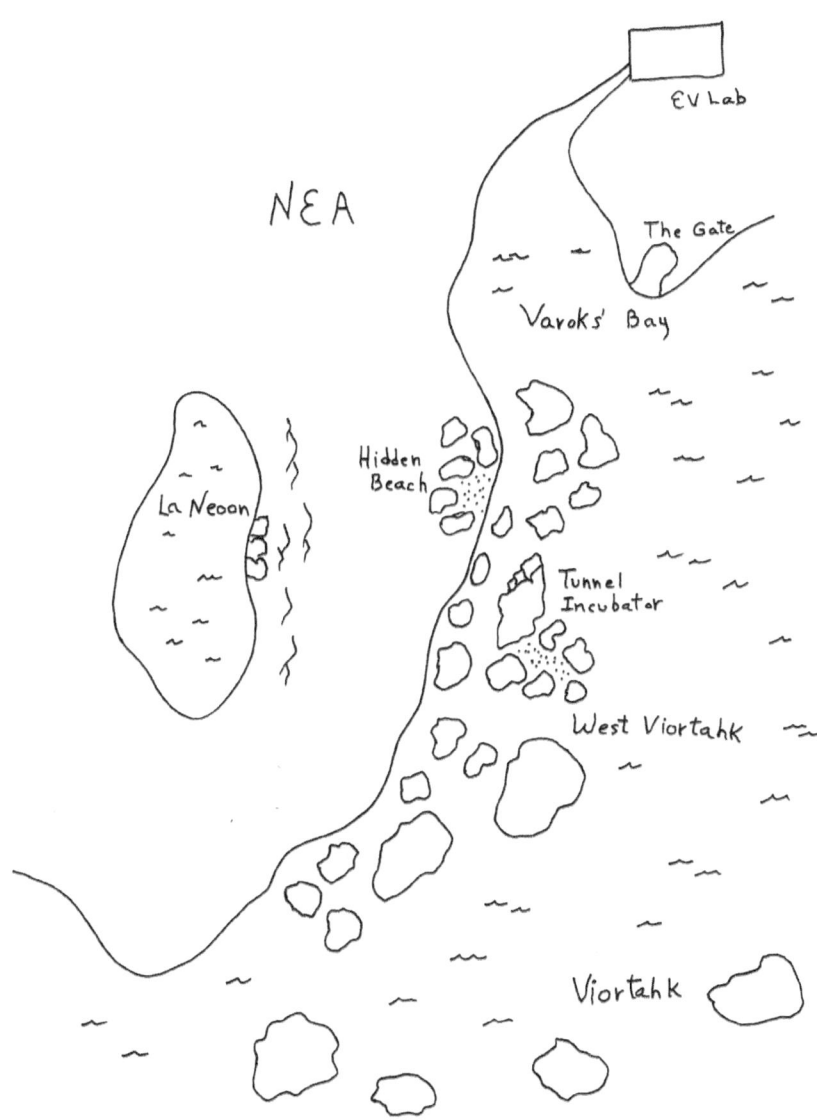

NEA

EV Lab

The Gate

Varoks' Bay

Hidden
Beach

La Neoon

Tunnel
Incubator

West Viortahk

Viortahk

"Show me the way down, my lovelies," Stringer smiled. "The master mechanic will open the boulder door. We can't pull Haralahn up here. Great-fish don't have lungs, you know."

"I feel so stupid," Nealla said. "I should have looked for the boulder mechanism when I first found you."

"We were just being cautious," Stringer said, kindly. "I still don't think the lock is accessible, to tell you the truth. The school doesn't want the incubator found. There are hundreds of fertile eggs in there—far more than would replace Cuffall's school and the hedge-guardians combined."

"We've got to get it open, Stringer," Shawne said. "We can't leave Haralahn in there."

"We might have to, for a while. He's got plenty to eat, and the water circulation is adequate from cracks in the rock, but let's give it a try."

They had just started down the rock chimney when three varoks appeared on top of the island thirty meters away.

"Dive," Nealla commanded, and the three jumped off the cliff feet first, preferring to break legs instead of heads, if something went wrong with their aim.

The jumps were successful. At least they hit deep water. They were soon at the overhang and into the tunnel. A quick search showed them nothing but a lever locked firmly in place with a code they couldn't break.

"Go," Haralahn insisted from inside the incubator. "I will survive here. I believe Nidok will lose the scuffle he started. You'd better find him first, then tend to Orram. Come back for the evidence here and for me when you have apprehended the two schools responsible for this horror. I can hear distress calls from the nursery. It has been left untended too long."

They swam as hard as they could toward the horrible sounds Nidok was making. They found him in a narrow channel between islands leading to a wide shallow bay, slashing away at ellls trying to hold him.

Shawne hooted to him, using the greeting they used whenever Nidok appeared over the fields at home on Varok. He struggled even harder, cutting elll flesh indiscriminately, until tempers flared out of control and a furious grab for his flailing right wing snapped it.

Pain roared through the ahlork's brain, and the terrible sound he made sent the school of ellls into flight. Mercifully, he lost consciousness.

When Stringer and Nealla reached his flaccid body bobbing like a cork on the water, they thought he was dead.

"Nidok!" Shawne screamed. She took his body from Stringer's arms and felt the ridge between his eyes for the rhythmic pressure of his circulation. "He's alive," she cried, and she bathed his thick neck. "But look at his plates. The joints are thick with moss. He's been away too long. He hasn't had enough of Killah's treatment. No wonder he couldn't defend himself."

Soon the hated cold water roused him, but Nealla whispered, "Play dead, ahlork. With your pain, the ellls' tempers are gone. Maybe we can take advantage of their empathic mood."

Stringer raced off. He soon caught up with Cuffall's school and stopped it with a sonar reprimand. "Is this how ellls are made on Ellason?" he voiced angrily. As he sped around the school, they hung quiet in the channel waters, their life-joy destroyed by the violence they had done. Nearby, a shallow bay roiled and sparkled with the electro-fizz of thirty new-legs, tads nearly ready for sale on the black market.

"Is this the example you set for your tads, disrespect for laws that protect their future? Leaving me to die on an *ahl* tree? And now violence? Who are you? You are not my cousins. My roots on Ellason have sprouted violent creatures I don't recognize. Surely you don't call yourselves ellls."

While Stringer kept the school busy trying to adjust to what they had done, Nealla stayed with Nidok. Shawne cruised near shore, hoping to spot TK. From the tide pools at one end of the beach, the child saw Shawne and struggled into the shallows. "Cuffall, look. It's Shawne," she hollered.

Cuffall swam in toward TK, but Talln was nearby on land. She caught the child, put her on her shoulders, and swam toward the school, hoping to lose Shawne in deeper water. She didn't reckon with Shawne's lifetime experience playing chase with Stringer. The elll was surprised when the human caught up with her and TK before they reached the distressed school.

Shawne dove for the elll's broad feet and stopped her with a painful grip to her widest toe fin. Talln was helpless, trying to keep the child above water. Her angry calls soon brought several females from the school. They interlaced arms and legs, making a raft for the child, and TK climbed on top of their backs so she could see Shawne better.

"You swim good, Shawne," TK said. "Take me on your shoulders."

"Of course, TK. Climb on my back. It's time to take you home to Varok."

"I quite agree, Shawne," Cuffall said, cruising around the elllonian raft.

"No," shouted Talln.

Before Cuffall could help Shawne with the child, Talln and the raft of ellls closed around TK, and, swimming as one, carried her toward the shallows.

"Later then, we will work together?" Cuffall asked Shawne.

"Where is Orram, *kaehl din*?" she raged. "Tell me that, if you want to work with us."

He said nothing, but swam quickly back to the school and disappeared.

Shawne, feeling utterly helpless, was about to swim to Nealla and help her with Nidok, when she saw four varoks moving away from shore into the rocks. One was Orram. She was sure. She knew his stance, his walk and the silver sheen of his hair.

She called, but the varoks disappeared. There was nothing she could do but make careful note of the landmarks on shore.

FORELOCK AND THE VAROKS

Soon after Stringer and Haralahn had left the young varok Korak on the small beach with his rover, he had realized he was being watched. During a short time of heavy mist, he had moved out of sight into the rocks. Since then, he had been eluding the hedge-guardians and some unknown varoks who were hunting him. He had retreated toward the water.

When he saw Nealla leaving Shawne, he joined her, and felt renewed hope at reconnecting with her. Then he climbed onto an outlook over the shallows to the north, and watched over her as best he could. He saw Cuffall's school struggle with Nidok. When he saw that Shawne, Stringer, and a lovely young elll were able to float the ahlork safely away, he continued his watch over Orram. Three varoks had disappeared with him into the rocks. Korak noted the place and decided he could do nothing more without help.

The idea of varoks partnering with ellls in the trafficking of tads was frightening to the boy from stable Varok. He had no idea what to do next. Apparently Shawne had found Stringer somewhere on the large island where the three varoks had gone. But where was Haralahn?

He dared not go back for his rover. As long as it was there, the beach would be watched. A vehicle would be of little use if one wanted to stay hidden in this wilderness of crags and water. His best choice, he decided, would be to work his way down to the shore where Stringer had said the nursery scent was strong. Perhaps he could find Haralahn and call the great-fish.

– Δ –

Within the star cycle of leaving the empty caves at lake Al Neoon, Tandra and Conn's group arrived at what they hoped was TK's beach. They were relieved to find Stringer, Nealla, and Shawne coming in with Nidok.

"Beating up on ellls again," Conn said. "Will they never learn, these ahlork?"

"You were off somewhere playing la la with Lanoll, Conn. Daughter Shawne fought good fight with son Stringer and mate Nealla," Nidok countered. "What you have in green paw? Smells like mosswash."

"It is mosswash, Bird Hips," Conn said. While Killah sprayed Nidok with the de-moss potion, he poured down the ahlork's throat one of the best *llaoon* grass brews he could find at EV Lab in his hurry to pack.

It did a good job of relaxing Nidok, so Killah set to work pulling his wing back in place. After some thought, Conn engineered a splint from metal trim off Korak's rover. His binding it in place to immobilize the wing made Nidok very unhappy.

"Now I am worthless as spy," he announced.

"But you'll make an excellent camp cook," Tandra said. "You can pick fat baby shells from the rocks with your good wing tip."

Everyone laughed and Nidok grumbled, but with Orram gone no one felt like eating. As the mists grew cold, they huddled together and made plans.

"I'm sure I saw Orram," Shawne insisted again. "Three varoks were taking him away from the shallows where Cuffall's school had TK."

"Then we had better go there first," Conn said. "We'll take the rovers for backup."

"I don't like the idea of varoks being involved," Tandra said.

"They were after us," Shawne said, "when Nealla and I pulled Stringer out of his hole. Haralahn is still in the incubator. We should try to get him out as soon as we can. There is a huge boulder that closes over the entrance about a *pallon* below the surface. It rides on a track that is locked electronically."

"I suspect Jesse and I have had the most experience with such gadgets," Charley said. "We will go over there first thing. We can go without sleep for a while longer."

"I don't like the sound of 'gadgets,'" Killah said. "It's another sure sign there have been varoks involved in this scheme for some time."

Lanoll looked at Conn, then Stringer. Conn nodded, and she outlined a direct approach with no offer of adjustment. "We drive right into the center of Cuffall's school, announce their arrest, demand Orram's release, and take TK. It will send their emotions sky high. Some will capitulate with shame. Others may run, but they can be tracked by the emergency team from the lab."

"You'd better wait until that team gets here," Charley said.

Orticon agreed. "It won't be long. I've been in radio contact with them."

"Then we have to assume the school knows they're coming." Stringer was not willing to take any chances. "They're very cagey. We think they're holding some females as slave nurses."

Jesse added, "We have to assume that an operation this big stays in radio contact and routinely scans the frequencies available."

"If that's true," Tandra said. "We'd better jump them now, before they run again."

Orticon checked his notes. "I suspect Elll Central and the lab emergency team are within minutes of backing us up. I'll stay in contact with them. Tandra and I will come in from the big island in one rover and cut off the varoks."

"Let's go," Conn said. "We're all too revved up to sleep. Let's go get Cuffall's school."

"So—here I am," Nidok grumbled loudly, "Everyone leaves me alone rotting. Foul sand gets in plates next to moss, drives me mad."

"Where is Forelock?" Conn asked.

"Who knows?" Nidok answered. "Probably halfway to Varok."

Conn considered taking Nidok along, but realized they had no choice but to leave him behind. With only one wing and an overload of moss, he was as helpless as a box kite in a hail storm.

Nidok gargled loudly, and he waddled clumsily over to a low rock, hopped onto it, and settled down to sulk.

– Δ –

In contrast to Nidok's bad day, Forelock was having a lively time—dodging into the mists and behind rocks to avoid being seen. He watched Nidok stir up Cuffall's school and Shawne challenge Talln for TK. He kept track of Korak, watched Conn and the gang arrive from Al Neoon, and saw that six varoks from the lab emergency team were close behind them. He guessed correctly that the ellls swimming in from the south were from Elll Central. Then he watched from high above when he spotted Orram's captors moving toward the shallows and back into the rocks.

He decided the varoks must have taken Orram underground somewhere. Though hating the risk of following them, he flew down across the cliff rock and soon found the entrance to a lava tube facing the shallows.

He decided to attack. The varoks would be surprised, he thought, because they hadn't noticed him.

He was nearly correct; Orram had seen him. Close association with ahlork on Varok, especially with Nidok and his family, had accustomed Orram to their odd noises and antics. He believed his captors had ignored the occasional clacks and box-kite vanishing acts that shadowed his transfer here and there in the West Viortahk. Orram's captors were far too worried about what to do with Orram to notice Forelock's movements. They would never expect to see an ahlork underground on Ellason.

When Forelock appeared in the steep entrance to the lava tube and flew at the three varoks with a flurry of sharp chitin plates, they didn't know what hit them.

Orram was ready. He had managed to loosen his reed bonds on the edge of a sharp rock. His hands came free the moment Forelock attacked. Quickly he untied his legs. As Forelock disabled one varok after the other, Orram was on them with the reeds that had bound him, securing their slashed arms behind their backs, then hobbling them, making it impossible for them to climb the sheer tumble of large rocks that made up the entrance to his prison.

When they reached the top of the rocks and breathed in the fresh mist, Orram laughed with relief and touched Forelock's lip in appreciation. "Thanks, my young friend. Excellent work. Now where?"

"Everyone meets in the shallows below," Forelock said. "I return soon. My sire has been injured."

True to ahlork form, he left Orram with no more explanation and flew directly to the hidden beach to check on Nidok.

ATTACK AND RELEASE

"When we get to the shallows, run in hover mode, straight at the school," Conn told Killah. Stringer and Nealla were on board with them and Lanoll, all ellls. "They'll dive or move out of the way. Let's play safe and stay in this boat. We can get in close and grab TK off the raft. The ellls won't try to take her to land."

Tandra, Tamilan, and Orticon were in the second rover. Conn gave them a signal, and both rovers took off toward the deeper water, where Cuffall's school was relaxing after their last meal before sleep.

"You're ignoring all decent protocol," Killah said.

"Our only chance is surprise," Conn answered, realizing with some angst that he was prepared to do violence if necessary to release Orram and TK and to rescue the sentient tads held for sale.

Where the channel widened, their rover picked up speed. Lanoll let out an ultrasonic distress call that would have raised dead great-fish at twenty fathoms if any had been around. They didn't realize that the ellls of the West Viortahk had not used such calls for a generation or more, because the *eefl* of these waters had learned to zero in on the call and gobble up all noisy, injured ellls in distress.

True to plan, Conn and the others were on top of the school before TK's ellls realized what they were doing. They slowed just in time to avoid swamping the raft of ellls carrying TK. The child didn't see them coming. She had spotted her beloved RamRam on the beach and was calling to him.

Conn saw Orram run toward her through the shallows, then dive. Before Conn could call him off, the varok was swimming hard toward TK. Like the rest of the visitors, he was naïve about the ellls of Ellason.

TK's raft of ellls took off for deeper water, leaving Orram far behind. At the same time a contingent of big hedge–guardians came at both rovers, knocking them over and throwing everyone into the water.

Conn feared most for Orticon and Tamilan. They were not strong swimmers. "Stay out of the fracas," Conn called to them. Shawne and Tandra would do fine. They would head for Orram.

– Δ –

Korak had seen Forelock emerge with Orram and had found the location of the incubation chamber by calling for Haralahn in Sonics, both underwater and in air, then following the continuous faint answer: "I'm here. Here. I'm here." With difficulty, the great-fish convinced the young varok to don his minimal scuba gear so he could guide him to the tunnel entrance.

When Haralahn heard Korak tapping a rock on the tunnel wall, he surfaced and called out in his difficult Varokian, "The boulder is on tracks shutting me in here. You're nearby. Look for a release. It could be electronic, probably coded."

"I'm looking," Korak answered in Sonics. "Are you all right?"

"A little sick. I need some fresh water."

"I don't see anything. Wait. Here's a loose rock. Yes. There's a control panel behind the rock. It has eight switches."

"Try single switches first, then simple combinations, systematically."

Korak worked at the panel and was nearly done trying combinations of two when he heard the scraping of a synthetic material against the rocks outside the tunnel.

"Hide," Haralahn clicked. "There are varoks about. Three or more are working with Cuffall's school and the hedge–guardians to raise illegal tads. You might get help from the females. I have heard enough to believe some are being held against their will. I will be all right here a little longer. Find the dry entrance to this tunnel. In a few meters it rises above water and continues on into the island. I have heard Varoks come in and never go back out again."

"I won't be gone long," Korak said. He swam quickly up the tunnel, took off his scuba gear, and hurried over the rocks and into the dry part of the tunnel where Orram had been held.

– Δ –

Did you hear something?" Charley said to Jesse. They spoke English, which was easier than Varokian or Elllonian for both of them, being their native tongue.

"It sounded like rock on rock, then someone moving away," Jesse said. "Let's tie up here. I think this is the place Shawne described. We'll have to dive to find the tunnel entrance."

They secured a rope around a boulder and donned the elaborate varokian scuba gear carried as standard equipment on the rovers. They dove and searched the sheer rock face underwater. "Haralahn, you here?" Charley called, when they found the tunnel entrance.

"He's a great-fish from Ellason," Jesse said into his radio phone. "Save your English. They communicate in Elllonian with ellls, and with mud sculptures."

"Oleyall knew some English, and some Varokian," Charley said.

"So, he lived his life as an immigrant to Varok."

"Don't you know any Elllonian, Jesse? You've spent nearly your entire adult life on Varok."

"I don't swim very well," Jesse said. "Ellls speak Varokian to me. Great-fish try, but I can't understand them."

"This tunnel must go deep into the island. Let's follow it." With that,

Charley took off at a good clip into the dark water.

"Hello," Haralahn screamed in Varokian. "Get me out of here."

"Did you hear that?" Jesse called into his microphone. "Come back, Charley. I heard some kind of noise coming from back here."

Charley retreated and hovered near Jesse, listening. "You're right," he said, as Haralahn repeated his demand. "The great-fish is supposed to be near the entrance. Look. This boulder is set on some kind of track up here at top."

"This is it," Jesse said.

"Turn up your communicator, Jesse. I can't hear you."

"Find the loose rock hiding the control panel," Haralahn said, straining hard to pronounce the Varokian carefully.

"I heard it again," Jesse said.

"That scratching sound? Just mice in the tunnel."

"Water mice, on Ellason? I don't think so."

"Find rock," Haralahn tried again. "Move rock. Search for controls." His throat ached with the effort.

"That sounded a little like Varokian," Jesse said. "Haralahn, is that you? Can you hear us?"

The great-fish clicked "Yes," hoping against hope Jesse understood at least that much Sonics.

Jesse clicked "Yes" in return.

"Find controls. Find controls," Haralahn said, then his inflamed throat gave out.

"I think you said, 'Find controls,' Haralahn. Is that right?"

Haralahn clicked "Yes."

"Here," Charley said. "This rock is loose."

"Take it out."

"There she is." Charley lifted the rock out of its niche.

"Damn. The door probably requires a coded sequence."

"No problem," Charley said. "I've done some code-breaking in my day. I'll assume that varoks, or at least ellls, are more into logic than memorizing numbers. Let's try a combination of every other switch starting at the top left."

"No," Jesse said, after trying the sequence.

"Top right."

"No."

"Every other switch; begin at the top left," Charley said.

"No."

"Top right, diagonally, every other switch."

"Bingo," Jesse said.

The huge boulder slid away, revealing the access deck, the incubation shelves, and Haralahn's triangular face smiling up at them in the water. After a quick lunge to the surface and a slap of his long tail fin in thanks, he dove and sped past them out the tunnel.

"Where's he going?" Charley asked.

"He's going to help, I hope," Jesse said.

"So what do we do? Explore the tunnel or get back in the rover and find the shallows?"

"We've got the coordinates from Shawne. We'd better get to the shallows and see what's going on."

Battle in the Shallows

Forelock landed on the hidden beach and looked around with black beaded eyes shining and anxious.

"Nidok, where are you?" he called.

There was no answer.

"Nidok," he called louder.

Still no answer.

"Nidok!" He punctuated his sire's name with an alarm call that echoed off three faces of rock before it quit.

"Shut your lips. I'm sleeping," Nidok grumbled. "You and Shawne need lessons keeping quiet."

"Where are you? I'll check out on you."

"I'll check out, all right, if you don't let me sleep," said the elder ahlork. "You check yourself. Go find Killah. Take his nasty bath, clean off moss."

"Here. Come out." Forelock probed under a rock where a few tail plates showed in the sand.

"Ouch. Leave me alone, cruel nestling. I try to heal wing." In spite of himself, Nidok crawled out of his nest and pointed the splinted wing at Forelock.

With an expert touch, Forelock checked Nidok's shoulder joint and the prehensile wing-tip. His temperature seemed normal.

"Now get gone," Nidok snapped. "Let me sleep. They need you at shallows. Go find Orram."

"I have released Orram."

"Well, good for you. Find him again."

Forelock flew off, satisfied with Nidok's robust bullying and pleased with the proud smile on his scarred greater lip.

– Δ –

While the rovers danced upside down in deep water, Conn looked around to be sure Orticon and Tamilan were afloat. He saw that Shawne and Tandra already had them on shore. Shawne had not been able to swim fast enough to catch up with TK and her elllonian raft. The attacking ellls had disappeared beneath the surface. Conn did an ultrasonic scan and saw that they were heading for the raft of females carrying TK.

"Let's get TK," he hollered to Stringer, Nealla, Lanoll and Killah. The five ellls went after the raft. They finned hard through the water, then they leapt across the surface to give themselves more speed.

For a few precious minutes the hedge ellls didn't realize they were being pursued. Then Talln, accompanying the raft and keeping a check on TK, saw the Varokian ellls leaping in at a right angle to their heading. She sounded the alert, and the live elllonian raft quickly reversed itself.

The hedge–guardian ellls dove under the raft as it came at them. Conn and the others found themselves face to fin with six of them. Cuffall joined them as the seventh.

"All right, buddy," Conn said to Cuffall. "It's time to own up. We know you want us to take TK back to Varok."

"I will give you TK," he said, "if you forget our little business enterprise here."

Conn laughed. "Tit for tat is a well-known computer model, Cuffall.

I do to you as you do to me—but not always. Not this time."

"Go to hell, Conn," Cuffall sneered in equivalent Sonics. "You're not ruining our business with your fancy theories." He made a violent pass at Conn's soft middle, which he managed to dodge with a quick somersault. Lanoll and Nealla leapt over the attacker. Killah helped restrain him.

Stringer didn't waste any words. He drew his knife from his waist pack and swam straight for an elll he recognized as one of his captors.

"Stop. Stringer. They are not armed," Lanoll shouted.

Stringer circled warily then, and Lanoll kept talking. "We must take TK in order to raise her as a varok. Elll Central is on the way, Cuffall."

"They will take you to trial for illegal trade in reproducing and selling young ellls," Killah added. "We know about the nursery and the incubator. Stringer and Orram will press charges for kidnapping, as will Haralahn. Your schools would be wise to cooperate."

Cuffall and his ellls said nothing. As Conn expected, two surrendered by leaving the tense circle and heading for the shallows. Enraged by the defection, the remaining ellls attacked with slashing hands and violent kicks at close range.

Stringer drew his knife again, but before he drew blood, all the ellls heard the warning calls of the Elll Central team as they entered the shallows from the east.

The hedge elll mob turned and fled south toward open water. TK's raft headed at top speed for the shore. As Conn scanned the waters to verify the criminals' retreat, he realized why they had fled so abruptly. At least three *eefl* were patrolling the waters, looking for supper.

– Δ –

Korak hurried through the rocky tunnel as fast as he dared. A footpath had been cleared, so he made good progress in spite of the dark. In less than a kilometer he saw light in the distance, then the tunnel opened into a large cavern. Groping his way toward the blinding light near the cavern's ceiling, he stumbled over a varok lying on the ground. The varok made a grab for Korak's foot, but he leapt free and fell over another varok. When the third started hollering irrationally, Korak rolled away, got up, and ran for the light.

He climbed up rotten rock and got out in admirable time, but he was breathing hard. As he gathered himself and caught his breath, he realized he was on a hill overlooking the shallows. He saw the varok, Orram, swimming toward shore. Not far from him, Shawne was running through the shallows toward—it must be the child TK. The eIlls of her elllonian raft had undone themselves and were racing back to deep water. The child stood alone in the restless water, screaming, and having difficulty standing up. Shawne was calling something to Orram. Tandra was making slow progress, swimming toward shore with another varok in her arms. As if irrational with panic, Tamilan was leaping through the shallows toward shore away from Tandra.

Then, just below where he stood, in the clear water of the shallows, Korak saw the terrible outline of an *eefl* heading toward Orram.

– Δ –

After what seemed an age of struggle through the shallows, Shawne got to TK and scooped her out of the water. The child coughed and cleared her throat enough to get her breath. As she made for shore, Shawne could see *eefl*, three now, converging on Orram. She slammed her feet on the water, trying to distract them, and she cried for help.

Tamilan sat huddled on the beach, shaking with terror, while Tandra brought Orticon to shore, saving him from a near drowning. She left him still coughing and ran to Tamilan, demanding that he help distract the *eefl*. When he saw her, Tamilan's patches closed down. He got up and ran for higher ground, shouting, "I can't swim. I can't swim."

Shawne's stomping had turned one of the *eefl* away from Orram. It was heading swiftly toward her and TK. For a terrible moment she felt shredded, torn between her love for Orram and her need to save the child. She had no time to help both. *I shouldn't have to make such a choice.* In her rage, she froze, and time stopped for her, while the *eefl* came on.

As if waking from a terrible nightmare, she forgave herself her humanity. She was no worse than the eIlls when they chose eggs to incubate, no worse than the varoks like Tamilan who did the best they could with what nature had provided. Her mind felt clear, her thinking sure, free of debris that could pull her into despair. Her choices were terrible, but she knew what she had to do.

She saw Forelock diving at the *eefl* with talons extended—and her feet took over. Clutching TK in her arms, she ran away from the *eefl*, reaching shore just as its long whip encircled one ankle, bringing her crashing back into the wet sand. TK landed on top of her. "Run, TK, run or crawl away from the water," Shawne said in distinct Elllonian.

The child was too young, her legs too weak. All she knew was that Shawne was her safety now. The ellls were gone. She clung to Shawne's neck, while Forelock's wings slashed dangerously close. The *eefl* slowly dragged Shawne and TK back toward deeper water.

"No!" Shawne shouted, "you will not have us," and she found new strength, determined to save her child. As she tore the *eefl*'s tail away from TK, she saw Killah enter the fray, while Forelock and two other ellls continued the assault. Then a wide fin knocked her aside and she lost consciousness.

– Δ –

Korak picked up a sharp rock and leapt down the path to the shore, ignoring the pain that shot through his heels. When he reached the cool water, he took the slab of rock in his teeth and dove onto the surface, swimming hard toward Orram and the *eefl*.

He had only one *eefl* to deal with. Korak reached it before it lassoed Orram, slicing its throat neatly with the sharp rock.

– Δ –

Conn's echo scan showed the third *eefl* zeroing in on Tandra. She was swimming blindly, using her full-face crawl, heading out to help Orram, unaware that Korak had already arrived.

Conn called to Stringer for help, took his knife, and they swam the surface with long leaps, trying to get to Tandra's third *eefl* before it got her. Even small *eefl* are difficult to disentangle from ones body after they get hold. Think six foot boa constrictor wrapped around your arm. It missed and got only a few of Conn's head plumes. His vanity or his life; it was a difficult decision, but vanity won. Conn skewered the beast before it rendered him bald.

"Where's Nealla and Lanoll?" Stringer screamed. "Scan for more *eefl*. They're running in schools."

Somehow Conn had missed Lanoll and Nealla in the confusion, and now he was consumed with fear for the elll ladies' lives. And where was Killah?

As he swam past Orram, Conn saw that all was well with the va-rok. Korak swam alongside him. He had redeemed himself ten times over. Tandra was swimming close by. They waved as Conn cruised by, and he could see they were dragging in Conn's dead *eefl*, not wanting good fresh protein to go to waste. Dangerous, foolish thing to do. Like sharks on Earth, *eefl* come to blood in water.

When he saw that they were near shore, he called to Stringer, visual-izing the worst for Nealla and Lanoll. "We've got to find them. Hurry."

Echoes through the water in every direction showed no female ellls. Where was the raft of ellls? Where were the hedge–guardians? Their scans showed nothing.

"No *eefl*, thank the Great Harrahn," Conn said to Stringer in Sonics as they cruised along. They swung their melons back and forth like dolphins, searching every ripple and rock, every shadow and sound, focused on spotting the familiar shape of their two feminine ellls. No Nealla. No Lanoll.

Then from below, in deep water, an *eeflin* got Conn by the legs, and another wrapped the lethal coil of his tail around Stringer's left arm.

"Use my knife," Stringer hollered.

"I got it."

He did some minor damage to the smallish carnivore. It hadn't been able to make a killing first strike. Then Conn heard the hum of a small motor. Two large splashes echoed from above, and suddenly the water went black with *eeflin* blood—he hoped.

No. It was his. Conn felt the nasty grip of *eeflin* tail about his legs. He thrashed out and caught flesh just as he came onto the surface. He grabbed a lung full of air for added strength, and struggled harder to get free—then he heard Charley's voice swearing a blue streak.

"God bless you, Conn, throw that damn knife in Korak's skiff here, or give it to me so I can slash your legs free of *eeflin* tail. You got my arm a good one."

Conn saw that Charley was bleeding, not himself. Then he saw Jesse, sopping wet, already in the skiff with Stringer, who was rubbing his squeezed arm to get the circulation going again.

Conn handed Charley the knife and held still while the human slid down the elll's body into the water and cut away the *eefl* tail still coiled tightly around his ankles. When Charley came back up and asked if Conn could move his fins all right, he nodded yes and nearly broke down. "You saved our lives, Red," he said. "Where the hell did you come from? Where did those *eefl* come from? Jesse, get Charley a rag to stop his bleeding. Where's Killah? Stringer, get out of the damn skiff. We've got to find Nealla and Lanoll."

Conn dove, still in a panic, leaving Stringer calling to him. He didn't have time to answer. He swam hard just below the surface, scanning again, every ripple and rock, every shadow and sound, focused narrowly, searching for any sign of elllonian life.

He raced for the shallows. Maybe the infrared scanner in the rovers would help. He blanched, so terrified he nearly fainted when at last he stood up in the shallows.

The first thing he stumbled over was Haralahn lying in twenty centimeters of water. Killah was busily wrapping a strip of white cloth around his tail and over the end of his right lateral fin to prevent *eefl* poison from spreading through his body.

Then Conn saw them—Nealla, Lanoll, and Shawne—talking baby talk to TK, who was busy combing bright blue plumes off Lanoll's face. A dead, tailless *eefl* lay on the beach a few meters away. Korak and Orram were busy cutting off strips of meat and hanging them out to dry on the rocks. Stringer, Jesse, and Charley stood near Korak's beached skiff, looking at Conn with bemused smiles.

Conn ran to Charley with an emotional explosion of thanks that sent them rolling in the sand, then into the shallows and on to the near deeps, where the human learned what brotherly intimacy with ellls really meant.

When they emerged onto the beach, thoroughly exhausted and reconciled, Tandra and Orram, Lanoll, Stringer and Nealla, and Shawne with Korak holding TK—all converged on Conn and Charley with a family hug. Before it was over, the celebration had plastered sand into all the ellls' hexagonal lines, each human's head of hair, and the varoks' patch organs. Jesse took photos when Nidok and Forelock joined the scuffle by sitting on heads.

Five Pieces of Advice

Shawne, Lanoll, and Conn—with Killah and Korak along as "observers"—accompanied Haralahn south to the City of Great-fish. Nidok and Forelock insisted on watching over them. Nidok had the good excuse of exercising his mended wing, and Forelock wanted to see his sire safely to the hospital near the great-fish's southern undersea metropolis for physical therapy.

Stringer and Nealla traveled with the Haralahn entourage as far as Rocky Deeps Ranch. Shawne, Korak and the rest of the team promised to see them on the return trip, after everyone had visited the site of the ancient elllonian library and breathed the wind of the Far Deeps.

Meanwhile, a conference of great-fish and elllonian elders had discussed the visitors' findings and passed the Loner-Schooler Reconciliation Act, modeled, on Tandra's suggestion, after the United States Constitution Amendment XIV regarding civil rights:

"All elllonian persons born or naturalized on the planet Ellason shall be guaranteed refuge, privileges or immunities by their nursing school of origin and any adoptive school. No school shall abridge the privileges or immunities of such person, nor deprive them of life, liberty or equal protection from harm.

"The rights to life's essentials—namely free access to water, food, clean air, shelter and health care shall not be compromised. Rather, these rights shall be guaranteed to all living beings, supported by fair and equitable revenues, and defended by courts of law."

"A nice tribute to the best in human governance," Orram said. "That should help things along on Earth, too."

– Δ –

Before Shawne's appointment with Haralahn, the Great great-fish, the Master philosopher who had driven all her urgency for this trip to Ellason, Shawne's team decided to throw a send-off party.

"I am so very thankful to you all for supporting my quest," she said, raising her glass to the team, "and will be forever grateful for your support through my illness."

Orram took Shawne's hand and invited her to sit close by on the carved steps. "You are in a good position to talk to Haralahn now. However, Conn and I want to say a few things that might help."

"I'll listen to Conn if he doesn't mention the word complexity." Her eyes twinkled with a thousand lights. Conn knew he had made a dent.

"We suggest you look at four underlying issues we all face, Orram said."

"I knew it. I knew you were bursting with something wise," she taunted.

Orram tuned in to her mood and spoke slowly. "First, ask yourself if you are willing to accept any authority outside of yourself."

"Ha!" Conn's gills flared with a snort. "Shawne accept authority? Isn't that an oxymoron?"

"The keyword here is *any*," Orram said. "You alone are the authority of last resort. You can't escape the fact that you will, and no one else can, make the decision to let others, individuals or institutions, dictate your beliefs or your declaration of faith."

Shawne looked at Conn.

"Done," he said. "I doubt that you'll have much trouble with that one."

"Now, Shawne my dear," Orram continued, "try on number two. It's a classical problem in philosophy. Ask yourself if the existence you experience approximates reality or is some kind of illusion. Do you trust your senses? Do you trust the information you were handed at the Concentrate?"

"I'll think about that one," Shawne said. "My first reaction is to say 'Of course I trust my senses,' but I will give it serious thought. Mom has had some very real spiritual experiences she can't explain. We can't know or sense everything there is, and our senses can be fooled. Next?"

"Number three," Orram said. "This is getting to the heart of theology, as I see it. Semantics is critical here, but not sufficient. We struggle to put God in the tiny bottle of our minds, when the reality of Existence—the reality of the observable universe and its meaning—encompasses far more than our collective experience."

"Is much larger than any of us can conceive."

"Sometimes only poetry will do," Conn said, "or long trips through ancient oceans."

"Or long lectures, like this one," Shawne teased. "On to number four."

"Wise beyond her years," Conn said, with a feeling of *deja vu*.

"Number four," Orram said, but Shawne read him before he could continue.

"Some concepts," she said, "are simply not falsifiable, hence outside the realm of the scientific method. Science asks *how*; religion asks *why*."

"Right. Simply do not confuse the two by extending their limits beyond workable definitions."

Shawne glowed with love for her alien dads and turned to look up at the elll. "Conn? Any summary advice from the peanut gallery?"

"All I ask," he said in his most serious tone, "is that you don't let doubt freak you out; it can unlock new possibilities and shape useful paradigms."

– Δ –

"We have news, Shawne," Nealla said.

On her way to meet with Haralahn, Shawne had stopped by the Rocky Deeps Ranch to visit with Stringer. He and Nealla had done good work finding homes for the sentient tads of Cuffall's school.

Nealla looked eagerly into Shawne's eyes. "Stringer and I are co-sponsoring one of Cuffall's tads. He will be ready to leave the nursery soon. We want you to meet him before you leave."

"Co-sponsoring?" Shawne asked. "How unusual—and exciting! Does this mean you are staying with the school, Nealla?"

"As an auxiliary loner. Stringer will always know where I am."

Stringer took Shawne by the shoulders, and she knew something difficult was coming. "We have wanted a tad of our own, like Lanoll and Conn. We have tried. Tamilan is right, Shawne. Ellls are splitting into two different species, maybe more. Nealla and I cannot produce a fertile egg."

Shawne reached to embrace her ellonian brother, but he shook his head and smiled. "We've decided to become family and use our Replacement Certificates to adopt two tads, one now and one when the first is speaking Elllonian."

In that moment, reality struck home. Stringer would be gone from her life. Shawne heard Orram's voice in her head, more than a Jovian year before. *If the Source of All is everything that is meaningful, both within*

our lives and in creation, then we must celebrate the eternal significance of
every moment we live.

Shawne smiled through tears, and Stringer wrapped his arms
around her. "What?" he asked.

"Do you suppose Tandra is ready to be a grandmother? It's almost
time for me to go home to Varok with Korak and TK."

Haralahn

Haralahn settled into the communication shelf in the wide, flooded
amphitheater above his cave home and offered Shawne a thick, chewy
stalk of *llaoon* grass candy. She sat next to him where the water covered
her lap and put one hand on the wide melon that peaked just behind
his wide-set eyes.

"So are we going to talk philosophy or religion, Shawne?" Haralahn
asked in Varokian.

"Both, if you don't mind," Shawne said. "I'm ready to talk about
anything, go anywhere. I have already taken some kind of leap."

Haralahn turned a questioning glance to her face.

"The details no longer matter to me, Haralahn. At last I understand why Conn's definition of God as 'Whatever' is not agnosticism.
It expresses a faith that goes beyond detail and recognizes our physical limitations. It means acceptance of creation and its Source—not
only as we experience them, but as they must be, whether or not we
understand them."

"I like that," Haralahn said. "Be sure to tell Conn you have adopted
a faith close to his. It will mean a great deal to him."

Shawne reached out for the prehensile end of Haralahn's left fin as
her eyes filled with tears. *I hope so. It's very hard to know when my choices
are too self-serving.*

Yes, the great-fish responded in mind. *Your personal experience speaks
volumes. Conn understands, you chose not to have an unwanted child. Indeed,*

is it not the kinder choice to produce only well-supported and healthy off-spring—whether by limiting reproduction or eliminating harmful genes?

Shawne nodded. *Many on Earth feel that's going too far, to take such control.*

I say it's wrong to let chance have its way, when one can make a choice to reduce suffering.

Shawne looked down, then out over the water. Haralahn's fin tightened around her hand. *I still feel your sense of failure in helping Earth. It may never entirely leave you, Shawne.*

How can it, when human beliefs continue to override well-tested information? She took a large bite of her *llaoon* grass and chewed it thoughtfully. *To make real progress, seems to me, we have to make a distinction between the love of our fellow beings and the love of our mind set.*

Fundamental change is always difficult, but human beings are beginning to see their part in the planet's fragile, complex whole.

Shawne couldn't help smiling. *Conn is right about complexity. Anything we do, no matter how small, could become significant in the long run.*

Haralahn nodded in assent. She released his fin and placed her hands on her hips. "So—what shall we talk about, Haralahn?" she said aloud. "I have not come all this way to preach to you."

The great-fish laughed. Shawne understood the laugh, and she started to giggle. They laughed together until the tears ran down Shawne's face, and beads of delight appeared on Haralahn's melons.

"Hop on my back, Shawne," he said. "There are ten moons dancing in the mists. Let me take you for a ride."

APPENDICES

A. A History of the Archives

3631 *ir* (**Earth 5000** BCE) - Events recorded in *The Unheard Song.*[1]

3634 *ir* (**Earth 4962** BCE) – Amanok writes his memoirs.

4225.8 *ir* (**Earth 2020** CE) – Tandra Grey born on Earth.

4228 *ir* (**Earth 2047** CE) – Shawne Grey born on Earth.

4228.3–4228.4 *ir* (**Earth 2050–2051** CE) – Events recorded in *A Place Beyond Man,*[2] revised as *The View Beyond Earth.*[3]

4228.4–4229.5 *ir* (**Earth 2051–2064** CE) – Events in *The Webs of Varok.*[4]

4229 *ir* (**Earth 2059** CE) – Aman Telariahn (Amantel) publishes Amanok's memoirs as *The Unheard Song.*[1]

4229.8–4230 *ir* (**Earth 2068–2070** CE) – Oran-ElConn-Grey family events recorded in *The Alien Effect.*[5]

4229.8–4409.7 *ir* (**Earth 2068–4202** CE and beyond) – Biological Events recorded in *The Alien Effect.*[5]

4230 *ir* (**Earth 2070** CE) – Events recorded in *An Alien's Quest.*[6]

1. Penscript Publishing House, 2022. 2. Charles Scribner's Sons, 1975.
3. Penscript Publishing House, 2014. 4. Penscript Publishing House, 2012.
5. Penscript Publishing House, 2014. 6. Penscript Publishing House, 2016

B. Bibliography

Included in this Bibliography are books that continue to enlighten us in our ongoing search for meaning and long-term solutions to current dilemmas on Earth.

A History of God: the 4000-year Quest of Judaism, Christianity and Islam by Karen Armstrong. Ballantine Books, New York, 1993.

America the Unusual by John Kingdon. Worth Publishers, Inc. (Bedford/ St. Martins), New York, 1999. A readable summary of why Americans can be so fiercely independent, hate government and fear regulation more than Europeans do.

Are We Smart Enough to Know How Smart Animals Are? by Frans De-Waal. W. W. Norton & Co., New York, 2016. If you substitute "Aliens" for "…How Smart Animals Are," you would have the theme central to the *Archives of Varok* series and the exploration of human identity reflected in religious thought in *An Alien's Quest*.

Betrayal of Science and Reason: How Anti-Environmental Rhetoric Threatens Our Future by Paul R. and Anne H. Ehrlich. Island Press, Washington D.C., 1996.

Chaos and Christianity: Questions to Science and Religion by John Polking-horne. The Crossroad Publishing Company, New York, 1994.

Christianity and Evolution by Pierre Teilhard de Chardin. Harcourt Brace Jovanovich Inc., New York, 1969.

Deep Future: The Next 100,000 Years of Life on Earth by Curt Stager. St. Martin's Press, New York, 2011. The author begins by noting that climate change may cancel the next ice age — which would give us all a better chance of survival.

Doubt and Certainty by Tony Rothman and George Sudarshan. Perseus Books, Reading, MA, 1998.

Enough Is Enough: Building A Sustainable Economy in a World of Finite Resources by Rob Dietz and Dan O'Neill. Berrett-Koehler, San Francisco, 2013. Recommended undergraduate text. The authors describe with concise, yet precise clarity the *why* and *how* of converting to a steady state economy like Varok's, complete with index and notes for sources.

Good Natured: The Origins of Right and Wrong in Humans and Other Animals by Frans De Waal. Harvard University Press, Cambridge, MA, 1996.

How Nature Works: The Science of Self-Organized Criticality by Per Bak. Springer-Verlag, New York, 1996. The definitive book clarifying the role of mathematical chaos related to complex systems.

Just Six Numbers: The Deep Forces That Shape the Universe by Martin Rees. Basic Books, New York, 2000.

Leadership and the New Science: Discovering Order in a Chaotic World by Margaret J. Wheatley. Berrett-Koehler, San Francisco, 1999.

Mistakes Were Made (but Not by Me): Why We Justify Foolish Beliefs, Bad Decisions, and Hurtful Acts by Carol Tavris and Elliot Aronson. Houghton Mifflin Harcourt Publishing Company, New York, 2007. A must-read about cognitive dissonance and why we are all more or less guilty of refusing to face facts when they challenge our beliefs.

Rare Earth: Why Complex Life is Uncommon in the Universe by Peter D. Ward and Donald Brownlee. Springer Verlag Copernicus, New York, 2000.

The Battle for God by Karen Armstrong. Ballantine Books, New York, 2000.

The Copernicus Complex: Our Cosmic Significance in a Universe of Planets and Probabilities by Caleb Scharf. Scientific American/Farrar, Strauss and Giroux, New York, 2014. A vibrant, readable and enjoyable history of astronomy, with a comprehensive overview of the current finds that suggest answers to the "ultimate" question, "Are we alone in the universe?"

The Gene: An Intimate History by Siddhartha Mukherjee. Scribner, New York, 2016. A fascinating review of how science answers difficult questions and challenges us with future options for moral integrity.

The Honor Code: How Moral Revolutions Happen by Kwame Anthony Appiah. W. W. Norton, New York, 2010. The story of how shame was needed to make lasting widespread changes in social behavior.

The Meaning of It All by Richard Phillips Feynman. Perseus Books Group, Reading, MA, 1999.

Thinking in Systems by Donella Meadows. Chelsea Green Publishing, White River Junction, VT, 2008. A masterful summary of the inherent complexity of nature and how to manage its interlaced systems, which are often driven by a lack of boundaries, by delays, non-linear reactions, and problems of addiction, low performance or escalation.

When Science Meets Religion: Enemies, Strangers, or Partners? by Ian G. Barbour. Harper, San Francisco, 2000.

C. Glossary

adjustment. Intense schooling of ellls, in which strong pressure signals, electro-sensing, magneto-orientation and ultrasonic messages are rapidly exchanged underwater so that accommodation may be made for the absence of a member of the school or for the addition of a new member or visitor.

aeo-o. Elllonian expression of intense pleasure.

aeyull. Elllonian expression of intense pain.

ahlrialka tree. Huge spreading, plant-like growth on the hot acid plains of Varok; it produces dense, tasty reproductive burls.

alahranon. The colorful, swirling mists that surround Ellason, whose surface is almost totally covered by warm oceans.

aloon. Elllonian noun, usually used with affection to mean something like wet slob or water bum.

alyakah. Varokian word for a mature, well-integrated female who would be desirable to any creature as a mother or wife.

arl. A large, brilliantly winged, moth-like creature of Varok, eaten by ellls and varoks and considered a delicacy.

brilln. The tiny, brilliantly-plumed water bird of Ellason.

challall weeds. Delicious, rigid, leafless plants which grow on the low hills of Ellason.

consummation. Total mind-link, achieved by varoks who have no mental reservations between them so that complete subconscious mind-scanning can occur.

dankah. A potent, intoxicating tea, made from the Varokian plant of the same name.

deacuh. Elllonian noun for isolation, quarantine, or loneliness and torture, all of which are synonymous in the minds of ellls.

directorate. Full title: Elll-Varok Earth Moonbase Directorate. The council of ellls and varoks at EV base, which makes policy decisions on behalf of EV Science.

effl. Large, fanged carnivores found in Ellason's seas. Their side fins span more than three meters behind a head shaped like a thick arrow and a ahead of a venomous, prehensile tail.

efflin. A piscoid species related to the *eefl* of Ellason's Viortahk, farmed by the ellls for food.

el eggs. The large, blue eggs laid by elllonian females about once every six Earth-weeks.

Ellason. A heretofore undetected self-heated planet of Sol with gravity equivalent to about twice Earth's. Its orbit is three times as far from Sol as Pluto, hence laser communication involves a delay of seventeen and one-half hours, Ellason being some eighteen thousand, eight hundred and seventy-seven million kilometers from Earth. Continental masses on the warm, black giant are small, and the deep, dark seas are enormous, glowing with ruby-red warmth near the heart of the planet.

elll. An adaptable, aquatic, life-loving species of Ellason, equipped with a formidable array of sensory organs.

Elllonian. The system of throat sounds laboriously devised by the varoks and ellls to be spoken by ellls in the varokian audible range in order to facilitate communication between those two species.

Elll-Varok (EV) Science. An organization of ellls and varoks that directs the scientific experimentation and observation conducted by those species and acts as depositor, summarizer, and interpreter of accumulated knowledge and verifiable fact.

EV base. Earth-moon observation station of Elll-Varok Science, set into the edge of a crater eleven kilometers in diameter, located north-west of crater Schlüter at 1.50° north and 89.5° west in the d'Alembert Mountains of Earth's moon.

EV Dictate. The working agreement between the species of Ellason and Varok, which defines obligations, responsibilities, options, and assumptions inherent in their dealings.

Generalist. Abbreviated as *G.* An earned varokian designation signi-fying the acquisition of thorough, detailed knowledge in a broad area of related studies, as, for example, physics, chemistry, astronomy, geol-ogy, from the area of physical sciences. Between Specialist and Master.

Gurahn. Mythological beast designed by the *ll-leyoollanl* to represent the total experience of the planet Varok.

hedonic glands. Sensory organs whose stimulation gives pleasure and often sexual stimulation to ellls.

hoats. A tangy, black edible root of Varok which sports feathery chartreuse leaves.

integrated. An elllonian concept to describe the state of being when an individual of another species becomes a part of the elllonian school in a way that implies total acceptance of the ellls; in general, to accept oneself as no different from others.

kaehl. A delicate, easily tamed Varokian animal with silky, pink, hair that drapes in long strands about its tiny body and over its large red nose, causing it to trip habitually as it attempts to run. It incubates its eggs in an abdominal pouch and protects itself with an acrid spray from its sour gland. The dried meat is tasteless but nutritious.

kaehl-din. Elllonian invective. *Din* means fecal matter, *kaehl* spray, and in general, any repulsive substance.

kaehloid. Literally, furry beast. The elll's nickname for species with hair.

la l lea. Elllonian; title of the tender mating duet of the ellls; literally— have a mating with me.

leel la oon. Elllonian; literally—female, you do water (swim, woman).

llaoon grass. A soft marsh grass of Ellason.

ll-leyoolianl. A species of creative great-fish of Ellason who perceive the significance of experience and express it in a manner most easily understood by their communicants, often by modeling clay represen- tations of their ideas as progressions of complex symbols.

lohn bird. A plump, football-shaped animal with large webbed feet, stubby wings, a ridiculously small, bill-less head, and a coat of deep red and pink parasitic moss that drips with a heavily perfumed liquid. One of two species on Ellason capable of flight.

L'Ran. The Elllonian word for the blue star-planet, Earth.

Lurlial. Varokian-built exploratory space cruiser, fourteen meters long, bat-shaped at full glide extension, with capacity to carry eight two-meter beings comfortably, eleven if necessary. The craft has an indefinite range, minimal noise, needs little landing space, and has an extremely low radar cross-section.

Master. Abbreviated as *M*. Highest honorary recognition by varoks of expertise in a broad area of study, with some understanding of all knowledge, demonstrated by wisdom and restraint in integrating and applying the acquired concepts to real problems. Artellian is one of twenty living ellls to have received the honor; Orram, one of two thousand varoks.

Mutilation. The period of time in Varokian natural history in which the varokian species mutated from magnificent and normally sensual winged intellectuals to unduly sensitive bipeds incapable of experiencing emotion rationally.

oeln. Edible fish of Ellason, large and gray, with cool arrow-shaped patterns visible to ellls as dark lines in the infrared environment of Ellason.

-oon. Elllonian suffix implying water or wetness.

pallonions. Ellasonian credits. A promise of postponed payment in goods or services whenever requested. Agreements are honored and enforced between all members of species capable of keeping promises.

pallons. Elllonian unit of measure, about twenty-three meters, the length of an elll's arcing leap over the water from a fast swimming start. The similarity of this word to the word *pallonions* is probably a result of the ancient ellls' sense of irony and humor.

patch organ. Round, featureless plate of tissue behind the ears of varoks that detects low frequency electromagnetic signals, often voltages produced by mental and nervous activity of nearby organisms.

Ranat. Thirty-meter varokian space cruiser designed to carry forty passengers over long distances.

reading. Sensing another individual's mood, emotion, or trend in thought. One function of the varoks' patch organs.

release. The ability to experience emotion and to function rationally simultaneously. An ideal state achieved rarely by varoks and only with the aid of a consummate partner.

school. Any number of ellls who inhabit a particular environs or locale and who relate by schooling. The ellls' normal social structure.

schooling. Functioning collectively and sharing awareness as if a group were one individual.

Sonarplate Apraxia. A debilitating disease affecting the hexagonal plates of ellls, caused by a viral-like agent. Untreated, it disrupts sonar meshwork function, hence ultrasonic reception and communication.

Songs to Life. Ancient varokian poems written anonymously during the Mutilation. The first verse of the poem translates as follows:

> *Though long denied Life's gracious gift of flowing free,*
> *In currents wild and lifting down, thrown tumbling,*
> *Lifted up, thrown down, and swept without control,*
> *Our minds unlocked, in gray mists swirling bright with crystal hue;*
>
> *Though elegance denied and flight subdued,*
> *We find Life's beauty in her gifts*
> *And take her favors where they fall.*
> *Though all our visions racked our minds with pain;*
> *Though sound grew dense and ruined quiet senses;*
> *Though mind-filling silence became unknown and unknowable;*
> *And new life came to us, imperfect yet yearning for consciousness,*
> *Heavily distorted, torn by savaged genes*
> *And thrown upon misery to writhe in horror for years denied;*
>
> *Though Life came not with joy or promise,*
> *But used us for her mindless purpose-*
> *Or too mindful — none can know —*
> *We still survive, thankful for new strength,*
> *Molecules still conscious in forms perhaps wiser.*

Specialist. Abbreviated as *S*. Varokian designation for those acquiring specific knowledge in one field of study, such as physics.

tad. An English word used by ellls to mean young being or new life.

tracking. Sensing and imitating the precise muscular movements of another individual, one function of the varoks' patches (in conjunction with spinal nerves).

udan. Varokian style bidet–toilet.

uleoon. Elllonian affectionate farewell, from *u* (go), *lea* (mating) or *leoo* (live) or *leoon* (love), and *oon* (in water, deliciously wet).

uuyvanoon (-l, plural). Sleeping basins designed by and primarily for ellls. They are made of a tough, flexible synthetic imbedded with a thick growth of moss, shaped like a bathtub, and provided with a warm water inlet and a sealed cover for space flight. From Elllonian: *u* (go), *uyan* (beyond), *van* (knowledge), and *oon* (in water).

uyen l'e advant. . . Elllonian; Furthermore, I am convinced that . . .

Varok. A dense, barely habitable, hidden satellite of Jupiter, thought to be associated, at least visually, with the Great Red Spot. At its closest, it is less than 600 million kilometers from Earth; communications delay is at least 32 minutes.

varok. The dominant intellectual species native to the planet Varok, formed by mutation from winged forebears, having lost their ability to fly and to tolerate emotion rationally.

Varokian Concentrate. An institution of Varok open to qualifying individuals of any species who are admitted as students to acquire— by high-speed microvolt implantation into the memory—established fact, non-interpretable information, and thought techniques. The integration and application of this knowledge is acquired through continuing studies, leading to the designations apprentice, specialist, and generalist.

Vrankah. A dance invented by ellls and performed by varoks only in close sympathy, usually in consummation; often used as a public announcement and celebration of legal commitment between varoks. The dance requires spinal anticipatory patch organ reading—tracking—by one partner as the other matches the rhythmic clapping of the ellls with his feet and tells a symbolic story with his hands.

wet-sweater. A shirt made of the most moisture-retaining, softest, and most delicious of Ellasonian mosses, kept alive by periodic moistening and feeding.

World Environmental Charter. A document signed by many nations of Earth to ensure the safety and cleanliness of the world's oceans, waterways, air, and soil, whose provisions were subsequently ignored or suspended for reasons of emergency shortages, international security, or economic disaster.

World Federation. A world government of Earth with limited sovereignty but growing enforcement capability, formed primarily out of economic necessity.

D. Principal Characters

The Oran–elConn–Grey Family

Humans

Adaptable technological bipeds, emotionally variable, sensually inhibited. Intuitive minds.

Tandra Grey – A microbiologist, born on Earth in the 21st century.

Shawne – Raised on Varok by the Oran-elConn-Grey family, originally adopted by Tandra on Earth in the 2040s.

Varoks

Durable but sensitive bipeds, emotionally fragile, senses easily overloaded; open minds and mood reading ability, instinctively focused on the long-term stability of the planet Varok. Strong hormonal links triggered by mental compatibility.

Orram – A highly respected Master of Life Sciences bonded in mind to the human Tandra Grey.

Orticon – Orram's son by planned procreation, now a teacher of local and global options to secure the future.

Ellls

Aquatic, playful, be-finned bipeds, native to Ellason. Emotionally vola-
tile, loaded with senses, with logic-driven minds, focused on moment-
to-moment experience.

Conn – A loner elll, lifelong friend of Orram, Tandra's first alien contact. Expert in Earth studies and lover of English slang.

Lanoll – Conn's elllonian mate, also a loner. An expert in Varok's ecology and recovery from Mahntik's treason in *The Webs of Varok*.

Stringer – A schooling elll, Conn and Lanoll's selected hatchling.

Other Characters

Humans

Jesse Mendleton – The ellls' first human contact on Earth, invited to
Varok on the elll Artellian's Replacement Certificate.

Charley Hazard – A former math professor, then fishing guide to the
Islas Revillagigedo, working out of Cabo San Lucas, Mexico, invited to
Varok by Tandra on Orram's Replacement Certificate.

Varoks

Korak – Koran Akrallon, a young graduate of the Concentrate on
Varok, specialist in elllonian studies.

Tamilan – Tamon Ilanor, specialist in elllonian genetics.

TK – Tahlee-Karal, varokian child rescued by ellls after a tragic accident on Ellason.

Ellls

Artellian – Retired Director of EV Science Observation Base on Earth's moon.

Bain – Also known as Old Bain. An elll of Varok's Lake Seclusion, respected for his wisdom in many matters but deeply prejudiced against loner ellls.

Cuffall – Likeable, complex hedge–guardian elll and protector of the varokian child, TK.

Nealla – Female loner elll in Stringer's adoptive school.

Talln – Female member of Cuffall's school, sponsor to TK.

Ahlork

Semi-literate flocking insectoids living in the cliffs of Varok, covered with chitinous plates and possessing prehensile wing tips; miners of the ancient urban ruins, with long-distance flight capability.

Nidok – Leader of the Greater Flock, bonded to the Oran-elConn-Grey Family.

Great-Fish

Marine mammaloids native to Ellason, immigrants to Varok; larger than Earth's dolphins, with prehensile fin-tips.

Oleyall – A Master of global health, immigrant from Ellason, recognized expert in holistic analysis of interactive living systems; respected for his wisdom.

Haralahn – Master of philosophy and religious theory, native of Ellason, descendant of the intellectual by the same name, author of

Reflections in Blood-stained Water after the history recorded as *The Unheard Song* by Cary Neeper.

Daramonts

Mild-mannered ungulateoids of Varok, larger than camels of Earth, with heads resembling Springer Spaniels; committed to providing ellls with transportation on land.

Big Dawn, Markup, and Pork Belly – Named by Conn; devoted to transport him and "Orserah's Family" in exchange for forage.

Light Hoppers

Tiny Varokian marsupialoids who love stories and thrive on imagination, ignoring reality unless threatened.

The Archives of Varok

In an alternate 21st century Solar System, Earth learns that we have neighbors too intelligent, too nosy, and too near to ignore. . . .

The View Beyond Earth

Two offworld species, disturbingly human and altogether alien. Microbiologist Tandra Grey finds new hope for an ailing Earth and her own future when she makes first contact. Revised and updated from Neeper's 1975 classic, *A Place Beyond Man* (Scribner's).

The Webs of Varok

Silver medalist, Nautilus Book Awards 2013; Finalist, ForeWord's Book of the Year Awards 2012. Tandra leaves Earth for the ancient sustainable culture of Varok, with its promise of stability for her young daughter. But a genius with a hidden talent sets her eye on Varok's wealth — and Tandra's alien soul-mates.

The Alien Effect

Raised on the Jovian moon Varok, Shawne returns to Earth to help her devastated home planet build a new civilization — one that can thrive for millennia. She and her mixed family face unexpected lessons in love and humanity, unaware of the long-term consequences of their collision with life on Earth.

An Alien's Quest

Only two decades after first contact, even Earth's people know of Haralahn, the great-fish spiritual leader on distant Ellason. Shawne seeks his guidance to tame a haunting disillusionment that followed her home from Earth. Her quest for meaning draws everyone she loves away to the Kuiper Belt and into a genetic mystery on the watery home planet of the ells.

The Unheard Song

In this Archives of Varok prequel, a humanoid invader and aquatic native struggle to communicate in their race to ensure peace and a sustainable future for the wild seas of Ellason.

Carolyn A. (Cary) Neeper, PhD raised her family in
the US Southwest with her husband and a friendly
menagerie of dogs, fish and fowl. An avid proponent
of sustainability and steady-state economics since
the 1970s, she studied zoology, chemistry and religion at Pomona College and medical microbiology at
the University of Wisconsin–Madison. Cary paints landscapes and animals in acrylics, including the cover art for *The Archives of Varok* series.

www.ingramcontent.com/pod-product-compliance
Lightning Source LLC
Chambersburg PA
CBHW022031240626
47154CB00007B/2357